Rich Woman's Fetish

a novel by Naleighna Kai

Macro Publishing Group
Chicago, Illinois

Macro Publishing Group
Macro Marketing & Promotions Group
888.854.8823
www.macrompg.com

Rich Woman's Fetish ©2015 by Naleighna Kai

Cover design: J. L. Woodson of www.jlwoodson.com

Editorial Team: Janice Pernell www.janicepernell.com
                   Katie Walsh Giannini ktwedits@gmail.com
                   Tanishia Pearson of Pearson Literary Group

Interior Book Design: Lissa Woodson of www.macrompg.com

ISBN e-book: 978-0-9754130-6-7

ISBN Trade Paperback: 978-0-9754130-7-4

ACKNOWLEDGMENTS

All praise is due to the Creator first and foremost. A special love and respect to my guardian angels, ancestors, teachers and guides.

To my spiritual mothers: Sandy Spears and Bettye Mason Odom; to my son, Jeremy "J. L." Woodson, who is the perfect example of determination and dedication. I love you more than words can ever say.

To the people who continuously inspire me: Renee Sesvalah Cobb-Dishman, Gretta Chamberlain, Debra Mitchell, DeMarco Suggs (my world famous "game master" nephew), Jennifer Cole-Addison (my beautiful niece), Laverne "Missy" Brown, Ehryck F. Gilmore; the best-selling author members of M-LAS: Joyce Brown (my "other" mother and my voice of reason), to Janice Pernell, Valarie Prince, and Katie Walsh, Tanishia Pearson-Jones, Martha Kennerson, Susan D. Peters, D. J. McLaurin, and Lorna L.A. Lewis. A special thanks to Sean Nash (for your male input and keeping me on the right path when it comes to representation), national bestselling authors Lutishia Lovely and Zuri Day, Christine Pauls and LaCeasha Banks Turner, Monique Chavers, Traci Denham, Quentin Daniels, and David Jones.

To the book clubs and avid readers who support my work—I LOVE YOU!!! (there are too many of you to name.)

To the Mighty Cavaliers who have supported my literary career and other endeavors--much love and respect.

To everyone I mentioned (and those that I may have forgotten to type), thank you for everything you are to me and have done for me.

Wishing you all—peace and love, light and joy.

—Naleighna Kai

DEDICATION

My mother, Jean Woodson
My grandmother, Mildred E. Williams
My brother, Eric Harold Spears
My niece, LaKecia Janise Woodson,

To Leslie Esdaile Banks (L.A. Banks),
one of the best storytellers in the world

To Anthony "Green Eyes" Johnson,
the real life "Dallas" and "Dinero"
By loving you, I learned to love myself more

to Derek V. Fields, my fallen Cavalier

"You only live once, but if you do it right, once is enough."
--Mae West

Part I

Song of the Siren

Prologue

Gina struggled for what she thought might be her last breath. Each gasp caused a rush of ice water to fill her little lungs, chilling her body to the point of unbearable pain. She sputtered, forcing streams of murky water from her mouth. Her efforts to remain afloat on the Chicago River were becoming weaker with each stroke, each splash against the tide.

Her daddy had taught her how to swim in the creek earlier that summer. Raymond Wright had held Gina lovingly in his powerful arms as he helped her float, then glide, then swim across the water on her own. He had bragged to everyone who would listened about his "big girl." A proud smile from that big bear of a man could make Gina's heart sing. Because of those lessons, Gina could stay on top of the water longer than her mother realized. But she wouldn't last much longer if the desperate woman kept trying to pull her under, trying to take her life.

God bless daddy and mommy and ...

Gina watched helplessly as Mayre's body was pulled into the current and disappeared. Their mother didn't even glance in the toddler's direction; instead, Faith gripped the edges of Gina's snowsuit and pulled with all of her might.

Gina fought back and was able to remain near the surface in spite of her mother's efforts.

Faith's voice had seemed so calm earlier on the bridge's steel casing. She had tried to explain. She couldn't take the pain any longer. And really no one would miss the three of them anyway. No one would care. Their lives had spiraled so far down into the abyss that nothing and no one could pull them to safety. Now Faith was determined to kill herself and take both of her little girls along for the deadly ride. One down. One last child to go.

Up on the bridge, men wearing gray jumpsuits, yellow hard hats, and hip boots were frantically trying to rescue them. They couldn't know that time and Faith were feverishly working against their actions. How could they know that this beautiful woman was deliberately thwarting every effort they made to bring them all back from death's certain clutches?

Gina stopped praying for salvation since God had already sent the answer. She raised her hands in the direction of the men shouting from the bridge.

God bless Mayre and Mama Bessie and ...

The moment Gina's fingers gripped the rope the men had tossed into the river, Faith yanked hard, pulling Gina's body down, hoping to take her under with the next current.

If I should die before I wake ...

Faith had lost the very thing for which she was named. She had seen the evidence of the worst life had to offer when Raymond was murdered in cold blood. Raymond had a big heart and was generous to a fault—and that generosity had him fighting a battle that some residents of the projects didn't want him to win. Faith had urged him to move them away from the place that had once signaled hope and promise but was now riddled with poverty and crime. But he couldn't run like everyone else. Black flight was equal to cowardice in his book. His strong convictions had left him lying in a burial plot. What they had done to him was vicious. But what happened afterward was something neither she—nor anyone else—could imagine, let alone explain.

Faith had held out hope that she would complete her education, receive the insurance and pension checks due to her from Raymond's death, then move from the projects into a three-bedroom duplex in Jeffery Manor within the month. Fate had other plans.

In Faith's mind, death had to be a better solution. Surely the world would understand that.

Gina caught the rope and clung to it. She felt herself move mercifully upward. Faith's grasp on her daughter's legs slipped. The four-year-old looked down just in time to see the lights in those weary green eyes go dim.

Faith closed her eyes and welcomed the darkness.

I pray the Lord my soul to take ...

Chapter 1

One week earlier

Faith didn't know why she was afraid, but instinct had kicked into gear. She glanced back and saw the men moving toward them. Eight of them. Anxiousness set in; terror was fast on its tail.

She quickened her pace. "Come on, Gina; get those legs moving."

The little girl didn't have to be told twice. Only one more block and they would make it safely to the eleventh-floor apartment of one of the yellow brick buildings of the Robert Taylor Homes projects. For a split second, Faith thought about crossing the street, but that would make the trip longer. Instead, she moved forward quickly, practically dragging Gina along.

It was so cold, Gina's teeth chattered their own song. Her mother had dressed her and Mayre for snow, but it was raining so hard she could barely see anything but her mother's gray wool coat and her sister's yellow one. But the one thing she could do was feel—and something was going on with her mother, something that frightened Gina too. She swished along in the Eskimo suit, though each step was more difficult than the one before. She didn't bother to wipe the rain from her face anymore.

"Hey, pretty mama. Need some help?" a gruff voice called out from behind them.

"No, we're all right," Faith replied, trying to keep the nervousness from creeping into her voice. Fear had never been a part of her vocabulary, but drugs, gangs, violence, and rape—practically unheard of when they moved in a few years after they were built—were now so common they barely got a blurb in the paper. She had every reason to fear for her life.

Faith looked ahead, keeping her eyes on their building. They were so close, but the fear that gripped her heart made the distance seem more like a mile. The bus had shuddered and come to a halt on 49th Street, forcing them to walk the rest of the way home in the worst weather Chicago had encountered all winter. She had moved closer to the curb to flag down the next car that came by, but none did.

Gina could barely turn her head, so she kept looking forward, pulled along by her mother's desperate, jerky movements, which were so unlike her usual confident glide.

"Why you running, Miss Lady?"

Another man taunted Faith with, "All we want to do is *talk.*"

A round of bawdy laughs ensued, but Faith didn't look back. "Have to get home to feed my babies," she said, then whispered. "Lord, why are city blocks so long?"

"Ain't so special now that your trouble-making man ain't around, huh?" a raspy-voiced man asked. Hatred dripped from each word as he circled like a hawk closing in on its prey.

"Thought he could run us up outta here, didn't he?" the tallest of the men growled.

Another tossed a beer bottle to the ground and quickened his steps. "Had your head all up in the air like y'all wasn't common folk like the rest of us."

Another man whizzed past Faith and stood in her way, causing her to halt and Gina to stumble forward and hit the ground. "We gonna show you just how common you really is."

They ripped the baby from Faith's arms. Shrieks rent the air as the men crowded around Faith and Gina, pushing them across the street and down toward the empty school yard.

"Run, Gina! Get help!" Faith yelled, struggling to free herself.

Before Gina could move, one of the men grabbed her, holding her in place.

And then the horror began. The men took turns abusing Faith. Her screams tore through the night until one of the men said, "If you don't shut your trap, she's next." His simple nod in Gina's direction left no doubt as to who and what he meant. And the terror of what *could* happen made Faith swallow her screams.

The heavy rain swelled to a thunderstorm, its roars covering the grunts of pleasure and whimpers of pain.

Gina shuddered at the horrific sight playing out before her. She whispered the only prayer she could remember, hoping that God would hear her. The look in her mother's green eyes brought a swell of fresh tears streaming down Gina's face. Something within her little soul shattered. Why was this happening? Wasn't God supposed to protect them from bad people just like her daddy used to do? Gina wanted her daddy. She wanted her grandma, Mama Bessie.

She could go to Mama Bessie! Yes, Mama Bessie would help. She had a gun. Gina yanked with all of her might, slipped out of the stocky man's grasp, and ran as fast as her little legs would carry her. She hid in the tiny opening between the rusty green dumpster and the brick wall on the side of the school, trying to catch her breath. Her heart slammed against her chest as she closed her eyes and prayed like Mama Bessie said she should any time she was afraid. Mama Bessie was too far away. The elevator was scary, and those men might see her. Then another thought came to Gina: The bus driver! He could help.

When she didn't hear any footsteps behind her, she scrambled down the street, nearly falling three times as she covered the long distance back to the bus. She banged as hard as she could on the glass door. The driver finally trudged to the front and stretched languidly as he yawned. He peered out at the dirt-covered snowsuit before flipping the handle that opened the door—but only partway.

Gina tried to squeeze in through the small opening. "They're hurting my mother! Please help!"

The driver scanned the area, then looked down at the soaked little girl.

Gina pointed toward the area where the school building stretched for half a block. "Please help. Please. Please. Please!" She ran up to him and yanked his sweater, trying to move him with her.

The driver quickly slipped on a bluish-gray coat, locked up the bus, and followed Gina down the street.

Another one of those bad men was on top of her mother.

"Get off her," the driver yelled, running toward the group. "I'ma call the police."

One of the men rushed forward. He whipped out a gun, cocked it, and grinned when the driver held up his hands. The man put the gun to the driver's temple. "Get outta here before we kill your lanky ass."

Gina's heart sank as the driver hightailed it away, leaving Gina at the mercy of the elements and the men who held her mother and sister. Before they could capture her again, she ducked behind the dumpster—too afraid to do anything else. It was too far to her building, and she didn't trust anyone but Mama Bessie. She would have to get across the street and go up that scary elevator all by herself.

She shivered, and not just from the cold. Bad things happened in those elevators. A very bad thing happened to her daddy in there. But Mama Bessie had a gun in her top dresser drawer. A big one. She wasn't afraid of nobody. Gina inched out but froze when the heaviest man of the group called out, "Hey y'all, I want some too."

He still held Mayre in his pudgy arms. He shifted the baby to his hip and licked his lips as he watched the man who was on Faith.

"Nobody wants to go behind your sloppy ass." The others hooted with laughter. "You go last. You just hold that baby and keep her quiet like you been doin'. You'll get a turn. Later."

The man mumbled, then turned his back and inched away. He looked over his shoulder to see that the others were paying him no attention. Gina pressed her body closer to the brick wall as he trudged toward the dumpster carrying her little sister.

What she saw next would have a permanent place in her nightmares.

Chapter 2

Mama Bessie waved a fist in the air as she shrieked, "It's an outrage!"

Voices from every corner of St. Mary's Church vehemently agreed with the stout woman. Once she retrieved Gina from Cook County Hospital, Mama Bessie had demanded a community meeting take place immediately so she could put everyone on notice. The sanctuary was filled to capacity with residents of the 5247 S. Federal building and a few representatives from each of the outlying projects. "What those men did to that woman and child ... I'd've gone crazy too."

Gina slipped into the room. All eyes were on her as she moved through the crowd and rushed to Mama Bessie, who leaned down and said, "I tol' you to stay outside wit' them other chil'ren."

Gina shook her head and took the old woman's hand.

"Baby, you got to stay outside," Mama Bessie insisted with a wry twist of her lips. "I got stuff to say, and this here's grown folks' talk. I might say somethin' not fit for yo' li'l ears."

"You mean like the cussin' you do at home?"

That little quip brought laughter that eased the steely tension in the room.

"The kids don't like me," Gina whispered as she lowered her head. "They're saying mean things. Was my mama a whore? She got what was coming to her? What's that mean?" She removed her hand and wrapped her little arms as far as they would go around Mama Bessie's thick thighs.

Mama Bessie sighed. She couldn't take time to deal with this little problem when there were bigger ones stirring. The sienna-colored woman tore her gaze from Gina, scanned the anxious faces in the room, and demanded, "What we gon' do 'bout it? The police ain't never cared what goes on up in here."

Those around her nodded, and some of them glared openly at the officers in the room, who were so engrossed in their own conversations that people near them had to strain to hear what was being said by Mama Bessie.

"They hurt a baby. A baby, y'all. That's just plain evil." Mama Bessie shook her head, trying to contain her anger. "And she still lived behind that madness." She swallowed hard, her eyes filling with salty moisture as she tried to meet the gazes of the other women's tear-stained faces. "I used to babysit her and her sister right here," she said, lifting Gina's tiny hand, which had slipped inside hers. "After what they did, that child wouldn't stop crying. All day. All night. I could hear her through the walls."

Gina peered out from behind the woman's floral skirt. Everyone was crying. Even the men had moisture in their eyes.

"And this li'l one." She stroked Gina's little hand as Gina's head whipped up toward Mama Bessie. "She's a strong one. Strong for being able to get through this. She already told us what we need to know." She released Gina's hand and waggled a finger at the audience. "And to make it ugly, those motha ..." she looked quickly at the wide-eyed girl before continuing, "they bragged about what they done to Faith. We know who they are. Question is, what y'all gon' do 'bout it?"

Murmurs echoed through the room. Some grumbled about justice, others mumbled about letting the police handle it, but no one said anything that mattered—at least not to Mama Bessie's way of thinking or hearing.

Her dark brown gaze shifted to the pale officer at the front of the room, who was whispering to the alderman—a man who did nothing more than keep the Black votes in line for Mayor Daley's political machine.

"Matter of fact, Officer Franks, you can take yo' leave."

The men's conversation and laughter trailed off as they looked at her and realized that the room's focus was now on them.

"We don't need y'all here," she said, putting a hand on her wide hip. "I don't remember invitin' yo' kind. Since y'all ain't done nothin' befo' now, ain't no need of y'all comin' 'round to see what we up to now. We gon' get this here problem under control—our way."

Officer Franks shifted in his seat before he stood and walked down from the small dais. He signaled for the rest of the officers along the side walls to follow him out of the room, but he tossed a pointed look at Alderman Dawson, as if to say, "I better know everything about this by end of day."

Mama Bessie didn't miss that look. She turned to Alderman Dawson. "Take your narrow tail on with 'em," she said through clenched teeth.

The beady-eyed man leveled a stony glare at Mama Bessie. "I have a right to be here. I'm a leader."

"You got the right to lead … somewheres else 'cause you ain't done a damn thing since Raymond Wright's been gone." She shooed him toward the door. "Now just go on."

Whistles and hoots of approval echoed throughout the room as he trudged past the first few rows and picked up speed on his way out.

Mama Bessie waited until the door closed behind them and said, "Ever since the gov'ment said the men couldn't be up in the house with they womenfolk, they been hangin' in the hallways, in the stairwells. Groups of 'em out in front of the buildin', forcin' us to walk 'round them as if they got the right to be here."

The women shouted in agreement, which was followed by a hearty applause.

"First they was hangin' 'round 'cause they say they can't find no jobs," she taunted, pacing the length of the center aisle. "That's what they said. Wasn't cut out for schoolin' and all that. Yeah, they said that too. Back then, they wasn't shootin' nobody, wasn't rapin' nobody. They was just out there," she said, gesturing to no place in particular. "Most kinda crime happenin' up in here was a li'l stealin' ev'ry so often, a man beatin' on his woman ev'ry now and then, fights and li'l dis'greements—nothin' we couldn't handle ourselves. Nothing we *didn't* handle ourselves," she said with a pointed look at Mr. Carter, whose permanent limp was a gift from the Mama Mafia—a group of grandmothers who had taught him a lesson about keeping his fists to himself.

"Then folks started invitin' peoples that don't live 'round here, didn't grow up 'round here, don't care 'bout us or nobody for that matter. Strangers that brought drugs. Then the shootin' come after." She gestured toward the buildings. "Those no-good hellions is just living off us. Call some of y'all they customers cause y'all done traded liquor for that heroin, stickin' all kinds of whatever in your veins."

She grimaced as her gaze landed on a few people before moving forward into the crowd, forgetting all about Gina. "I say that since the men who's shackin' up wit' womens up in here ain't workin' or doin' nothin' else, some of 'em need to be helpin' themselves to more than just nookie."

A roar of approval went up from the women; some stood and applauded as some of the men cringed, and others shared looks that told of their unease.

Mama Bessie pointed a finger at the group of women nearest the aisle, then to ones on the other side. "Your husbands, common-law husbands, or whatever you callin' 'em this week, need to be 'bout helpin' to keep us safe."

"We ain't no police," one of the men shouted as he stood. This outburst garnered the thundering support of the men who had remained strangely silent through Mama Bessie's speech. Even a few of their women nodded, but then withered under Mama Bessie's hard glare. "Gina, go on outside, baby. Now."

Gina inched away but didn't make it past the last five rows before she ducked back and hid behind Mrs. Burroughs, who looked over her shoulder and gave Gina a quick wink.

"Y'all ain't no police," Mama Bessie taunted, her deep voice dripping with sarcasm. "Y'all ain't no police." She cut a simmering look at some of the women who had the nerve to agree with Joshua. "And this here don't concern you, right?"

She glanced at the beautiful, sharply dressed woman sitting next to the man who had spoken up. "You loves you some of that high yella woman, Joshua?" Mama Bessie gave a low, throaty chuckle. "Be mighty interestin' if they think they want some too. Catch her on the way home from that hospital she works at. Corner her in the stairwell and take what you been gettin' on the regular.

"How you feel 'bout sharin' her with 'em? They not gonna stop at one time. You didn't." The old woman's lips spread into a sly smile. "Nathan lost his mind over this woman. Almost killed hisself 'cause she ain't want him no mo'. Wanted your tired ass instead." Mama Bessie rounded the third row to stand in front of him. "And you felt all proud about it, like you had some prize 'cause folks think purtiest one in here—at least that's what they say. Now that Faith Wright's gone."

She stepped to the right and leaned in so that her face was mere inches from Nadine. "How'd you feel if it was *you* they raped? Hmmmm? You want some no-count sucker who say *he ain't no police* laying it to you after that? A man who'd just let it ride like it don't matter? Is the lovin' that good, baby?"

Low whistles punctuated that statement. Nadine cast a wary glance in Joshua's direction, pulled a shawl around her shoulders, and moved away from him as though he carried some sort of contagious disease. Joshua glared at Mama Bessie as he slumped down, scowling.

Mama Bessie's eyes flashed as she thrust her fist in the air. "They. Raped. A. Baby. That's an evil the Bible never spoke nothin' 'bout. That's evil to the core. Evil to the bottom of they souls." She scanned the people in the room. "First it's women, then girls, then babies, then old women like me. If we don't make a stand right now, no female'll ever be safe 'round these parts. Mark my words."

Mama Bessie frowned as she locked gazes with a wide-eyed Gina, who wasn't normally disobedient. She wanted to stay, needed to know she would be safe. Even she understood that Mama Bessie was saying something important, something that was about making sure what happened to her mother and sister that night wouldn't happen to her.

"I've gots one thing to say." The woman focused on the anxious crowd caught in thoughts of the real consequences they could personally suffer. "By sundown t'morrow, if them evil mothafuckas ain't six feet under ... I'm goin' on a li'l shootin' spree. Start wipin' out e'erybody who got som'thin' hangin' between they legs. Me and George gonna take matters into our own hands. Y'all don't want that. My eyes ain't so good these days." She wiggled her fingers. "My aim might be a little off."

Charlotte leaned over to Geneva sitting in the pew in front of her and whispered, "Who's George?"

"Her .38 special revolver. She only used it once—on her husband. Trust me, her aim was dead on. Had him running down sixteen flights of stairs butt-naked, nuts swinging in the wind."

Charlotte did a double take at Mama Bessie, a brand new respect forming for the woman who was rumored to be the head of the Mama Mafia.

"Next time it could be yo' chil'ren," Mama Bessie pointed to Gloria. "Or Bobby Jo," she said with a quick look at Laverne, Christine, and Susan. Then she locked a gaze on Cleopha Jean. "Oh, I wouldn't want to see anything happen to yo' li'l Ruby. Have her laid up in the hospital, insides all messed up." She paced the center aisle, her heels clicking along the industrial brown tile. "These animals won't stop if we don't stop 'em." She paused and swept her gaze over the people once again. "So what y'all gonna do?"

Chapter 3

Mama Bessie walked the center aisle of St. Mary's Church after she posed that question to everyone, letting their thoughts simmer for a while. The crowd was silent enough for Gina to hear Mama Bessie's sharp intake of breath. The little girl ran to the front of the church.

A flash of heated conversations followed. Mama Bessie smiled down at Gina who said, "Ooooh, Mama Bessie, you said a bad word."

The old woman simply nodded and moved forward. "Gotta use words that gets the point across."

"Did they know what you mean?"

"They heard me loud and clear." She cocked a brow at the little girl. "And I'ma spank your li'l tail for not mindin' me."

Gina's soft brown eyes widened as she froze. "Those kids … they said some mean things about my mommy and daddy. I couldn't make them stop." She lifted her chin. "I wanted to be in here with you. I'm glad you said those things. If I wasn't so scared of that elevator, I would've run to you first."

Mama Bessie bent down and hugged Gina to her bosom. "It's all right, chile. You were mighty brave that night. You did come and get me. So don't think no mo' 'bout it." Mama Bessie sighed in frustration. "Come on, let me get you home. Fix you some vittles."

Mr. and Mrs. Tucker cornered the aisle and stood in their path. "We've been thinking," Mr. Tucker said with a quick look down at Gina then at Mama Bessie. "Maybe we should keep Raymond's daughter. We can raise her."

Mama Bessie maneuvered around them. "We gonna be fine."

The tall, broad-shouldered man blocked their exit once again, saying loudly, "But you *too old* to be caring for a child that age."

Conversations nearest them came to a halt, and people slowly looked in their direction. Soon everyone else in the room was silent. Martha Tucker lifted her chin as she inched closer to her husband and folded her arms across her slight bosom.

Mama Bessie pulled up to her full height, which was still only five-foot-six. "Ain't too old to watch yo' little hellions sometimes." Mr. Tucker blanched at her caustic tone. "'Specially when your wife's runnin' a few … um… *errands* while you off at work," she said with a pointed look at the missus, who inched back under Mr. Tucker's questioning glare.

"Like I said, we's doin' jus' fine. You wanna do somethin' for this girl? Handle the biz'ness you charged with. Be a man 'bout that, then we can all sleep good 'round here."

She scanned the crowd , which still had its eyes locked on the couple across from her, who were still in her way.

"The Mama Mafia can only do so much," Mama Bessie said, referring to the group of older women who kept the children while the younger women went to work, to school, or to run errands. They also did a little "dirty" work now and then. "Taking out the trash" is what Mama Bessie called it—and it meant that somebody was put six feet under. "So we need to put you men to work. Good men—trustworthy men—who only fear God. Men who can do what needs to be done. Or do I really have to put this here task to the Mama Mafia? Are we the only ones with some balls 'round here?"

Every woman over fifty moved forward one by one in a blatant show of solidarity.

Mama Bessie smiled and nodded with relief. Every woman standing was packing the best kind of heat—the kind that ended disagreements permanently. "God helps those who help themselves. And this is war. The same way they did it in the Bible; same way they did it in slavery—kill and weaken the men, and take the women and chil'ren—put fear in 'em. Control 'em. This ain't nothin' new." She shook her head. "Next they'll be movin' into our homes sayin' we part of they ter'tory too."

Quite a few gasps echoed around the room at the statement; murmurs followed.

"See, here's what y'all ain't thinkin' 'bout," she said to everyone as her gaze swept over the people in the room. "The real problems. We went from a place of promise to a place of hell. Went from men and women keepin' the family together to a buildin' full of lazy-ass heifers lyin' on their backs so they can get checks for every chile they push out. And I ain't faultin' them." She waggled a finger at no one in particular as she sauntered back up the aisle. "I'm faultin' y'all. Cause y'all didn't listen to what Raymond Wright was sayin' 'bout how they was tryin' to tear us down by bringin' in folk that don't know what an honest day's work is. It's *they* kind that bring the rest of them up in here.

"I say let's put religion on the table for a minute and get that eye-for-an-eye thing workin'. Or is it, if thy right hand offend thee, cut it off?" She lifted her hands, then tilted her head to the right as though studying those weathered digits. "Naw, y'all. My right hand works jus' fine. It's my shootin' hand, yes, indeed. Praise the Lord and pass the ammunition."

The men in the room bristled as she looked at them one by one.

Mama Bessie strolled back up the aisle "So anybody else think I'm *too old* to take care of her?"

No one mumbled a word as she cut a stony gaze at Mr. Tucker. "Anyone else jus' tryin' to get they hands on the money she got coming?"

Mr. Tucker turned beet red as the silence enveloped them once again.

"That's what I thought," she spat. "This child saw what they did. She gonna need a whole heapin' of love and 'tention to get past all this. And I be jus' the one to give it to her. I'ma raise her like she was my own." She stroked a pudgy hand across Gina's face. "This here's a strong child. Been through too much." Mama Bessie looked out to the crowd. "We didn't do right by her daddy, her mama, or her li'l sister, but we damn sho' gonna do right by her."

She continued her walk up the center aisle to the wooden doors with Gina on her heels. "We a community—ain't the best, ain't the worst either. Unless'n that's how we allow it to be. Won't happen if y'all *take out the trash* before they get too strong in numbers." She lowered her gaze, then glanced at the older women who had lined up along the wall to file out behind her. "All it'll take is groups of two or more men, a few weapons, other men to walk the women to and fro to get the word out that we ain't puttin' up wit' no mo mess. This our place, our home. We better start actin' like it."

Mama Bessie's lips pulled into a scowl as she continued with, "Like I said, y'all got 'til sundown tomorrow. If a single one of those demons draws a breath beyond that, George and the Mamas and me won't discrim'nate. And we'll start by takin' out the useless ones sittin' right here in this room." She took Gina's hand and moved forward. "And with that, I bid y'all goodnight now."

Gina smiled up at the woman.

Mama Bessie crouched down with quite a bit of effort; her joints cracked loudly in protest. "Maybe I should've asked. Whatchu wanna do? Who you wanna live wit'?"

Gina wrapped her arms as far around Mama Bessie's body as she could and squeezed with all her might.

Mama Bessie lifted her chin and stood, patting Gina's back as she looked out to everyone. "It's settled then. I'll leave y'all to handle thangs. This one's tummy is growlin' louder than Otha's old Chevy." She moved forward, pressing toward the door. "Come on baby, let's go home."

Gina could feel the eyes of everyone on them. She lowered her head to avoid making eye contact with anyone.

Mama Bessie pulled her to a fast stop. "No baby, you hold yo' head up high. You ain't done nothin' to be 'shame of."

Gina took a few moments before she lifted her chin, same as she had seen Mama Bessie do, same as her mama and daddy had done. Tears pooled in her soft brown eyes, as she said in the clearest voice she could manage, "Yes, Ma'am."

Mama Bessie nodded and walked on. "Now show me which one of them li'l heathens had somethin' to say. I got somethin' for 'em, too."

Gina wiped the tears from her face as she smiled and ran to catch up with the spry old woman.

* * *

The days following that community meeting in St. Mary's Church resulted in eight men laid out execution style in the school yard across from 5247 S. Federal.

The local news didn't report a single word. The police didn't bother to look for the killers.

Chapter 4

Robert Taylor Homes
Monday, April 14, 1980

Gina navigated the groups of thugs in the dark, crowded stairwell. The first bunch was passing around a bottle of whiskey and smoking a joint on the second floor landing; others were playing craps on the third floor landing. She struggled up the stairs with her book bag in one hand and groceries in the other. The acrid stench of urine slammed her senses the moment she reached the concrete area leading to the fifth floor. Dice rolled along the ground as another group of men traded what money they had, along with insults for good measure.

She hurried past them, ignoring the string of profanity that came out with every sentence. Gina wished she could take the elevators. Unfortunately, hopping in those metal boxes meant certain death; the stairwells provided at least a fighting chance if there was some sort of attack.

Rakim, one of the leaders, tore himself away from the game, halting everyone's conversation as he moved toward her.

Gina swallowed hard as he pressed up against her and placed a blocking hand on a wall that was colored with more gang tags than the original paint job. "I've been waiting to get me some of this," he said loud enough for his boys to hear. "That old woman was keeping you all up in the house, so I know nobody ain't been up in it yet."

She looked into dark brown eyes that were as cold and lifeless as a day-old corpse. She couldn't stop the anger that ripped through her. She shifted her books, reached into her back pocket, and felt the cold metal against her skin. "Let. Me. Pass," she growled through clenched teeth.

"Naw. We needs to talk."

"There's nothing I need to say to you." Gina flicked the switchblade she kept on her at all times and pressed it toward his groin until he flinched and backed up a little. "I can let Little Gina do all my talking for me … or you can let me pass. Either way works for me."

His crew broke into hoots of laughter as Gina inched away, making certain to keep the switchblade ready. She slipped under his arm and walked toward the apartment near the opposite end of the deserted landing. The same landing that the women once proudly took turns mopping every day was now littered with empty soda cans, bottles of liquor, and all kinds of rubbish.

"Friday," Rakim shouted. "After that old woman's funeral … that ass is aaaaall mine."

Gina did her best to ignore him and the taunts that followed. Tomorrow she would start carrying George to school. It was still in working order, and Mama Bessie had taught her how to use it well. If she had to take out one of those thugs to send a message, so be it. If they killed her in the process, that was fine too. They had already taken her mother, father, and sister. They would not take anything else from her—not before she was ready to give.

The madness had started again. Was it just twelve years ago when Mama Bessie stood up in St. Mary's Church demanding justice for her family? Now Gangs now overran RTH at an alarming rate. One weekend spawned three hundred separate shooting incidents with twenty-eight killed. Fighting for control of the buildings had claimed more innocent lives than intended targets. The place had become part of a multi-million dollar business with nearly $45,000 in drug money flowing through those sixteen buildings daily. The police received their cut off the top; politicians were paid in drug-infested currency off the bottom. No wonder criminal activity thrived—everyone who mattered had a good reason to look the other way.

All the other members of the Mama Mafia had died; Mama Bessie had been the last woman standing. Without them or anyone else who cared enough to make a difference, the place had become a den of poverty run by drug lords who wanted to keep the tenants living in fear and utter helplessness. Some tenants even had to turn over their entire welfare or Social Security checks to the new "landlords," because they owed money for drug habits that couldn't wait for the first of the month.

Gina had survived untouched while Mama Bessie was alive and still commanded some semblance of respect. Now that the spirited woman was gone, the vibe had changed. Thugs and grown men made open passes at Gina, undeterred by the fact that she was sixteen. Then Ted and Patricia, Mama Bessie's estranged family, had come out of the woodwork like the vermin they were, demanding that Gina turn the apartment over to them by the end of the week. Friday.

What was it about four days from now that made everyone think she would give in to their pressure? Ted said she could stay, but Gina would have to earn her keep, and he wasn't just talking about cooking and housework. Patricia had slipped Gina some money so she could leave. But where would she go? She had no other family. She only vaguely remembered Raymond Wright's relatives in Natchez, Mississippi, and there was no way to connect with them even if she wanted to.

Friday ... become Rakim's woman or Ted's woman. Both were equally appalling. Giving Ted what he wanted wouldn't guarantee that she could keep a roof over her head. But it was certain to create one hell of a problem with Patricia, who for some reason loved his useless ass.

Rakim would start off with showing Gina around because she was a "prize" that everyone had wanted and no one could have. Then when he tired of her, he'd eventually pass her down to his other men. When they were done, she'd be just like so many other teens in the building—pregnant and sporting a tribe of babies, or addled with some type of disease, and forced to get on welfare either way. She owed it to her parents and to herself to live a good life, and that meant she had four days to execute her plans and get the hell up out of RTH.

Gina ambled through the front door of the apartment and froze. The scurrying sound caused her heart to pound as she quickly covered the distance from living room to her bedroom in a few short moments.

"What are you doing?" Gina demanded of the tall, slender woman who had barged into Mama Bessie's home the day the wonderful old woman slipped into a diabetic coma.

"Oh, I'm just cleaning up around here, that's all."

"The place was already clean," Gina said dryly, her gaze darting from the slightly open dresser drawer to the small familiar object in the woman's hand. She did her best to keep the place tidy and to Mama Bessie's standards. Something that Ted and Patricia didn't seem to know anything about

"Well, I was close to Mama Bessie and thought I'd have a piece of her jewelry as a keepsake."

Gina glanced at the necklace that her father had given her mother for a birthday present—a gold chain with a tiny diamond drop.

"That's not Mama Bessie's. That belonged to my mama."

Patricia blushed, stalled for a moment, then placed it gently on the cherry wood dresser and looked up at Gina. "Sorry about that. I didn't think something this beautiful could be yours."

"It was in my room."

"Well, I said I was sorry," Patricia snapped as she brushed past Gina and hurried toward the master bedroom.

Gina sighed and took a quick look around, then went back out to place the groceries in the refrigerator. She was thankful that one of the few remaining mom-and-pop stores still offered credit to those who needed it and allowed regulars to pay it back when they could. Thanks to Patricia's special little gifts, Gina had been able to keep Mama Bessie's account square at State Street Market and make purchases of her own.

She whipped up some bacon, eggs, biscuits, and grits and left a plate for the intruders. Then she cleaned up the pots and pans, poured a glass of apple juice, and took the meal into her bedroom.

"Mind how you talk to my wife," Ted growled as he came to stand in the doorway.

"Mind that your wife keeps out of my room," Gina shot back, rifling through some of the items in her dresser to find out what else Patricia thought "belonged" to Mama Bessie. She glanced at Ted's right arm and took a deep breath to quell her anger. "And you can return my daddy's watch too."

"Oh no. This right here belonged to *my* daddy. He got it from working the railroads all those years." He tapped the gleaming gold piece and gave her a sly grin.

Gina closed her eyes, remembering that Mama Bessie's husband had never worked a day in his life after a car accident rendered him unable to stand for long periods. Mama Bessie said she could put up with his not working; it was his drinking and raising his hand to her that gave her no choice but to help him see that leaving would keep him breathing.

She tried to picture what Mama Bessie would do in this situation with Ted. Then she leveled a simmering gaze his way. "Let's hope that your daddy's watch doesn't ... *fall off* one night when you're sleeping on the couch." She gave him a matter-of-fact shrug, sat on the bed, and fingered the switchblade. "Might have to remove a few fingers to help it slide off," she said with a grin. "Whether you're wearing it ... or not."

Ted flinched; he balled his fingers into fists as his eyes flashed fire.

"Give me my daddy's watch. Now!"

Ted bit his lip as he glowered openly. "Somebody's gonna take the bite out of you one day," he grumbled while he slipped the gold watch from his arm.

"Not if I take a bite out of them first."

He tossed it her way. She caught the watch in midair and kept her focus on him as he sauntered from the room. He tossed a final look at her over his shoulder. His eyes were vacant, but the parting lift of his lips was predatory and spoke a warning. She might have the upper hand now, but things were about to change. Friday.

Gina crossed the room, slammed her door, and slumped onto the full-size bed. Despite Mama Bessie's absence and the presence of people she had labeled "the intruders," the place still felt like home.

Tears filled Gina's eyes as she thought fondly of a woman who had loved her despite the fact that they didn't share a single drop of blood. Mama Bessie had stressed getting a good education and survival, along with being a lady and fearing no one but God. Gina had taken those lessons to heart; others in the building weren't quite as fortunate. But then again, they now had good reason to be afraid.

The violence was so bad that schools were closed some days and only re-opened when a gang truce could be reached. On the weekends, Mama Bessie would often have Gina sleep in the bathtub to protect her from the random rounds of gunfire. Gina stopped that a year ago. When Mama Bessie questioned why she would defy her, Gina simply replied, "If there's a bullet with my name on it, it might still meet me in the bathtub or somewhere else. If it's all the same to you, I'd rather die sleeping or fighting than fearful and hiding."

Mama Bessie definitely understood that.

No one took the elevators anymore; the most violent crimes took place there. People on nearby floors would listen to a victim's screams for hours on end and not lift a finger to help. Even the paramedics and firefighters wouldn't enter RTH without police protection. People died waiting for emergency help to arrive.

Even Gina knew one thing: you can't go from a community of proud, hard-working people to an invasion of non-working families who didn't believe in their own value and expect the community, the fabric of the projects or its daily life to remain the same. But far be it from Gina to continue the fight that a majority of the remaining residents had never wanted her father or Mama Bessie to win.

Gina had four days to put her plans in motion—a place to live, a way to finish her education, and money to survive. She would not be just another statistic, collecting government checks, living in squalor, and raising children that were born too close together to receive the kind of love that was due them—the kind of love that her parents gave her, the kind of love Mama Bessie gave her. If she had children, it would be in a place where they would be well taken care of and loved, and they would not want for anything. Her children would be wanted, instead of accidents, mistakes or worse—little humans that translated into cold, hard, first-of-the month cash.

Gina retrieved George from his hiding place in the concrete wall. She might have to sleep with the damn thing. In the short time he had been staying in the apartment, Ted had already tried twice to come in her room at night. Thank God Patricia was a jealous woman and a light sleeper.

She lifted the pillow to place George underneath and found another wad of cash.

Four days. Friday seemed too close for comfort.

Chapter 5

Tuesday - 4:38 p.m.

Rakim stood outside of the screen door and held up a brown paper bag before giving Gina a toothy grin. She peered at him a moment, then smiled back and flipped the latch. The wonderful scent of Chili Mac's wafted in with him.

"I brought your favorite stuff."

"Thank you, Matthew," she replied softly. "You want to come in and have some with me?"

Rakim walked past her into the living room. His gaze swept the area, and he nodded, seeming to approve of how neat and orderly the place was—as always. When Mama Bessie approved of her work, she would simply nod and kiss Gina's forehead. That one gesture meant more to Gina than anything Mama Bessie could buy.

He watched her go into the kitchen to retrieve two porcelain bowls and a pair of glasses from the white metal cabinet.

"You need to call me Rakim."

"I'm going to always call you by the name your mama gave you," she replied, opening the fridge and taking out a carton of juice. "I don't know this Rakim person. I've loved Matthew Jones since I was in first grade. You were just going into third. He was sweet and kind and smart." Her soft brown eyes locked on his. "Rakim frightens me. He's into all kinds of stuff I don't even want to know about. So I won't call you by that name. That's not who you really are."

Rakim looked at her for a long moment before she turned and handed him half the things she was carrying.

She moved her schoolbooks off the bed so he could have a seat, then spooned the hearty chili with macaroni from the carton into the two bowls. They ate in silence for a while before he focused on the notebooks and the scribbled information on the pages. He frowned as he looked her way. "School ain't about nothing no way. You need to get on some real money."

"You're only saying that because you stopped going," Gina countered around a mouthful of food. "You were good in English, even better in math."

"The only math I need to know is dollars and cents."

Gina shook her head, waiting until she finished another spoonful before she said, "There's more to life than just drug money, Matthew. And what do you spend it on? Cars? Clothes? Liquor? Partying? You're not buying a house or trying to get your mama out of the projects, so what are you doing with all that money?" She set the bowl on the nightstand. "I know exactly what you're doing. Making some other man rich. That's what. Folks making the real money don't live up in here. They live in fine homes; their children go to private schools; they're driving nice cars; they have bank accounts overflowing with cash. Those are the real players. Every day one of you all gets killed, and for what? Someone else's money."

Rakim stiffened at her verbal assault—mostly because she mentioned things that were true, but he had pushed all that to the back of his mind because none of it concerned him. He couldn't change things even if he wanted to. "You don't know what you're talking about."

"I know more than you think," Gina replied in a soothing tone as she touched a hand to his cheek. "And what was that all about yesterday? Why do you have to act like that with me in front of your boys?"

"Sorry about all that. It's the only thing that's keeping you safe." He reached up to softly stroke her face in the same manner as she had stroked him. "They know I want you, so nobody's gonna touch you."

Gina leaned forward and pressed a kiss to his lips. She heard him gasp in surprise.

He placed his empty bowl on the floor and soon held her in his arms, exploring her mouth relentlessly as she melted into him. Tingling sensations ripped through her body as she returned his passion measure for measure. She wrapped her arms around his neck and pulled him even closer. The kiss deepened, and moisture pooled between her thighs.

Finally, she put a little distance between them and looked in his dark brown eyes as she whispered, "Why don't we just go, Matthew? Just leave tonight. Let's get out of this place and never come back. We can make it on our own. You could finish school, do something real nice, do something right."

"I'm already doing something right," he said huskily, his erection straining against his jeans. "I'm loving you."

Gina closed her eyes, taking in that half-truth. She laid her head on his chest, and he wrapped his arms about her as he tried to bring his breathing under control. Her hands reached under the white T-shirt and splayed across tight abs. She inhaled the musky scent of him, which told plenty about where he'd been and what he'd been up to. Weed, liquor, cigarette smoke—all things he had tried to hide under the fresh clean scent of Irish Spring soap. He had showered before coming to see her. Inwardly, she smiled at another argument won.

Everything about him now was wrong, but she still loved him— always had, even though they were a few years apart. Unfortunately for Matthew, Mama Bessie had always said, "It's better to have a man be mo' in love wit' you than you is wit' him." Matthew fit that description. Rakim did not. She wanted to appeal to Matthew in the worst type of way. Wanted someone to walk that new road along with her rather than having to make it outside on her own.

Rakim inched up her blouse, then her bra to expose the cinnamon nipples. She trembled with the unexpected pleasure as he gripped her bottom, kneading it in his hands as he called out her name. "Gina, awwww Gina. I need you, baby. Just let me ... just let me this one time... it'll be good. I swear to you. I'll make it good for you ..."

She couldn't just yet; she had to know—did she have him for real, or did she need to lock it up tight and keep it moving? Gina pulled away, tried to come back to her senses as her breathing hitched. "You have to go before Ted gets back."

Rakim stiffened and took a deep breath before his head snapped up. "Why? He ain't nobody." Then he sat up, checking out her entire body. "Is he messing with you?"

She straightened her clothes as she leaned back among the feather pillows. "It's nothing I can't handle. Thinks he's in charge because Mama Bessie's gone." She gave him a sly grin as she zipped up her jeans. "Just like you."

Those words did not placate Rakim, who growled, "Say the word and his ass is over the top."

Gina froze. *Over the top* meant they would drag Ted up to the sixteenth floor, slip his body through the fence that served as a barrier of safety, and watch him plummet to his death.

She stared at him a moment before saying, "I can handle him, Matthew."

Rakim pulled her back down onto the bed and lowered his head to her breasts. "If you stay here with me, baby, I'll treat you right."

She stroked his short-cropped hair, then planted a soft kiss on his forehead. He would mean it—at first. Then she would become no different than his other girls. Most of the teen pregnancies at 5247 were because of Rakim and his boys. She wanted more from life than being some man's woman. She wanted the kind of life that meant she would never have to depend on anyone but herself and the good Lord.

Three days.

If he didn't still respect Mama Bessie in some way, he would have taken her right then, and Gina knew it. He would allow her the time to get through the funeral on Friday, but that night ...

Rakim pulled away and stared openly at the bulge in her book bag. "Why did you start carrying her gun?"

"Hasn't felt too safe around here since she's been gone."

His handsome features pulled into a deadly scowl. "I wish some fool would put his hands on you."

"I wish they would too," she replied calmly. "My aim is just as good as Mama Bessie's—if not better."

Rakim grinned and looked away, muttering, "Crazy old woman."

She could only smile. Mama Bessie was far from crazy—the woman was too smart, too strong. And the woman had a heart as wide as Lake Michigan. There wasn't anything she wouldn't do for the people in 5247; there wasn't anything she wouldn't do for her little girl.

Gina remembered when they would make the trip to get their hair done at Stormy Clark's every Saturday, then go down the street to the South Center Department Store for a little shopping. The day would end on 47th & Michigan with a special treat at Chili Mac's. Later that night, Mama Bessie and the rest of the Mama Mafia would have a little fun at Jerry's Palm Tavern, where they could hear some live Jazz, or sometimes they hit Club DeLisa's on 63rd Street. Mama Bessie knew everything about working hard and playing hard and showed Gina that there was nothing wrong with balancing life that way. No, there wasn't a damn thing crazy about that old woman; she had commanded respect until her dying day.

Rakim twirled a finger around one of Gina's auburn curls that hung past her shoulders. "She did a lot of good around here. She was a true gangster. Still was crazy though."

Gina looked down at him and stroked a thumb across one of his sharp cheek bones. "She always said that you could put your brains to good use. Be a businessman, own things, property even, make some woman a good husband. Would make me a good husband."

He shrugged and focused his gaze out of the bedroom window to a sky where clouds were beginning to form. "Would be nice, but that ain't me."

Stung by his rejection, she said, "That's because you don't want it to be, Matthew. You're taking the easy way doing what all those other boys are doing—drugs and dying. Exactly in that order."

Anger flashed in his eyes. He stood and looked down at her spread out on the bed, lingering on her curves as though committing them to memory. "Gotta go. Duty calls."

"I love you, Matthew," she whispered.

He softened instantly, closing his eyes against the crush of emotion that flooded him. He licked those sensually curved lips as though wanting to return those words and her love. Then his eyes opened, and it was Rakim, not Matthew, who said, "If you really loved me"—he leaned over to press his hands inside her jeans and cupped a hand over her hot mound—"you'd give me some of this."

She slapped his hand away and sat up. "You don't need no more of that. You have enough girls around here. A vagina is standard equipment on every female."

"But … they … ain't you."

Gina paused as she took his meaning and gave him a wide smile. "No, I guess you're right about that." She stood and scooped up their dishes. "I'll walk you to the door."

"You actin' mighty strange tonight," he said as he stretched out on the bed again instead of following her out of the room. His gaze narrowed as though trying to piece together some unspoken clue.

"You're the only one I have left, Matthew," she said softly, trying to keep the tears from falling.

"You think I don't know that?" he asked, his expression softening with his tone.

She trembled a little, her steps faltering as she tried to turn and leave the room.

Rakim took the dishes out of her hands and set them on the floor before he pulled her down next to him.

Gina let the tears flow. She cried for her father. She cried for her mother. She cried for Mayre. And she wailed for the loss of Mama Bessie. Sobs tore through her in violent spasms. Rakim held her through it all and didn't say a word, just stroked her back and wiped away as many of the tears as his T-shirt could hold.

Finally, the sobs trailed off into silent sniffles, and she said, "You want to do right by me, then marry me, Matthew, like you promised, and let's get away from here."

Rakim didn't say anything for a long while, as though he, too, wanted that very same thing but couldn't voice it to anyone. At seven, Matthew had promised that he would be the one to take care of her so she wouldn't have the nightmares any more. At eleven, he had promised that he would marry her and they would have that house in Jeffrey Manor that her mother had wanted for the family so long ago. He promised that they would be somebody. The two of them.

Rakim wiped away his own tears—the few he allowed to fall when Gina's pain had touched his heart and made him think of things he had lost. His father, who walked out on them when Matthew had turned seven. His brothers, who had met untimely ends that weekend when death had swept through the projects and left a trail of bodies behind. His mama, who was now so strung out on drugs that her day began with a needle to get her out of bed and ended with a pill to make her fall asleep. Dreams were for other people, people who didn't grow up in the projects.

Gina knew that the gang leaders would kill his mother in a heartbeat if Rakim disappeared. But even then, that would be a more merciful exit than the slow death she had chosen.

"Naw, baby, I can't leave here. People respect me around here." His expression hardened, along with the look in his eyes. "I'm a soldier, baby. Soldiers don't leave they posts. Once a man's in the life, he's in for life. I got obligations--"

"You're not obligated to no one but God," she snapped.

"Yeah? Well sometimes God be forgetting that He made it so that people need a drug just to forget the parts of them that hurts. He forgets that we need a daddy just like we need our mamas. He don't have nothing for people in the projects. God's for people who got a different type of life. God ain't done a damn thing for me."

Rakim inched away from her and was suddenly enraged and unable to keep it inside. He paced the ten free feet of space of her bedroom.

"And don't tell me about who I should be obligated to," he said through clenched teeth. "And don't talk to me about God. God stopped hearing project prayers when my brothers were killed—all five of 'em." He looked over at her with an expression that was as mean as it was lethal. "You think that God was listening when them people killed your daddy?"

Gina gasped; her hand flew up to cover her mouth, and a fresh well of tears sprang to her eyes.

He moved to stab a finger in her chest. "Your mama wasn't thinking about God when them men did what they did to her. And she wasn't thinking about God when she took y'all ass over the edge."

Gina shook with a rage of her own as she slapped his finger away. "You didn't have to bring my mama and daddy into this." She swiped away the last of her tears and turned away from him.

"And you didn't have to bring God into it at all," he replied, satisfied that she felt exactly the way he always had. "I was just making a point so you'll get my meaning."

She kept her back to him as she walked over to the window to look out at traffic crawling along the Dan Ryan—that great concrete divide and permanent ten-lane separation between The Low End and Bridgeport, between Black and White. "I hear you loud and clear, Matthew."

"It's Rakim. Matthew ain't here no more." He stood in the center of the room, refusing to cover the few feet between them. "And Friday, Gina, it's a whole new game. By choice or by force. I'm done playing with your ass."

She turned to face him, then leaned against the concrete wall as she shook her head and just stared at him. "It's always all about what you want."

"If it was about what I wanted, you'd be on your back right now," he countered. "I wouldn't be waiting for nothing." His gaze shifted to Mama Bessie's photograph on the dresser. "Didn't want that crazy old woman to put a bullet in my ass." Then he roared with laughter. "No, what she said was that she would slice off my balls, have one for breakfast, the other for lunch and use my dick to stir dinner." His grin widened as flickered a leering look over Gina. "But I don't have to worry about that no more."

Gina leveled a stony gaze at him, her voice low and deadly. "You sho' 'bout dat li'l nigger?"

Rakim flinched and stepped back, his eyes wide, his mouth gaped in surprise as he took in her meaning. Gina sounded and actually felt more dangerous than Mama Bessie ever had. Several moments passed before he relaxed and let out a nervous laugh. "Bitch, please. You wouldn't shoot me."

Gina didn't bother to answer. Instead, she lowered her gaze to hide the fury that had filled her heart. She loved him, but she would put a bullet in his ass faster than a whore could straddle a dick at sunset. And she would have the balls to come to his funeral to make sure she had done it right.

She took a deep breath and tried to push all signs of her anger aside. Then she gave him a humorless smile, batted her lashes at him, and softened her stance while thinking, *Mama. Daddy. Mayre. Mama Bessie. My life. My way.* Her heart had glazed over with purpose.

"It doesn't have to be this way," she said in a deceptively mild tone, while her brain was clicking out her plans; none of them included surrendering to Rakim or Ted. But she had resigned herself to the fact that it might take putting a little hot lead in into one of them to get her point across.

"This is the only way I know how to be," he said simply. "You keep talking about leaving. Ain't nothing out there for a young Black man. So I'm doing just what everybody else's doing—making a living."

Gina folded her arms across her ample bosom. "You call that living? I call it a funeral just waiting to happen. There aren't that many of you left."

Rakim glowered angrily at her because he didn't have a quick comeback. He had lost twelve men over the past few weeks. Since 5247 produced more cash from drugs, prostitution, and others who paid them for "protection," the Mickey Cobras—a rival gang—wanted this particular building in the worst way.

Her lips lifted in a slow, sly smile that rankled his nerves. Gina had a point and he knew it.

"I have to go. But remember what I said. Friday, your ass is mine." He walked to the threshold but paused when he heard a whispered, "Goodbye, Matthew."

His head whipped around so he could lock a steady gaze on her. "You mean, goodnight, Rakim."

She arched a single brow and relented. "Yes, goodnight ... Rakim."

By choice or by force? Bitch? Ah, yes, the real Rakim had come out to play. Any trace of Matthew Jones was long gone. In his place was a cold, hard, ruthless boy named Rakim who was hell bent on destroying his own life and taking Gina along for the ride. "Give a man a li'l power and some money, and his true self will shine through."

Truer words were never spoken by the master gunslinger herself.

Gina would not make the mistake of thinking she could appeal to his good side again. *By choice or by force* were definitely fighting words. And she would fight to win or die trying. George would give her a six-bullet head start. One of them had Rakim's name on it. Actually, they probably all did.

Rakim looked at her for a long while and didn't reach out for his normal hug. Instead, he walked out of the bedroom, then the house, and left her standing near the window.

Chapter 6

The bedroom door creaked open. Gina inched her arm under the pillow and relaxed, waiting. He had rigged the lock so it wouldn't catch all the way. Nothing she had done to reverse it had worked.

Mama Bessie's funeral was two days away. If Ted continued to make the wrong moves, he would join his father on the wrong side of glory. She slowly moved the gun down by her side under the comforter.

"And I hate to say it," Mama Bessie had said, "but if somethin' happens to me, even my son ain't gonna do right by you. He ain't gonna see takin' care of you as carrying on my obl'gation; he's gonna see you as another piece of tail he can get his hands on. Like his weak pitiful wife. Heifer should've left him the first time he hit her."

"But he's always been so nice to me," Gina protested.

Mama Bessie scoffed, "That's 'cause he ain't had no power over you ..."

Ted halted at the edge of the bed. Gina forced her breathing to stay even. The smell of whiskey and musk overpowered all other scents in the room. He lunged toward the bed and pinned her body with his weight. Gina cocked George and jammed it right at Ted's exposed genitals. "You'll have a hard time explaining what happened to your nut sack."

Ted froze; only his eyes moved as he locked on Gina's hard glare and growled, "If you ain't giving up no ass, then you got to go."

"I think I got that message loud and clear," she replied dryly, keeping her eyes focused on his. "So why did you feel it was necessary to come in here at two in the morning to say it again?"

"Put the gun away," he said through his teeth. "And let's talk about it."

"Put your dick away or George will be the end of the conversation."

"Ted..." Patricia's soft whisper echoed behind them.

He scrambled off the bed and stumbled backward into the dresser, knocking over the tiny bottles of perfume and Mama Bessie's picture before landing on the floor. He struggled to stand as Gina reached out and switched on the lamp next to her bed to unveil his limp dick greeting the early morning chill. Gina's metal friend was gripped tightly in her right hand.

"Oh, oh, sorry." He grabbed his head as though a headache was coming on. "I ... I ... um ... I stumbled into the wrong room."

"Again?" Patricia shot back, leaning on the door jamb as she tightened the belt around her robe.

Ted shook his head vigorously and swallowed hard. "I was on my way to the bathroom and I just ..." He reached down, pulled up his zipper, and turned to his wife. "Why aren't you asleep?"

Patricia's hands were balled into fists; a vein throbbed at her ivory temple. "Go back to bed, Ted."

He threw one last scathing look in Gina's direction as he stalked off, brushing past his wife on the way out.

Patricia inhaled deeply and waited until she knew he was out of hearing range, then walked further into the bedroom. She perched near Gina's feet and stroked a hand over the soft pink comforter. "What have you been doing with the money I give you?"

"If I didn't buy food, none of us would eat." Gina shifted and placed George back in his resting place before sitting up so she was eye level with the slick-haired woman. "And it's going to take more than a hundred dollars for me to get up out of this place. I don't have any place to go. No family. Nothing."

Gina slipped off the bed and righted Mama Bessie's picture. She frowned at the cracked glass that now marred the woman's image. She could replace the glass; the woman herself was one-of-a kind. She picked up the perfume bottles and placed them back on the dresser one by one. Sand & Sable, Mama Bessie's favorite, had spilled but at least the scent swept away Ted's pungent odor. Gina cracked the window to let in some fresh spring air.

Patricia bent down to help Gina with the rest of the bottles, then reached out to place her hand over Gina's. "You could stay with my people."

Gina snatched away. "I don't know your people." She turned her back to the woman and continued cleaning up the mess Ted had made.

"Staying with them would have to be better than living on your own."

Gina stood. Her gaze shifted to the window and to the darkened sky; a flash of light blinked as an airplane seemed to inch across the darkness as it left Chicago. Stay with Patricia's people? Another set of strangers, a whole new set of rules that would put her back to square one instead of several steps ahead. She had been through enough hell. The rest of her life wasn't going to be about struggling or about someone else making choices on her behalf.

"If that's such a better choice for me, then why aren't you and Ted moving in with *your people*?"

Patricia lifted her chin and squared her shoulders. "This place suits us just fine. We have more right to be here than you do. You're not even related."

Gina shook her head as she looked over her shoulder and took in the woman's beautiful face. Gina knew from the way the woman spoke that she was educated. "You don't have any children, and you're a nurse. The only thing Ted works on is turning up his next bottle. You could do so much better than him."

Patricia moved from the bed and fingered one of the broken bottles on the dresser. "He's not so bad. He just drinks a little too much. Sad about his mama and all." She opened the Love's Baby Soft and inhaled deeply.

"If he missed his mama so much, why didn't he come see her more often? He didn't bust his ass to get here until she wasn't here anymore."

Patricia replaced the clear pink bottle and picked up the next one. "He's got his finer points." She had actually said that with a straight face.

Gina pursed her lips against the smart remark that threatened to spill out.

Patricia locked gazes with her through the dresser's mirror. "I guess you can't see any of that."

"Uh ... no."

Patricia moved to stand in front of the closet and fingered the soft, flimsy material of the black chiffon dress that hung on the door. "People move in here all the time without a lease or anything."

"And CHA has the police escort them right out."

"We'll put in the proper paperwork later. They'll let us stay because he was her son. They loved that old woman." She ran a hand over the smooth concrete walls, which had been painted a bright blue. "This place is something I can afford on what I make. We were losing the apartment anyway. So the timing's perfect."

"So he just lays up and lets you do it all?"

Patricia's silence was an answer in itself.

"So what good is having a man if he's not pulling his weight?" Gina asked, using her bath towel to wipe up the spill. "That's one thing Mama Bessie always taught me—how a household works." She stood, put a hand on her hip, and mimicked her grandmother, "Those who ain't bringin' in as much as other folks have to c'tribute in other ways. Even a dog's gotta work, bring in a bone or somethin'."

"Then she should've taught her lazy ass son that same thing," Patricia shot back.

"Hard to teach a man who resents you for running his daddy off."

Patricia whipped around to face Gina. "He blamed her for that?"

Gina shrugged, placing the towel on the floor next to the bed. "I heard that Ms. Franks in 812 wanted to take him in and put him to good use, since she was a widow and everything. But he was too ashamed to stay, and she was scared of what Mama Bessie might do."

"He sure wasn't worth a bullet," Patricia quipped.

"Mama Bessie wouldn't have shot her over him. Though the woman might have taken a bullet *accidentally* if Mama Bessie made a second attempt at shooting her husband."

Gina giggled, and Patricia joined in. When the laughter died away, Patricia sighed and said, "I'm going to try to get a good night's sleep though the night's already gone." She walked to the threshold. "And speaking of gone, Gina …"

"I hear you, but in the meantime, do what you can to keep your husband from mistaking *mine* for yours."

Taking Gina's meaning, Patricia whirled around to face her. "I can't protect you from him. You have to find someplace else." She steadied herself and said softly, "I can get you to my sister's house."

Gina slipped under the comforter and laid her head among the pillows. "Does she live alone, or does she have a man?"

"She has a …" Patricia's eyes widened with understanding.

Gina switched off the lamp. "Goodnight, Patricia."

Patricia didn't bother to answer as she walked out and closed the door.

Gina was too wired to sleep, so she stretched out on her bed and worked her mind around Plan A—one that Mama Bessie would never have approved of. If the girls of RTH were baby-making machines, collecting thousands of dollars a year just for spitting out mostly unwanted offspring, then why not do it in a way that mattered for people who would cherish the little human outcomes?

Weeks before, when Mama Bessie first slipped into that coma, Gina had seen an advertisement from a mixed-race couple who wanted a Black female surrogate to carry their child. Gina did her research and found that the couple was offering a substantial amount of money—but there were also some problems she would have to address:

The surrogate needed to be eighteen or older. Gina had found someone in the print shop at school to alter her birth certificate. So according to that piece of paper, she was eighteen; not the seventeen she'd be in a few weeks from now.

The surrogate should already have a child of her own. Big problem. Gina was still a virgin; she'd had every intention of staying that way until she was married, and she had never really wanted children of her own. RTH's residents had soured her on that idea a long time ago.

The primary motive for the surrogate could not be money. Fat chance. The *only* reason she was considering the idea was that she needed money desperately. What they offered would certainly tide her over until the insurance policies from Mama Bessie and other money left by her father came to her when she turned twenty-one.

Surrogates were required to go through one or several medical procedures. Gina hated hospitals and needles, not exactly in that order. The child would need to be conceived in the natural way or not at all.

This couple wanted the surrogate to be middle class—and could not be on any form of government assistance. Gina had class, but her income was far from putting her in the middle bracket. She hoped the couple was desperate enough to make an exception.

Surrogates had to be non-smokers, healthy, and want to help people have families. Done deal.

Gina was certain she could renegotiate for what she required most—a place to live, to finish her education, and have enough money to carry her until she was able to make it on her own. If she could work around their stipulations. If they were desperate enough to resort to advertising, then she might have an edge.

She had used the phone in the principal's office to set up an interview with the Meisters, a couple from an upscale suburb of Chicago, for Friday, right after Mama Bessie's funeral service.

Gina pulled out her book bag and packed the last of the items she would need to take with her—some underwear, a couple of changes of clothes, the remaining pictures of her family and those of Mama Bessie.

The day the "intruders" showed up, she had secretly removed Mama Bessie's valuables and her own; the majority of them resided in an hidden compartment in her science class at school.

Gina wasn't as worried as she should have been. *If* things worked out, she would give the Meisters what they wanted most—if, and only if, they were prepared to give Gina Renee Wright what she needed in return.

Two days.

Chapter 7

Wednesday - 8:06 a.m.

Gina inhaled, frowning at the scent of rain that threatened to break at any moment. All week the clouds had gathered, but nothing had come forth. She adjusted the suitcase in her hand, locked the door behind her, then turned and ran smack into Rakim's hard chest. She kept a good grip on the items she carried and stood firm as his gaze roamed her body, then locked onto her book bag.

"What's in there?"

"School stuff."

Rakim glared at her for a few moments. "Open it."

Gina thought about resisting, but then slipped the bag off her right shoulder and exposed the stack of papers inside.

"What's in the suitcase?"

She balanced the beige leather case on one knee and cracked it opened to show it was filled with papers.

Rakim cocked a brow.

"Need it for a school play."

He turned to the two boys flanking him, then looked back at Gina. "We ain't heard nothing about no play."

"Why would you? You're not in school," she snapped.

"We know everything that's going on around here."

A door slammed from an apartment down the hall. Ms. Pitchford struggled with her three children, ushering them to the elevator. She punched the call button. Moments later when nothing happened, the woman's gaze swept to the end of the hall where Gina, Rakim, and his boys were standing.

Gina shook her head to answer the woman's unspoken question.

"Damn! Broke again?"

Gina nodded and watched as the woman dragged her kids to the stairwell, muttering her displeasure along the way.

"Well, I have to go." Gina moved around Rakim but only made it a few feet before his hand snaked out to hold her in place. "Tino and Man Man, y'all take Gina to school."

She couldn't keep the alarm from gripping her heart, but she tried to keep her expression neutral. "They don't have to do that."

"Them fools over there," he said, gesturing to the next building, "been acting real stupid since we put some of our people up in there." He passed the suitcase to Tino. "They're gonna take you there today and tomorrow. Be waiting for you when you get out of school." His eyes searched hers for a moment. "And Friday, baby, I'll go with you to the funeral. I gotta pay my respects to that crazy old woman too."

Rakim gave her a sly grin and winked as he stroked her arm.

Damn. Just what she needed. Rakim all up in her business. Gina shrugged off his touch, which only angered him more. She walked a few steps with the men trailing her before Rakim said, "Oh yeah, and you can let me hold onto George."

Gina didn't turn around. "But I need him for protection."

"Ah, don't bother with all that," Rakim countered smoothly as he came to stand in front of her and held out his hand. "I can protect what's mine."

She looked at his open palm then back up to his face as she smiled.

"Actually, George is in the house. You said I was safe, right? I didn't have to be afraid of no one but you, right?"

Rakim's jaw twitched, matching the throbbing vein at his temple. "I'm going to be real glad when I can put my fist in that smart ass mouth of yours."

"Big bad Rakim," she taunted, lifting her chin so they were eye level. "Have to hit a girl to have some power."

He grabbed her shoulders and pulled her so they were nose to nose. "Don't try me, bitch!"

The two men rifled through her bag again as Rakim shoved her, pressing her back to the yellow brick wall while she kept her focus on him. They didn't turn up the gun, so they reached for her and jammed their hands into her denim jacket. Gina smacked their hands away, but they came right back at her. At that moment, Ms. Williams exited her apartment dragging a checkered print area rug and a broom. The silver-haired woman halted, peering down at them with a questioning expression.

"Oh, so that's how y'all do it now?" Gina said in a voice that carried down the hall. "Just molest me right out in the open. Damn, that's deep." Gina turned, went to the wall, and spread her legs out. She placed her hands against the brick, looking more like a criminal being shaken down by the police than a young girl on her way to school.

"Stop that," Rakim yelled, venturing a quick glance at the old woman, who had called for others inside their apartments to come out and watch. "Turn your ass around."

"I just wanted them to check everywhere."

Rakim didn't take his eyes off her as she faced him. "Why don't we step back inside and get him?"

"And wake Ted? And Patricia too? Two days before the funeral? Oh that should be reeeeeal interesting."

Rakim scowled his displeasure. Finally he pushed her toward his men. "Take her ass to school. And if she tries any stupid shit—like running away—put a bullet in her ass ... No. In her foot." His lips spread into something that was neither a smile nor a frown. "I want that ass perfect."

Gina smiled back, thinking, *if they shoot me, someone will have to take me to the hospital, and I could leave from there.* But she sobered instantly. She didn't want to show up at the Meisters' that way. Explaining a bullet wound would not be easy. She already had enough going against her.

Ms. Williams glowered at Rakim and stopped the group from moving past long enough to hug Gina to her. "Thanks for that bed. It's so comfortable, I think I snore even louder now."

"No problem, Ms. Williams," Gina replied, giving her a smile. "She would've wanted that for you."

Rakim peered at her for a moment. "What did you do?"

Gina didn't bother to answer as she moved around him.

His face darkened with anger. "You gave away all that old woman's shit? Why?" Then he relaxed and grinned. "You thought you wouldn't need it no more." He nodded at his own observation. "That's all right. I'll get us some better furniture."

Rakim trailed them to the stairwell. "I'm moving in Friday night, Gina. I got people down at CHA who's gonna lose the paperwork on that apartment. It's not gonna be available to nobody else. It's all done, baby."

Gina navigated the stairs without looking at him, though her heart stilled at the fact that he had gone to such lengths. She could only wonder if it was the same person she had contacted to tell about Ted and Patricia's untimely arrival. Respect for Mama Bessie aside, for the right amount of money anyone could be bought.

"You gonna live the way I say you should live. You gonna learn to take care of your man. So after Friday, no more school. 'Cause your ass is mine."

Gina swallowed hard and didn't say anything as she trudged down the stairs to the third floor.

"And I want breakfast every morning," he said, as though warming up to the subject. "Yeah and dinner too. Them lazy ho's can't cook. Can't do nothing but spread 'em wide. Oh, and have babies."

Tino and Man Man bellowed with laughter.

Gina walked down the final flight of stairs. Still, she didn't look at him.

Rakim maneuvered in front of her and tried to catch her gaze, but failed. He stood in her path, forcing her to stop as he tilted her chin so their eyes met. "It'll be better for you than my other women. And I'm not gonna get you pregnant," he whispered into her ear. "I'ma put that schooling to good use. You gonna be my bottom woman and collect my money from the other girls. Give 'em just enough money to pay CHA and keep the lights on. I already put them on notice. They're gonna respect you like they respect me. See, it won't be so bad."

She tried to keep her expression blank—void of fear. But she was afraid. Very afraid. And that was certainly a foreign feeling.

Gina continued to make her way out of the building with Tino and Man Man trailing behind her. Rakim was at her side, scowling as he said, "But get out of line, and you'll learn what I do to the others." He stroked a hand across her face. "I don't want to do nothing like that to you, but I will. Actually, I'll be moving some of my shit in tonight. Don't worry about my man Ted. We'll get him straight. You're gonna learn that I run this. We're gonna take over all three of these units."

Seeing that she still didn't respond, show fear or any emotion, he added, "Maybe I'll get that fine house that you want, but you gotta show that you can obey me and only me."

Rakim licked his lips and pressed them to hers. She turned away and wiped her mouth. The action caused his expression to darken. He shoved her away. "Get this bitch outta my face."

The two men moved to her side and walked up the sidewalk out to the car.

Gina's mind was awhirl with thoughts. She could ask the principal for help, but if she involved him, Tino and Man Man could bring reinforcements and then innocent people could get killed. She wouldn't put it past Rakim. He was still alive when so many others had been gunned down. That didn't happen by accident or by being slow on the draw.

In Rakim's Chevy Impala on the way to DuSable High School, Tino asked Man Man, "How long you thank befo' we get some of that?"

Tino shrugged, looked at Gina in the rearview mirror, and grinned. "He loves this one. Might be a minute."

"Naw man, he always feel that way in the beginning. They all fall in love with his ass. She ain't gonna be no different. I bet she'll feel good too."

After that, neither of them said much, but they had done plenty to confirm what her life would be like once Rakim tired of her.

When she arrived at school, she gathered her items from their hidden places around the school and held them against her chest as she walked to the principal's office. She kept thinking about Mama Bessie and her life lessons. Mama Bessie had given her the tools and the will and had broken down the ways of life in a way that Gina would never forget:

"When you look at life, you gotta look at it from all sides, baby. This place is a concrete slave ship. We're stacked on top of each other just like we was when they took us from Africa. Folks can't see it for what it really is. They don't know they past and the future's playin' out the same way all over again."

But Gina wasn't going to be trapped in that concrete prison. She carefully placed her new birth certificate, all five of Mama Bessie's bank books for accounts that listed Gina as beneficiary, and every one of the insurance certificates in her book bag.

Gina stroked a thumb across the batch of report cards from kindergarten to the last grading period. Tears rolled down her face as she remembered Mama Bessie talking about her life and how she handled even the toughest situations.

"I only went to school until the sixth grade 'cause I had to work in them cotton fields to help my family. Spendin' all that time in them fields taught me to hear what's really bein' said when somebody's lips is moving and they brains is spillin' out into their ass. It taught me to listen to what they ain't saying and see past all the bullshit."

Education would be Gina's first plan of attack, then everything else would follow. Gina's child by the Meisters would know love, would know what it was like not to want for anything. Would not have to be afraid or make it alone in the world.

As Gina sat in the office, tears began to stream down her face, and she closed her eyes picturing the one woman who had given her almost everything she needed so that Gina would never be afraid...

"The Bible speaks on all types of women. Virt'ous women, and it speaks on the so-called bad ones, but there's a whole lot of gray in between—and that's where all the real lessons is." Mama Bessie looked Gina straight in the eye. "Make yo' way in life—yo' choices, Gina. Let it be *yo'* choices, and not because of some boy—or man." Mama Bessie had cupped Gina's face in her hands, then pressed a gentle kiss to her forehead. "Get that schoolin', baby. Make somethin' of yo'self; do whatever it takes to survive, but make no mistake about it—make the rules yo' damn self."

Point taken. Two days. She used the principal's phone to make a call to the funeral home, putting her first line of defense into play.

Chapter 8

Rain. Why did every major event in her life begin and end with water? The funeral was well underway. Unity Funeral Parlor was packed wall-to-wall; Gina hadn't seen some of the people in attendance since they had moved away from RTH years ago. They greeted her warmly, and though her heart was heavy, it lightened when she remembered how much they had loved Mama Bessie too.

Ted and Patricia sat in the front row. Ted stared openly at the life-sized portrait of his mother. He had been angered, and others had been taken aback, to find out that Mama Bessie had requested that she be cremated. She had said to Gina, "It's cold down there. Sprinkle me in front of the buildin' and call it a damn day. Don't make no kinda sense to put all that money into some box that people don't halfway come visit no how. This way I can hang around and keep an eye on things."

Gina was glad that Mama Bessie had put her wishes in writing and had paid for the services many years prior. Those who wanted to take one last gander at the old girl, whose spunk was legendary in all of the RTH units, would just have to remember her the way they last saw her. Gina was grateful for that. She hoped her mentor was looking out for her at this very moment. She didn't leave Ted a single dime. He didn't take the news well.

Since their encounter the other day, Rakim had staged an around-the-clock watch. Anytime she peered outside to see if her "guards" were asleep or had taken a break, they were right there, laughing it up loud as hell all hours of the night long.

Rakim and a good majority of his crew had showed up at the apartment hours before the funeral. He had dressed in a brand new black pin-striped suit that draped his slender frame to perfection. Almost all of his women had shown up at the parlor, their unruly tribes in tow. He had them sprinkled throughout the congregation. Each of them had cut angry glares in Gina's direction. She took the time to study each one of them, taking in the hardened expressions, the eyes that were tired and weary. She sensed an overwhelming feeling of hopelessness about them—the same feeling that was weighing her down at the moment.

One of them locked gazes with Gina who couldn't believe the change in the young woman. The girl was twenty but looked more like forty. Shallonda checked Gina's perfectly styled curls, the slight touch of makeup, the classically tailored A-line dress, and her shiny black pumps. Shallonda smacked her lips, rolled her eyes then looked over to Rakim, who had been watching the entire exchange.

He gave an almost imperceptible nod, and the girl visibly softened and smiled before turning back to her three hellions and attempting to get them in check. "Didn't I tell your little asses to be quiet!"

Gina cringed along with others around them and shook her head. Rakim flicked a gaze between the children and Gina's obvious disapproval. His lips pursed into a straight line as he glowered at Shallonda, willing her to miraculously get the children under control. Evidently, his reputation on the streets hadn't reached the ears of his children. They ignored him and any attempts the brassy haired woman made to keep them quiet.

"Folks ain't as stupid as they let on," Mama Bessie had said, "We know what's being done around here. What kind of sense it make to give a woman somethin' for nothin? Can't raise the first chile right, 'cause the next one knockin' him off the tit. Can't love 'em really, 'cause they ain't even know themselves. What kind of foolishness is that? Get mo' money to lay up with some no-good man than to go to college and make som'thin' of themselves?"

Gina looked off to another of Rakim's women, who must have felt Gina's eyes on her. Rage rolled off Trina in waves that matched her weave as she growled, "Fuck you, bitch. Think you all that. You gonna be a ho' just like the rest of us."

Murmurs of agreement echoed from all of the women who belonged to Rakim. He crossed the distance to the girl and raised a hand to strike. The other guests around them gasped and inched back. He took a deep breath, then yanked Trina up from the seat, pushing her toward Tino and Man Man, who dragged her out. Rakim's gaze swept the room, flickering to the remaining women in his unlikely little harem. They seemed to wither under his hard glare. He had gotten the point across: Gina was the new main lady and any disrespect would not be tolerated.

Gina turned away from him and all the onlookers, who now whispered among themselves. She focused her gaze on Mama Bessie's picture, wondering if that was what her life would become. Worn out and without any end in sight? The lover of a man who would use her, then have his boys run up in her? Would she still beg for his occasional attention as if she was some love-starved child?

She sat stoically through Ms. Charles' heart-stirring rendition of "I Won't Complain." Gina didn't look at anyone else who took the podium during the service. Her mind was far from the kind words that people spoke about Bessie Mae Slaughter. She knew more about the woman than anyone in the place ever would.

Mama Bessie had taught Gina there was always a choice in everything. Even the slaves had made a choice when taking those ill-fated trips across the Atlantic. Some had taken their own lives rather than face the unknown and allow someone else control their fate. Some had chosen to risk getting killed as they ran from the plantation and the brutality they faced. Now that was a straight-up Mama Bessie type move. And then there were some who conformed, just gave in to whatever—no matter how unhappy it made them. Thanks to Mama Bessie's strength and courage, there wasn't a conforming bone in Gina's body. Rakim could take his plans and stick them where the sun couldn't give him a tan.

She scanned the parlor to find that his men were posted at every exit. Their guns were hidden underneath their suits, but Gina could spot heat from twenty paces.

Trina stumbled back in as all eyes focused in her direction. Some gasped at the additional bruising coloring her face. At first she glared at Gina. Then she thought better of it, lowered her gaze to the floor, and growled, "I'm sorry, Gina," before being led away to the back pew.

Embarrassed that this would happen in the middle of service, Gina glared at Rakim, who gave her a small smile that Gina didn't return. He came to sit next to her and tried to hold her hand.

Gina snatched it away, folding her arms across her breasts. She took another gander at the rest of his women and could see the differences and the similarities. Anger ripped through her at the fact that one man had compromised the lives of so many women. Correction—all those women had allowed one man to take them over—take over their will and their dreams. They had made a choice that Gina never could.

She stood the moment the minister came to the lectern to give the eulogy.

Rakim caught up with her and grabbed her arm. "Where you going?"

"To the restroom."

"You can hold it 'til he gets through."

Gina moved forward so that she was a breath's length away. "You want me to tinkle all over your brand new pants?"

Chuckles rang out around them, causing Rakim's face to darken with anger.

Rakim nodded toward Tino, who moved forward and hooked his arm under Gina's. She didn't make eye contact with any of the people sitting in the pews as they made it to the door. She held the funeral director's gaze for as long as she could.

Gina slipped into the bathroom stall and waited a few moments to get her bearings and her breathing under control. She didn't have a gun. They had ransacked the house Wednesday night and found George nestled in his hiding place in her bedroom wall. Ted had tried to stop them, but they made short work of his protests with a quick but convincing ass-kicking. No switchblade either. Rakim himself had searched her body for that piece of weaponry. She could swear that his fingers lingered in her panties, playing with her a few moments before extracting Little Gina. Instead of passing it to his boys, he had pressed the silver to his nose, inhaling her feminine scent, then stuffed it into his jeans pocket.

A honk outside the bathroom window snapped her into action. She ran out of the stall, removed the frosted glass panel and gently placed it on the floor. She hoisted her body upward and scaled the red brick until she was halfway to the ground.

At that moment, Shallonda burst in and screamed, "Rakim, Come quick. She's gettin' away."

Gina pushed hard and tumbled the rest of the way out of the window, landing face first on the ground. She rolled, jumped up, and scrambled into the front seat of the hearse. "Go! Go! Go!" she shrieked at the gray-haired driver, who took off before she could close the door all the way.

The wheels squealed in protest on the rain-slicked pavement as he tore down Michigan Avenue. Gina crawled over the seat, clawed at the casket, and opened it. She fumbled inside, searching for her suitcase and her book bag, while her heart hammered in her chest.

The hearse lurched to a sudden stop, tumbling Gina into the back. She ducked down the moment she heard the click from a gun.

"Get your old ass out. Right now."

Gina closed her eyes and said a prayer, then lifted the body enough so she could slip underneath. She stretched out her arm, struggling to reach the casket's lid, but only managed to get it down most of the way. She covered up with the silk lining and peered out of a sliver of the opening.

The rear door swung open.

"Open that up."

"I'm not touching that," Tino shrieked.

Man Man shook his head before Rakim could bring the request his way. "Don't look at me."

"This is the only place she could be."

"You didn't see her get in here. And one thing I ain't down with touching no dead bodies."

"I know she's in there."

Tino threw up his hands. "You wanna know for sho' then your ass is gonna have to do it, man. I ain't touching no dead body."

Rakim growled, "Get the driver."

Man Man dragged Mr. Wheeler to the rear of the hearse.

"Open it up."

"I don't have a key," he answered in a dry tone that barely hid his nervousness.

Rakim cocked his gun at the man's head. "You think I'm stupid? What it need a key for? They ass is already dead. They ain't getting out unless you let 'em." He struck the man's forehead with the butt of his gun. "Open this mothafucka or you're gonna take one to the head."

"Man, why are you attacking me?" Mr. Wheeler yelled. "I could lose my job for opening that casket."

"You can lose your life if you don't. Where she at?"

Mr. Wheeler held up his hands to deflect another blow. "I don't know who you're talking about."

Rakim cocked his head, nostrils flaring. "Don't play. I ain't got time for dumb shit."

The man closed his eyes tight and waited. If he was afraid, no one could tell.

Rakim scanned the area and saw that people had come out on their porches. Witnesses. Every single one of them.

"Gina. Listen up. I will kill him and won't think twice about it. Come out right now, or it's his life."

She took a deep breath then used all of her strength to push her casket mate to the side and crawl out. She grabbed her suitcase and bag just before Rakim gripped her arm and backhanded her so hard she dropped everything. Tino and Man Man caught her as she stumbled into them, and they kept her from hitting the ground.

Gina wiped the blood from her mouth as Rakim moved forward until they were eye to eye. "You think I'm playing with you? See, I tried to do right by your ass and let you put that old woman to rest. Now you ain't gonna get to do that." He gestured to the open door. "Put her ass in the car. We're going back to the house."

"What about him?" Tino asked, pointing his gun at the driver, who threw an apologetic look her way.

"Please don't kill him," Gina whispered. "Please just let him go."

Rakim snatched her up. "You should be worried about your own ass, not some crusty old fool."

He dragged her to the Impala a few feet away. She ventured a look back at the driver who had risked his life to help her. And it was all for nothing. The old man glared at the young men, his hands balled into fists as he watched them take her away. Rakim shoved her in the backseat, and she flinched when four shots rang out.

Gina's heart came to what seemed like a complete stop. She peered out of the tinted windows to find the driver still standing, but the hearse was lower than it had been. They had shot out the tires so he couldn't follow. But they had left him alive. At least one prayer had been answered.

"I said you was gonna be different, but that's changed now," Rakim growled at her. "I can't trust your ass. I gotta treat you just like them other ho's. I loved you, bitch. I *loved* you." His shoulders flexed, and he glared down at her. "Yeah, now I gotta show you some things."

They turned onto 47th and made a right as Rakim raised his hand to smack her again.

She froze and closed her eyes to absorb the blow that never came.

Instead, he lowered his hands to his side. "I was gonna make it good for you—being your first time and all. But you don't deserve that. Made a fool outta me in front of my boys."

Tino and Man Man exchanged a knowing glance and grinned.

"When I'm done, you're gonna make me some money."

They pulled up in front of the building, as numerous other cars were pulling in from the services. A number of Rakim's men filed out along with his women and their children, who fell in step with the rest of the group.

Rakim gripped her arm and half-walked, half-dragged her across the concrete walkway, yelling at her the entire time. They were almost to the stairwell when Shawn—leader of the Mickey Cobras and several of his men crept out of the laundry room, guns drawn as they rolled up on Rakim and his men. Gina saw them spreading out from the corner of her eye, but didn't alert Rakim to the fact that he had unwanted company.

"Yo, dawg, what's up? '47 ain't enough for you now?" Shawn asked as his men fanned out around them to cover Rakim's crew. "You tryin' to take what's mine? That ain't happening."

Rakim's men moved into a defensive position. They outnumbered Shawn's people by just a few men, but it wasn't the count that mattered; it was fire power. And the newcomers had it in spades.

"Move the fuck out the way before we ghost all y'all," Rakim growled. "Next time, come with something more serious than your preschool crew."

The smart residents scurried back into their apartments, and the women and children hightailed it back to the cars and to the other buildings. Others poured out onto the landing, boldly looking down at the exchange.

Gina inched back and tried to make a mad dash for the street.

Rakim put a solid grip around her neck. His gun whipped into his right hand, and he pointed it at Shawn. "We need to talk 'bout this some other time. I got business to take care of. Ain't nobody trying to kill nobody on the day of that old woman's funeral."

At that moment, Gina sank her teeth into Rakim's gun hand.

Reflex made him pull the trigger. Shawn sank to the ground, clutching his chest. A volley of shots followed. Chaos ensued.

Gina hit the stairwell at top speed, scaled the first flight three stairs at a time. She rounded the third flight and heard Rakim yell, "I'ma beat your ass, Gina."

She kept moving. The gunshots had died down some.

"Cover that other stairwell," Rakim yelled.

Damn. Now she couldn't cross the landing and go down the opposite stairwell and back to the ground. A stampede of sounds thundered behind her, but she kept it moving.

Gina rounded floors eight and nine. The adrenaline coursed through her, fueling her with renewed energy. She had to make it to the top. At floor ten she kicked off her pumps and picked up speed. She tore up flights twelve, thirteen, scrambled up to fourteen, fifteen. Her chest tightened with pain; her legs were on fire; tendrils of pain shot through her head, but she kept pushing.

Gina hit the sixteenth floor and hauled ass across the landing to the middle section of the mesh wire fence that stretched the length of the hallway; the only protective barrier that kept residents from falling sixteen stories to the ground. There was a small part cut in the center, curled back far enough to allow someone as small as Gina to fit through.

"Are you crazy?" Rakim screamed. He came to a halt and held out an arm to keep his boys from passing in front of him.

The sky had darkened to a dusky gray. The heavens opened up and rain poured down, blurring her vision. She wiped her face with the back of a shaky hand. "I always thought my mama was weak for checking out on life the way she did." Gina tried to calm her erratic breathing and rapid heartbeat. "It took courage for her to decide she didn't have to take what life was throwing her way. She could say to hell with everybody and exit stage left."

Gina gripped the silver fencing and looked down.

"Come on now," he demanded. "Get back from there."

Tino and Man Man yelled at people, telling them to go back into their apartments.

For once, the residents ignored them, as the scene unfolding before them held more interest.

"You said by choice or by force," she shouted to him. "I choose death, Rakim. I would rather die than to live the way you want me to live."

"I didn't mean it, baby. Come—"

"Oh, you meant it, all right. And I believe you." She looked over to him. "You actually think I would allow you to control me? That I would be happy to be nothing more than your whore? That I have no other potential in life but to spread my legs for you and do what you tell me to do?"

"Okay … wait … wait. Let's talk about it." Rakim inched closer, gesturing for everyone else to stay back. "I can go back to you just being my bottom woman. That's not so bad. I mean, you'll still be above everyone."

Gina laughed, but it was a sound devoid of mirth. "That's what you want for me. I'm not living my life for you." She looked out at the cloud-filled sky, the rain pelting her face like tiny bullets. "Mama Bessie's waiting on me. My mama and daddy's waiting on me. Mayre … they're all waiting for me."

People had gathered on the ground level and looked up at the scene unfolding above. Bodies were scattered across the concrete—some in the grass, some in the area leading to the stairwell. With a single leap, she would be in perfect company.

She inched forward.

"Gina. No!"

"I can end my life on an exclamation point instead of you making it a question mark. I want to live on my terms. I can't do that with some man who doesn't love me."

"I love you, Gina. I do love you," Rakim pleaded, taking another step in her direction. "I want to take care of you."

Gina slipped forward, but her grip on the fence held her steady. "The only person you love is yourself."

"Move back. I'm not playing with you," he growled.

"I'm nothing to you, so this shouldn't be a problem, right?"

"Okay, I'll let you go." He spread his arms, inching toward her a bit more. "Just don't jump. Please, baby. Don't jump."

"Goodbye, Rakim."

Gina released her steadying grip on the fence, spread her arms wide, tilted her head to the rain and smiled. She stuck one foot off the platform and prepared to fly.

Rakim ran and reached for Gina, but he could only grab a handful of material. He held her in place, one foot angled dangerously on the edge of the concrete.

"Gina, pull back."

"Let me go!"

The dress ripped, and he sobbed as she struggled to pull away, almost forcing him to lose his grip.

"Gina."

He pulled on the material like a rope, hand over fist until, with one final yank backward, she tumbled in his direction, slamming into his body, taking them both onto the yellow bricks and landing them on the cold ground.

Rakim rocked back and forth with her in his arms, holding onto her as if for dear life.

"Gina," he finally whispered, his tears mixing with the rain on his face. "Baby, you're all I got left."

Gina tilted her head so that her gaze locked on his. A single tear dropped from his eye right into hers as she whispered, "You think I don't know that?"

"If you can't handle me at my worst, then you sure as hell don't deserve me at my best."
--Marilyn Monroe

Part II

Sins of the Mermaid

Chapter 9

Friday- 3:39 p.m.

Doctor Christopher and Alana Meister lived in a three-story mansion in Evanston, Illinois, right along Sheridan Road. He was the youngest surgeon at Loyola Medical; she, the newly appointed VP of Finance at a Fortune 500 company headquartered in downtown Chicago.

Their home was furnished simply and elegantly, but everything—from the tan, blue and eggshell color scheme, to the Egyptian and African artwork—had been contrived to give a feeling of warmth and class.

Gina sat on a dark leather sofa in Christopher's library, where the surrogate contract lay on his desk. The handsome blond man, with eyes the color of a clear morning sky, towered over his wife and Gina by a good five inches. He had a slight but muscular build and strong hands.

"I know you're desperate to have this child," Christopher said softly, finally breaking the silence that had gone on for longer than fifteen minutes. "But there's no way we could pull this off. She's still a virgin," he whispered as though amazed that a young girl from the projects could still be *virgo intacta*. "Any doctor in their right mind would have both of us committed."

"It should be easy to take care of the virginity issue," Alana replied, venturing a look in Gina's direction. "I'm sure she has someone who could share that special moment. A boyfriend perhaps?"

"No boyfriend," Gina countered quickly, focusing on Alana's soft-brown eyes, which shimmered with kindness. "I don't date anyone where I come from." And she certainly couldn't tell them about her near-death experience with Rakim to make the point.

Gina thought back to a few hours earlier. For all the remorse Rakim felt as he carried her down the flights of stairs, he hesitated when they approached the fifth floor. She looked into his eyes, witnessing the struggle between letting her go and taking her into the apartment.

Finally, Gina had ended his dilemma by saying, "Whether it's today, tomorrow, or the next day, by knife, rope, or in the tub, the end result will be the same."

Rakim resigned himself to the fact that he would not have what he wanted. But she soon learned that what angered him most was not that several of his men had been killed, but what message his failure with her would send to everyone. "Now all my bitches are gonna try and pull that," he growled as he continued toward the first floor. "They ain't gonna be so lucky if they do."

Gina doubted any of the girls would have the balls. She had seen the looks that Shallonda, Trina, and Bebe and the rest had given him. They loved him—as misguided as it was.

His boys had retrieved her shoes, returned her suitcase and book bag. He maneuvered through oncoming police who had swarmed the area. One of them waved him through the madness and toward the line of ambulances stretched out along State Street. Then he watched her slip on her heels and walk away. She didn't turn back for a single moment. She'd taken the State Street bus downtown, slipped into Berghoff's Restaurant, changed clothes, and waited for the Meisters to pick her up.

The interview was now in its second hour. She had explained

away everything else and presented the few pieces of satisfactory documentation, but they were stuck on one issue.

"I was saving myself for marriage, but I have other plans for my life now," Gina said. "And at this point, I don't think you would want to take a chance that I'll get pregnant by someone else. That could set you back a couple of years, even longer if you try for someone else. It's been years. Haven't you waited long enough?"

The classy, slender woman, with skin a couple of shades darker than Gina's took a long, slow breath. "Well, I guess that's true, but my husband's right; we can't let you be examined by a gynecologist and let him find out you're a virgin. It'll be almost a sacrilege for him to inseminate you while your hymen's intact."

"Inseminate? Needles, right?" Gina shook her head at that prospect. She had already stated her aversion to those little silver things.

Alana took a sip of the tea that she had brought in at the beginning of the interview, but it was cold by now. "Yes, lots of needles involved with that process." Her gaze kept moving over Gina's simple white blouse, tailored black slacks, pumps, and the single strand of pearls and matching earrings that Mama Bessie had given her for her sixteenth birthday—even now the woman was still sizing her up.

Alana glanced at her husband who scowled.

"I hate needles," Gina reminded them. "And I already told you that it's natural or nothing."

"Isn't there some young man who you've taken a liking to? You seem like a responsible girl. You can use a condom to protect yourself."

"Ms. Meister, you know where I come from. If there was someone I … *liked*, we wouldn't be having this conversation right now." Christopher blushed a bright pink and looked away. He ran a hand through his whisper-soft hair then perched on the seat nestled along the window.

"There are only two alternatives," Alana said, going to stand next to her husband. She looked over her shoulder at Gina. "But I'm not sure you'll accept them. You can use a sex toy and break your own hymen."

Gina frowned at that scenario and shook her head.

"Or … my husband could do the honors." He flinched, and she placed a hand on his shoulder as though to calm him. "We'd pay an additional fee, of course."

This time the man turned bright red as he stood and whirled his wife around to face him. "Have you lost your mind? She's just a child for Chrissakes."

"A child who is willing to give you the one thing your wife cannot."

Gina crossed one leg over the other. "How much money are we talking about?"

"Darling, we've spent thousands. I've had procedure after procedure." She splayed a hand over his broad chest as she whispered, "I can't have children, and I've accepted that. The other women were nowhere near as acceptable. This is the only way."

"You mentioned an additional fee," Gina interjected.

"I'm not comfortable with it, honey." His gaze locked in on his wife. Both continued to ignore Gina. "She's practically a baby herself. A smart, determined one, but still … we can't do this. We could always adopt."

"I don't want some stranger's child," Alana responded, pressing her body to his. "Someone's remedy for getting rid of their mistake. I want a child from at least one of our bloodlines. What's so wrong with that?"

Slowly, he moved his hands to her hips. And that single movement caused a flash of desire to spark in his eyes.

"You mentioned money," Gina ventured cautiously, taking a seat on the sofa and retrieving the papers from the cushion to place on her lap. "But I would like something else …"

Both of them finally focused on their guest. Alana's eyes narrowed to slits. "Exactly what are you asking for now?"

"I want room and board, for you all to put me in school so I can finish. I'll sign whatever you need me to sign, but I need an answer tonight, or I'll have to move on to the next couple." She tapped the edge of the document in her hands.

Christopher peered at her for a moment as though she had spoken a foreign language. He took his hands from his wife's hips and walked over to Gina. "Room and board? You're … you're homeless?"

Gina briefly weighed playing hardball versus telling the truth. "I am as of a few hours ago. I could have a roof over my head, but I'd have to pay for it in ass—literally."

Alana came to sit next to Gina and settled back among the cushions. "Well that certainly puts things in perspective. And just how do you propose we pull off the education part of your requirements?"

Christopher peered at her intently. "And how old are you really?"

Gina locked gazes with him, but lowered her eyes under his hard glare. "Didn't you check my birth certificate?"

He stared her down and Gina felt the enormity of her mistake. She should have waited until things had progressed to far before bringing up the school issue.

"I'll be seventeen three weeks from now," she mumbled.

"Sweet Jesus." He threw up his hands and stormed away with his wife right on his heels. A long, heated exchange ensued.

From what Gina could tell, Alana was still all for it; the husband had every argument against it. Though Alana was a stock queen and negotiator for a living, Christopher was holding his own. Words like *statutory rape* and *losing his license* were tossed around. Things that Gina hadn't considered. The husband did, though, want to give Gina some money and help her find a place to live. That alone spoke volumes. How Gina had gone from being ready to tip over the edge to landing on the rich side of town wheeling and dealing with people who could buy her many times over—was amazing.

"I want a baby," Alana said in a wavering voice. "I want a child. We've tried for so, so many years. I want a child. Your child, while we're still young enough to enjoy it."

Gina inched toward the door and peered around the corner into the living room. She saw Alana had laid her head on her husband's chest.

"Please, sweetheart," she said, stroking a hand across the broad length of him. "You've given me everything I could want. Please, don't deny me this one thing I ask …"

Christopher gently wiped away his wife's tears. He softened

considerably as he looked down at her with a love that Gina could feel across the room. "Honey, we can't fulfill her requirements. She's underage."

"We could become her legal guardians and work from there."

Christopher looked up to see Gina standing before them. "I won't touch her until she's eighteen. Can you at least wait that long?"

Alana paused several moments, then nodded as he stroked her back.

He continued to focus his attention on Gina. "She needs to learn about her body, know what sex really is about. You teach her about that. I never have liked inexperienced women. I detest causing a woman pain."

"I know that, but at least we know she's pure and has a pure heart."

"Not so pure if money's a motivating factor," he countered dryly.

That comment caused Gina to look away.

Alana pulled on his lapel and forced him to look down at her. "You haven't been listening. Survival is what drives her. Same as anyone." Alana stroked his smooth face. "And you have to give the girl some credit. Look at what she's really requesting—a roof over her head, food to eat, education, *then* money." This time Alana looked over her shoulder at Gina. "I admire that in someone so young, especially given where she was raised. She knows exactly what she wants and how. If we don't accept her, then she'll go to another couple who might not be so ... discriminating. At least we can take care of her, really care for her, and she'll be a happy pregnant woman, which means she'll give us a happy, healthy child."

Alana pressed her lips to his. It took a minute before he returned the kiss. He kept his focus on Gina, who held his gaze steady and sure.

She smiled and took a good look around her new home.

* * *

They enrolled her in a magnet school, one that would challenge her and give her a solid foundation for college. Christopher insisted she attend other schools on Saturdays to learn Spanish, French, and even etiquette—as if Mama Bessie hadn't taught her. But Gina saw if for the move that it was—a way to keep her out of his sight. Alana made good on Christopher's demand that Gina learn about pleasure and her body. Masturbation wasn't half bad, but she still wasn't using one of those damn toys to do away with her virginity just to "get it out of the way."

Christopher constantly tried to talk Gina and Alana into an artificial insemination procedure. She did try to do it Christopher's way, but every time she saw the length of the needles they would use, she would tremble so badly her blood pressure would soar, heart rate would go out of control, and she was out of commission for at least an hour.

Gina had barely made it through blood draws for tests, but during the first times, Alana had held her hand. Only then did she tell Alana what had happened so long ago. The time she spent in the hospital after her mother and sister had been raped was the source of vicious nightmares. Only when Mama Bessie had come to the hospital and sat by her side, singing and humming, had sleep taken her. But the nightmares had lingered. And those days after leaving Robert Taylor Homes, the nightmares had returned.

Two months before Gina's eighteenth birthday, Alana came up with a plan of her own. She had charted Gina's fertile times, then stopped having sex with her husband, using a busy schedule as part of her excuse. The day before Gina turned eighteen, Alana was "called away" on business.

Only when Christopher realized that his wife had sent away the maid and cook did he understand that something was up. On occasion, he was on edge when it came to Gina. He made it his business to stay in the study to try to avoid too much contact with Gina. Unfortunately for him, that played into the women's plan.

Before Alana left the house, she told Gina, "It's up to you now. I've taught you everything I know—and actually learned some things I didn't know." She smiled warmly. "I learned something about my husband. He's not going to come to you even when you're nineteen, or twenty, or twenty-one. We have to force his hand. You promised to keep your word."

Gina came to him at midnight dressed in a flimsy negligee, smelling of his wife's perfume, her hair layered into a love knot with curls spiraling down in a style that he loved on Alana.

At first, Christopher's eyes lit up with pleasure, but he soon lowered them and tried to focus on the paperwork in front of him.

"Christopher, it's time."

He shook his head vigorously as she walked toward him. "I can't do this. I love my wife."

"I don't doubt it," Gina whispered huskily, making her way to him. "And if you really love her, you'll give her the child she wants."

"They could put you to sleep for the procedures. You wouldn't feel a thing."

Gina used her knee to inch his chair away from the desk, giving herself room to slip onto his lap. She stroked his face, then leaned in slowly and pressed her lips to his.

He did not return her kiss, but after several moments his erection throbbed, and that was all the encouragement she needed.

She traced the outline of his thin lips with her tongue. When his breathing hitched, she parted his lips so she could gently explore his mouth, teasing the inside with soft licks. Gina moved her hips slowly, stirring him until his erection became fuller. She wound her arms around his neck and pulled him to her.

Their kiss became harder, more passionate as she took his hand and placed it near the swell of her full breasts. Christopher looked down and fingered the lacy material before moving it to expose a cinnamon nipple. He took it into his mouth. And she splayed her fingers in his hair while drawing him even closer. She inhaled the essence of his cologne, could feel his covered erection pressing near her bare bottom. Gina lowered the zipper; he shifted his hips upward, allowing her to remove both his slacks and briefs. She parted her thighs so she could straddle him properly. Christopher reached out, gripped the round globes of her ass, and sighed as he centered her over his erection.

Then just as suddenly, he froze and tried to push her away. "Gina, we can't do this."

She locked her thighs around him. "We can, and we will," she answered in a breathy whisper. "It's the only way." She took his hand, pressed it to her moist core, then kissed him until his erection was so stiff she could barely touch it without eliciting a hiss of pleasure from him.

Soon he teased her pearl, which caused her to arch toward him. Then she reached down and gripped him in her hand, stroking the shaft until his head went back. His eyes closed as he tried to maintain some control.

"Please," she begged in a voice husky with promise. "Please don't make me wait."

He pressed a finger into her, gently exploring that hot center, letting her rain on him. Gina unbuttoned his shirt to expose a hairless chest and lowered to his nipple, taking one into her mouth then tasting the other.

Christopher gripped her ass, spread her cheeks, then guided that throbbing member to the heated tip of her and paused. "Are you sure?"

"Yes," she whispered. "Very sure. You all have been so good to me. I want to be good to you."

He pressed into her heat, bonding them slowly inch by inch until she gasped with a sudden onslaught of pain. Christopher froze and buried his head in the smooth curve of her neck, waiting for her to adjust to the intrusion.

When he didn't continue after several moments, she took over. Gina stood and turned her back to him, braced on the desk, and guided her way down the shaft until she heard him cry out. He thrust into her heat, then raised out of the chair, pushed it out of his way, gripped those creamy globes, and stroked into her with thrusts that heaved her forward, the sounds erupting from his throat nearly as animalistic as his movements.

"Yessssss," she encouraged. All pain was totally forgotten.

The feeling was powerful.

Christopher almost lost his footing on the final thrust as he released his seed deep into her womb and shook with an orgasm that seemed to go on forever.

When she could catch her breath, she said, "Thank you, Christopher."

He blinked his blue eyes as though coming to an understanding. "I should be the one thanking you."

Christopher turned Gina to face him and kissed her before he scooped her up, carried her to the bedroom, and made love to her once more.

* * *

Alana arrived home on Sunday evening to find her husband wrapped securely in the younger woman's arms.

Gina stroked his soft hair as she looked at Alana and gave her a small smile.

Alana tried to smile back, but it faltered some as she wondered if in sacrificing her husband to have the child she so desperately wanted, had she also given up something in her marriage to her surrogate.

But it was too late for regrets.

When Gina conceived and had a child, it would all be worth it, right?

Alana resisted the urge to wake her husband and ask him to come to their bed. Instead, she closed the door behind her as she walked to the master bedroom alone.

* * *

One month after graduation, Gina had the pleasure of telling her guardians, "I'm pregnant." And for once Christopher looked more pleased than worried.

Eight months later, Gina gave birth to a healthy baby girl with whisper-soft blond hair and surprisingly blue eyes—nearly the spitting image of her father.

Chapter 10

Alana Meister brokered a surrogate contract with another couple on her behalf before Gina turned nineteen. Mostly the same stipulations as theirs—natural conception, medical expenses paid—but this time, the couple would pay for two years at the University of Chicago and an upscale apartment near campus. Gina would also receive a sizeable cash allowance.

Christopher fussed throughout the entire process, and after Gina signed the deal, he grumbled, "I feel like a pimp." Gina locked gazes with Alana, knowing the woman had two ulterior motives for brokering the next arrangement so quickly; it would essentially separate Gina from her first-born daughter and also from her Christopher, who had gained an intimate attachment that he consistently tried to deny.

With Alana handling Gina's investments, the money they had paid her in the beginning had nearly tripled—something that pleased Gina to no end. She had also graduated at the top of her class, only missing valedictorian because she hadn't attended the school all four years. They didn't count her honor roll status and grades at DuSable High School because, they argued, the schools probably used "different scales". Sounded like crap to Gina, but at least they had given her recognition and awards for all her other accomplishments. And it was getting into college that mattered most, so Gina and the Meisters let it ride.

Gina's initial goal to be a millionaire by the time she was twenty-one was close. Ted had contested Mama Bessie's will, so access to the money from the bank accounts had been tied up in probate—and there was no telling how long that would take. If Gina had her wish, she wouldn't need the money—from Mama Bessie's insurance and what was left by her parents—that was coming to her when she turned twenty-five. That money would only go so far, so she increased her goal to earning three million and that meant adding three more surrogate contracts to take care of her basic needs. She signed them willingly, then would bank all of her money so that she'd never be poor. She would never set foot in the projects again.

Gina sat across from Sanjay and Michelle Bhandari in their Skokie home. The affluent area had a sizeable Jewish population, so she expected the couple to be from that ethnic background. She was wrong.

Sanjay, an East Indian with chiseled features etched in a handsomely rugged face, had a medium but muscular build and dark silky hair. He was as mesmerizing to look at as he was passionate about life. There was a confidence about him that showed in his bearing and in his walk. But there was also something darkly dangerous about him. In some ways, he reminded her of an olive-skinned Rakim. His wife, a slender, caramel woman with a curvy body and killer instinct when it came to trying court cases, was a share partner at Leonard, Steinmetz, and Esbrook. The couple was desperate, having gone through several other methods to conceive, and failing with each attempt.

Seven months into her pregnancy, the couple requested for her to come to their home. For some reason, Michelle wouldn't make eye contact, and Sanjay seemed less confident than usual. Gina rubbed her extended belly as she peered at them. They couldn't change their minds this far into things. Could they?

Michelle ushered Gina into the living room where she took a seat across from Sanjay and said, "My husband has something to ask you."

Sanjay stole a glance at his wife, waiting for her to continue. Instead, she stared back at him, crossed one leg over the other, and smirked as she waited for him to speak.

Gina shifted uncomfortably on the chaise. She was already pregnant. What more could they want?

After what seemed an eternity, he took a deep breath. "This might sound a bit strange," he said in thickly accented English, "but I assure you it is not."

She looked at him, tried to cross one leg over the other as Michelle had done, and quickly remembered that she couldn't. The baby made even simple things impossible. Like a full night's sleep or getting through a full meal.

"I would like …" He paused as though unsure if he should go on. Then he looked directly at Gina, trying to hold his gaze steady. "I wonder if you would consider another request."

"For a second child?" Gina asked, relishing that thought for her own selfish reasons.

Michelle perked up, her eyes wide with excitement as she said, "No, nothing like that, but would you consider that?"

"Possibly." Gina arrowed her gaze back at the husband. "But what is it you really wanted to ask?"

Sanjay rubbed his chin as though still in deep thought. "I wonder if you would allow me to …" He stole a glance at Michelle, who looked off at nothing in particular, then found a pointed interest in the color-splashed Jackson Pollock painting on the living room wall. No mistaking her expression for anything other than slightly amused.

"Will you stop this," Gina screamed at him. "You're scaring me, Sanjay. What is it?"

"I'd like to have the breast milk."

Gina blinked to give herself a moment. She couldn't understand what all the embarrassment was about. "Okay, so you'll want the baby to be breastfed. That's something I can do. No big deal."

Sanjay gave her a small smile. "I do not think you understand," he said, biting his bottom lip. "I want the milk."

Gina looked from husband to wife and back to the husband.

"For me," he added, bringing the point home.

She froze. Seconds later, one eyebrow shot up. Gina blinked to clear her vision and her thoughts. For a long while she stared at him, watching as his expression changed from uncertain to confident and then to vulnerable. "Okay, so I'll pump some for you after the baby has had its fill."

"Actually, I prefer to have all of it," he countered smoothly.

"The baby needs some milk for the first month at least."

Sanjay licked his lips and added, "All right. I am willing to concede that."

Gina couldn't even look at him. What had she just committed to?

When Michelle spoke, it was in an edgy tone so low, Gina almost didn't hear her say, "Actually, he's not finished."

Gina looked at her, frowning at the woman's taunting tone before searching Sanjay's face. "What do you mean *he's not finished?*"

"Go on, ask her," Michelle urged, this time with a sly smile as though relishing her husband's discomfort. Gina had never witnessed this type of exchange with them. They were always so loving; that was one of the reasons Gina was happy to have their child. Well that, and the other obvious reason. She now had more than enough money to get her through the next year or too. But since she aimed to never be anywhere near the poverty line, those other two contracts were still on deck. Sanjay cleared his throat, snapping her back to the present. "Well, I was wondering if you would be amenable to letting me draw the milk … from the source."

Gina cocked her head, her eyes widening before narrowing to slits. "Bring that by me one more time."

Michelle uncrossed her legs and slipped back in the chair, folding her arms over a slight bosom. Her expression was smug as she watched her husband squirm his way through the conversation.

"We'll pay you for the inconvenience," Sanjay offered.

"You mean, *you'll* pay her for the inconvenience," Michelle snapped. "None of my money's going into that ... *project*."

This man wanted to draw substance from her breasts like he was some newborn babe?

Gina stood, walked over to the cathedral windows, and leaned on the wall so she could take in the full weight of the request. What harm could it do? It wasn't as if she hadn't already allowed the man full access to her body so he could plant his seed within her. And sweet Jesus the man was a skillful lover. It had been the most pleasurable experience she ever had.

When Christopher lost control and actually enjoyed his time with her, he apologized immediately after he was done. Sanjay had no such inhibitions and had taken her on a sensual journey that left her breathless. He seemed to be more interested in making sure that she took pleasure in being with him. She was almost saddened that she had become pregnant so quickly. A few more sessions with him, and she would have been easier to melt than freshly churned butter.

Gina didn't turn away from the window as she asked, "How much money are we talking?"

He replied.

She whipped around to face him and almost lost her footing. The amount was more than what they had paid to have the baby!

"For how long and how often?"

"Two months ... three times a week?" Sanjay posed it more as a question than a statement, as though he wanted more, but was testing the waters first.

Gina turned to Michelle. "And you agree with this?"

"He recently told me that he's always had this strange ... I don't know what to call it." She flipped her hand, waving away the rest of her thoughts. Then she looked off as though ashamed of it herself. "I can't understand it, but he wanted to try it at least once ... so here we are."

"Yes, here we are," Gina whispered. With a damn near insatiable Indian man who was handsome as hell and wicked in bed. She was getting wet just thinking of him lying next to her—those strong arms wrapped around her, his hands playing in her hair. He smelled of frankincense and the freshness of citrus, combined with the warmth of labdanum and sweetness of honey. Intoxicating. She couldn't get enough.

"All right, three times a week, two minutes a shot—*after* the baby has been fed."

Strangely enough, they hadn't discussed having Gina breastfeed the baby at all, but she would be damned if she would let the milk flow just for him. The baby had to benefit from this little exchange and so would she—since it would allow more time with her child. Michelle shrugged as if to say, *not my call*. But Sanjay frowned at the limited amount of time allotted.

"Take it or leave it."

He nodded, but quickly asked, "What if I need more than just two minutes?"

Gina locked gazes with him, and there was no mistaking the hunger in his eyes. "Sounds like you're about to come up with some more cash. But I can extend it for a few more weeks as well."

"Name your price."

Gina walked back to the window again and looked out at their lush green gardens for several moments. She reassessed her financial goals, made a quick set of mental calculations, then let loose with an outlandish sum. She told him she would double the amount of time, but she still hoped in some small way that the amount would deter him.

When he let out an enthusiastic, "Done." Gina gripped the ledge of the window to steady herself. She looked over her shoulder and found his intense eyes focused on her. *This man really has it bad.* But the move had reduced the amount of pregnancies she would need to go through. She had originally counted the need to have seven children to make the amount she wanted. With this new development—two more and she would hit her goal.

She folded her arms across her chest and pressed her back to the wall as she faced him. "My only requirement is that the baby gets it off the top; you'll have whatever remains, regardless of whether it lasts for the duration."

"Agreed."

Michelle's jaw tightened the moment he said the word. She was probably noticing the huskiness of his voice. Then her lips lifted in something that was neither smile nor frown. She looked at Gina for a long moment, her expression closed and unreadable.

For a split second Gina wondered if she had made a major mistake.

* * *

The night those "special" sessions with Sanjay was set to end would be a time Gina would never forget. Sanjay stroked a hand across the feather soft hair of his baby daughter, watching as she took nourishment from her biological mother. Gina looked at him, searching for signs of jealousy that never materialized. She wondered what he really felt in all of this. But he never rushed her in the process. Never seemed to get impatient when their baby girl needed a little more each time.

The moment the soft pucker of lips ceased its movements, Michelle approached the bed and reached for the baby. Gina held up a hand to halt her, allowing the baby to fall into a restful sleep. Then Michelle took the baby in her arms, looked down at Gina, and whispered a teary-eyed thank you before she hurried to the door and closed it behind her. It seemed as though she was afraid Gina would somehow change her mind even this late in the game.

Sanjay searched Gina's face as he always did before they began. She tried to keep her expression neutral, but there was something different about him this time. According to their arrangement, this would be his last night, and she wondered what was going through his mind. Normally, he would have already laid the groundwork to extend his sessions again. So why was this time any different?

Sanjay undressed slowly, allowing his silk robe to fall to the floor. Her gaze roamed his body, which was as beautiful in its symmetry as it was in strength and agility. He loved pressing his skin to hers, holding her as she held onto him, playing in his hair the entire time. She loved the way it felt—this taboo thing that they did—but she would never say so out loud. He lowered to her breasts, which were engorged to the point of pain just from inhaling his masculine scent. He kissed them, taking his sweet time as though he had all the time in the world. Gina looked over at the clock on the night stand and mentally began keeping time. Five minutes.

His piercing dark eyes focused on her; his lips lifted in a small smile that didn't quite reach his eyes. Something about it made her uncomfortable. It was as if her body responded to him of its own accord. The moment she inhaled him, her breasts filled to capacity—even right after she had nursed the baby.

Why was he taking so long?

Sanjay smoothed a hand over her skin, trailing it from the concavity of her abdomen down to her heated thighs. He kissed her breasts, but didn't draw from them. Instead he stroked the outer areas of her thighs, creating a soothing rhythm that made her breath catch.

As though sensing her impatience, Sanjay looked into her eyes and smiled. This time he stroked a tongue across the nipple, which caused her to arch toward him. She wanted him in a way that she shouldn't. He pressed his erection into her thigh, but nowhere close to her center. He whispered how much he wanted her, then asked for a permission she could not give. Michelle paid her twice the amount he offered for her *not* to let him make love to her. When he left Gina's room after their sessions, hard and unsatisfied, he took his frustrations out on his wife. Her screams of passion filled the air for most of the night.

Michelle was no dummy, and neither was Gina.

Sanjay continued to tease Gina's body, soothing her breasts with his hands. He watched her through hooded lashes as she began to feel a different type of heat flow through her. He settled his body between her thighs just at the moment she said, "Your time's almost up. Why don't you get down to business?"

"No, actually ..." He pulled away and slipped off the bed. "It is all right. I do not need for you to take care of me tonight. I thank you for what you have done." He grabbed his robe and strolled toward the door.

A swell of disappointment filled her.

"Sanjay, you can't leave me like this."

He tied the sash tight and gave her a shrug that signaled his indifference. "Leave you like what, Gina? This is only a business arrangement. You have said that many times. And tonight that business is now concluded." He had one foot out of the door.

"Please," she whispered, sitting up on an elbow. "I need you to—"

"To what, Gina?" He didn't turn to face her.

The pain in her breasts was damn near unbearable. Nothing provided the relief that he gave her each and every time. She never admitted it to him or to Michelle, but the amount he pulled from her had increased her flow to nearly double what the baby actually needed. She enjoyed the pain to some degree because she knew the pleasure that awaited when Sanjay went to work. And it was a labor of love. He seemed to enjoy the act more than the substance itself.

Sanjay looked at her and said in a low tone, "Sometimes when I come to you, I feel two things—need and shame. Tonight, you will need to release one or the other. My wife already makes me feel …" He grimaced, unable to come up with a word. "Because of this. I do not want you to make me feel that way too. Especially when I know you enjoy it as much as I do."

She lowered her gaze, and when she finally could look up at him, he had crossed the distance and was now at the edge of the bed.

"Sanjay. I never meant to—"

"I know, sweetheart." He placed a finger to her lips. "You are thinking with your head and not going by what you feel."

"I need you. Please …" She reached for him, but he pulled back a little.

"If I touched you down there, would it be moist?"

Gina thought about lying to him, but only for a second. "Yes, I'm wet."

"And if I want to make love to you, will you …"

Tears sprang to her eyes. If she allowed him that access she would be betraying Michelle. But would she? This time money wouldn't factor into it. He was asking her to admit something she had never wanted to say out loud.

His lips pursed in a thin line before he moved from the bed and walked toward the door.

Her voice was a shattered murmur, "Make love to me, Sanjay."

Seconds later, Sanjay dropped his robe, rushed to the bed, and settled between her thighs. He looked down at her breasts but didn't touch them. She angled toward him, ready to take him in, but still he waited. For the first time ever, he pressed his lips to hers, then kissed her with an intensity she never thought possible.

When he pulled away to search her passion-filled eyes, Gina pursed her lips and held her ground. The desire was so overwhelming, it made it impossible to catch a solid breath. But she would not beg him again.

His gaze settled on her breasts. "I can make the pain go away, but I will need this for more than just tonight and the next night. I want you as my woman."

She focused on his erection, which was so beautiful, so strong, the veins angry in its effort to hold back his release.

"Tell me how much you want me," he whispered.

"Sanjay, please stop this. You know I want you."

This time he lowered, pressed his lips to her breasts, and at that same moment he thrust into her heat, filling her to the core. She cried out with pleasure. The orgasm whipped through her in rapid succession as the need for him intensified. His second thrust went so deep she screamed but held onto him so he would not stop. His pelvis moved in a circular, deep rotation that took her on a whirlwind of pain and pleasure—so much so that she passed out and came to, only to pass out once more. She went limp in his arms as he continued his sensual assault.

"You are mine now. Only I will take care of you."

Gina couldn't form a coherent thought let alone a protest. This was not what she wanted to be—another man's possession.

"Do you hear me?"

He thrust into her again and again.

"Yes!"

"I did not hear you. Who do you belong to?"

"I'm yours, Sanjay," she cried into the smooth curve of his shoulder that was peppered with perspiration. His arms wrapped around her and he slowly, methodically made love to her until she was nothing more than a wilted mass of pure bliss. And then he did something that he had never done before. He held her in his arms, whispering words of comfort and love until she passed into a sweet, restful sleep.

Gina woke in his arms just before dawn and Sanjay made love to her again and again. She received him with no reservations. His possession of her body was so complete, she knew at that moment that she would have serious trouble with Michelle Bhandari.

* * *

Later that day, Gina hurriedly packed her things, left Michelle's last bribe in a place she was certain to find it, then hit the door without giving the place a backward glance. She ached for the daughter she would never see again, but she had betrayed the woman who had been so good to her. People just shouldn't do that.

Gina had been forced to take all that extra money the Bhandari couple had given her and place it into a special account since she couldn't tell Alana about the circumstances surrounding it. The first time she had passed Alana a subsequent check from Sanjay, Alana had bombarded her with non-stop questions, demanding to know what she was doing to make so much money. Even Christopher was angered by it and watched her to see if she would lie in giving an answer.

"It's none of your business," she had told them.

Christopher had glared at her, flickered an ice blue gaze over her body, then stormed toward his home office.

Gina had scrambled after him, yelling, "I'm a grown woman, Christopher."

He froze in his tracks but didn't turn around. "If you can't tell us, then it must be something depraved," he said through clenched teeth. "What is he forcing you to do?"

When she didn't answer, he growled, "Trust me, I'm going to find out."

"And what difference would it make if you did?" Gina fired back, while coming to stand in front of him. "It won't change anything."

The room was charged with an energy she couldn't name. Silence swirled around them, and she watched the range of emotions play across his pale face.

An eternity later, Christopher reached up to stroke a gentle hand across her face. He moved in slowly, almost as if it was against his will, drawing her toward him. His voice was full of sadness when he said, "If he's doing … if he's touching you … if he's—"

"Sweetheart, stop," Alana screamed, shoving him away from Gina, instantly breaking his trance-like stare. "You're beginning to sound like a jealous lover."

Christopher turned bright red as he righted himself, glared angrily at Gina one last time, then stormed out of the house. Alana had turned to Gina, her eyes filled with concern as she said, "I don't want to know the details, but I do need to ask … is Sanjay Bhandari hurting you?"

"Far from it."

And that was putting it mildly. What she felt for Sanjay was beyond her own understanding, and she left their home before she got in any deeper. Being with Sanjay and being mentored by Michelle made Gina understand what it was like not to be alone; what it was like to be needed; to be valued. But no matter how good it felt—no matter the promises that Sanjay had made—she would not be *that* woman.

* * *

A persistent knock roused Gina out of bed. She slid out of a Palladian stone bed, slipped on a paisley silk robe, and froze the moment she pulled open the door.

Michelle Bhandari gave Gina a critical onceover, then moved forward, forcing Gina to step aside whether she wanted the woman to enter or not.

That sharp gaze swept across the suede semi-circle sofa, the intricately carved glasswork on the coffee table, the multitude of books along the glass shelves, the artwork which displayed varying stages of motherhood, then to the photographs sitting along the mantel above a marble fireplace. Approval came alive in those dark brown eyes, which finally focused on the young woman standing in the center of the room.

Before Michelle could open her mouth and explain her presence in the Hyde Park apartment, Gina simply said, "I'm not coming back."

"Why? The baby needs you."

"Which one?"

Michelle gave her a small smile. "Touché." She settled on a chair near the window and crossed her legs. "I'm talking about the one you gave birth to."

Gina could not look Michelle in the eye. She leaned on the threshold as though it would hold her up under the enormous weight she felt. "Michelle, I … he … we … I let him …"

"I know."

A teary-eyed gaze focused on Michelle. "I thought I had better control than that."

Michelle shrugged and chuckled. "Sweetheart, I'm surprised you lasted as long as you did."

Gina wiped her tears and glared at the woman across the room. "So it's all one big game to you."

And all this time, Gina had cared, had held back because she loved Michelle too. She admired her style, her confidence. Wanted her approval as much as she desired Alana's.

Alana and Michelle had insisted she take good care of herself, and Gina had begun to emulate those two classy women in several aspects of her life. She loved taking trips to the spas and shopping at malls that catered to people with rich tastes. She embraced the fact that she had choices—when it came to education, when it came to her life, when it came to who she allowed in her bed. The only downsides to the surrogacy were visits to the doctor—and needles of any kind, but Michelle went with her each time, just as Alana had done. There had been a great deal of comfort in that.

"You don't think I know what drives him? I love him even with all of his flaws."

"Not so flawed," Gina retorted in Sanjay's defense. "Do you know how many men saw me nursing your baby at the park and asked if there's enough to go around?"

Michelle's eyes widened in shock; she took a few minutes to absorb that tidbit of information.

"Even though I have something covering us, they know exactly what I'm doing. Other men have approached me to do the same thing for them." She shook her head. "It's not a flaw; it's a fetish. And if I wanted to, I could bring in just as much money in breast milk as I do having babies."

Michelle seemed stunned by that interesting fact, but she recovered quickly. "He's a good man, but he's a hell of a lot more sexual than I could ever be. That man gets a hard-on just from hearing my voice."

Gina could definitely believe that. "So why would you want me involved?"

"Because my focus should be all about the baby right now and, to be honest, all about my business, too."

"I don't like the fact that he feels that I belong to him that way," Gina admitted. "He said that I'm his woman, but I can't be that to him. You're his wife."

Michelle covered the few feet separating them and tilted Gina's chin so that they were eye to eye. "When you're in his bed, in his arms, you are his—for that moment. Play that game with him. It's all about control or giving the illusion of control. The real game is in making a man want you more than you want him."

Gina remained silent, taking that in as it sounded similar to what Mama Bessie had once said.

"There are many types of love, Gina. He *loves* you, but he's *in love* with me."

Gina shook her head as though unable to digest what Michelle was trying to tell her.

"I don't take it personally that he wants you. You're beautiful, you're determined, you're sensual. And he likes that. But you're here for the moment." She paused, giving Gina a pointed look. "But I'm in it for the long haul. Whether you give in to him or not, he *always* comes back to me. And truthfully, he's more satisfied now than he's ever been. I like it that way. For everything he's done for me, I want him to be happy."

Michelle walked over to the fireplace, lifted the black and white picture of Mama Bessie, and looked at it a long while before moving on to the ones of Raymond and Faith Wright, then Mayre. Gina watched the woman's gaze fall on the two baby pictures on the mantel of the Meister child and the Bhandari girl.

"Now I have a child, a husband who loves me, and a top position at a firm that's raking in billions. There are a lot of women who would kill to be in my shoes. If my only sacrifice is that he needs to indulge in a little … unorthodox sex, then baby, like my mama used to say, 'That ain't no major. Put your big girl panties on and deal with it.'"

"But you both took vows," Gina protested, searching Michelle's face for a moment and finding nothing close to concern. "It was different when we were making love to produce a child. That was almost Biblical. You know, the surrogacy thing."

Michelle ran a hand through that signature shoulder-length hair. "The thing you're not getting, Gina, is that I gave him permission to have you. We're all adults here. Nothing is being done behind my back." When Gina did not move or acknowledge the statement, she continued, "The baby needs you. She cries for you. Sanjay needs you. He hasn't said a single word since you walked out. He's afraid that he hurt you in some way."

Gina shook her head vigorously. "I can't go back. I love him, and it's just not right."

"It's as right as we make it," Michelle countered smoothly. "He told me that he loves you."

Gina whipped her head toward Michelle, her gaze searching Michelle's face for any sign of … what? Deception? But Gina knew she had no reason to lie about something as serious as that.

"And for what you've given us, I can totally understand that. Now, if he said he was *in love* with you, then I'd have to whip your little ass. But that won't ever happen."

Gina lifted her chin and leveled a stony gaze at Michelle. "True, because I can give as good as I get. I won't take an ass whipping lying down."

"I don't doubt it, but I'm talking about the 'in love' part, Gina." Michelle walked toward the window and parted the sheers to look out at the deep green waters of Lake Michigan.

"Sanjay gave up his family because he loved me. They disowned him because he wanted a Black woman. He was heir to a textile fortune in India, and he gave that up when he married me instead of the woman he was supposed to marry. He struck out on his own to start that chain of restaurants and became successful on his own. But what I admire is that he didn't hold me hostage to his dreams." She gently pressed her fingertips to the window as though touching her husband's face. "At first he worked two, sometimes three jobs to put me through college, then law school so I could live my dream and he could fulfill his own. For that, I will always love him. Always."

Michelle left the window and went to the fireplace, lifted the baby picture of her daughter, then traced the outline of the gummy smile. "I love his passion, his drive. It's exciting; you can feel it rolling off him— it's like he's made of it. And I've never had a man who worships the color of my skin, worships my very essence as though I was a goddess." She looked over her shoulder at Gina. "You understand what I'm saying?"

Gina nodded. It was exactly how Sanjay made her feel—as though everything about her mattered. As if there were no color barriers.

Michelle replaced the picture and picked up the one of the Meister's child. "The very thing you're striving for in your life is something I already have. There's nothing I can't do, nothing I can't be, no place I can't pick up and go on a moment's notice." She turned to face the younger woman. "And that's power, Gina. That's being in control of your life. You make choices; you bend and flex sometimes, and it all comes down to what you want in the end. What are you willing to give to get what you want?"

Michelle traced a finger over the handsome features of Raymond Wright. "And to have a husband who doesn't deny me anything, who never doubted me when so many others had, who has pushed me beyond my fear of failure... There is *nothing* I wouldn't do for him if I could. I just couldn't give him that … what he wants."

Gina walked to the foyer and grabbed up her purse. She poked through the contents for a moment, then came back in the living room and held a small bottle out to Michelle.

"What's this?"

"Pills," Gina answered simply.

"I can see that," she shot back, eyeing the translucent orange bottle suspiciously. "Why do I need these?"

"Now you can give him *exactly* what he needs."

Michelle stared at the bottle for so long, Gina thought she had turned to stone.

Tears filled Michelle's eyes—only the second time Gina had ever seen the woman shed them. The first was the night she had given birth to a raven-haired child with a powerful set of lungs which announced her arrival to the entire maternity ward in a few solid blasts.

"Where? How?" She shook her head as though to clear it. "When? Where did you get this?"

"My doctor."

"Why would you do this?"

"Because I need to let him go." Gina paced the length of the Persian rug. "Sanjay makes me feel things I've never felt before. And I'm afraid. When he touches me, I get wet. When he looks at me, I get wet. When I think about him, I get hot. I don't like it."

"Oh, you like it all right," Michelle said with a low, throaty chuckle that rankled Gina's nerves. "That's what scares you. I think the only thing that worries you about all this is me. If I wasn't in the picture, it wouldn't be a problem, would it?"

"I'm not that way. I'm not *that* woman."

It had been easy to just have those times with Christopher and leave. But Sanjay Bhandari had made moving on damn near impossible. She could not go back to him, no matter what Michelle said. She knew her limits, and he was one of them.

"Sweetheart, I've given permission for you to be with him," Michelle said, pulling Gina down with her on the sofa. "He's the happiest that

I've ever seen him."

"But aren't you jealous?"

"Why would I be? His wanting to be with you is no reflection on me. I give him one-hundred and fifty percent." She stroked a manicured hand along Gina's silk-covered arm. "Sanjay is more virile than any man I've ever known. Before you came along, we'd make love three times a day and practically all night. He'd even show up at my job for lunch. I couldn't focus and was slipping up. It took a toll on my work because I was so damn tired." She sighed deeply and folded her hands in her lap. "Now it's only once—at night, and that's something my body can actually handle. It's as if having you fulfill that wild desire has calmed him; it's made him less demanding. I was worried because as much as I want him, I couldn't keep up with his demands." She pressed a hand to Gina's face. "So I need you to stay … for me."

Gina thought it over for a while, then shook her head.

"Will your being"—she crooked her fingers as quotes—"'in love' with him keep you from moving on with your life?"

"I don't think so."

Michelle shifted to kneel in front of Gina and gently rubbed her hands along the younger woman's thighs. "It's the vows thing, isn't it?"

"Mama Bessie said a woman was supposed to keep her word. And I can't seem to do anything right here. That's why I left. That's why I can't come back."

"One thing you'll learn, sweetheart, is that marriages are complex; they're about compromise. It's in his best interests and mine that you are with him." She laced her fingers with Gina's. "And tell me you haven't benefitted from it as well."

Gina looked away and tried not to smile.

Michelle looked down at the pills. "You cared enough about me to make sure that I could pick up where you left off. I never even thought about asking if there was something that could make me able to fulfill that desire for him."

Michelle settled in the place next to Gina and reached out to wipe the younger woman's tears. Then she gently pulled Gina's head down until it rested on her shoulder. "You're young, sweetheart. Love will come and go for you. Believe that. That man loves me and always will. Nothing you do will change that."

They were silent for a long moment. Each woman allowed her individual thoughts to simmer.

"Do we have an understanding, Gina?"

Gina nodded slowly but still couldn't meet Michelle's gaze.

"What?"

"When he leaves the bed, I feel so empty and alone," she whispered. "I don't like that feeling either."

Michelle looked at her for a long moment, then smiled with understanding. "All right, we'll see what we can do about that too."

Gina stared ahead, the enormity of what transpired filling her with a small sense of trepidation.

"How is school?"

"Statistics is kicking my ass, but it's aces for everything else."

Michelle brushed a hand across Gina's face. "You know, we're not so different, you and I. I grew up in Stateway Gardens."

Gina focused on Michelle, whose hand was now playing in her hair. The soft touches alone were distracting. "You were raised in the projects?"

"Oh yes," she nodded as though filtering through her memories. "And one thing about girls who leave the projects, they're a different kind of smart. Exactly what I expect you to be in all of this." Michelle extended her hand; Gina placed hers inside. "Come home, Gina. Be with us just a little while longer."

Home? Yes, home—it had truly felt like that. Gina said, "I'll stay only until your milk comes down. Then he won't need me anymore."

Michelle's smile was fleeting, and for a moment Gina felt that maybe Michelle believed that she had missed the point. Instead, she gripped the bottle of pills, turned them out onto her palm and seemed suddenly vulnerable. "Suppose I don't like the way it feels?"

"Trust me; he'll make sure that you do."

Michelle gave her a smile that reached all the way up to her eyes. "I could definitely live with that."

Chapter 11

Gina waddled up the brick path to the Kham's home, struggling to carry her suitcase and matching overnight bag. Her heart was truly heavy. Sanjay had protested the fact that she still planned to fulfill the contract she had with the couple. His words still weighed on her even seven months into her pregnancy.

"Gina, whatever you need, I will provide," he had whispered. "Please don't do this."

"Before I even met you, I made a promise."

He looked at her for a long moment. "One you do not have to keep. You do not owe them anything."

"Supposed I said that to you? To Michelle?"

Sanjay didn't have a comeback for that question.

"I do not approve," he whispered as she drew him to her breasts and replied. "You don't have to."

But she did. She would honor her promises, no matter the cost. And when she was done, she would no longer make promises that would alter the course of her life.

The phone was ringing at the couple's home so she rushed into the foyer, snatched the phone off the hook, and answered, "This is the Kham's residence. How can ..."

She froze the moment she took in the black metal contraption which had been rigged across the entire expanse of the living room. The piles of rope on the floor—different colors, textures, thicknesses—could stretch around the length of the house and back.

"Uhhhh … they're a little … tied up right now," Gina whispered to the person on the other end of the line. "I'll have them call you back when they become available."

As Gina placed the phone back on the charger, the suitcase slipped from her hand and dropped to the marble floor. She weighed turning around and running straight out the door, but curiosity held her rooted in place.

Ms. Kham was suspended mid-air in a trapeze-like system, bound and tied so tightly she could barely move. A black blindfold covered her eyes, and some type of vibrating mechanism was wedged in a tight area between her thighs. Her body was spinning counter-clockwise while swinging back and forth in a way that made Gina dizzy just watching. The only sound in the entire house was a shaky buzzing noise.

The lattice work of the ropes crossing Ms. Kham's body was as beautiful as it was intricate—almost like the woman had been caught in a spider's web.

Mr. Kham stood speechless, anxiously looking at Gina while trying to come up with words—anything to explain what their young guest could only perceive as madness. "I am not quite sure how to help you make sense of this."

Gina nodded, still trying not to laugh—or run. He looked absolutely ridiculous in a tight black outfit more suited for deep sea diving. But maybe this explained things. Her time with him was the least pleasant of all of the fathers. He didn't seem to enjoy any aspect of sex. Now she understood why. This freaky Laotian man was into a little slap and tickle—and she wasn't talking about the between-the-sheets kind. He certainly wasn't the everything-goes type like Sanjay or a go-for-the-gusto-then-apologize type like Christopher for that matter. She might have gotten a rise out of him if she had spanked that ass and *then* had sex with him.

Ms. Kham shook uncontrollably, twitching as though trying to get out of the ropes or off the black metal wiring system that held her. The twirling and swinging had slowed some. Gina's eyes went wide with alarm as the frantic movements seemed all wrong. She glanced at Mr. Kham, who did nothing. Moments went by, and the woman was still shaking. He remained in place, not even making an attempt to help. Something had gone wrong. Maybe she was dying.

Gina rushed toward the machine, touching the pulleys and putting forth an effort to get the woman out of whatever the hell it was called.

"No," Mr. Kham shrieked, yanking Gina off her feet and away from the suspension system. "She is not finished with her orgasm."

"Orgasm?" Gina shook off his hands and inched away, her eyes locked intently on the petite woman whose locks had been banded as tightly as the rest of her body. "Orgasm? From this? Are you serious?"

"Will you two shut the hell up," Ms. Kham snapped. "You're blowing my high."

Gina swallowed her next words. She moved just enough to perch on the edge of the talking bench in the foyer, staying as close to the door as possible. These people seemed nothing like the conservative couple she met several months ago.

She glanced at the items on the table nearby—paddles, whips, cat-o-nine tails, then wooden spoons, and other kitchen utensils. What the hell? And she had eaten dinner with them almost every weekend. Yikes.

Mr. Kham kept watching as Gina took it all in.

The woman finally came to a complete stop, and a breathy sigh echoed loud enough to carry across the two rooms.

Gina grabbed her suitcase and overnight bag and rushed toward the door. "I'm getting the hell up out of here."

"Gina, wait," Mr. Kham yelled.

She had her hand on the knob but looked over her shoulder at Ms. Kham, who was now being lowered toward the floor. He slowly unwound her, removed the huge vibrator that had been wedged on the outside of her dark outfit, then took off the blindfolds. The woman actually smiled. It was probably the first one Gina had ever seen. The husband stood by as Ms. Kham walked past him, saying, "Looks like that will be all for today."

"But … but we … did not … I …" Mr. Kham sputtered and came to a halt under the redhead's hard glare.

"Did you hear what I said?"

"Yes, Mistress." He lowered to one knee and bowed his head in submission.

Well, damn. That's how they're rolling? Gina placed her back on the door and watched as Ms. Kham slipped off a pair of black leather gloves and tossed them on the toy table.

"You told us you weren't coming this weekend," she said in an almost accusatory tone.

"I needed a break, and I wanted to let you know how the baby was doing."

Ms. Kham removed her thigh-high boots but looked up at Gina, awaiting an answer.

"She's fine. I'm having another girl."

Ms. Kham kept her focus on Gina, taking in the incredulous expression that she couldn't manage to mask. "You've never seen anything like this before?"

Gina tried to avoid looking back in the living room. "Maybe on television, but it still wasn't anything like this."

"We're into sensory play. A little bondage and discipline." She nodded toward the contraption. Then to the toy table. "A little S&M." She flicked a gaze at her husband, who had not moved from his kneeling position. "You can stand now."

"Yes, Mistress."

She kept her eyes on Gina as she told him, "Why don't you put our things away?"

"Yes, Mistress."

He scurried to do her bidding, looking nothing like the confident, reserved man Gina had first encountered several months ago. He had seemed hard then, with very little warmth, and it had almost made her reluctant to sign the contract with the couple. It was the beautiful, caramel woman with green eyes that reminded her so much of Faith Wright, that had changed her mind. Unfortunately, that woman was nowhere in attendance at this point.

She liked how Ms. Kham seemed to be in control and was even turned on by the power she wielded over her husband. This chick was more like an underground superhero.

The Meisters would never be into anything like this; they were as conservative as they came. And even still, Chris was totally turned on by seeing a Black woman's ass, and Alana had this thing about dressing up as a little girl. Sanjay's fetish was a little off the meter, but it wasn't something that she couldn't handle. But this?

Gina swept her gaze across all of their toys and asked, "Is it painful?"

"Contrary to what most people believe ... no. A Dom"—she grimaced as she saw the confused expression on Gina's face. "I'm sorry. A *dominatrix* has to know her Sub's"—she paused again—"*submissive's* tolerance and stay within those limits. People have different thresholds. So pain and pleasure depend on the person giving and receiving."

Gina nodded as though she truly understood, but she was actually more confused than ever. "Were you all doing this while you were pregnant? Is that why you miscarried so many times?"

Pain flashed in those green eyes.

Gina's heart constricted, seeing the woman's expression go from amused to sorrowful, "I'm sorry, I didn't mean to—"

"It's a valid question," Ms. Kham countered.

Mr. Kham was instantly at his wife's side, consoling her as he explained to Gina in softly stilted English, "My wife's womb was not strong enough to hold our offspring. Only once did she carry to term, and that child was not her own."

Gina looked at Ms. Kham, waiting for a further explanation.

"The fertility clinic had impregnated me with the embryo of another couple. It was a mistake that wasn't caught until I was in my fourth month and ..." Her voice broke on that note. "I couldn't bring myself to end the pregnancy. When I gave birth, they were there, and I gave them their child ..."

Mr. Kham stroked his wife's back and said, "The only time we stopped our sensory play was when she became pregnant. This did not cause the other miscarriages. I was able to continue with another Dom at The Castle while my wife was with child."

"The Castle? What's that?"

Mr. Kham parted his lips.

Ms. Kham gripped his arms. "Don't."

"She needs to know," he countered smoothly. "I never agreed to that kind of silence."

Finally, Ms. Kham nodded and turned her back to Gina.

"It is a place where anything and everything is possible," he said, keeping a hand on his wife's shoulder, his fingers squeezing lightly in a gesture of reassurance. "It is where every fantasy known to man is fulfilled. It is where I met Tory—the love of my life."

Ms. Kham returned his look of open admiration as she added over her shoulder, "It is also where we found out about you."

Gina took the nearest seat before her legs gave out from under her.

Ms. Kham's gaze narrowed on Gina. "You didn't know that?"

It was Mr. Kham's turn to admonish his wife—and he did so with a pointed look.

"But you opened that door," she said to him, causing him to avoid straight eye contact.

Gina looked at him as he shook his head slightly, and this time it was the missus who lowered her gaze. Suddenly, she was no longer the Dom; she was the wife—or was it the submissive? This was way too much for Gina to follow.

"It is not fair for her to find out this way."

Ms. Kham paused as though taking his advice under consideration, but seconds later she said, "Alana Meister spread the word at The Castle about your particular ... ability. Several couples met in the Red Room, and she sent all but three couples away. We were one of the few that met their requirements. And we were guaranteed not to have the problem that we had with surrogates before. That was worth any amount of money."

Gina was stunned, but she tucked that away as something to deal with another time and instead, pointed to the metal and pulleys. "So what's that?"

"It's called a hoist," Ms. Kham said, looking at the contraption with such longing that Gina could only stare at her. "It gives me a feeling like I'm flying."

Gina went over to the table. "And that thing?" She gestured to the purple and white plastic contraption with the bulbous head.

"Oh, just the basic body massager. Nothing special about it."

"I'd like to—"

"Absolutely not," the couple chorused, causing Gina to flinch at the intensity of their words.

"Damn, I was just asking," she whined, feeling somewhat disappointed.

"Wait until you have the baby," Mr. Kham said softly, giving her hand a gentle pat. "Then we'll talk."

She gave them a pointed look. "And I want to know more about this Castle you're talking about."

"I'm going to make us some coffee," Ms. Kham said. She headed toward the kitchen with her husband following right on her heels.

Gina mumbled, "To hell with coffee. After all this, I need a drink."

They both whirled to face her.

She held up her hands to ward off the verbal lashing she knew was coming. "I mean juice. For real."

Mr. Kham peered at her as Ms. Kham pursed her lips in obvious disapproval.

"I'd like to visit The Castle."

A looked passed between the Khams, and then they both smiled as Ms. Kham purred, "We'd be *sooo* happy to prepare you for that."

* * *

A few months after Gina had given birth to another baby girl, she stood partially naked in the center of the Khams' Wilmette home. Ms. Kham laid out the rules for the sessions and for any time Gina spent at The Castle.

The petite woman bound those reddish-brown locks with a small band and gave Gina's body—particularly her rear end—an appreciative review. "For your preparation sessions, no bodily fluids are exchanged. It's really not about sex. We'll see what you respond to the most. For your days of service to me, you'll wear absolutely nothing." She unlatched the lace bra that held Gina's full breasts. "What turns me on isn't sex or penetration."

The woman then led Gina through the enormous living room, a dining room large enough to seat an army, past the solarium, and finally into a private office. She gestured to the plaques and awards on the wall. "As the dean, I deal with naughty little girls and boys all day long. When I get home, I'm ready to whip somebody's ass." She gave a longing look at Gina's rounded buttocks. "Right now, *your* ass will do nicely."

Gina almost laughed, but it died in her throat the moment the woman extracted a small wooden paddle out of the top drawer of her desk.

"And I want it totally exposed to me at all times."

Alarm had shot through Gina. "So, I'll just stand here, and you'll hit me all day?" Gina snapped. "And that's supposed to make me feel something? And orgasm or something?"

"No dear, there's a lot more to it than that. But I *will* have to spank you from time to time," Ms. Kham replied in a husky voice, as her husband looked on from the leather sofa. "Because I can already tell that you're going to be a very naughty girl."

Gina gasped as Ms. Kham planted a soft swipe on her buttocks. Sensations rippled through her, causing an unexpected thrill.

Ms. Kham sauntered to the window, lowering the shade. "What turns me on isn't in the 'normal' range of things."

Gina felt her heart slam against her chest. What the hell did this woman want from her? And what did this have to do with her ultimately having an intimate experience at The Castle?

Ms. Kham came over and stroked a hand across Gina's buttocks softly, almost lovingly, until she elicited another breathy moan. "But if someone's washing my dishes, cleaning my house, working in my garden—you know, that sort of thing—it really gets my juices flowing."

Gina favored the petite woman with a small smile.

Ms. Kham raised a brow. "What's so funny?"

"I have a maid who cleans my place and a cook. So at this point in my life, I don't have a domestic bone in my body. You're out of luck with that." Gina's gaze swept across the already immaculate room. "But if you have some filing, typing, or a Power Point presentation to be done, I'm your woman."

Ms. Kham laughed. "I'll teach you everything I want you to know."

Well, that certainly had an ominous ring to it.

That day, the couple established a safe word as Ms. Kham taught Gina how to be the perfect domestic goddess—everything from polishing silver to doing laundry. The occasional sting of the paddle on Gina's cheeks served to provide sensations she never thought she'd welcome. Ms. Kham followed each sting with a course of petal soft touches to soothe the areas, which lead Gina through a series of tiny orgasms. Later, Mr. Kham took his turn, binding her wrists then her body in a rope display that was so elaborate that she marveled at his skill.

At times throughout the day, Gina closed her eyes and thought she couldn't tell whose fingers were making her cum, but upon further reflection, she realized that it wasn't Mr. Kham. He had already made things clear on where his boundaries lay.

"I love my wife. I think the other men, the other fathers ... I believe they forgot that, but I will not," he told her. "I promised my wife if she gave that child she carried to its rightful parents, that I would do whatever it took to give her the child she wanted. You brought that about, but that's where it ends. This ..." he said, gesturing to their toys and tools. "Is sensory play, but I will never sleep with you in that way again or touch you in a sexual manner."

Indeed, but Ms. Kham had no such boundaries. By the time Ms. Kham brought her mouth to Gina's full breasts, a feeling of overwhelming solace and release filled Gina to the point that it reduced her to tears.

One night she was at the house when the couple had their entire stock of gear hooked up in the living room—the hoist, the ropes, the tools. The couple was dressed in all black. Candles had been strategically placed through the house, providing the only light in each of the dim rooms. The couple had Gina bent over the workbench, her ass totally exposed. First, Ms. Kham started with a small session of feather soft taps which became a little harder, then heavier. Mr. Kham sprayed a mist of freezing water on her cheeks and massaged them from time to time.

Gina looked over her shoulder and asked, "What's that for?"

"To cool things down a bit."

The zeal they seemed to have for her rear end was laughable; almost reminding her of Christopher. All her life people were trying to get *in* that ass, but this couple was excited just by getting *at* that ass.

Then the real session began again—soft taps at first and several harder ones between to heighten the experience, nothing that caused Gina any alarm or pain. And in between, the cool mists created another type of sensation—she went from hot to cold, then hot again, and her tolerance built with each blow. Then there was a final paddle swat to her behind that sounded as if Ms. Kham had used as much strength as her petite body could muster.

Gina looked over her shoulder again at Ms. Kham. "Is that all you've got?"

Ms. Kham cocked an eyebrow at her husband and grinned. "Oh yes, we've got a live one here."

After the spanking, Gina lay down on the bench as Mr. Kham gathered his ropes and placed them across Gina to start his part of the process.

"I'm not feeling this," she said softly.

Mr. Kham halted and peered over at her, a flash of disappointment in his eyes. "You can sit up on the bench if you like."

"Okay, let's do it that way."

His smile could have lit up the entire south side of Chicago.

She sat up and he created an intricate web across her body. He focused on the lacing, tightening them as he went along. It came to a point where she couldn't move anything except her head. She looked into the mirror across from the bench and thought his handiwork was absolutely beautiful.

"Are you okay?" he asked again, as he had done in nearly every step of the process.

"This is cool, but when am I supposed to get an orgasm?"

Mr. Kham actually chuckled, then placed a blindfold over her eyes. The world went black, and fear clutched at her heart. She was bound and now deprived of all sensory input except sound. She could hear that his footsteps were taking him from the room.

Gina tried to keep her voice calm and steady, when she felt anything but. "Mr. Kham, I'm about to panic right now."

He hurried back to the bench and snatched off the blindfold. Gina took a deep breath and relaxed.

"It is strange that you did not freak out when I tied you up, but you almost lost it when I put on the strip." He tapped his chin. "Hmmmm, strange. Very strange indeed."

"You're calling *me* strange? Please."

Mr. Kham chuckled, which brought a smile to Gina's face.

This time he situated the massager between her thighs, but nowhere near her core. Gina pursed her lips and smiled and asked in a dry tone, "Am I there yet?"

The couple passed a knowing look between them, then they both roared with laughter.

"Sweetheart, we're just getting started."

Mr. Kham switched on the vibrator and the orgasms shot through her. Gina's entire body vibrated as she tried to focus on him. Ms. Kham was also watching closely, but her eyebrow arched as though to ask an unspoken question.

The moment it all ended, Gina smiled at them, saying, "I could learn to like this."

Chapter 12

Sanjay pressed Gina's back to the wall of his office, parted her thighs with his knee, then placed the tip of his finger on her clit before teasing it to the point where Gina was begging for mercy. The soft strokes and his skilled fingers had her melting instantly.

His hand slipped under her skirt and gripped her buttocks. The contact made her cry out, and only seconds later did she realize that was not the thing to do.

Sanjay pulled away. His gaze narrowed at her, which caused her to shrink under its intensity.

"Turn around," he demanded.

"Sanjay, it's nothing." She held her hand out to him, but he moved it away.

"I said, turn around!" His dark brown eyes flashed fire, and as much as she wanted to resist, Gina turned slowly and placed her hands against the exposed brick wall to steady herself.

He reached up her skirt and slipped the lace panties down to her knees. She looked over her shoulder at him, biting her bottom lip so she wouldn't say anything else. He lifted the skirt, exposing her bare bottom. Sanjay growled an obscenity and whirled her around to face him, but he was too angry to form a question.

"It's not what you think," she protested.

"Oh? What am I supposed to think, Gina?" He stormed away from her and paced the area leading up to his desk before coming back to stand in front of her. "Pull them up or take them off. Either way, we are leaving."

"Just hear me out." She placed her hands on both sides of his face. "You have to listen to me. It's not what you think."

He glared at her so long, she eventually let her hands fall to her side. When he didn't budge, she slid her panties back in place.

Sanjay grabbed her arm and rushed her out of the office, past his anxious-looking employees and guards, and finally to the front seat of his Lexus.

"Please listen to me. If you—"

A vein at his temple throbbed as he tore out of the building's garage and hit the Eden's Expressway at an alarming speed.

"You're scaring me," she shrieked, trying to grip the dashboard for balance.

He glared over at her, then lowered his speed, but he remained silent the entire drive. Gina again became alarmed when the roads he traveled were the same ones she used when making the trip to the Kham's home. Sanjay turned into their circular driveway and whipped around the curve leading to the entrance. She held her breath. He threw open the driver's side door and took off for the entrance. Gina tried to keep up with him, but to no avail. She had never seen him so angry.

The frantic knocking was finally answered by Mr. Kham, whose normally expressionless face immediately pulled into a scowl.

Sanjay's fist slammed forward, sending the smaller man sprawling into the nearest wall before crumpling in a heap on the floor.

Ms. Kham ran the rest of the way down one side of the spiral staircase and rushed to her husband. She glared up at Sanjay. "Have you taken leave of your senses?"

"He has caused her great pain," Sanjay growled, his chest heaving in an effort to control himself. "She has welts and marks all over her buttocks."

"Sanjay, if you had just listened to me, you would understand," Gina screamed, finally getting his attention. "They didn't hurt me."

"Are you mad? Do you know what that looks like? He beat you."

"Actually, I did," Ms. Kham countered smoothly, getting to her feet. Sanjay's eyes flashed with rage, but he didn't lash out at the woman.

"And if you would have listened to her you would know—"

"She is *my* woman. Mine!" He shook his fist in the air, causing Ms. Kham's eyes to widen in shock. "You are *never* to touch her again!"

"It's my body," Gina shouted at him. She moved to stand between him and Ms. Kham. "I do what I damn well please."

"*Your* body? Woman, you belong to me. What part of that do you not understand?" He moved until there was only a breath separating them. "Every inch of you is mine."

Ms. Kham arched a brow and grinned. "She never told me it was like that." She bent down to help her husband to his feet.

"It wasn't your business," Gina said without taking her eyes off Sanjay. "Just like what I do with you is not his business."

"I don't know what kind of sick games you play," he growled at Ms. Kham, "but she is not to be a part of it."

"Agreed."

Gina glared at both of them. "He doesn't have a say on what goes on in my life."

Ms. Kham's gaze stayed locked on Sanjay. "Honey, he has more say than you know."

Sanjay whirled her around to face him. "If you have any belongings here, get them now."

Gina folded her arms across her full breasts and huffed, "I'm not leaving."

"Oh yes, you are," Ms. Kham said softly. "You are his property, and as such, he has every right."

"He doesn't own me." Gina stamped her foot. "No one owns me."

Sanjay came to stand in front of her, crushed her body to his, and used his tongue to outline the curves of her lips. Gina stiffened and tried her damndest not to let it affect her. He leaned in to whisper, "You are mine," while gently stroking his other hand along her back. "And I will not allow anyone to hurt you."

"What I'm trying to tell you is that they didn't hurt me," she said in a voice hoarse with defeat. "I like what they did. I like it—a lot."

He lifted her chin, searched her eyes a moment, then looked over at Ms. Kham, who was whispering to her grumbling husband, holding him at bay.

Sanjay didn't realize that he could've gotten his ass kicked if Ms. Kham let her husband loose. The man was a martial arts expert but was as peaceful as anyone she had ever known. Violence was always a last resort. But self-defense was of the highest order. After that sucker punch, Sanjay had it coming.

"You like being beaten?"

For some reason, the way he worded the question shamed her, and she looked away.

"What is wrong with you?"

"This is where you are wrong," Ms. Kham interjected. "It is sensory play. It is not about us abusing anybody. Although, I'm curious as to how she became your possession. I'm sure it involves something equally as ... interesting," she said with a sly grin that spoke volumes. "Apologize to my husband. He has never raised a hand to her. I was the one who administered any and all spankings."

Gratefully, the woman had left out that Gina had also been taught the proper way to administer a spanking. Mr. Kham believed their young charge was a natural, as evidenced by the erection he got whenever Gina took the paddle to him. There had to be a reason Ms. Kham didn't mention that little fact. Probably for the same reason Gina had chosen not to mention Sanjay's particular fetish, which would have really made for a fascinating round of conversation.

"Apologize, Mr. Bhandari."

Sanjay's jaw throbbed as he kept his hold on Gina and looked over at the man. "I apologize for striking you."

Mr. Kham nodded first to Sanjay, then locked gazes with Gina before offering a small, bitter smile.

Gina felt that silent goodbye, and her heart constricted. Though nothing sexual had transpired between them after she had conceived, she had actually come to love the Asian man. "I'll be right back." Gina scaled the spiral staircase, went straight to the room she had there, and gathered the few items from the closet and dresser. On the way back, she went in to see her little girl one last time. She held the little one and almost cried at the grin the infant gave her. Then she kissed that soft forehead before passing her back to the uniformed nanny, who quickly glanced at the suitcase. "You're leaving for good?"

"It's for the best."

"I've never agreed with this whole scenario," the salt-and-pepper haired woman continued, adjusting the baby in her arms. "A mother should be with her child. I know you're young and all, but it's obvious that you love this child."

"They can give her a better home, a better life."

"You're just a child yourself. What do you know of what you could do?" she asked angrily. Then she softened as her gaze swept across Gina's tear-streaked face, over the lips trembling in an effort to hold in her pain. "But I promise that I'll help them take good care of her."

"Thank you. Thank you so very much."

She hugged the fleshy woman, kissed the baby one last time, and managed to walk away on unsteady legs.

Gina slowed when she hit the staircase. Sanjay was in a deep conversation with the Khams. He turned, walked across the marble tile, then met her at the bottom and retrieved the suitcase. He took her hand in his, but she broke from his grasp and ran back to Ms. Kham, who embraced her. Then Gina reached for Mr. Kham, bringing him close. His eyes were filled with moisture that he refused to release.

"Go on now," Ms. Kham said, nodding toward Sanjay, whose gaze was deadly in its intensity.

"Before I have to kill him," Mr. Kham added in a lethal tone.

Both of them grinned slyly at Sanjay, which only served to piss him off even more.

Sanjay slipped into the driver's seat but did not take off immediately. Instead, he gripped the steering wheel until his knuckles turned white. For a moment Gina felt a stab of worry.

How had she fallen in love with another woman's husband? It could be the fact that Sanjay took such good care of her. She never had to spend a single dime of her own money. Not for clothes, not for living expenses, or for her car.

She now carried a Platinum American Express card in her name, but on his account. She held a well-paid position in his corporate headquarters, putting her business degree to work and gaining some experience on her résumé. But the real perk was that Sanjay had total access to her at any time. She never knew what to expect from day to day or from one hour to the next. And she loved every single minute of it.

The moment the man walked into the office, moisture pooled between her thighs. She submitted to him because it felt right, because she wanted to. Gina belonged to him in a way his wife did not—even if she was afraid to admit it.

She looked up in time to see that he wasn't taking her to his home.

"Where are we going?"

He didn't bother to answer.

Minutes later, they were checked into an elegant suite at the Hyatt. Sanjay entered the room just ahead of her, scanned the area, put her things at the door, and gestured for her to go into the bedroom.

Gina stood at the edge of the bed, awaiting his next move. He paced the length of the bedroom like a caged tiger, which only made her worry all the more. Finally, he came to stand in front of her, his eyes locked on her as he stroked her face. She had never witnessed a time when Sanjay wasn't controlled—and the fact that he had lost it was not lost on her.

"Sanjay," she whispered, trying not to unravel.

He pressed a finger to her lips and used the other hand to travel up her skirt and rip off the lace panties. He kept his eyes on her as he unbuttoned the blouse, but he quickly became frustrated and tore the rest away until it displayed the red lace bra that barely held her full breasts in place.

Keeping focused on her, he reached behind her, his breath whispering across the heated skin as he flicked a finger, released the clasps and allowed her breasts to go free. The blouse landed on the floor, the bra fell right after. He ripped off the skirt, and it joined its fabric cousins on the plush carpet.

Sanjay tilted his head and pressed his lips to hers, his restraint barely evident in the tightness of his jaw. She tried to steel herself against what was coming.

A single tear slid down her face, followed by another, and yet another. Something within his hardened expression crumbled. He leaned in and tasted the salty moisture. It seemed that some of his anger had left, but he was still determined to teach her a lesson. She just wanted it to be over.

Sanjay lowered her to the bed, pulled her body to the edge, then dropped to his knees. Petal soft kisses trailed the inner skin of her thighs until her breath quickened. He gripped her buttocks, then as though remembering what had happened, he softened his hold. He favored her pearl with feather-like touches, which caused her body to thrash and a moan to escape her lips despite her best efforts not to show him how much his efforts moved her. His tongue encircled her core as though drawing sweet nectar from the ripest fruit, creating an avalanche of pleasurable sensations. Sanjay teased, taunted, and tortured. She gripped the comforter so hard, her nails nearly ripped into it.

He became more virulent in his ministrations, the pressure more demanding with each pass of his tongue. She called out his name, reached for him, only to have him slap her hands away. Rejected, Gina let her hands fall to her side.

Sanjay slipped out of his pants and briefs in one smooth movement, then pulled the shirt over his dark waves and tossed it to the floor. She tried to wrap her arms around him, but he pulled back and glowered at her until she placed her arms on the bed. Only then did he grip his erection, placing the tip at her core, moving it just that bare half inch, teasing her, making her arch upward, demanding that he take her. Instead, he grinned as he left the bed, went into the bathroom, and closed the door behind him. The next thing she heard was the water streaming from the shower.

She wanted to scream at him, cry out her frustration. But she clamped her mouth shut, allowing herself time to process what had transpired over the last few hours.

Sanjay came out of the shower fifteen minutes later toweling off his body. That glorious erection was nowhere in sight. He rolled in her suitcase and commanded, "Get dressed."

Gina slipped off the bed, a trembling mass of nerves. She sifted through the case for something to replace her damaged clothes.

He watched her as she barely held on to the material long enough to take it out completely. She sank to her knees, resting her buttocks on the back of her heels.

Gina's heart was so heavy, she could barely think straight. She had ended a relationship with the Khams, relinquished one last precious month with her baby girl—and all because he wanted to prove a point. *And then to top it off, he didn't want me anymore? When did she become his property? When did she become so enthralled that he could control her life this way?*

The moment she fell in love with him. That's when. And she couldn't shut it off now, no matter how hard she had tried.

Gina steadied her breathing, willed her body to stop trembling, and reached for a pair of faded jeans and a simple blue blouse.

She stood and got her bearings before making her way toward the bathroom.

"Dress out here."

Gina froze and willed her voice to stay steady. "I made a serious mistake today, and it's too late to change it." She gestured to the bathroom. "But I'm going to take a nice long bath and make some choices about my life." She finally made eye contact with him. "Whatever you want to do, go right ahead. I'm done. It doesn't matter anymore."

On legs that barely wanted to move, she turned toward the bathroom. Gina only made it three steps before he swept her from the floor, tossed her on the bed, straddled her and thrust into her.

Winded, she could only look up at him in shock. She saw that familiar fire in his eyes as he pulled back, then buried himself inside her.

Gina gripped him as he moved within her. She forced him to change positions so that she was on top and rode him until his breathing became ragged. The moment his eyes closed and his head tilted back on the bed, she reached down and slid her hands down to the base and applied a gentle pressure that stopped his release.

Sanjay's eyes widened with understanding, but he failed at gaining a solid breath. He was prevented from saying anything.

Gina then moved off the bed and threw a glance over her shoulder as she hurried to the bathroom. She smiled, winked, and closed the door behind her.

A frustrated groan echoed as he called out her name again and again. She locked the door, and soon a roar of laughter rang out on the other side.

She turned on the shower, but didn't step in. Instead, she pressed her ear to the door.

"All right, Gina. You have made your point. Come on out."

She didn't answer or move.

"Gina, enough of this now," he said more firmly.

She smiled, imagining the scowl that probably matched his threatening tone.

"Little woman, if you do not come out of there right now, I am going to spank your little ass."

Gina unlocked the door, yanked it open, and said, "Now you're talking my language."

Chapter 13

Gina entered the Steinberg's home in Niles. Sanjay was right on her heels. A chill passed through her, and it wasn't because of the bitter cold in the air. She had a sense of foreboding that she couldn't shake off. The maid led them through a labyrinth of plush white carpeting, bright white walls, and white marble floors, which were as austere and unwelcoming as the sterile surroundings. And if Gina had thought the maid was cool, the woman of the house was a veritable ice queen.

Joan Engstrom Steinberg was dressed in a white Versace pantsuit that hugged her slender, athletic form, which didn't have a single womanly curve. Her ivory skin was pale; her lips were the barest pink. Her eyes were an ice gray that could freeze one's blood with a single look. Her features were classically pretty, like that of a prima ballerina. She looked more like a model than a world-renowned photographer and artist. Something about the woman made Gina want to turn and run, but Sanjay's determination for her to fail made her push forward.

Sanjay had canceled an important meeting with a round of private equity investors to accompany her on this trip. He was angered that Gina had failed to inform him of this final contract, especially since he had commanded after the Khams child was born, "No more babies, Gina. Your womb needs a rest."

He would not tell her what to do with her own body. Of that, she was certain.

That day Sanjay set out to "teach her a lesson" in ownership, Gina became pregnant with his second child. She remained with him and Michelle for another six months after the birth of another baby girl. Sanjay became a slight bit possessive, and she constantly sought ways to put some distance between them. The best way to achieve that was to fulfill this final contract.

Without telling Sanjay, Gina had accepted payment from Solomon Steinberg and refused to give it back, which sealed the deal. Now she only needed to flesh out the details, but Gina was having second and third thoughts. She had insisted that the third meeting take place in their home so she could meet the wife. Upon first glance, she understood why everything to this point had transpired in Solomon's office.

As far as Gina was concerned, the woman didn't have a warm bone in her body. How the hell did Solomon think she would make a good wife, let alone a good mother?

A handsome, robust man dressed in a Bill Blass suit draped a proprietary arm around the ice queen as she took a seat next to him on a stark white leather sectional. Solomon's green eyes twinkled with warmth, and the smile that lifted the corners of his lips caused Gina to relax, but only a little. Another man, tall, with skin the shade of smooth ebony and whose chiseled features were so striking it hurt to look at him, sat on the woman's right with his hands laced in hers. The look in his dark brown eyes as he gazed appreciatively over Gina made her quickly look away, but not before she saw the flash of anger in the ice queen's eyes, who witnessed the exchange.

"Which one is the husband?" Sanjay asked after Gina had mentally spent several minutes trying to come up with her own explanation.

Both Joan and the second man pointed to Solomon.

"So who is he?" Gina asked, gesturing to the man on the woman's right.

"My lover. His name is Edgar." She rubbed her hand along the lover's thigh, and her lips lifted in something that was neither smile nor frown, as though she relished Sanjay's and Gina's shocked expressions.

Gina blinked, absorbing everything at once. "What kind of craziness is this?"

"The kind you signed up for just to spite me," Sanjay whispered so only she could hear. He leaned back, but made a concerted effort to catch the wife's eye.

Gina shrugged him off. "So who's actually going to raise this child?"

"We both are," the men replied in unison.

"But I only agreed for Solomon to get me pregnant."

"True, but think of the possibilities if we both tried," Edgar countered in a rich baritone that commanded attention.

Solomon scowled. Sanjay went rigid. Joan colored all the way to her dark hairline.

"Out of the question," Sanjay snapped and gripped her hand.

"Absolutely not," Joan said with a pointed look at Sanjay, who tried to get Gina to stand with him, but relaxed his hold when he glanced at Joan. Gina saw the look that passed between them. Something made the hairs on the back of her neck stand at Army attention. The woman's features were as controlled as she had seen from anyone—even Sanjay.

Solomon was a plastic surgeon whose services were well in demand with celebrities and the very rich. How much of Joan's beauty was man-made? Then another question surfaced. If Joan was Jewish as she had claimed, why was Solomon so set on having a Black woman have their child? She scanned the woman's face for any signs of an answer and came up empty, but a red flag had been raised in her mind.

"She travels a lot," Gina said to Solomon. "So who's going to actually raise the baby?"

"I will," Solomon replied, glowering at his wife, who cocked a single eyebrow. She almost seemed amused by the whole process. "And I'll have a nanny too. My son or daughter will be well taken care of. I promise you that."

And she believed him. He was the one to initiate the contract and had added all kinds of things to sweeten the deal. It was Joan who now gave Gina pause, but the woman's nature seemed to imply that she wouldn't be the primary caregiver or have much to do with the child.

Then a thought hit her—being Jewish was merely about religion, not ethnicity. Gina took a chance and threw out, "How is she going to take being considered the mother of a Black child, when it's obvious she's passing for White?"

Joan's eyes flashed fire. Finally some form of life from that side of the sofa. "I resent that."

"Resent it all you like, but ..." Gina began, then paused once she saw Solomon's frozen expression. "You didn't know?"

The wife shifted her gaze, took in Edgar's stony expression, and squirmed in her seat. Gina had made an instant enemy. Then it hit her all at once—Joan had forced Solomon to choose a Black woman, thinking he wouldn't go through with it. Evidently, she didn't know her husband as well as she thought.

"Why do you want this baby so badly?" Gina asked, taking in Solomon's stilted expression.

Solomon grimaced, then looked away, as though searching for ways to voice his desire in words. "A child is not a do-over moment in life. I don't want to be seventy and say I wish I had." Then he looked at Gina, and his eyes and voice softened as he searched her eyes for some form of understanding. "I want to go to Disney World ... and water parks and ballet recitals or piano recitals. Baseball games. Things I couldn't do as a child." Solomon looked down at his hands; the wedding band sparkling under the bright white lights. "My parents were plumb out of money, but they were plenty ready with a whole heaping of love." He moved to stand in front of Gina, then lowered to his knees. Sanjay stiffened the moment he touched Gina. "I can give my child both. And I'm not ashamed to say that I'll spoil my son or daughter absolutely rotten."

Gina smiled at that statement, remembering how her father had done the same. She reached out and touched his face gently, a move that wasn't lost on Sanjay, who scowled but remained silent. "Then why didn't you choose a woman who feels the way you do?"

"We can't always choose who we love," he whispered, and the sad tone touched a corner of Gina's heart. "I love Joan, and one day, I truly believe she'll come to understand what unconditional love is all about. Then she'll return what I give to her so freely."

Gina moved away from Solomon, wandered to the images displayed along the walls—pictures of the interior and exterior of elaborate architectural designs, plated cuisine, and photos of famous models taken at exotic locations around the world. How could a woman who was so cold produce pictures that were so vibrant and full of life?

"So why can't you have children?" she asked Joan over her shoulder before turning full frontal to read the ice queen's reaction.

The woman's head whipped up, and she glared at Gina. She opened her mouth to snarl a reply, but Solomon intervened. "It's not that she *can't*; it's that she *won't*," he said bitterly. "Just like she refuses to give him up ..." His voice lowered to a breathy, but shame-filled whisper, "And I refuse to give her up."

Edgar grimaced at Solomon's discomfort while Joan settled back on the sofa and sighed impatiently.

"I loved her long before you did," Edgar said, linking his hands with Joan's. "I just didn't have the money to compete with what you offered. You can let her go anytime you want. Or we can continue to share her as we've always done."

So there it was; the ice queen married Solomon for his money and kept Edgar because he loved her. But now that Joan made her own money, why didn't she just leave? What hold did Solomon have on her?

"I've always wanted a family," Solomon said softly. "A big one. That dream will obviously never happen."

"Exactly," Joan snapped back, folding her arms across her chest. "One is all I'll allow. Children are work; they demand too much time. Women have messed up their careers by having those things."

"You knew how much I wanted children before we were married," Solomon countered as he went to stand in front of his wife. "We took vows. I take them seriously."

"Looks like you're the only one." Gina stood and let out a long, slow breath. "You know, I signed a contract years ago, and I know you waited for me, but I think this might not be such a good idea."

The victorious glint in Sanjay's dark brown eyes was enough to make her dig in her heels. But this family was too off center. Children needed two parents who loved them. And she wasn't feeling it from the mother. The father couldn't do it all himself, even with help from the lover.

Solomon caught up with her at the door. "Please, do this for me … not for her. I want a child—someone to carry on long after I'm gone. That will bring me all the happiness in the world."

He continued with his plea for her to change her mind, as Sanjay leaned against the foyer wall and took it all in.

His gloating made her decision much easier. "You must promise me that you, and only you, will be responsible for the child's upbringing. That woman doesn't have a loving bone in her body."

"You're wrong about her, Gina," Solomon said softly, his green eyes filling with sadness. "She does love me … in her own way, as much as she can love anyone." When she didn't respond he said, "I understand your concerns. But I am the one who wants a child, and I will be the one who gives him … her ... the love and attention a child deserves." Solomon reached out, placed his hand over Gina's, and gave her a smile that melted her heart.

"Promise me," she said, locking an intense gaze on him, "if anything happens to you, you make sure my child comes back to me."

Solomon's shoulders tensed as he took her meaning. "She's not so decrepit that she would hurt a child."

"It's the only way I'll consider it. I trust you, but if you're not around," Gina replied, looking him in his eyes, "I don't trust her."

"But I'm fit as a fiddle." He gave his belly a pat. "I'm not going anywhere."

Gina grinned up at him. "Humor me. I have that little clause in all of my contracts. If anything happens to the parents, I become the child's legal guardian and all rights revert back to me. But for yours, it'll have to be if something happens to you—" She held up a hand to halt his protest. "I certainly don't envision that, but I have to be realistic. I like you … a lot, but if you want me to go through with this, then I have to feel more comfortable about everything."

Finally his shoulders relaxed, as he said, "All right."

Sanjay stormed back into the family room with Solomon and Gina on his heels. "Can I speak with you a moment?" he asked Joan, who was sitting so close to her lover, it was as though she had become a second skin.

Joan lifted a single brow, extracted her hand from Edgar's, and led Sanjay to a room just off the dining room. Edgar came to stand next to Solomon a few moments later, and they conversed in hushed tones. The two men seemed to get along fairly well, at least on the surface. What was it about that woman that she could hold the love of two men? Why didn't Solomon just let her go on with Edgar? And why did Edgar stick around when it was obvious that Solomon wasn't going to leave his wife and that she wasn't going to leave him?

Sanjay and Joan came out ten minutes later. He gave Gina a sly smile, and Joan had a smug air about her that was more pronounced than before.

"I've made some adjustments to the contract." Joan held it out to Gina, who snatched it, looked at the handwritten changes and said, "Insemination or turkey baster method. I'm not agreeing to that."

Joan's thin lips lifted into a smile. "Well, that's the only way it's going to happen."

"Or it doesn't happen at all," Sanjay added with a sly grin of his own.

"And trust me," Joan continued with an almost unreadable expression thrown in her husband's direction, "you might find it a hell of a lot more pleasurable."

Gina glanced at Solomon, who glared at his wife then looked back at Gina with a defeated expression, who kept her peripheral gaze on Sanjay. She gave Solomon a wink, which cause a wilted smile to form on his thin lips. "You know what? Turkey baster's fine with me. Solomon will be worth it."

The grateful look in Solomon's eyes and the fact that his shoulders visibly relaxed let Gina know that she had spoken the right words to ease the pain of his wife's venomous blow.

Sanjay's dark brown eyes went as wide as saucers, then a scowl marred his handsome features. Joan shot an angry gaze at Sanjay, who was so boiled over with anger he couldn't form a single word, let alone a full sentence.

"As long as Solomon does the honors," Gina said to Sanjay in a breathy whisper. Then she turned to the wife. "And since he's so interested, your lover can watch. We might as well make it a family ... affair."

Joan stormed out of the room, and soon a door slammed loud enough to cause a crystal vase to crash to the floor.

Gina took in Solomon's wide smile and the confident set of his jaw as she said, "Sweetheart, I believe your wife is a tad bit upset."

He took her outstretched hands in his. "You don't say?"

Chapter 14

The turning point in her life was making a decision to defy Sanjay, and follow through with her promise to Solomon Steinberg. They discarded the contract that Alana had drafted, and replaced it with one of their own. Soon they were meeting for candlelight dinners, romantic walks on Navy Pier and the lakefront, and excursions to the theater and ballet. Gina tried to get him to see that there was more to life than being with a woman like Joan. And she had succeeded, but her plans nearly backfired.

The night Solomon came to her so they could create the child he wanted, Gina undressed him slowly, peeling the suit from his robust frame, before draping her fingertips across the smooth expanse of skin. The moment she trailed up his thighs and reached his erection, she could only wonder what had happened to the rest of it. Now she understood Joan's taunting words. Gina looked up and saw the stricken look in Solomon's eyes and knew right then and there that she had the power to destroy what was left of his self-esteem or do something that would give him a confidence that would last beyond their coupling.

Gina released him, and stretched out among the layers of pillows, allowing him to take control of their love-making. She needed to see *how* he made love and only then could she know what direction to take them in.

Surprised that she had not turned him away, or laughed at his lack of length, Solomon straddled her, spread her as far open as she could go and aimed at pressing himself inside. Gina halted him and whispered, "Solomon, if you'll let me, I'll teach you how to please me. And *any* woman."

A look of uncertainty crossed his handsome features before he pulled back and waited.

"First, let's start with foreplay, then I'll show you the best position for you to work with, so you can please a woman and find pleasure too."

Solomon swallowed hard, nodding as he kept his gaze on her.

"You have to get a woman so aroused that she's fulfilled long before you even attempt to put this," she stroked his hardened member, " inside her."

Gina took his hands in hers, and worked him through soft, searching, teasing touches across her body and lingered on her erogenous zones, followed by a session of tastes over several points that was the catalyst for an orgasm. She taught him to use his hands, fingers, lips in a way that prolonged her pleasure and brought some to him as well. He was patient, open to exploration and the moment she brought both of her legs over his right shoulder, giving him full access to her heated core, he pressed in slowly, allowing the tightness and heat of her to guide him in.

"Sweet Lord, it has never been this good for me," he whispered.

Gina could actually believe him. "Yes," she whispered back. "This is the only position where you should attempt penetration."

She guided his hips into giving her direct penetrating thrusts that concentrated on that small tangle of nerves which provided the ultimate pleasure. Solomon's release was like a downpour of rain after a lifetime drought in the Mohave Desert. He gently lifted her legs from his shoulder and wrapped her into his arms for an embrace that seemed to go on for an eternity.

She could actually pinpoint the moment that Solomon's desire for her turned into an admiration and love so deep that he would do anything for her. After that night, Solomon redirected his attention and affection to Gina in a way that could have proven dangerous for both of them. She didn't want to become anyone else's kept woman.

* * *

Gina had not choice but to stop working for Sanjay's company. The rift between them was nearly impossible to remedy. Sanjay learned that she was pregnant by Solomon and he walked out without saying a single word. She felt a sense of loss; a sense of hopelessness, but this was even more of a sign that she needed to go her own way and live life on her own terms.

When he finally got over himself, she refused to take his calls or answer her door the many times he showed up. Then she finally moved into one of the apartments of the high-rise building he had purchased for her after she had given birth to his second child.

Mermaid Towers was being renovated, and eventually it would be the place she called home. He had acquired it for a steal from the previous owners because it needed extensive repairs. She alone had been responsible for the renovation plans and the management of the various stages of construction. She was adding a valet service, a sun deck with comfortable patio seating and tables to hold a hundred people, a fitness center, and elegantly designed parlors for residents to use for entertaining a large number of guests.

Working on this project, she fell in love with the idea of owning property. She completed the courses for her real estate license and made a different plan for her life—buying and renovating distressed properties.

Investments had rendered her a multi-millionaire, and a secure future meant she would never be at anyone's mercy—well except God and the IRS. Now she was ready to do the one thing she had always dreamed of: travel to England, Paris, Switzerland, Ghana, Senegal, India, Greece,

Italy, and many other countries she had read about as a child. Once she had this little one, she would be free. And in some ways she regretted this pregnancy because it had not been done for all the right reasons.

But the moment that Solomon said, "Don't leave me, Gina. I need you. I love you," she almost wavered. This time she would have a man who loved her, cherished her and she would be able to raise her child with him. She almost gave in. Almost.

"Solomon, I can't break your heart a second time."

He looked at her for a long moment. "What do you mean?"

"No matter how much I love you, I'm not in love with you," she said, cupping his face in her hands. "I'm still in love with Sanjay. I can't do that to you. I can't hurt you that way."

What Gina didn't say was that she would not be the cause of the man leaving his wife, no matter how much she hated the ice queen. Why couldn't she have met him under different circumstances? She loved Solomon almost as much as she loved Sanjay. Well…not quite, but it would have been enough for her. Almost.

Chapter 15

Gina was packing her things for the day so she could leave her real estate office in time for a seminar. Buying rental property had become her new passion. Thanks to Sanjay's gift, she had used the high rise as leverage and had now amassed a series of courtyard buildings in South Shore, Bronzeville, and Chatham.

The phone rang, causing her to halt her movements. The display indicated that Alana was on the other end. She would not have anything else to do with Alana and Christopher, since it was obvious that they were exposing more of her private life to people who were members of the Castle than she preferred. Now they were stalking her for some strange reason.

After the Steinberg child, Gina's time as a surrogate was done. Seven million, the results of investments and surrogate earnings, was enough cushion for anyone to live on. After having to leave so many of her children in the care of others, she realized that she did want children of her own. The next children she would have would be with her own husband and ones she would keep.

The phone rang again, and she balanced her briefcase in one hand and property surveys in the other so she could take the call.

"Alana, I don't have anything to say to you," Gina snapped. "You betrayed my trust. How could you do that to me?" Gina heard the sharp intake of breath, but cut Alana off before she could reply. "And exactly when did you leave your firm to do this baby brokering thing full time? I was that much of a cash cow? What, exactly, is your cut?"

The silence that came after that question was an admission unto itself. The amount was too exorbitant to put into words. But they had gone too far. Alana had ambushed her with a set-up for a couple who wanted a child strictly to use the genetic material to keep another child alive. Unthinkable. And for all his jealous anger against Sanjay Bhandari, how could Christopher have been a part of this?

"Gina, I know you're angry at me, and you have every right to be." She sighed softly as though amazed that Gina let her get those few words out. "Christopher would like you to meet him at his office. There's something he needs to ask you. It's important. It's *very* important."

"And you can't tell me what it is?"

Alana hesitated, and that let Gina know that something was very wrong.

"So you're letting him do your dirty work? Because after what you did, you don't have nothing coming."

"I don't know what you're talking about," she replied slowly.

"Why did the Khams and that other couple know so much about what I've been into? They're from The Castle, too?"

Silence.

Amazing. The woman—once a top lawyer—was always ready with an answer for practically everything. Before then, Alana had never interjected her opinions about Gina's life or her decisions. But because it suited her purpose to put a wedge between Gina and the man who loved her, Alana had spoken against Sanjay at every turn, hoping it would free Gina to do what she wanted—give them a second child.

Gina had been grateful for everything the Meisters had done for her, even going so far as to allowing her time with that beautiful little girl with whisper soft blond hair and eyes the color of a morning sky— anytime she wanted.

The child she carried now, more than any of the others, required more sleep, more food, more care, more everything. One last child. Freedom. No, she couldn't give them what they wanted.

"I think this should be discussed in person," Alana Meister said softly, snatching Gina from her thoughts, which included kicking herself for answering the phone in the first place.

"What's going on? Is something wrong with my ... I mean ... your daughter?"

Alana's breath caught at that little slip. "Just go see him. Please. Today if you can."

She disconnected the call before Gina could further protest.

* * *

When Gina arrived at the hospital, she was promptly escorted to an office in the ICU wing. Christopher looked up from a stack of documents; his smile was fleeting while he slowly checked out Gina's body, as though trying to verify an answer to some unspoken question. He removed his white jacket, revealing a tailored blue shirt stretched across a toned physique. Christopher focused on her face and smiled when she continued to watch him.

"I'd like you to reconsider our request for a second child. Whatever you want ... whatever you desire ... it's yours."

Gina sighed her frustration and took a seat in one of the wingback chairs across from the mahogany desk. "I can't do that."

"Give me one good reason why." He went over to the door and locked it, then placed his back against the frosted glass.

"After one more child, I'm done with having children for other people."

"Whose child?" he growled. "Sanjay Bhandari's?"

Gina stared at him, surprised more at his bitter tone than the question itself. She followed his movements until he was behind the desk.

"Oh yes, I know all about him," he spat, his blue eyes flashing pure fire. "Asshole."

"You know what?" She moved from the chair and toward the door. "I think I should leave."

"How is it that you're still sleeping with him?"

That question held her in place. She hadn't been with Sanjay in a long while, but that wasn't any of Christopher's business. She released the knob and turned to face him. "I'm not going to have this conversation with you."

I would've taken care of you," he whispered hoarsely, then made his way over to her and stroked a hand gently along her arm as he pressed a kiss to her forehead. "You didn't have to leave me."

She slapped his hand away. "You were too busy feeling guilty to manage that. Every time we made love, it was like a shadow was hanging over your head. Sanjay has no such inhibitions."

Christopher's blue eyes went dark, and he closed them while taking a steadying breath. Finally he took a seat, then looked at her for a long time. He patted his lap in that familiar way that she had once known. "Come, just let me hold you one last time."

Gina hesitated a few moments. As she peered at him, she felt a familiar twinge of longing. She then moved onto his lap and laid her head on his chest as he held her, stroking a comforting hand across her back. It had been a long time since she had been in a man's arms, and for a woman who was used to making love every day, sometimes several times a day, going off the program had been hard as hell.

Christopher had always felt wonderful to her. The way he held her, the way he kissed her, the way he—

"We've been good to you, haven't we?" he whispered, lowering his hands to her buttocks and massaging them through the soft material.

"Yes, Christopher."

"We gave you a great start in life."

"Yes, that's true."

"We did whatever you wanted us to do."

"Yes," she said, stroking a hand across his chest.

"So ... you'll do this for us," he said in a voice so husky it sent a tingle of pleasure whipping through her. "We're not asking for too much. Just one more child. Please, sweetheart?"

This time she didn't get a chance to respond as he moved his hands and lifted the skirt, slid his hands under the thin material until he reached her bare cheeks. He stroked a gentle hand across them, relishing the feel of them. The man had always become turned on by the mere sight of that part of her anatomy alone.

"Alana sent me here for this?"

"Yes," he said, massaging those warm globes until she moaned, then he slipped off her panties, pressed his fingers to her core, slipping one of his digits into her moist heat. When she whimpered with his rhythm, he grew bolder, pressing another digit inside, stroking her until she began to move against him of her own accord.

Gina looked up at him, feeling a tenderness and heat well inside her. She longed for this, for a time when he would let himself go and be into her in a way that made him forget everything else. The desire he felt for her was in his strained expression, the wildness of his eyes. He wanted her, and this time there would be no holding back—no timid touches as though she would break at the slightest movement.

His lips went to hers, kissing her with a softness that stirred her. She moved on him, urging him to finish what he had started, but he hesitated as though he was not quite ready.

"I've missed you," he whispered, holding her to himself as though she would fly away at any given moment. "God knows I'm not supposed to, but I have. I never wanted you to leave me. I need you with me. Come back to me. I will take care of you ... better than he can."

Gina lifted from him, turned and braced her body on top of the desk, exposing herself to him the way he liked.

The hiss of pleasure that escaped him gave her a power that she loved more than anything. He pried into her moist center and played with her at his leisure. "Awww sweet Jesus. You're so hot, so wet."

"You've always made me this way," she said softly as he continued to press his way inside her. "I don't know what you're waiting for, but if you're not willing …"

He was unzipped and on her in an instant. With every ounce of strength he could manage, he thrust inside, then trembled at the pure power of it. Her body heaved forward with every lunge of his hips, sending his paperwork sprawling to the carpet.

Christopher gripped her body and pulled her back toward him, going as deep as her body would allow until his seed spilled into her and he came in spasms that jolted through him and into her.

She glanced over her shoulder just in time to see his eyes roll heavenward and his head thrown back as the pleasure overtook him. He moved within her until a moan became a growl, and that growl became a mighty roar. The liquid sounds of his flesh entering her was overshadowed only by the voices on the overhead speaker.

Finally, he looked down at her, then himself. She saw the instant the guilt began to creep in. Christopher lowered his gaze under her heated glare. He staggered backward, slumped in the chair, and closed his eyes. The crisp blue shirt was partially stuffed in his slacks, and he righted the rest of his clothing as best he could, but still left them in apparent disarray.

"Christopher, you know as well as I do that I can't come back to you."

In a voice colder than she had ever heard from him, he said, "Then you'll let me know if you conceive."

Gina chuckled as she straightened her blouse. "Oh, is that what this was all about?"

Christopher glared at her as though she was the one who had done something wrong. Then it clicked for her. She alone had handled the new contract with Solomon. The Meisters didn't know anything about it. Alana was the one to track her cycle for all of the times leading up to her pregnancies. It was like clockwork. On a normal basis, she would be fertile right now. Evidently, they were going on false information.

"I could've saved you the trouble, sweetheart." She leaned in so they were nose to nose, "I'm already pregnant."

He froze. His face became flushed with anger. "With … with that Indian fucker's child?"

She shrugged and tilted her head as she looked at him. "And if I am?"

He gripped her, slammed her down on the desk, and fumbled to get his dick back out of his pants as she laughed once again.

"What do you propose to do? Screw it out of me?" She spread her thighs, offering him instant entry. "You could always try, but I don't think you can last that long."

Christopher backed away. He turned and faced the wall, trembling with equal amounts of anger and remorse.

Gina was gone before he could offer the apology she knew was coming.

*"In three words, I can sum up everything
I've learned about life:
it goes on."*
—Robert Frost

PART III

Eyes of the Starfish

Fourteen years later – January 2003

Chapter 16

Nalina flinched as her husband gripped her arms so hard his fingernails dug into the skin. "You're my wife," he said through clenched teeth. "I forbid you to work in those slums any longer."

"Sri, you knew what I wanted to do for a living before you married me," she replied, trying unsuccessfully to break his hold. "I wanted to be in this field long before our families decided that we should marry. I'm not giving up my dream for you, your family, or anyone."

Nalina pried his fingers from her arms and snatched away from him as quickly as she could manage. She walked from the living room and quickened her steps up the hallway. They had been arguing for nearly an hour, and she realized that they would never reach a happy medium. Nalina needed to put as much distance between her and the man her father had chosen for her as fast as possible. Luckily, their massive home—a house that had never been to her liking—afforded her that luxury.

Srinivas Kasturi was most women's idea of a dream—rich, handsome, with tawny skin, thick dark hair, piercing brown eyes and boyish good looks. Nalina had never warmed to him because of his controlling and demanding nature. Their nights were often spent locked in an old-world way of doing things and a "you'd-better-recognize" American woman tug-of-war. In three years, neither side had gained any ground. But she was about to settle things once and for all.

As she maneuvered past the master bedroom, she stopped short of opening the glass door and walking out to the lush garden. Instead, she pressed forward to her small bedroom right next to the solarium and pool—a section of the house closely connected to a series of residences which belonged to the other members of the Kasturi family.

Since they had married, she had not been allowed to alter a single thing. Only her clothes and sporadic presence signaled any sign of change in this house and in his life. She would not share his bed, so at first Sri and his mother forbade her to use any other room in the house. They changed their tune when Nalina began to stay at the office instead of coming home. She was finally relegated to the one small bedroom until she "came to her senses." Fine with her. She was not for fending off her husband's advances in the master bedroom every night.

Every attempt at gaining some small concession she requested to make her feel welcome was met with, "My mother would not like for you to do that."

Nalina only wished she could reply, "Then you should've married your mother!" However, that would have been impolite.

Sri followed her to her private sanctuary, invading even that special space.

"You're my wife. You need to learn that means you must do as I say."

Nalina turned and stared at him as though he had spoken a foreign language.

"You will not work with those ... those lowlifes, those degenerates," he said with a haughty lift of his chin. "And let us be very clear about things. When we have children, you *will* stay home and raise them. Then if you want to work, it will be within my family's business." He nodded and leaned on the door as though that was the end of the subject.

Nalina couldn't help the laugh that escaped her lips. "That's never going to happen, stud."

His shoulders went stiff with anger as his gaze narrowed to slits. "What do you mean?"

She walked to the closet, lugged out two large suitcases, and dropped them on the bed. "Staying home. Giving up my business. My father arranged for me to become your wife, not your slave. Somehow you've confused the two. Either you come at me when you grow some balls or file for a divorce."

Sri threw his hands in the air, grumbling, "This is what I get for marrying a fucking half-breed."

Nalina went stock still, then slowly lifted her gaze to him. "What did you call me?"

"A half-breed," he snapped, unfazed by her near deadly tone.

She snatched a knife from under her pillow and motioned for him to step her way. "You want to come a little closer and say that again?"

"You're not a pure Indian woman," he snarled, inching back toward the door. Then he paused as though realizing that his action showed weakness. "You should be grateful that I married you. No other men in our family would have anything to do with you."

"Grateful?" she shot back, moving around him to make a quick trip to the dresser and extract the first of many items she would need. "And what exactly should I be grateful for? I didn't need you to marry me." She tightened the caps on the lotion, perfumes, and face creams before placing the toiletries into a clear protective sleeve. "I was doing just fine without you or your damn family. It wasn't my choice. *You* were never my choice."

His gaze followed as she whipped out a few unmentionables and used them to wrap the framed pictures of her father, mother, and sister.

"Half-breed," she spat, pausing long enough to look over up at him. "And if you feel that way about me, how will you feel about our children … if we even got to that point. What will you call them? Fourth-breeds?"

Sri's face was frozen in a comical expression of bewilderment. He was actually trying to process that insult!

He became suddenly still as his gaze swept from the closet, to her cases, to the small number of items left on the dresser. "They say that I have been too lenient with you," he countered smoothly, trying to block her path to the bed. "I should have gotten you pregnant right away."

"You haven't earned my virginity," she fired back, maneuvering around him to retrieve the small package containing her identification and school records. "My father said I had to marry you. He didn't say I had to fuck you."

"And that mouth of yours. Such filth. They raised you and that hellion sister of yours as uncivilized women."

"If I'm such a barbarian, what does that make you?" she taunted. "I'm well on my way to a master's in social work; and my sister's right behind me on the path to become a psychologist, while you barely received an associates in what is it called … um … what were you studying?"

"Art History."

"Uncivilized my ass!" Then she gave him a sly look. "And your brother doesn't have a problem with treating my sister the way a woman should be treated."

"That's because Anil's a weakling. He's too busy trying to gain favor with your father." Sri shifted uncomfortably as she came within a few feet from him. "If it were not for that, I assure you, she would be treated like the half-breed whore she is."

Nalina's hand snaked out and slapped him so hard he staggered backward. "Say it again and you'll lose your tongue. I guarantee it."

Sri backed into the wall so hard a picture fell, but he continued to glare at her with an anger she had only felt from him once—the night he had tried to enforce his marital "rights." He soon learned that Nalina would not be an easy conquest.

Somehow, he refused to accept the inevitable: either he would have to meet her halfway or they would be housemates. Since the relationship between Nalina and his family was so volatile, she only came home to sleep, change, and leave before anyone else was up and cracking. Tonight, Sri was waiting on her when she walked through the front door.

Evidently, the Kasturi family had put on the pressure—again. They wanted offspring—proof that her claims about their marital bed were untrue.

"You treat me like I have no right to speak my mind, no say in my own life." She poked a finger in his chest. "Listen up, stud, I'm not your property. I don't even carry your last name." Nalina bypassed all of the intricately designed wedding garments, selected the rest of her business attire and gently placed them inside the second suitcase. She looked over at him. "You weren't raised in a cave somewhere. Learn how to treat a woman."

"You refuse to be reasonable," he shrieked. But when she focused on him, he inched back from her. "You're too much of an American woman to make a good Indian wife."

"And you knew that from the start," she shot back, continuing her efforts to pack—noting that he was so angry that he hadn't commented on her movements. "I didn't see you trying to get out of the marriage. You had a choice. They would have listened to you." Then she grinned as another thought came to mind. "And actually, your brother Kalyan was all for marrying me. And that man ... Lord, I would've wanted him in the worst way." She shrugged, trying to hold in a laugh at the flare of jealousy that flashed in his eyes. "Maybe my father set me up with the wrong brother. I could call him and have him rectify that situation, since I'm *still* a virgin. Kalyan could more than handle me. He would have courted me like you should have. He has style, class ... and I bet he could do more than demand I do something. He might actually deliver in the marriage and in the bedroom." She relished the heat that flushed his cheeks. His thin lips had pursed into an angry line.

The first suitcase clicked shut before she lowered to the floor and reached under the mattress for the gun she had hidden there, and then stuffed it in her open case. "Three years later, and I'm still intact. Hmmmm," she mused, looking heavenward. "Might lend some weight to those *equipment failures* I mentioned at the family dinner last time."

"I will tell them that you still refused to fulfill the terms of the marriage contract."

Nalina turned to her husband and didn't miss a beat. "Tell your family—and mine—whatever you like because I'm going to do me." She rolled the cases through the hallways of the house and made it to the front door, completely ignoring the fact that he yelled her name several times. He was sure to wake up everyone in the adjoining Kasturi houses, and then the real fun would begin.

"Where the hell do you think you are going?"

She opened the foyer closet, slipped on her synthetic fur, and traded the house slippers for a pair of boots. She turned to him and said, "Sweetheart, I'm done with this dance. You have two left feet, and I'm tired of mine getting stepped on. There are better things I can do with my time and my life, and I can't do them here."

Sri whipped past her and put his back to the door, shutting it. "You can't leave me. I will lose my stipend," he whispered.

"Stipend? Ahhhh, now we're getting to the real deal," she taunted, then opened the door, moving him with it,. "But the thought of losing that money didn't make you want to treat me any better than you have, so it couldn't be all that important." She nodded then walked out, maneuvering up the icy path to the car to put that first suitcase into the trunk.

"There has never been a divorce in the Kasturi family," he yelled, trailing her to a pearl white Lexus.

"And probably not any married virgins either. There's a first time for everything." She went back in, grabbed the second suitcase, and schlepped it to the car. He watched as she situated that one beside its mate. "You can blame it all on your half-breed wife," Nalina said, giving him a sly grin as she slipped into the driver's seat. "Surely your precious family will understand that."

* * *

Nalina drove toward downtown Chicago and at first thought of checking into the Westin. Instead, she hit the Dan Ryan, took the 55th Street exit, drove over to State, made a right and went up four blocks.

She parked in front of a two-story gray stone building. As she exited her vehicle, she looked with pride at the banner which read, NEW PATTERNS, NEW LIFE.

She had worked for the organization for the past few years, first as an intern, and then in a role she never thought possible at her young age—director of a social service agency. When the owner of Nalina's firm suddenly took ill, she turned the reins over to her spirited young protégée who was encouraged to change the name of the agency, keep the current contracts and follow her own dream—which meant continuing to help families transition from the developments—the new, "politically correct" term for projects—into the private housing market. She had hoped that the name alone would be a ray of hope for the people she served within the Bronzeville community—or the "Low End," as some still called it. Her company was all about helping people change their patterns so their lives would be different—through education, training, and positive support.

She removed the cases from the trunk and rolled up to the steel security gate. When she locked the entry door behind her, she made a mad dash to disengage the alarm. The office was her haven, her real sanctuary—a place she looked forward to coming to every day and dreaded leaving at night. The place had twelve offices, a small training room, a fully equipped kitchen and cafeteria, file room, conference room, a waiting area that could accommodate ten people, and a receptionist desk for the part-time students who worked there during the week.

The residents' initial contact with Nalina's agency was where the wheel of fortune began to spin. Some people who had never held a job in their lives had to be taught skill sets for not just getting the job, but maintaining that job and their households—including budgeting, maintaining good credit, and staying in compliance with their current leases. But the major issue for Nalina's team was getting many of the women to understand they had to choose between having a man in their beds or keeping a roof over their heads.

Nalina would often advocate for marriage, which made her very popular with the women—not so much with the men. The same men who didn't have a problem planting three, four, five, and sometimes more children in a woman's womb would cringe at the idea of marrying that very same woman. The moment the men said, "I do," Nalina had her pro-bono lawyers start working on clearing any criminal records they might have, while she also worked to get them some education and the training they needed to land good jobs and bring in a decent paycheck. Those men became her biggest advocates.

Nalina and her employees were really starting to make a difference in the lives of the residents of the neighborhood. They were well respected, and word was spreading that they, in turn, respected the people they served. Unfortunately, because of dirty politics, their time was coming to an end, and Nalina's staffers were out of work. The deputy director of the CHA had been gunning for Nalina because she didn't carry the credentials of the previous owner. Now he had slated the relocation contract to go to one of his cronies. Nalina could rant and rave until Lake Michigan dried up, but the end result was the same—the doors to NEW PATTERNS, NEW LIFE would have to close.

Nalina had no one to turn to in her time of need. She couldn't even call her mother and tell her what she was going through. The woman hadn't uttered a single word when Nalina and her sister, Anjali, were parceled off as though they were chattel. Nalina went through with the arranged marriage, but she would be damned if it would change who she was at her core.

Sometimes, when she was confused or something didn't feel quite right about her life, she would close her eyes, and this picture of another woman she had called Auntie would come to mind. The woman had showered her with so much love and attention she still felt the sincerity of it to this very day. She wondered what had happened to the woman with long auburn curls, a beautiful heart-shaped face, soft brown eyes, and a smile that warmed the heart.

The one time she had asked her mother, Michelle Bhandari had flown into such a rage that Nalina had hidden in her bedroom until her father came home to get her. Only then did her mother have the patience to say, "Never, never speak of this again. Not to me and especially not to your father."

"But why?" Nalina inquired.

"He would not like to be reminded of her. I certainly do not wish to remember her."

"So the woman *does* exist," Nalina whispered, her heart soaring with hope. "Why won't you tell me who she is?"

Her parents exchanged a speaking glance before her father walked away. They didn't hear from him for three days, and her mother was a weeping mess the entire time.

Nalina saw the mysterious woman every time she looked in the mirror and at times when she looked at Anjali. There seemed to be more of her in Michelle's daughters than the woman they called their mother.

She had not dared bring the subject up again, but she would the moment her parents took her to task about her failed marriage to Srinivas Kasturi. They would want answers, but this time, so would she.

Nalina turned up the heat, took off the fur coat and boots, set the alarm, then stretched out on the sofa in her office. The rickety sounds of the Green Line rolling across the train tracks lulled her into a not-quite peaceful sleep.

Chapter 17

Kasturi Residence - Skokie, Illinois

Anjali Kasturi searched her husband's eyes, trying to decipher what could have brought on such a thunderous expression. He placed the cordless back on the charger and stared straight ahead. Even with mere slivers of light streaming in the bedroom window, she could tell all color had drained from his face. Only one person would call them at nearly two o'clock in the morning, knowing the children were asleep. Srinivas Kasturi. She would bet that whatever it was, it had something to do with her sister. Only Nalina could get that man's boxers in an uproar.

She reached out, touched a hand to her husband's arm, and asked the dreaded question, "What's wrong, Anil?"

After a few moments, her hand fell away. Then he seemed to realize she had asked him a question that deserved an answer. "Sri's freaking out because Nalina left him. Your father has threatened to wring his neck if he doesn't find her and do whatever it takes to bring her home."

Anjali grimaced but didn't speak.

Anil turned his head, his gaze narrowed as he took in her lack of reaction. "You *knew* she was going to do it?"

"I'm surprised it didn't happen long before now," she answered carefully. "You were at the wedding. Everyone knew those two were not going to make it."

Anil sighed and had no real comeback for that kernel of truth.

The day of the wedding, Anjali cringed as Sri and Sanjay had shared a knowing look that caused Nalina's gaze to narrow on her father. Sanjay gave her a sheepish smile as he patted Michelle's hand. Michelle looked first at her husband, then over to Anjali's stricken expression. Realization swept across her mother's features and Michelle looked away, as though resigning herself to what might happen.

Only then did Anjali feel a pang of regret for her part in things, believing that once her sister saw the time, money, and creativity that went into making their combined weddings a glorious event, she would be on board with the program.

Sanjay had planned something quite different and had enlisted Anjali's silence, hoping that Nalina's sense of decorum would not embarrass him and the Bhandari family. He should have known his older child much better than that. Anjali should have known her sister much better.

Anil and Anjali had started the first of *Saat Phere*—the seven vows that the *Pandit*—a spiritual scholar—had them recite.

Suddenly, the Pandit stopped the ceremony, nodded to Sanjay and smiled at the audience, then spread his arms out as he said, "I understand that we actually have two brides here today."

Everyone in the immediate family, and the entire Kasturi clan looked at Nalina.

"Nalina Bhandari," he said, gesturing toward her in the front row.

Nalina pulled the lehnga—a dress a deep shade of ruby—from about her ankles, so she could stand, then turned to the attendees, gave a little Miss America wave, pulled the head scarf over her upswept hair, and simply returned to her seat.

Sri moved forward, hooked his arm under Nalina's, and jerked her forward, ushering her toward the Pandit.

Nalina struggled against his efforts, but her gaze focused on Sanjay, who smiled and nodded his encouragement. Soft brown eyes flashed pure fire, and Anjali's knees went weak. This was going to backfire in a major way. Nalina would probably go down in history as changing that little part of East Indian history forever.

Sri stood next to Anil and Anjali, lifted his chin, and gave Nalina a sly smile. She slowly returned that smile with one of her own.

Anjali's spirit sank to her toes.

The Pandit clasped his hands in glee as he said in thickly accented English, "So, we will have a wedding for *two* couples today."

"No you won't," Nalina shot back. She snatched her arm from Sri's grasp, lifted her skirt, and turned to face all of the guests. "I'm only here to support my sister's wedding. Papa knows that. If you'll excuse me."

Sri gripped her arm and held her in place. "Just do it," he said through his teeth. "Everyone's watching."

"How unfortunate that everyone wasn't privy to our little discussion. I have to marry you, but I'm not doing a ceremony." She pinched him with her free hand, causing him to yelp and release her altogether. She graciously tipped down the stairs and went back to her seat.

The Kasturi brothers and cousins chuckled, and Srinivas turned red with anger.

This time Sanjay came forward and ushered her in front of the Pandit, and growled, "Stay put."

The Pandit began again, and when it came time for Nalina to repeat Phera—the prayers to God for plenty of nourishing and pure food—she simply turned and looked at all of the expectant faces, and said, "I do."

Sri leaned over to Nalina and said, "You must say *all* of them. All seven of the vows or we're not considered officially married."

Nalina lifted the silk scarf covering her hair and answered in a voice that everyone could hear, "Look partner, I signed that *isaivu padimaanam*." She looked at a panic-stricken Anjali and asked, "Did I say that right?"

Anjali could only nod.

"The wedding contract," she added for clarity. "And that's all I'm required to do. I'm not standing up here seven whole hours in heels, while some Swami dude speaks all manner of whatever in a language I don't understand and expects me to say words I can't halfway pronounce or believe in." She placed the sheer silk shawl around her shoulders. "*I do* is it for me."

"I told you to wear flats," Anjali whispered, trying to hold back her tears.

"And the result would still be the same." She moved away from them and tossed a few final words over her shoulder. "I'm going to sit it on down. Y'all go right ahead." She perched on a front row seat as Sri appeared at her side and he said, "You're making this more difficult than it has to be."

"Difficult for who?" she snapped, oblivious to her father, who gestured for her to go back to the dais. "Our families got what they wanted. I don't have to do anything more than that. Unless, you'd like to repeat those words you said to me a little while ago. I'm sure everyone would like to hear how you really feel about things."

Sri glowered at her; a vein throbbed in his temple.

"No?" She gloated. "I didn't think so."

She shooed him back toward the place where Anjali and Anil stood, as the Kasturi parents looked on in utter shock. Everyone was stunned silent at the spectacle.

Then he locked gazes with Nalina's equally angered father, who gestured for him to sit down next to Nalina so things could move on without them.

* * *

Anjali slipped out of bed, put on her silk robe, and walked toward the hallway. She turned when a thought hit her. "What makes him think she's gone for good?"

"He said she took pictures, her passport, all of her clothes—except her Indian wedding and formal garments. She only had two suitcases and an overnight bag." Anil shook his head in frustration. "Why did she have so little in their house?"

"She never felt it was *her* house. He made her feel like a stranger." What Anjali didn't add was, *the same way I feel like a stranger in this house.* She went to the nursery to check on her toddler son and infant daughter, who were thankfully still asleep, then continued past another set of bedrooms before moving on.

Anil caught up with her at the dining room and breezed past their two golden retrievers, who stirred then trotted behind him to the kitchen. "Why didn't you tell me things had gotten that bad? I would have spoken with him."

"Any of your other talks had any lasting results?" She rinsed her hands under a cool spray of water and looked at him for his answer.

He let his head drop and took his time answering as he stared at the green marbled tile. "That's beside the point."

"That's *exactly* the point," she countered, wondering how he could be so concerned with his brother's marriage when their own wasn't exactly the stuff of love songs.

Anil's tawny skin darkened to a deeper shade as he grasped her meaning. He had never been effective at helping his brother rein in his hellcat of a wife—Sri's words. Sri, a former playboy and world traveler, was too arrogant to listen to his younger brother—or anyone, for that matter—when it came to matters of the heart or the bedroom. It was his way or nothing at all. Secretly, Anjali cheered for her big sister. She only wished she had the courage to do half the things Nalina did.

Nalina had been a challenge to Sri from the day Sanjay announced the marriage that would join the Bhandari and Kasturi households. And Anjali knew that Sri would never win points with Nalina if he treated her like he treated all of his other women. Leaving was the best thing she could have done for both of them. At least he hadn't ended up in the hospital this time. Or the morgue.

Thankfully, Anjali's marriage to Anil had fared better in most ways. On the night that Anjali and Anil arrived at the Kasturi family's home where she and her husband would reside, she was ushered in by her mother-in-law and a still-barefoot Anil.

Anjali took care to cross the threshold with her right foot first, which she used to gently knock over a vessel filled with rice that had been placed there to ensure good luck and plenty for the new family. So far, their luck was holding out, but Anjali had a feeling that things were about to get pretty damn interesting. Anil was starting to show signs of concern over their marriage. Could she somehow use that to her own advantage?

Anjali moved about the kitchen, gathering up the items needed to sweeten the chamomile tea to calm Anil's nerves. He was still angered by her statement about his lack of success with Sri, as evidenced by the scowl on his handsome face. He hadn't bothered to put on a night shirt, so the expanse of tawny skin stretching across his well-defined body was illuminated by the moonlight pouring in from an array of windows. She glanced admiringly over his body, before catching his lingering gaze.

"Your sister has always been so difficult, so wild," he said with a weary shake of his head as she turned off the boiling water and poured some in the cup. "My family will forbid us to have anything to do with Nalina."

Anjali nearly spilled the hot liquid on her hand. She placed the pot on the oven mitt, looked up at him, and said quietly, "They will forbid *you* to have anything to do with her. She's my sister. I've known her a lot longer than I've known you or your family. My relationship with Nalina is *not* negotiable."

Anil stared at her for a long moment. She had never spoken to him in such a manner.

She slid the cup his way.

Tense minutes passed before he dropped in a few cubes of sugar for good measure, then peered at her over the rim. "Your sister is not good for our marriage."

"There are a lot of things that aren't good for this marriage, but I endure them."

He quickly placed the cup on a coaster she put in front of him. "What do you mean?"

"The only real voices in this house are yours and your family's.

I have no place here. I'm just visiting. The place doesn't reflect me; it reflects your mother. I do what you tell me. I do what she tells me. My happiness has never factored into it." She paused, realizing how bitter she must sound, which was exactly what she felt at times. "They used all the normal criteria—wealth, diet, height, age, city of residence, education, language, and family reputation. Our parents were so hell-bent on their approach to this marriage and bringing the two families together that they forgot that I have feelings."

She looked into Anil's panic-stricken eyes. There really was no easy way to express things.

"But you were raised in America," she continued. "You speak the king's good English and know the norms here. I find it amazing that as forward-thinking as you claim to be, even now my feelings aren't considered. You just told me that I would have nothing to do with my sister as if it were law." She locked a steely gaze on him. "And this is supposed to be my existence for the rest of my life?"

When he didn't reply, she folded her arms across her breasts and said, "I'm here to tell you that it's a brand new day, my brother."

Anil winced at the term that Nalina used quite often—especially when she bringing a point home to Sri.

Anjali looked out at the star-filled sky. "I only wish I had Nalina's strength. I would have walked a long time ago, long before I had that first child."

He flinched and almost knocked over the cup.

There. She had laid down the gauntlet.

Anil was by her side in an instant, gripping her arms. She looked down at his hands, then up at his face and saw worry filling his expressive brown eyes. "I don't want to lose you."

She could hear Nalina's voice whispering in the darkness, "Look for an opening, Joy. Press your point, and make things work for you too."

"Are you willing to make some changes to make sure that I stay?"

"Sweetheart—"

"Yes or no," she snapped. "Simple question."

"You're my wife now. Of course I want you to stay."

She sighed softly, broke his hold, walked back to the stove, and poured out the last of the water. "It doesn't matter."

"What are you saying?"

"If having peace means keeping my thoughts and opinions to myself, so be it."

Anil came to stand next to her, his eyes searched hers; she'd never seen him more confused.

Well, that made only one of them.

Chapter 18

New Patterns, New Life

An urgent knock on the door roused Nalina, and her heart slammed against her chest. Darkness stretched as far as she could see. There was no reason for anyone to be at her office so early in the morning. She tossed off the heavy coat she had pulled on as cover, grabbed a bat from the closet, and inched her way to the door. She peered out to see Dinero on the other side of the security gate.

His handsome features were pulled into a scowl as he thundered, "What the hell are you doing here?"

Nalina ran to turn off the alarm, opened the entry door and security gate, and he brushed past her, his black leather coat fanning out behind him. His two guards gave her a brief head nod and remained outside.

"My soon-to-be-ex husband and I had a difference of opinion."

Dinero's right eyebrow shot up, before his expression became guarded. "You left him?"

"Yes," she whispered, feeling a weight lift from her with just that simple admission.

"He's straight-up stupid for letting you go. If you were my woman—"

"Good thing I'm not your woman," she countered quickly, taking a huge step backward at the intensity of his glare. "So there's nothing for you to worry about."

Her gaze swept over his warm brown skin, dark piercing eyes, closely cropped hair, tall, muscular build, and broad chest that filled out a maize-colored shirt. A pair of black slacks draped over a firm ass that made her do a double-take every time he walked away. The man exuded power and authority, and was as handsome as summer days were long. Something about the way he licked those sensuously curved lips sent a tingle to places she didn't think could feel a single ounce of heat.

Nalina followed him as he moved with unbelievable speed, taking a quick tour of the place as though checking for signs of trouble—or to confirm that she was definitely alone. She tried to hide a smile at his obvious intentions.

When he turned to face her, her heart lost a bit of its rhythm.

"You can't sleep here, baby," he said in that deep melodious voice that always sent a shiver of pleasure up her spine.

"How did you even know I was here?"

"The moment you hit my hood, I know it. The moment you leave, I know it. The moment you make your way to South Shore, I know that too. Nothing happens with you around here or there that I don't know about." He nodded toward the suitcases. "You said you wanted to stay in the projects, learn what makes us tick ... so let's make that happen tonight."

"Really, I'm fine here." She gestured to the alarm system, trying to hide the panic rising within her. "There are locks on the door and security too. It's fine."

He zeroed in on the bat she held by her side. "And what's that supposed to do?"

"Even the odds if someone thought I was easy prey."

Dinero grinned as he removed a pair of leather gloves, then held out his massive hand for the weapon.

She hesitated a few moments before placing it in his open palm.

"Get a steel one. This one will splinter on contact." He placed it on the desk, scooped her fur from the sofa, and held it open. "What did I tell you about wearing fur around here."

"But it's fake," she protested.

"And someone who puts a target on you is going to know the difference? "

Nalina lowered her gaze.

"You're not staying here tonight."

"Dinero, I can't spend the night with you."

His liquid smile nearly made her melt. "Trust me, baby. I know your limits."

"I'm fine here. Really."

They locked gazes for what seemed like minutes, but in reality was only seconds. Finally, she moved forward and allowed him to help her into the coat.

* * *

Fifteen minutes later, they arrived at a freshly painted apartment on the fifth floor of the 5135 S. Federal building. The place was neat as a pin; the floors had been mopped and shined to perfection. The heat alone was enough to make Dinero peel off his jacket two seconds after crossing the threshold. A spun silk spread and layers of fluffy pillows suitable for a queen covered the bed in the largest bedroom.

The other three bedrooms and the living room were set up as mini-classrooms. The kitchen had a dining set that could seat six. A system of file cabinets had been set up along the walls in the hallway.

Nalina looked at him, trying to comprehend everything at once. She scanned the living room, taking in the care and attention that had gone into the vibrant colors, the warmth and functionality of the furniture and the décor.

"I thought you might like to hold some of your classes here until you get another office."

Moments later, she looked up at him. "Thank you," she whispered so softly she could barely hear it herself.

"No major." His gaze shifted to the living room floor, studying the speckled pattern on the industrial tile so he wouldn't make eye contact. He actually seemed embarrassed by her gratitude.

She leaned in, tried to press a kiss to his cheek, but he turned so that it landed on his lips. When she didn't move away, his tongue trailed the smooth outline of her lips before he went in for a soft taste that became an exploration of moist heat, wet expectations, and small sighs.

Nalina instinctively wrapped her arms around him. She allowed him to hold her, kiss her, tease her until her legs almost gave out.

As quickly as that passionate kiss began, Dinero pulled away, pressed the keys into her hands, and said, "Sleep tight, baby."

"You too," she managed in a shallow, shaken breath.

"Now you know that never happens." With one last lingering look, he walked toward the door.

Nalina's gaze swept across the school supplies stacked up against the wall, the new books along the floor, and the canned goods and groceries on the counter. She knew without looking that the fridge was already fully stocked. He was thorough like that. Tears came faster than she could close her eyes and hold them back. This man understood her in a way that her husband never would and more than her father ever tried. The work she did here affected people for the rest of their lives, and their children's lives. She meant something to the people, and they meant the world to her.

With this one act of compassion, Dinero had done more than he could ever know.

"Oh no, baby, don't." Dinero rushed from the door and came to hold her. He rocked her in his arms, crooning soft words of comfort until the sobs subsided. "Baby, please don't. It's gonna be all right." He brushed the strands of hair from her face and pressed a kiss to her temple. "Come on now. None of the water works."

She held onto him, trying to stem the tide that was too heavy to hold back. She cried because in a single gesture, this man, who wasn't related to her in any way, had shown faith in what she was trying to accomplish. He knew her value. He understood her dream. And she would never have thought that he could the first time she had come into contact with him.

* * *

Everyone in RTH pitched in when times were hard—rent parties, collections for graduations, funerals, and so many other things. Nalina learned that the residents had created a village, and everything they needed was close by. Mrs. So and So down the hall kept the kids, or Ms. What's Her Name fed the people who were out of work or down on their luck. If a family was in trouble in Skokie where Nalina had been raised, they were too embarrassed to tell anyone or ask for help. The people of the small village within the Windy City worked together, and that made all the difference in their lives.

But even in such a village, there were some major issues. Regardless of what the powers that be at Chicago Housing Authority chose to believe, gangs still had a stronghold on the buildings. At the beginning, Nalina's biggest roadblocks came at the hands of D'Angelo "Dinero" Michaels. If he told his people not to let her people into the building, they didn't get in. If he told the women not to relocate, they didn't move an inch.

Finally, fed up with the lack of results, Nalina had called him to have a "come to Jesus" meeting—a term she had learned from one of her clients, but it fit the situation to a tee. One of the senior citizens told her that she had to "speak the language" of her listener. She would do her best to speak Dinero's language and rake him over the coals at the same time. They sat outside of a Harold's Chicken in his SUV, and she began with, "Listen, I'm not trying to fuck with you on your grind, and I don't need you fucking with me on mine."

Dinero's right eyebrow shot up, and he stopped eating long enough to give her a serious side-eye. "Oh, it's like that?"

"Most definitely," she answered. "They're going to tear these buildings down whether you want them to or not. If my people keep having problems, the CHA's going to bring in SWAT or some other force. They'll sweep these buildings every day until you're all out of the way."

Dinero leaned back onto the leather seat and watched her from under hooded eyes.

"But I don't want that," she continued, softening her tone. "Because that might mean a few gunfights here and there. Innocents might get hurt."

He tilted the bag he held toward her, offering a wing lathered in mild sauce. She hesitated a few seconds, then plucked one off the top, slipped a napkin off the side, and took a bite.

"So let's keep the police out of your business," she said around a mouthful of food. "And you let my people do their damn jobs."

Dinero's gaze followed her movements as she reached over and snagged a few of his fries. "Feisty little something, ain't you?"

She shrugged and finished off her part of the meal.

Feisty wasn't the word. Strong was a better fit. Nalina had expanded from two employees to nearly fifty workers. If she didn't start producing results, she would lose the contract and everyone would be out of a job. She understood Dinero's reluctance, but it didn't change the facts. The Plan for Transformation was being orchestrated by an even bigger gang—the people she termed "poverty pimps," politicians and their cronies who made a substantial amount of money off the residents who lived in the area. They wanted that land, and nothing would stop them in their quest to get it.

"We can do this the easy way and let things ride or the hard way, where you and your people will end up in prison," she said. "Either way it goes, we're both running out of time. I'll respect your boundaries, but you'll need to respect mine and have your people leave mine alone."

Dinero continued to eat as he thought this over. "Okay, I can get with what you're saying. But there are some things you'll have to do."

Nalina's gaze narrowed on him. She extracted a wet nap from her purse and cleaned her hands. "I'm listening."

Dinero offered her another shot at his meal. She gave him a regretful shake of her head.

"It's a six piece."

Nalina grimaced at first and put away the wet nap. "Well, since you put it that way." She snagged another wing and some fries and ignored his victorious grin. "Thank you."

"You can't walk up in here all times of night."

She took in his meaning. She knew that the place was not safe, but she felt as if she was smart enough to handle the situation. "I'm not changing who I am for anyone."

"You're asking us to change; you need to give a little too. All that jewelry and those fur coats have got to go."

Nalina fumed. She didn't worry that people would take anything from her. Some of the women who lived in RTH had their own fur coats and better jewelry than she wore. Why would her wearing them be an issue?

Sensing her anger, he placed a hand over hers, and it made all thoughts flee in an instant. "You're not just rolling up in RTH, you're also going into other places, and some people's intentions aren't good, baby."

Nalina opened her mouth to protest, but was so taken aback at the electricity of his touch, she couldn't form a single word.

"Either I'll have my boys pick you up when you have to come in here late, or you'll have to do it at a different time. Bottom line."

She didn't say anything for a while.

"Lina, it's called moving in wisdom. It's not wise to make yourself a target. You don't live here; you're not from here, and people can tell. And I can't keep putting my boys on surveillance to watch over you. They can't go into some buildings for obvious reasons. And I don't want anybody to think you're on some other agenda because most of your work is done in RTH where the GD's hold ground."

Nalina lowered her gaze, then sighed softly as she said, "I don't need your protection."

"Woman, you have no idea," he shot back in an edgy tone.

She looked at him, taking in the fire that flashed in his dark brown eyes. No harm had ever come to her when moving throughout the area. Did he actually have something to do with it? After a few minutes, she inclined her head.

"And I'll need your number."

Nalina pursed her lips, trying to come up with some excuse that would suffice for not complying with that request.

"If I call you and say your people can't come in at all one day, respect that."

"I can't do that."

"Lina, I mean it," he said forcefully. "Some things won't stop, even for you, Miss Feisty."

The fact that he had shortened her name without asking wasn't lost on her. He felt comfortable enough already; maybe she should too. Nalina passed him her phone, and he plugged in his number and called himself to lock it in.

He had only used it twice for that reason. Both days had ended with news cameras in front of a red brick RTH building and body bags being wheeled from the grounds.

* * *

After that day, Dinero would drop by her office from time to time to check on her. Sometimes he'd bring their favorite food, or introduce her to some other South Side specialty. Soon the visits became a daily thing. They'd discuss everything from the ebb and flow of project life, to the ways she needed to go about doing things to get her work done. With every conversation, she realized that the man's intelligence and perception was unparalleled.

And now she was deeply attracted to him, and she knew he felt something for her as well. How could that have happened? He stood for the very things she was against. There was an element of danger around him but little by little, he had chipped away at her heart.

Maybe her sister had found a way to deal with her marriage to Anil, but from this point on, no one would dictate Nalina Bhandari's life. She would marry for love or not at all. She would be with a man who loved her and respected her mind and body, or she would be alone for the rest of her life. There were no gray areas on that score.

Nalina tried to push the trouble with Sri from her mind. She finally pulled away from Dinero and wiped her face. "I apologize for the tears. It's been a rough night."

He lifted her from the floor, carried her to the bedroom, and gently set her down on the bed. Then he slipped off her boots, removed her simple jewelry and placed it on the nightstand. When he lifted the corner of the spread, she slipped under the soft sheets, settled among the plush pillows, and drew in a steady stream of breath before reaching out for him.

"You know I can't stay, baby," he said in a husky whisper.

"Just for a little while. Please." She held onto the edge of his shirt. "You're always there when I need you. And I'm not ashamed to say that I need you right now."

Dinero thought about that for a minute and went to the front door. She heard hushed whispers of conversation but couldn't make out what he had said. When he returned moments later, he removed his shirt and tossed it on the chair near the window, took off shoes, then his slacks and let them slide to the floor. He slipped into the bed and gathered her into his arms. For the first time in a long time, Nalina felt at peace.

She could swear that just at the point she slipped from consciousness into dreamland, she heard him whisper, "I love you, Lina."

Chapter 19

Anjali let Anil stew in his own thoughts as she cleaned the pot, dried it, and placed it back in its original spot. Finally, she said, "Your parents are more traditional than my parents ever were. They come from a different cultural background. It's required a lot of compromise on my part. I couldn't register for this semester, which puts off my dream of becoming a family therapist. Marriage hasn't benefitted me one single bit. I don't have a single ounce of privacy in this house now that I am under your mother's constant scrutiny."

Anil thought about that for a moment, then inched his hand under the cookie jar and slid a blue envelope in her direction. "This came for you."

"What is it?" she asked, taking it in her hands and checking the postmark. "This says it was mailed weeks ago."

"It says personal and confidential," he answered cautiously. "I didn't open it."

She looked at him, wondering why he would have hidden it instead of giving it to her right after his mother gave it to him. Anjali wasn't even allowed to get her own mail.

"And you weren't sure if you wanted to give it to me," she said.

He didn't bother to deny her words.

She looked at it for a few moments, taking in the vibrancy of the silver ink, the elegant script, and the beauty and texture of the envelope before putting it to the side. "Thank you. I'll get to it later."

Anil's eyes narrowed to slits. "There should be no secrets between us."

"So you tell me *absolutely everything* that's happening in your life? Those little 'private meetings' with your family. Do you share what goes on in them?"

"That's family business."

She leaned against the cabinet and grinned. "Exactly. Meaning no matter what I do, I'm. Not. Family."

"I didn't mean it the way that it sounded," Anil quickly added, running his fingers through the thick shock of dark hair.

"So exactly *how* did you mean it?"

"I tell you what you need to know."

"Right," she drawled, gesturing to the fancy envelope on the counter. "And this is something you might not need to know."

Anil turned his back to her and took another long sip of his tea as he carefully thought about his next words. "I really would like you to limit your involvement with Nalina because she buys you those … things."

Anjali tried not to smile. "I never know when they might come in handy."

His expression became close to murderous. "I am perfectly capable of pleasing my wife."

"All right," she said with a mild shrug before looking away.

"Now it is you who is being difficult."

"No, I'm being honest," she shot back, lifting her cup in mock salute. "You said you please me; I said all right. That's all." But the smirk she gave him said otherwise.

"Do you really want to leave me, Anjali?"

"Does it matter?"

Anil walked over to the kitchen table and took a seat. "Yes, it does."

"Do you want the truth or the version that will rest well with your ego?"

Anil slumped in the chair. "If you have to ask it that way, then maybe I should be worried."

She took a few more moments before she gave him a non-answer. "I've been as happy as I could be, given the circumstances. But what Nalina did last night has put a lot on my mind." She poured the rest of her tea down the drain and washed the cup. Only then did she look at him. "Do I have your permission to return to bed? You have an early day, and as a good little Indian wife, I have to be up at three in time to fix your breakfast and your lunch. Fresh only," she waggled a finger and said in an accent that mimicked his mother. "Only fresh meals every day for my son and my family."

She walked toward the door, the dogs trailing behind her. She halted when she heard, "How can we make things better?"

Anjali closed her eyes, feeling a small pang of hope enter her heart. She faced him, searching for any signs that he was being less than sincere. She was surprised at what she saw—genuine concern and worry. And that was enough to make her cross the distance between them and cup his face in her hands as she answered, "By being my friend and not a dictator. By recognizing that I want to be more than just your wife, a mother, and your mother's whipping girl. Her zeal to make sure I learn all things Indian is draining me." She gestured to the spotless kitchen, the rows and rows of spices and cooking supplies. "I'm practically at her mercy all day. And I don't deserve it. Only once have I complained. Even then you said, 'It'll be good for us.' What us? The only person who it's good for is you."

And then it happened against her will. The tears came—the ones she only dared shed in the shower when she had some type of privacy. "And I'm tired, Anil. I'm so, so very tired."

Anil reached out and pulled her into his arms and held her for a long while. Then he wiped her tears with his fingers. "What is it that you want to do?"

"I want to finish school and get my bachelors, then my masters, then maybe a PhD. Then I want to do counseling. Help children and families. It's something I could do from home or at a nearby hospital. Not too much time, but it'll be something I do for me."

Anil lowered his gaze for a moment, then looked back at her.

"I have a brain, Anil. I'd like to use it for more than compiling recipes, managing the household schedule, and taking orders from your mother."

"I never knew you felt this way."

"You never asked," she whispered. "And I only think you're asking now because of what happened between Nalina and Sri."

His gaze lowered to the marble tile—an admission if she ever saw one. "I want this to work, Anjali. I want to find love."

She smiled at his statement, but was unable to say the same—at least for now. "Really loving me might mean going against your family sometimes."

"I realize that," he said, pressing a kiss to her temple. "We'll deal with it as it comes. I understand that I'll have to make some sacrifices too."

"Let's start with this house." She gestured to the kitchen, which was beautiful but enormous and difficult to manage. "I want a house that we choose together. And I'd like to put some distance between us and your family; I want to give us a chance to breathe, to grow, to become … us—whatever that means for us."

"Built from the ground up or something else?"

The fact that he posed the question—and so quickly—meant he had been thinking of it too. "What did *you* have in mind?"

"I kind of like condos that have old world character and a lasting charm."

"Me too. Lots of room and beautiful views, maybe of the lake and downtown Chicago?"

Anil grinned down at her. "I'll call a real estate agent this morning."

She turned and wiped away a tear. When she looked back at him, she smiled.

"I think that's the first real smile I've ever seen from you," he whispered as though amazed that she could do such a thing.

"It's the first time that I had reason to. And—"

He reached into the garbage and pulled out a large plastic item. "We need to talk about the reason your sister feels you need this."

Anjali gasped at the sight of the vibrator in his hand.

"It's nothing really."

She reached for it, but he raised it over his head. "We just talked about sacrifices. You don't mind if I toss this one, right?"

"Actually," she began, but thought better of it when she saw the stricken expression that shadowed his face, though he had tried to mask it. "No. Go ahead and toss it. But we need to talk about some things in that area too."

Anil actually froze for a moment, took a deep breath, and relaxed. "Okay, give it to me straight."

"You're long on equipment, but short on delivery."

"What the hell does that mean?"

Anjali swallowed hard, trying to come up with a way to say it without hurting his feelings even more than she already had. She had thought that "long on equipment" line should have worked. "Anil, I need you to take your time," she said slowly. "It's not a race. By the time you get to the finish line, I haven't even made it to the gate."

Anil's cheeks flushed as his lips pursed in a thin line. "That sister of yours ..." he finally said with a light chuckle. "I'm so glad they married me off to the right one."

She smiled at that statement. "And you'll need to keep your family out of this marriage if you want it to last. You'll have to learn it's about what *we* want, not what *they* demand." She took a deep breath. "They may have put us together, but we have to find the best way to stay together."

He nodded and laced his fingers in her hair as he smoothed it down. "I returned your father's dowry money last week. He gave it back to me, and I put it in your personal bank account."

"Why would you do that?"

"I would have married you if there wasn't any money involved," he said softly. "When I first saw you, I was happy. Then I met you, and I knew it was the right choice."

"Then why were you on that old," she lowered her voice, "'I'm the man, I'm the man, I'm the man,' macho man trip?"

Anil laughed at her attempt to sound masculine. "I was listening to my asshole brother about how to keep you in line. He said if I didn't, you would be just like Nalina."

"He was wrong."

"You are nothing like your sister. You are kind"—he kissed her forehead—"and sweet"—he kissed the tip of her nose—"and loving"— he finished with a kiss on her lips.

"She's kind and sweet too," Anjali protested softly, relishing his touch.

"On what day of the year?"

"Watch it," she said, giving him a playful punch in the gut. "That's my sister you're talking about."

"I still know that you're the right one for me."

"You're just feeling that way because you're glad they didn't saddle you with the Gupta sisters."

Anil's eyes widened in horror. "How did you know—"

"Oh come on now. Nalina sat next to them for the entire reception. Women talk."

He shuddered at the thought.

"I'm pretty to look at," she said in a teasing tone. "The lesser of two evils."

"Never say that." He cupped her face in his hands. "You could have been homely, for all it mattered. What matters is your disposition. Your sweet nature. And you're beautiful because this"—he placed a hand over her heart—"is beautiful."

She laid her head on his chest and held onto him. This time because she wanted to, not because she felt it was expected.

"Why couldn't your brother be this way with Nalina?"

"Because he is not me. He doesn't see a woman's worth other than money and offspring. I see a lifetime of friendship, family, and fun and growing together. We're young, and there's so much we can do ourselves."

Anjali looked up at him. "Your family and my father each built their own empires. Why can't we do that?"

"I've never thought about it because I always knew that I would join the family business. There was no other choice."

"Until we figure things out, why not do both." She looked up at the clock, extracted herself from his embrace, then went to the stainless steel fridge, and pulled out the makings for the next meals.

Anil scooped them up and put them right back inside. "Not today. You get some rest. I'll catch the buffet at India House."

"Your mother will have a hissy fit."

He failed in an attempt not to smile. "I'm going to talk to her, tell her that times have changed, and to cut you some slack. When we have our own place, it won't matter, but for now, I'm going to back your play."

She embraced him; this time the tears that came were ones of joy.

Anil led her back to their bedroom. "My family's going to say that *you're* a bad influence on me."

"And what do you say?"

"I say they're right." He wiped away her tears as he pulled her in for another kiss. "And that's a good thing."

Chapter 20

Nalina awoke early the next morning to find herself still wrapped in Dinero's arms. She watched him as he slept, taking in the rise and fall of his broad chest. His breathing was slow and easy, as though rushing the process was out of the question. She reached up, traced a line across his thick eyebrows, then to the strong jawline and down the fullness of his lips. He pursed them to kiss the tip of her finger. Startled, she snatched her hand away.

Dinero's gaze locked on hers as he stroked a hand across her hips and shifted so she rested completely along the powerful hard lines of his tight muscular frame. His erection was pressed against her inner thigh, ready to take exactly what she was only too willing to give.

She parted her thighs, wrapped them fluidly around him, and pulled him closer.

"Woman, don't start nothing you can't finish," he said in a husky whisper.

"Who says I can't finish?"

"You're not ready, baby. You've got too much to figure out right now. And I'm not going anywhere." Dinero kissed her forehead and untangled himself from her embrace. He crossed the room and gathered his things.

She sat up and watched him straighten his clothes, while taking in the smooth muscular beauty of his body. Her mouth watered in expectation of tasting him, touching him, feeling him.

"But I thought you said you weren't going anywhere?" she said in a playful whine.

"You know what I meant," he answered, putting a careful distance between them.

"Thank you for ... everything."

"No major, baby. I'll see you later, all right?"

Nalina nodded and went to him. She wound her arms around his neck, pulling him to her for a warm embrace. The throaty moan that came from him made her look up. Massive hands splayed across her back, then lowered to her buttocks. He released one last moan, and she could feel the heat rolling off of him in waves.

"I gotta go, baby." He looked down at her and almost smiled, but he seemed more concerned than anything. "You gonna be all right?"

She could only nod. The longing she felt for him was more troubling and overpowering than she could put in words. He embraced her again. Nalina couldn't think straight.

"I say a prayer for you every night," she whispered, pressing her hands against his chest. "God, please don't let anything happen to him before he makes love to me."

Dinero grinned and placed another kiss to her temple. "Baby, that's not a prayer; that's a promise."

And with that, he was gone.

* * *

An hour later, Nalina was in her office, packing the last of the crates of files. She filled one, taped it shut, and walked it to the front door. As she did so, her mind kept drifting to Dinero. *Why does he keep putting this thing between us to the side?*

The phone rang, breaking into her thoughts. Her sister's voice was enough to blow even the best of moods. "Nalina Bhandari Kasturi, have you lost your mind?"

Nalina angled the phone between her cheek and shoulder, mumbling a weak, "And good morning to you too, my dear sister. And it's Bhandari, sweetie. I never took his last name." She struggled to keep the phone in place so she could finish. "Hold on, let me find a headset."

She ran to the front of the office, grabbed the silver set off the receptionist's charging station and slipped it on her ear. "All right, I'm back."

"Papa's spitting mad. He told me to talk some sense into you."

"Well, at least he didn't send mother to do his dirty work. He knows I don't have anything to say to her."

Anjali gasped, and there was silence on the line for a long while. Anjali and Michelle were close, so she would take those words personally. Nalina had no warm feelings left for her mother. She felt betrayed by the woman who says she gave birth to them. She didn't stand up for her daughters when it counted, so she had nothing coming.

"Why are you still so angry with her?"

"I'm angry with both of them. Why shouldn't I be?" Nalina snapped, while carrying another box toward the door and dumping it on top of the pile. "And for that matter, why shouldn't you be?"

"I've made a commitment to my husband."

Nalina paused and ruffled a hand through her unruly hair. "That's my point; he's really not your husband. You didn't make the choice; it was made for you."

"Regardless, I went through with it, so it *was* my choice. We have to play the hand we were dealt—"

"No, *you* have to play the game that way," she replied, stacking another box on top of the last row. "I'm so done with Sri, it's not even funny."

Anjali lowered her voice to a whisper. "Now his family will be looking at me strange because of what you did."

"I apologize if that happens, but I'm not going back to Sri. Ever." She moved another set of files into an open box on top of a metal file cabinet.

A shriek in the background made Anjali drop the phone and scurry away. Soon, Nalina could hear gurgling sounds. "Is that my nephew?"

"Greedy little sucker," Anjali said softly, cooing to her son. "I swear, the moment I think of taking a break, his radar kicks in, and he's ready to eat."

"And yet, you're going to get pregnant again and again."

"Anil wants a big family," she protested, but there was no mistaking the weary emotions around that statement.

"And what do you want, Joy?" Nalina whispered, using the nickname she'd had for Anjali since they were little girls.

"To be happy."

"Are you happy?"

Nalina closed her eyes at the answer her sister's silence provided. She suddenly pictured the faint bitter smiles that her sister now gave everyone, instead of the tinkling laughter that could warm even the coldest heart. Anjali was now almost always on the verge of tears. The sun-kissed skin that once was smooth as silk was now a bit dry, and hair once as dark as the midnight sky now had a lackluster off-black tint that showed she barely had time to do anything for herself.

But what really disturbed Nalina was Anjali's lack of enthusiasm for anything. Her sister once had an unquenchable thirst for knowledge, as though learning was sweet rain and she was the Sahara Desert. Now Joy's schooling was on indefinite hold. At first, when the two sisters landed in the newly built mansions that were situated in the Kasturi compound, Nalina would go to bat when it came to Joy. But soon the arguments would escalate to near blows, and there was only two of them and nearly sixty of the Kasturi clan. Sheer numbers were against them, but that didn't keep Nalina from trying.

Anjali succumbed to her mother-in-law's demands of cooking and cleaning for the entire family, with no one in the Kasturi family lifting a finger to help. As though they were forcing Anjali to make up for all she hadn't learned about the culture since she had been raised in a mixed household.

Nalina knew ways of evening the odds and putting that family on notice that the Bhandari sisters were not to be toyed with, but Joy wouldn't hear of it. She wanted peace, and embracing that peace sometimes made her less of what she had once been. And that angered Nalina all the more.

"I will be happy," Anjali said softly. "After our talk this morning, which, I might add, came on the heels of you leaving Sri—there are some things we're going to do differently."

"That sounds … promising," Nalina said, noting the difference in her sister's tone.

"Marriage takes work. It takes compromise," her sister said in between coos to quiet the baby. "You, my dear sister, do not know a thing about the C word."

"I married him, didn't I?"

"Yes, but you didn't really marry him," Anjali replied softly, as though someone was listening in. "You wanted it all on your terms."

"I gave in to the marriage. Why shouldn't something go my way?" Nalina sighed as she pushed another round of boxes toward the wall. She checked the clock over the secretary's desk and noted she only had three more hours before the movers came to take the rest of the boxes to the new agency who would be taking over the social work aspect of her world. She should have taken the staff up on their offers to come in and help. Packing was no joke.

She slipped into the seat behind the front desk to take a breather. "I wasn't asking for much, Joy. Respect is too much for his little brain to handle."

"Are you going to call Papa? He'll want to hear your side of things."

"I doubt it," she replied, wiping the edge of her sleeve across her forehead. "There's only one side that matters to him in this—his."

Joy didn't bother to protest that unhappy fact.

Nalina's gaze shifted to the classy invitation she had tacked to the message board.

"At least let him know that you're all right."

"In due time. I'm not up for a lecture on learning to be a good Indian wife. If he wanted us to be Indian wives, then he shouldn't have married a Black woman. It's the Black side of me that's not taking any crap from him or any man."

"Ooooooh, you are sooo bad," her sister said with a giggle. "Where are you staying?"

Nalina grinned as she flashed to an image of her new abode and that wonderful pillow top mattress which had given her an excellent night's sleep. Or was it the man who had spent the night wrapped around her that made for that blissful event? "I'd rather not say, Joy. I don't want you saying anything to Papa or your husband."

"I promise I won't tell a soul."

And if she promised, she actually wouldn't, but still …"Joy, as much as I love you, I'm not going to put you in a position to have to lie for me. You did enough of that when we were in high school." She peered out of the front windows as the blues and reds of a police bar flashed across the street. Harold's Chicken was bustling with activity, but it paled in comparison to the line forming in front of the liquor store. "What's for dinner?"

"Chicken Mahkhani, Saag and corn, Vegetable Briyani, Naan and Rice Khir."

"Ahhh, the good little Indian wife," Nalina taunted as her stomach grumbled in protest at not having eaten since yesterday.

"You're just jealous because you won't cook."

"Keyword—won't, not can't." She snatched a blue envelope from the whiteboard. "Put some in the freezer for me; I'll slide by and get it this weekend."

"Hey, I have to go. Anil's on his way in. I don't want to hear another word from him about you being a bad influence on me."

Nalina roared with laughter. "Am I, little sister?"

"He found the vibrator you gave me."

"Oh no." Nalina draped her fingertips across the silver ink and couldn't keep from smiling at that mental picture. "What did he do?"

"He threw it out."

"I'll hit the toy store and slide you another one tonight."

"Actually, I have a feeling I might not need it anymore."

"Well, I'll slide by the toy store and bring one just in case. I'll call before I come, and you can meet me outside. This time, hide it better."

Anjali's tinkling laughter caused Nalina to smile. At least she could manage that one little pleasure for her baby sister.

Nalina ended the call, grabbed more boxes, then went to the front of the office and began the tedious job of packing up the parts of the files that would need to go to her apartment. Minus the documents that were created beyond the scope of her contract. She would not give them that satisfaction. The new people would have to figure things out on their own.

Things didn't have to be this way. If she had been a little less vocal about the way the deputy director ran things, or the fact that her people had better results than all his preferred contractors, or the fact that less deaths had occurred under her watch she might still have the contract.

But being silent was not in her nature.

* * *

Nalina's first meeting with Dinero had set the stage for how she would deal with the other gang leaders. She didn't think she was doing anything wrong. Sometimes there was a price to pay for getting things done. But she soon learned that reality and perception were totally different beasts.

An intercity panel comprised of agency leaders from New Jersey, New York, and Los Angeles came to Chicago to share ideas and learn how her agency had become so successful. She didn't think to lie about what she'd been doing. "Well, it's like this ..." she had said, scanning the expectant faces of the distinguished group. "The gangs aren't going anywhere and neither are we. So in order to get my people into the buildings, I've had to sit down with their leaders and—"

Nalina's microphone was cut off, and her voice trickled to a halt when she realized that no one could actually hear her words.

The deputy director finished with some drivel about working within the community, with tenant leaders and community organizers to get great results. He glared at Nalina, who looked right back, trying to figure out why he had glossed over her answer with politically correct chatter when folks really wanted to know the truth.

Only later, when she had a conversation with one of her staff members, did she realize her error. Wandra, her right-hand woman, had said, "First of all, none of those paper pushers want to do any real work that will actually help the residents. Some are perfectly content with making a hit here and there, and doing just enough to get by. But going into the units in person is totally out of the question."

Nalina was taken aback by that statement. "How can they connect with people that way? One-on-one contact doesn't work by phone."

Nalina's workers had a passion for people and were as tough as good case managers came. They would climb sixteen flights of stairs if necessary. They would go back day after day until that "no" became a "maybe," and that "maybe" became a "yes."

She was amazed at how many residents hadn't heard words of encouragement—that they were special, that they were worthy of love, they could exceed beyond even their own expectations no matter how young or old—until she or one of her employees said them.

Nalina learned that the deputy director took issue with her methods. Admitting that the reason for much of her success was that she had tenuous agreements with several gangs was not acceptable. "Work with your local neighborhood thugs" was not a popular option for people who were unwilling to even work closely with the average residents.

No one wanted to admit how much power the gangs had. Unfortunately, the buildings' residents didn't have the option of turning a blind eye. Those who had lived there generation after generation and were there day in and day out knew that towing the line when it came to gang members and respecting affiliations was a matter of life and death.

Nalina attended meeting after meeting, telling everyone who'd listen, "You cannot take people from a building that's run by the Gangster Disciples and put them in a place run by the Mickey Cobras or Vice Lords."

That tight-assed deputy director blasted her with, "The gangs don't run things. We do!"

"Tell that to the people who suffer the consequences," Nalina snapped at him. "They're getting killed down there."

"You don't know what you're talking about," he said through clenched teeth, though his colleagues on the podium began to talk amongst themselves.

"I don't know what I'm talking about? Then neither do you." She slammed a huge set of manila folders in front of him and waited for him to look at the evidence. He didn't move, so one of the other members reached around him, grabbed the stack, and passed them to everyone else on the dais.

The folders contained gruesome crime scene photos of the victims. "There have been twenty deaths within the last two months because you all didn't listen." She gestured to a silver-haired woman sitting on the front row. "Ms. Markham watched her husband being beaten to death, all because you all are too stubborn to listen."

She walked forward to stand in front of a bushy-haired, mustached member, then flipped open the top file to a wedding portrait. "That man was sixty years old. He wasn't in a gang. They did it to send a message—one you're not getting. Don't move those people into their buildings like that. You have to respect the code, or you'll have more deaths on your hands."

When the murmurs of indifference continued, Nalina leveled a stony gaze at each one of them. "Nicole Meister, an investigative reporter at the *Chicago Sun-Times,* contacted me. She would love to do an *in-depth* story about it." She went to stand next to Ms. Markham, linking her hand with the woman's weathered one. She turned back to the executives. "Do you want more innocent blood on your hands?"

After this, Nalina was viewed as a troublemaker and rebel, and the deputy director went out of his way to ensure she was silenced. When he put the next relocation contract out to bid, although Nalina's bid was the lowest, and although her agency had consistently been ranked number one for their success in relocating RTH's residents, she wasn't awarded the contract. The deputy director said that he wanted an agency with a leader who had experience. Because of her age and the fact that Nalina and most of her workers didn't have higher-level degrees, he awarded the contract to one of his friends. Nalina didn't have the energy to fight it because the result would be the same—he wanted her out and did everything in his power to make it happen.

As she polished off her meal, then closed her eyes, reflecting back on the day she sat in her office contemplating the error of her ways after the deputy director had delivered the news that her contract had been awarded to someone else. Dinero had walked in while she was still in aftermath of her verbal sparing with the deputy director. She was itching for a fight. Unfortunately, she picked the wrong one. And definitely with the wrong person.

Normally they talked about politics, education, world affairs, local news, and relationship issues. Sometimes, she even asked him about which men she should put in her program, and he'd let her know if they were too far in the life. But this day, for the first time, their discussion treaded into the dangerous waters of how he made a living.

Dinero had given her food for thought by simply saying, "The police aren't really trying to clean up the drugs and the gangs, baby. That's how they stay in business. They do just enough to make it look good on paper, but on the real, they're building jails faster than they're building colleges. If they wanted to get rid of the problem, it would happen. But let me tip you to the real game. If there wasn't any crime, they would be out of a job. And where's the fun in that?" He frowned at her, taking in her silence for a moment. "Think about it," he added. "They're not about protecting and serving. It's all about law enforcement. They take some to jail but leave just enough seeds to grow a new crop month after month." The light in his dark brown eyes suddenly dimmed, and his gaze narrowed at her. "Now that I've said all that, this part of my life is something we can't discuss, baby. You feel me?"

She hesitated and didn't look up at him.

"Nalina, from this point on, don't ask me a question if you won't be able to stand the answer."

"You're right," she said, lifting her gaze to meet his dead on. "I don't want to know."

But she did. She wanted him to understand the damage he was doing. He was intelligent, witty, a strategic thinker and planner—but it was all wasted on being on the wrong side of the law, the wrong side of life.

Dinero took in her anxiety-filled expression and sighed. "Okay, we'll have this one conversation so you can speak your mind."

She stood, came around the desk, and leaned against the edge. "There are jobs out there that would challenge you—"

"Women have that choice. You're hired faster than we are. There's a reason for that. You're not a threat."

"Don't give me that white-man's-keeping-us-down crap," she fired back. "You have a choice, Dinero."

"A choice to do what?" he snarled, his eyes flashing with fire. "Give my time and energy to some fat-cat cracker who couldn't give a damn about me or mine?" He came at her so they were toe to toe. "Forty years to come up with the same kind of money it takes me five months to make? Then be at the mercy of whoever and whatever every damn day and have them fire me before the benefits kick in?"

Then he tilted his head as he gave her a forced smile. "Oh, and let's not forget the end game, where I have to wait for some little payout for the rest of my life while they're hoping I die before I can actually get it all. Or should I mention the fact that it might not even be there with the way they're running through Social Security." He gave her a smile that didn't quite reach his eyes. "For real, lady? For real?"

Nalina maneuvered away from him and went to perch on the chair behind her desk. "Are you coming up with this to justify your lifestyle?"

Dinero was on her in an instant. "Let me tell you something. I own up to my shit. I do it because I want to. I do it because I like the money. I don't have to come up with anything to justify my life to you or nobody. People buy what we're selling because they want to."

"They wouldn't buy it if you didn't make it available," she countered, standing so that he didn't tower over her so much.

"And that's where you're wrong. Just like the people who created the system make sure it works for them, people will always find a way to beat the system and make their own money. This is just one of them."

"You make your living off the very people you're supposed to respect and protect."

"They have a choice, Lina."

"And so do you," she shot back, locking a steely gaze on him. "It would be a wonderful thing to see you put all that intelligence into something greater than lining your damn pockets." She stormed out of her office.

He trailed her to the water cooler and turned her to face him. "Bottom line is I don't make excuses for what I do. And I don't need a woman who feels that I should."

She jerked away, drew down a cup of water, and took a long, slow drink before finally offering him some. He hesitated at first, then drank directly from her cup and passed it back.

"Right and wrong are subjective depending on who's telling the story." He paused, allowing her to absorb that little tidbit. "Drug money is A-okay when the government's using it to purchase weapons or for covert operations. The government is in on the deal, just like the police and FBI are in on it too. That's how it gets here in the first place."

Damn, she couldn't argue with that either. It was like the people who instituted the war on drugs were talking out of both sides of their mouths.

"The problem won't go away until the need goes away," he said, softening his tone as he looked at her, imploring her to see his point. "The need won't go away until the reason there is a need goes away."

"And as long as the desire needs to be fed, you'll be the one supplying the—"

"Watch it, Lina."

"Oh, so now I can't be honest about what I say?" She poked a finger in his massive chest. "I have to filter my shit with you? Is that how we're rolling now?"

Dinero took a long, slow breath. He looked annoyed. "This subject is way too touchy for you," he said, making his way to the front door. "We won't go there again."

"But that's not fair. We talk about my life."

Dinero whirled around and nearly bumped her off her feet. His arms reached out to catch her just in time. "That's different."

"How?"

"You don't see me getting bent out of shape about things that bother me."

"Like what?"

In a warm flash, the normal expressive lines returned to his face. His gaze lingered a little too long, and he radiated a sensitivity that nearly knocked her for a loop. "Like the fact that you're attracted to me, but you go home to your husband every night."

She winced and drew in a sharp breath, which wasn't nearly enough to steady her. "I haven't done anything against my vows."

"But you want to," he said in a low tone, his face twisted with defeat. "What's the difference?"

"I didn't choose my husband."

Dinero failed in an effort to smile. "You married him anyway."

"I didn't have a choice," she shrieked and pushed him away.

"There's always a choice, Lina." He bore down on her, backing her against the wall. "You chose to please someone else at the expense of your own happiness. That was a choice. I wonder where all that *feisty* was hiding when that happened."

She punched his chest, growling, "Fuck you!"

"Yeah, that woman right there," he said with a sly grin, catching her hand before it landed a second time. "You must have sent her ass on vacation or something."

"You know what? We're so done with this conversation."

"Oh, so now I have to filter my shit for you?" he taunted with a low chuckle that set her nerves on edge.

Nalina glared at him, trembling with equal parts rage and frustration. "You can't use my words on me. It only works when I say it."

"If you're gonna take me there, be prepared to ride shotgun." Dinero returned her angry glare measure for measure.

Nalina closed her eyes against the pain that pierced her heart. For as kind as he was, Dinero could be as cold-hearted as they came. How could she ever give her heart to him? How could she give herself to him?

"No more of this, Nalina," he whispered. "It disturbs you too much."

She nodded and folded her arms across her bosom, trying to keep the tears from coming. "You're not there when they're struggling to get off that mess. You're not around when those babies are screaming, withdrawing from a drug they didn't choose to take. You're not around to see people go from hope to despair."

"You have no idea," he growled, placing his hand against the wall to block her in. "My mother's day began with a prayer and ended with a curse. Started with a needle in her arm and ended with a prick between her toes. Don't tell me what the hell I don't know."

"And yet, you're perpetuating this madness," she whispered, blinking to clear her vision. "What kind of sickness is that?"

They stood in heated silence for a long while. He watched her through hooded lashes, but the vibe radiating from him said that maybe, just maybe, her words had penetrated through that hard shell of his heart, had sunk into that deep well of indifference that was as much a part of his existence as the confidence and danger she found so attractive.

Nalina moved away from him and looked across the street to the empty lot filled with abandoned cars and a blanket of waste that the workers for Streets & Sanitation could never seem to clear.

Dinero came to stand behind her. Instinctively, she leaned back, and he held her in his arms.

"There's something about you," he whispered, trailing his lips over the smooth expanse of her neck. "This thing that drives you—it's sexy. Your strength is sexy. Your passion for doing what you love is sexy. I stopped believing in God a long time ago, Lina. But I believe in you and what you're doing." He splayed a hand across her belly. She felt his breath against her skin and closed her eyes against the crush of pleasure that overwhelmed her. "Some small part of me knows that by helping you do what you do, it'll balance out something. I won't spend the entire eternity in hell. Maybe just the first half."

She turned to look up at him, searching his eyes for some form of guile, but the vulnerable expression on his face, the uncertainty that she saw in those dark brown depths opened her heart once again. "The moment you decide to take that step, you'll be believing in you. I believe that Dinero is stuck in the game, but D'Angelo Michaels could do anything he sets his mind to."

His eyes narrowed at her use of his given name. "The moment you break free from all that binds you, then I know it can be done," he said. The words were more than a thinly veiled challenge; they were an olive branch—a promise of things to come.

"It's my family, Dinero."

"It's my life, Lina," he countered smoothly. "When you make that change, I'll be right behind you."

Well, it seemed that was one challenge she had met head on.

Now, she had to wonder where would life take them.

Chapter 21

Nalina had finished packing the last box in her office and snatched up her lunch from the counter. She sprawled out on the sofa in the reception area, propped her feet up on the cushion, and chowed down on a Chicago-style turkey polish and hand-cut French fries lathered in barbecue sauce. She was practically seething with anger. The movers were late, and if they didn't arrive by the time she finished her lunch, they would have to come back whenever she felt like making time for them.

Dinero knocked on the glass and she opened to him. He came in carrying a package from Harold's along with a familiar bright white, pink, and brown paper bag. He settled into the sofa, slipped off his shoes, and looked at her for a long moment.

"Dee, don't you have a life or something?" she asked.

He shrugged at her concerned expression. "Or something. I just came to check on you."

"I'm fine. And I've already had lunch."

"So, I'll just take it back with me."

"The hell you say," she shot back, extracting the bag from his hands. "This is going to be dinner."

Dinero laughed as she took a seat next to him, laid her head on his shoulder.

"About last night …" he began.

"Oh, it was nothing. I—"

Dinero lifted a single brow, and the flex of his mouth showed that he was struggling to hold back a sly smile. "When you come to me," he said in a voice so low she almost didn't hear him, "it'll be because you want to be with me. And you won't have to make up an excuse for it. And you won't have anything standing in your way or anyone holding you back. When you're mine, you're mine."

Nalina stared openly at him, unable to voice what was on her mind and in her heart. She wanted to be with him in the worst way, but she was courting danger and knew she might not be strong enough to withstand the consequences.

"You're always so serious." he whispered, draping a single finger across the tip of her nose.

Nalina shivered from the ting of that simple touch. "There's just so much on my mind right now."

Dinero lifted the second bag. "When was the last time you had an ice cream sundae?"

"Mmmmm," she moaned, smiling at the image it brought to mind. He placed the bag in her hand, and she peered inside. "Whipped cream and cherries too."

"Woman, you can't be moaning like that around me. I'm having it hard enough as it is."

"Why?"

"If you have to ask that question, then you're not paying attention." Dinero zeroed in on a photo of a man, woman, and two children laying on top of the counter.

"Who's that?"

"My sister and her family."

He picked it up and scanned the image. "She's pretty," he said with a pointed look in her direction. "Not as pretty as you."

"Are you stroking my ego?" she asked around a spoonful of strawberry ice cream.

"Baby, there's too many other things I'd like to stroke …"

Nalina's spoon stopped midway to the container as she nearly choked.

"That came out exactly the way I wanted it to sound. I'm not taking it back."

He walked over to the shelf near the door, fingered a book on the top of an open box, then closed his eyes as he recited from memory:

"Leaving behind nights of terror and fear, I rise. Into a daybreak that's wondrously clear, I rise. Bringing the gifts that my ancestors gave, I am the dream and the hope of the slave."

Nalina looked at him, noting that he hadn't cracked open the book. "You read Maya Angelou?"

Dinero shrugged and grinned at her perplexed expression.

"Then why on earth are you—"

"We said we wouldn't talk about that, remember?"

Nalina looked down at her treat, dropped the spoon inside, and placed the round container on the desk. She opened her mouth to protest but thought better of it as she remembered that their last exchange about the touchy subject of his lifestyle hadn't been quite so pleasant. It had almost ended their friendship.

* * *

Dinero's gaze swept the wall of her office, taking in the rows of certificates and awards.

"I hate that this had to end."

He whirled to face her, scowling as he asked, "Why does it have to?"

"The deputy director had it in for me the moment Janine turned the agency over to me. He awarded the contract to another agency, even though I had the lowest bid. I'm paying my workers until the end of the month, then I'll have to officially let them go. Right now, I let them have time off so they can find other work, so they won't have too much time between paychecks."

Dinero held her away from him as though what he heard couldn't be true. He lifted her chin with a single finger. "And you're going to let it ride like that? Let some suit tell you what to do?"

Nalina remained silent. There wasn't anything she could say.

"Didn't your husband try that?"

She nodded slowly.

"And how's that working out for him?" Dinero cocked his head as he looked down at her.

Nalina smiled at first, then she laughed so hard she nearly cried.

He took her hand in his and led her back to her office. Then Dinero stretched out on her sofa and polished off his sundae. Around a mouthful of chocolate he managed to say, "This means you have to come up with another game plan, right?"

"No shit, Sherlock."

Dinero grinned at her sarcasm. "What I mean, Lina, is what is it that you do that the other agencies won't do?"

She blinked for a moment, swirling the pink spoon inside the melting ice cream. "All they're concerned with is getting the people out of the building, knocking them down, so they can put those high-priced condos and a lighter ethnic group in their place. There's so much more to it than that."

His gaze shifted to a whiteboard that listed the upcoming seminars and workshops Nalina had been forced to cancel a week ago. "So why do you do all the life-skills, credit-repair stuff, and budgeting?"

"You can't just transplant people from one life without preparing them for the next. It's not just about having a place to live, but maintaining that place, getting off any type of government assistance, becoming more self-sufficient so they don't have to live in a development again. Bottom line?"

He nodded.

"I want them to be successful."

"So the money for the contract they gave you covered all of that?"

"No, the grant was just about relocation and compliance. I found that all the other things were necessary for them to continue to live within the new framework." She took a small bite of her treat. "Pretty soon, thirty percent of the people we're relocating will need to move back into the development, or the CHA will be out of compliance. I want to make it so that the residents don't have to come back unless they want to."

"So none of the other agencies do all of that?"

She shook her head.

"Hmmmm," he mused, popping a cherry in his mouth and letting it swirl around. "Sounds like you've got your new gig, baby."

"I don't follow you."

He watched her swirl the spoon in the container and leaned forward. "Are you gonna eat that?"

"Damn straight." She shot him a threatening glance. "Leave my ice cream alone."

"But it'll melt if you don't eat it right away."

"Even when it melts, it'll taste even better…"

Dinero's grin widened as Nalina looked away and she whispered, "That soooo did not come out like I wanted it to sound."

He left the sofa and perched his gorgeous rear end on the edge of the desk close to her. "Sounds like they're going to need to come to you eventually. You just have to set yourself up right." He placed his empty container on the desk. "And who says there isn't some type of grant out there for the things you do now? Go after some other type of money. People aren't going to need relocation forever. But people are always going to need job training, education, and life skills."

Nalina stared at him, blinking as she really thought about what he was saying. She could keep her workers if she shifted the focus of her agency. Especially, since not having those added elements is what made every other agency less successful. Why hadn't she thought of that? Because she was too busy throwing a pity party and sending out invites for people to join her—that's why.

"Don't fire your people," he said. "Lay them off so they can collect unemployment. Tell them it's a paid vacation. By the time their money runs out, you'll have it all in place." Dinero stood, cracked his neck left then right, and rolled his shoulders first forward then back before slipping into his leather jacket. "Seems like you have work to do."

"Yes, it does seem that way, doesn't it?" she said, smiling up at him. "Next time, Harold's is on me."

"I got you faded, baby."

"And Dinero ..."

He looked at her over his shoulder.

"Thank you."

Dinero gave her a mock salute and said, "You're looking at me like you want to kiss me again."

"Am I really?" She snapped her fingers, teasing him as she said, "I have to do something about that look."

Dinero walked back to the desk, pulled her to him, and pressed his lips to hers, exploring her mouth with teasing licks that had her breathing rapidly in no time.

When he pulled away, he smiled at her dazed expression. "We can't do this love thing, baby," he whispered, looking in her eyes. "We're too different."

"Then can we do the lust thing?" she asked with a grin and a comedic lift of an eyebrow. "That would work for me."

Dinero threw his head back and laughed. She gestured to his empty container on her desk.

"Hey, I brought the food," he protested with a grin. "The least you can do is wash the dishes."

She chuckled, dropped the remains of their treats into the waste can, and escorted him to the front door.

"Somebody spent a lot of money on that."

Her gaze followed his to the invitation on top of the pile of mail on the receptionist's desk. "How would you know?"

Dinero's expression darkened, and his eyes narrowed to slits. "Don't ever insult me that way again."

She froze at his harsh tone and searched her mind for why he would feel insulted by that simple question. "I meant have you worked in a print shop or something ... I didn't mean for it to ... I didn't ... I'll be right back."

Nalina made a beeline for her office, but he caught her before she cleared the hallway.

"I'm sorry, baby. I took it the wrong way," he whispered, rocking her in his arms. "I know the differences between us. I made something out of nothing."

"I would never try to make you feel—"

"I know, baby." He pressed a kiss to her temple and held her. "That invite has real silver ink, the color and heavy weight of the paper is custom. The writing—calligraphy—was done by hand. Somebody wanted to get your attention, and it's been sitting there for at least two weeks."

The fact that he noticed at all was a testament to his attention to detail—attention to her. She extracted from his hold, walked back to the receptionist's desk, plucked the envelope from the top of the pile and offered it to him. "Why don't you open it?"

"No baby, that's on you."

Nalina flipped open the royal blue card and fingered the velvet along the edges. She scanned the date, time, and place as he looked over her shoulder.

"Are you going?"

"I don't think so."

"Aren't you curious?"

She grinned up at him. "You're more curious than I am."

"Right now your options are open, baby. Take the meeting. See what this Gina woman wants. What do you have to lose?"

"I should do it," she said, making it more of a question than a statement as she looked up at him.

"The feisty woman I know loves a challenge. I dare you." Then his grin widened as he added, "No, I double-dog dare you."

"No you didn't just say that."

Dinero raised a finger to trace an outline of her lips. "So when I come back, I won't see you looking so sad, right?"

"Why does it concern you?"

"Baby, everything about you concerns me." And with that, he moseyed out of her office, leaving her more confused than ever.

Chapter 22

Robert Taylor Homes, Apt. 510

Nalina's cell blasted the theme from Sanford & Son, jolting her from a mouth-watering dream about Dinero that she wanted to go on for an eternity. "This had better be damn good," she mumbled into the phone.

"Ms. Bhandari, I'm sorry to call you so late, or should I say, so early, but we have a problem," the deputy director said.

"What do you mean 'we', white man?" she shot back.

"I'm not white."

"With the way you sell out your people, I can't tell." She settled under the bedspread and turned on her side.

"Someone is still inside one of the buildings scheduled for demolition today."

"Then it sounds like *you* have a problem. Amy should be all over it. It has nothing to do with me."

She disconnected the call and hugged the body-length pillow Dinero had bought her, then closed her eyes. He had refused to come inside the apartment after that first night. She missed him. Especially at night. When she asked him why he wouldn't come, he said, "That's your grind, remember? That apartment's just a satellite office until you land something better. I'm not going to fuck with you on your grind, if you don't fuck with me on mine."

Nalina didn't find her words so funny when he threw them back at her that way. "But it's lonely at night," she whined into his ear. "I need something to hold onto."

Dinero came over later that night and presented her with a body-length pillow that had his name airbrushed along the front.

"This is sooooo not what I had in mind."

He had laughed and gave her a small kiss. "You'll get over it," he teased, giving her a sly glance as he walked away.

The pillow was a damn poor substitute for his warm body, strong arms, rippling abs, finely tuned ass, and—

Sanford & Son echoed again. She snatched up the cell. "Yes."

"Ms. Bhandari, I know you're upset about losing the contract."

"Oh, I'm not upset," she snarled, throwing her legs over the side of the bed so she could sit up. Evidently, the man was not going to let her get any sleep. "I'm pissed. You didn't do it to benefit the people, as you told the mayor. It wasn't because of my lack of experience or the fact that I don't have my masters yet. You did it to get back at me for making you look bad. All these years, the people you placed to serve this area didn't do jack, even with all those letters and degrees behind their names. So the mayor insisted you choose someone else. I was able to deliver, and you felt some kind of way about that. Get over yourself."

"Ms. Bhandari, I'm begging you," he pleaded. "Come talk to Ms. Rose. Things can go pretty bad very quickly if she doesn't cooperate. There are news cameras out here."

Ms. Rose was the woman who had struggled but finally received her GED at sixty-seven. She had given Nalina's workers a tough time since she wasn't required to do it as a part of her relocation, but she was one of the agency's greatest success stories. Ms. Rose should have been out of the building long before now. Unfortunately, the woman had been caught in the transition period between the end of Nalina's contract and the beginning of the new agency's responsibilities.

"Give me a minute." Nalina strolled to the kitchen, washed her hands, and put on a pot of coffee. "So, where do you plan to put her?"

"A nursing home."

Nalina laughed and said, "Goodnight, Mr. Watson."

"Wait. Wait! What did I do wrong?"

She made her way toward the bathroom. "If you can't recognize the fact that you can't take senior citizens who are living just fine on their own and stick them in a place where they're forced to become dependent on nurses and staff to get things done, then I know that hotshot director of the new agency you chose must have slept with you to get that contract."

"I resent that."

"Resent it all you like," she shot back, "but do it on your own time."

Nalina disconnected the call a second time and placed the cell on the edge of the sink. She looked into the mirror and noticed that for the first time in a long while, worry wasn't making her look tired and drained. She was actually enjoying the fact that her schedule was a blank slate and that she had time to put her new game plan in motion.

The cell rang again.

She barely answered when he blurted, "You know what will happen if I have to bring in the police."

Nalina closed her eyes, picturing that prospect. But she also knew that they wouldn't manhandle the old woman. And the director wouldn't want the whole episode captured on film either. "She won't want to live in a nursing home."

Mr. Watson let out a long sigh. "All right, I promise. We'll find an apartment for her."

"No, *she* gets to choose," Nalina countered smoothly, putting a dollop of toothpaste on her spin brush. "Someone should've been up to her place long before now. The kind of place she wants should be on record." She managed to get the brush across the front row of her teeth. "What's the name of the caseworker who went to see her?"

"Actually, we called him first," he said, then cleared his throat. " He's only spoken to her once. He's never been in the building ..."

Nalina closed her eyes, took the brush out of her mouth, and tried to contain her anger. "So let me get this straight—he hasn't followed up on her case? We sent all the active files first."

She looked up at the mirror, then turned away, placing her buttocks against the sink. "And how, exactly, am I going to cover your ass on this one?"

"Well, it's not really covering—"

"That's bull. You know it, and I know it," she snapped, waggling her brush as though he were standing there in front of her. "Your *friend's* agency isn't getting results because her staff looks down on the people in the projects. They can't get off their bourgeois asses to handle the process. So please have your *friend* learn to handle her business—and leave me alone."

"It's only the older residents giving us issues right now."

"Why do you keep saying us?" she said, freezing as a few things clicked into place. "Are you tied to that woman's agency in some way?"

The silence on the other end confirmed her suspicions. The man was getting it from both ends—literally. Ass *and* cash.

She finished brushing her teeth, letting him sweat it out, then bent down to rinse her mouth. When she came up and looked in the mirror, she gave herself a triumphant smile, and went in for the kill.

"Mr. Watson, let me lay it out for you," she said smoothly. "Several of the older residents died shortly after being relocated by her agency. Why? Because you all didn't think about what *they* needed. You all didn't think about their emotional well-being. Word spreads fast, so now none of the older residents trust the new workers. You are moving people, people with feelings. This isn't about money for them; it's about money for her and you."

Mr. Watson let out a long, slow breath and finally admitted, "I get all of that now, but it's not going to change what happens today. I realize my mistake in letting this get personal, but I need your help. Let's put personal issues aside for once."

Nalina relaxed and released a small sigh before she said, "Okay, I can play ball. The same way you played with me. What's in it for me if I help you?"

"What do you want?"

She looked at her reflection for several moments, then grinned. "I want an employment contract for at least thirty of my workers."

"Amy would have to fire some of her people to do that."

"Sounds like she's about to make some people really angry. Probably the ones who didn't take the time to go into the building and do their damn jobs. Start with them. That's only fair."

Still he hesitated, so Nalina went to the bedroom and pulled out a pair of jeans, a blouse, and underwear. "Here's what I know, Mr. Watson. If it comes out that the new agency didn't send someone up to get Ms. Rose situated in her new place, or better still, that they were about to tear the building down *with her inside*, Amy will lose the contract, and it will go to the agency who underbid her—mine.

"That will not look so good for you or her, especially if an oversight committee opens her files and compares those with what my workers did and what hasn't been done." Nalina sighed heavily. "And you know I have electronic copies of all the files I transferred to her—in exactly the state we left them in, so she can't put it on me.

"Ahhh, justice," she taunted, blinking at her reflection in mock innocence. "I'd say you have more to lose than Ms. Rose does. I could bail her out of jail in a heartbeat. She can even come live with me until it's all sorted out. But you, *my brother*, would lose big time." She ran a brush through her hair, smoothing it back into a ponytail. "Call me back once you've made up your mind."

Nalina moved the phone from her ear but heard, "Okay, okay, okay! How many people?"

"Thirty."

"Employment only, and that's all," he fired back.

Nalina gathered up her coat, scarf, and gloves and tossed them on the sofa. "Amy needs them more than you think. It's employment with full benefits or nothing at all."

"Jesus!"

"Leave him out of this," she countered. "He has better things to do than clean up your mess."

"You've got my balls in a sling here."

"Evidently, I'm not squeezing them hard enough because you're still talking, and I don't hear anything worth listening to." She pulled out a face and bath towel and placed them on the edge of the sink. "I'm about to go back to sleep. I won't answer my phone again."

Moments later he relented and growled, "All right; I'll do it."

Nalina turned on the water as a thought hit her. "Oh, and I'll need you to go ahead and approve that new grant proposal I submitted.. I wouldn't want it getting lost in all the red tape down in your department."

"Done."

"And I don't *reeeeeeally* have to give up that building on 59th, do I?" she said, loving what Dinero had done, but knowing that with her new purpose, she would need more space.

"I'll have the department extend your lease," he growled.

"Five years and you all pick up the tab."

Mr. Watson hiccupped on the other end, then let loose with a string of curses before Nalina interrupted, "Meet me in the 5135 Federal lobby with a written contract and my approved grant. I'll give you the names to put in," she said, lathering the cleanser on her face. "Then we'll go to the other building. Bring Amy with you so she can sign too. I don't want any bull about how she didn't know anything or didn't agree to this." Nalina bent down and splashed the cream off her face. "These are good people, Mr. Watson, good workers. I didn't hire people who look down their noses at the very people they're supposed to serve. If one person tells me that she's giving them a hard time, I'm going to be all over you like liquid shit in a baby's diaper."

"Fine. How soon can you get to the building?"

"Fifteen minutes. I live in the development."

"What???!!!!"

"See you shortly," she said with a little laugh. "Should I say, it's *been* nice doing business with you or *it is* nice doing business with you?"

Chapter 23

Robert Taylor Homes
Friday - 5:32 a.m.

Moving trucks, utility vehicles, and demolition rigs were staggered along State Street while groups of men sat around drinking coffee, smoking and chattering about sports and women.

Nalina finalized her grant, extended lease along with the plan, terms, and living arrangement for Ms. Rose with the deputy director before heading toward the building. She climbed the five flights of stairs, said a silent prayer as she crossed the icy concrete landing, then knocked on the steel door to Ms. Rose's apartment. The woman opened it and peered outside, looking first to the right, then to the left of Nalina.

"It's just me, Ms. Rose."

Weathered hands unlatched the locks, opened the security gate, snatched Nalina inside, and slammed the door behind her. A full set of locks clicked into place. Then the spry old woman pushed a chair to the door and hooked it under the knob. She placed a 12-gauge shotgun by the door and slid a small silver handgun into the pocket of her housedress.

Nalina swallowed hard. This was going to be a lot harder than she originally thought.

"They tryin' to get me up outta here," the silver-haired woman said between ragged breaths. "They gonna have a fight on they hands."

"Ms. Rose, may I sit down?"

"Oh, sho', baby. I'm sorry. Where's my manners?" She gestured to a sofa draped in a rose print slipcover. "Would you like some tea?"

Nalina didn't want to ask what the woman would use to heat the liquid; instead she said, "No tea, but water would be nice."

Nalina's gaze shifted, following the woman into the kitchen. Candles were everywhere, providing the only light in the place. A kerosene heater was holding off the chill. A quick sweep of the area showed that the woman hadn't packed a single thing. Another major issue. If she didn't leave today—actually in a few hours—all bets were off. No new apartment, cleaning service, new furniture and first six months rent that wasn't covered by the voucher—all of which were slated to come directly out of Mr. Watson's pocket.

"Ms. Rose, you need to leave with me right now."

"Uh uh, can't do it." She shook her head so hard the pin curls came loose. "I ain't goin' nowhere. If we'd all jus' stuck t'gether, then them folks couldn't've done nothin'."

Nalina took a sip of the cool water and placed the glass on the wooden coaster. "This morning they shut off the heat, then the electricity; next it will be the water. They're not going to keep this building going for one person, Ms. Rose. Especially for someone who was supposed to be out of here already."

"Where am I gonna go? Huh?" she snapped, her weary brown eyes flashing with anger. "I ain't got nobody. Everybody's gone. My husband. My chile. Ain't nobody left." She glared at Nalina. "Since you left, almost ev'ry old person them peoples take from here dies right after. They's killin' us off."

Ms. Rose shook her head, trying to bring her anger down a notch.

"Bertha Jean wasn't out of here a month. Gone. Louise? Kaput. Bice? They put him up the street. Died two weeks later. They been living here all this time and wasn't nothin' wrong 'til they took them from this place."

She folded her arms across her slight bosom and huffed. "They gon' put me in some old folks' home with some old rickety heathens that ain't tryin' to do nothin' but die." She gave her heart a soft pat. "I got some life in this old body. Ain't gonna see the grave 'til I say so."

Nalina smiled, picturing Ms. Rose taking up a fight with the grim reaper. Her bets were on the gun-toting old woman. Nalina held out a manila folder from her private files and opened it so the contents were displayed. "I have three beautiful apartments all picked out for you to choose from. They're really nice, easy to get around, and they're on the first floor. You won't be in a senior citizens' building. I promise."

The old woman's gaze swept the pictures but kept going back to a gold brick three flat. Nalina knew that the location would be perfect, since it was only a couple of blocks from the lake and the park.

"That looks nice. But who's gonna look out for me, baby?" she asked in a voice just above a whisper. "Ev'rybody always came by to see if I need somethin'. Check on me ev'ryday." Her gaze narrowed on Nalina. "Where y'all send me, they gonna do that?"

Nalina thought about that for a moment, then she took the shaky hand in hers. "I'm not going to lie to you and promise that I will do that, but I can have someone drop in on you. It might not be the same person each time. I won't let you be alone like that. All right?" Then she gave the woman a sly smile as she said, "I could move you in with Annie, but you two would get to fighting like two pit bulls."

"Damn straight! That old heifer cheats in Bid Whist."

Nalina gave Ms. Rose a pointed look. "Heard tell, it was *you* that was quicker on dealing off the bottom."

Ms. Rose's lips spread into a sheepish smile that vanished as fast as it appeared. "I don't know who told you that." She lowered her gaze to their clasped hands. "You a good girl. Kinda sweet on that Dinero, ain'tcha?"

Nalina opened her mouth to protest.

"Oh, don't bother lyin', girl." Ms. Rose sighed softly. "He is kinda handsome. Fine young piece of chocolate. Reminds me of Jeremiah in his better days." She grinned at some unspoken memory. "That man was a pistol, sho' nuff. I loved me some Jeremiah Jackson." She stroked a finger across Nalina's hand. "And your Dinero, he got a good heart. He jus' fell in with the wrong crowd and stayed there, that's all. But you know something, there's more to him than what he's showing folks. Remember that." She looked into Nalina's eyes. "He makes sho' I got everythang I need. Gives presents to the kids who ain't got no daddies. Ain't been as much killin' 'round these parts since he's been here. He ain't all bad like they say."

Nalina raised a brow and pursed her lips against saying what actually came to her mind.

"Now, don't get me wrong," Ms. Rose added with a little chuckle. "He done plenty bad too. But I don't know too many people who ain't got some bad and some good. There's always some typa balance. Some swing one way or another—he a little bit of both."

Her gaze lifted to the framed black and white photo of a handsomely rugged man on the end table. "My Jeremiah used to run moonshine when we lived down in Vicksburg, Mississippi. The sheriff ran him off, and we came to this place. Jeremiah got a job and became a church goin' man." She lifted her eyebrows in a conspiratorial manner. "Ain't nothing like a bad boy turned good. Means they know the good, the bad, and the downright ugly. Means they know the Good Lord, and He sho' don't want no punks."

Nalina could hear the voices outside of the apartment—the women she had called in to help if she was successful. She studied the yellow piece of paper sitting on the end table. The number scribbled on it was one she knew by heart.

Ms. Rose took the slip in her hand and stared down at it. "You know he said you'd come for me."

"Who?"

"Dinero," she whispered, leaning in as though someone outside might hear. "He told me not to leave here unless you came. And if you didn't, I was s'pposed to call him, and he'd take me." She gave Nalina's hand a gentle pat. "But he knew you'd come. Knew you'd come and make thangs right. Them peoples wouldn't listen to me. Now they gots to listen."

Nalina closed her eyes and tilted her head back as the realization hit her full force: *Sweet Lord. The man had found a way for her to force the deputy director's hand.*

"He said use them news cameras downstairs. Tell them what them new peoples ain't done for us. Tell them what you used to do for us." Ms. Rose reached out to touch Nalina's hair, stroking it with trembling fingers. "Got that thick, pretty hair like my baby girl." Her eyes glazed over with tears. "That breast cancer took my baby. I only had the one. I couldn't have no mo chil'ren after her. Since they gave me one of them Mississippi appendect'mies."

"What's that?"

Ms. Rose released Nalina's hand and placed hers in her lap. She looked out of the window at the sun trying to make that first break on the horizon. "Some of us in the South went to the hospital for one thang and they took our women parts without tellin' us. Happened to a lot of us down there. Took our 'bility to have more babies. Took away my choice."

A single tear slid down that wrinkled brown face before those eyes lit with that familiar spark. "Like them bastards out there. We was doin' alright in here 'til they want this land. Now we gots to go. They ain't thought 'bout us all this time. Now we high prio'ty." She nodded at her own assertions. "Nobody's gonna take nuttin' else from me. Nobody."

Nalina moved closer to the old woman and put her arms around her shoulders. "Ms. Rose, I'm going to make sure you have something better."

The trembling woman pursed her lips and just looked at Nalina for a long while.

"If you don't come with me, they're going to send in the police …"

Ms. Rose glanced at that shotgun and looked back at Nalina as though to say *I ain't scared of them. They need to be scared of me.*

"I don't want anyone to get hurt. I promise you; I'll see to it personally that you're in one of these new apartments." Nalina looked around, then added, "And with some new furniture too because it's too late to take this all with you—only your personal items, clothes, dishes, and things like that."

Ms. Rose's gaze lowered to the area rug under the coffee table.

"It won't be like it is here, Ms. Rose, but you're going to meet new people who need you. People will listen to you, your wisdom, your stories. They need to hear about that woman you're always talking about. What was her name?"

"Bessie Mae Slaughter," Ms. Rose said with a wide grin. "I was a young woman when that old biddy set this place on its ear. Mama Bessie was one bad gun-slinging woman. Betcha they wouldna got her up outta here."

"Well, someone's going to need to tell that story."

Nalina reached for Ms. Rose's shaky hands, as Ms. Rose looked over to the cherry wood dining set in the middle of the kitchen.

"Ev'rybody came here on Sundays. I'd cook all day long and ev'rybody would be in and out of here. Some slipped me a few dollars for a plate. Some didn't have money, but they knew they could always eat here. Always. And they ate good, baby. Real good. They loved me. They loved me ..."

Nalina used the edge of her blouse to wipe away the tears that sprang to the rheumy eyes. "I'll come for dinner, Ms. Rose. The first Sunday you cook it in your new place, I'll be there."

"For sho'?"

"As long as you're fixing some greens."

Ms. Rose grinned. "Sho' nuff. And some sweet 'tatoes and fried chicken, too."

Nalina stood, went to the front closet, retrieved a hat and scarf, and held out her coat.

The old woman stopped Nalina's movements and scanned the place one last time. "You know folks gonna forget about this place. Gonna forget what this place was supposed to be about."

"There are history books on the Robert Taylor Homes, Ms. Rose," Nalina said, angling one sleeve of the coat onto her arm.

Ms. Rose nodded, looking back toward the living room. "Robert Rochon Taylor was who this place was named for."

"I know," Nalina said, trying to get the woman focused on putting on clothing that would protect her from the Windy City chill. "He was an architect and housing activist in Chicago who became chairman of the Chicago Housing Authority."

Ms. Rose slowly looked up at Nalina. "Where you learn all that from?"

"I live in 5135. I had to find out about the place where I lay my head."

She took the wool hat from Nalina's hands and slowly perched it over her pin curls. "So you know they pissed him off, and he didn't want to be chairman no mo', right?"

"Yes, ma'am."

"You know why?"

Nalina sighed softly and leaned in to secure the buttons because Ms. Rose was having a hard time of it. "He resigned when he found out that city leaders voted to put the projects in all Black neighborhoods. They named the buildings after him, even though he wouldn't have approved of the project. He was all for integration and scattered site housing."

Ms. Rose nodded her approval. "Hmph. And he said you was smart too."

Nalina grinned at the woman and at the fact that Dinero had said those words.

"Taylor also started the Illinois Fed'ral Savin's and Loan," Ms. Rose said, patting the small tattered purse she slung over her arm. "That's where I still keep the rest of my money. If I don't keep it up here"—she slid a wad of cash in her bra. "Don't trust none of these new fangled banks. They's crooks."

Nalina tried to keep from laughing.

"So they *are* tellin' some of the real story in them books."

"And on the Internet, Ms. Rose," Nalina added, tying the scarf loosely around the woman's neck.

"Internet? What's that?"

Nalina grinned, knowing that Ms. Rose was going to finally put her GED to good use. "Something that will give you a lot of information at your fingertips. I'll make sure it's available on that brand new computer you're getting."

At the door, Ms. Rose—who had to be nearing seventy years—bypassed the boots sitting on the mat and slipped on a pair of high-heeled shoes. Nalina would not point out that there was at least six inches of snow on the ground and the weather was more suited to those cozy boots. Ms. Rose was known for her heels. She would sit out on the porch sometimes, telling stories to people how she had made her living in heels and they had better bury her in them.

The two of them walked out together and were greeted with a round of cheers as they made their way up the concrete walkway. A small group of women carrying empty boxes and bubble wrap spoke to the older woman, then moved into the apartment to quickly be about their business.

Nalina escorted her past the next set of empty apartments, but paused long enough to look out toward the snow-covered lawn, taking in the familiar form along the walkway. Dinero, wearing his trademark leather coat, black slacks, and black shirt, gave her a mock salute, then turned to walk toward the SUV that was parked between the demolition crew's vehicles.

Ms. Rose scowled at the men hanging about on the fifth floor walkway and asked, "Who's that? The welcome wagon or som'ing?"

"Something like that," Nalina answered, grinning at the stocky man in front of the pack of men. Ed was the first to confront her when she came to start work in RTH, saying, "You're not going to last long up in here." Three years later, she had proved him wrong. He tipped his hat to Nalina and gave her a brief nod.

"Y'all be careful with my stuff," Ms. Rose warned as she passed the men. "Somethin' come up missin' and it's yo' ass."

The men grumbled as they rushed past her to go into the apartment.

"What's wrong with y'all?" Ms. Rose called after them, pausing at the end of the walkway. "Y'all can't help us ladies down the stairs? Ain't no gent'men 'round here no mo'?"

The men froze and looked to Nalina for direction, who looked back at them as if to say, "Well, she does have a point."

The men mumbled something that Nalina couldn't quite catch, put their packing supplies on the ground, then trudged back to where the two women stood. One hooked an arm under Ms. Rose's arm on one side and a co-worker did the same on the other side.

The group escorted Ms. Rose down the stairs as if she were royalty.

*"I may not have gone where I intended to go,
but I think I've ended up where I need to be."*
—Douglas Adams, *The Long Dark Tea-time of the Soul*

Part IV

Whispers of the Goddess

February, 2003

Chapter 24

Mermaid Towers

Gina Wright walked through the parlor one last time, making sure that everything was perfectly situated for her guests. An array of East Indian, West Indian, and Soul foods were spread over a set of serving stations that stretched the entire length of the space.

A trio of patio doors led out to the building's sun deck, giving way to a view of a snow-covered city and the icy waters of Lake Michigan. Around the dining table sat four brown leather chairs along the sides, while Gina's red suede seat sat the head of the table.

She had chosen to hold the gathering here, rather than in her penthouse apartment. Too much would have had to have been hidden away if she wanted to keep her anonymity. And she did have to keep her relationships secret if she didn't want to open herself up to a world of questions and judgments by the very women whose approval and help she now sought.

Gina was more nervous than she had ever been in her life. What if they said no? What would make them extend themselves for a total stranger?

She had come a long way from her humble beginnings in the Robert Taylor Homes. She now had several investment properties along the Lake Michigan shoreline, along with courtyard buildings and complexes in Bronzeville and Chatham that were rented mostly to women with children. She was also director of an organization that specialized in rehabilitation and job training for ex-cons who truly wanted a new start.

She had everything a woman could want—money, status, and power. Everything except love and her own child. She had given up on love when an unexpected tragedy had proven to her that the world's most coveted thing was as fleeting as a breath of air. That tragedy had also taken away an ability she had always taken for granted.

* * *

A year after giving birth to Solomon's child and placing that sweet baby girl in his arms, Gina put her most important things in a lock box at her bank and slipped out of her apartment. She didn't tell anyone her plans to live from moment-to-moment, to try to forget about the man she loved almost more than life itself. She had expected Sanjay to return the moment he figured she was breastfeeding, but even that fetish did not bring him back. Sanjay wanted her to plead for his forgiveness. Begging had never been a part of her nature.

Gina had almost been swayed by Solomon's offer to share the responsibility of raising the baby. When she refused him, Solomon had again optimistically stated that his wife would certainly soften once she was more involved with a child. Gina hated to be the one to inform him that there was nothing that could open that woman's heart. So she left the door open for him to contact her "just in case." She still had misgivings about the ice queen, but watching the robust man fall in love with his daughter was all she needed to feel comfortable.

She had spread a map before her, closed her eyes, and let fate choose a destination. She traveled a few years before returning to The States.

The management company that handled all of her real estate interests had everything well in hand, so Gina threw herself into more altruistic endeavors. She had met Scott Mandrake at a fundraising dinner for Cabrini Green Legal Aid. He was a striking blonde venture capitalist and real estate mogul who had grown up in an affluent area of Birmingham, Michigan.

They had a great deal in common, but held differing ideologies on certain topics—namely politics and ethics. She believed in doing things above board, and he believed in doing whatever it took to close a deal. Their differences, however, didn't keep them from tying the knot in a private ceremony in Madrid, Spain.

Eight months later, fate reared its ugly head.

They were traveling along the Dan Ryan, listening to Motown tunes on the way to a gala benefit for college scholarships when a truck's tire unraveled. The rubber peeled off and flew into their window, causing Scott to slam into an embankment on one of the Dan Ryan's most dangerous curves. Gina had rounded that curve healthy and pregnant with twins, but she woke up in Rush Presbyterian Hospital with a flatter stomach and minus a few vital female organs.

Scott came to her hospital room and delivered a final blow. "I'm really sorry for what happened. No one could have predicted it."

Instead of sitting by her bedside consoling her for their loss, he walked to the window and looked out onto the bustling traffic. The man she had married didn't have a scratch to show for all the damage that the vehicle sustained.

"The doctor explained everything," he said, unbuttoning his coat before loosening the silk tie. "I just think it's best that we make changes in our lives sooner rather than later."

Gina pressed the button to raise the bed so she could get a clear look at him. "What are you saying?"

"I need to be with a woman who can give me children."

Her heart slammed against her chest, and her mouth went dry. When Scott turned so she could look in his eyes, she saw none of the warmth she had come to know. The massive loss of blood and the subsequent transfusions and surgery to save her life had weakened her body but not her mind.

She carefully worded a statement that would set the record straight. "We could always adopt."

"I don't want anyone else's children," he said in a voice so cold it sent chills through her. "If you can't give me an heir, then what good are you to me?"

Gina was too stunned to reply.

Scott took her silence for agreement, walked toward the door, and held it open. "You'll have the divorce papers by Monday."

She closed her eyes against the crush of tears that threatened to come. How could she have misjudged his character that way? Had she ever really known him? She hadn't loved him; her heart belonged to Sanjay. Still, she had believed that she could have a wonderful life with Scott. When he left, she lay in that bed, barely watching the shows on the television screen. Gina didn't shed a single tear that day or in any days that followed.

As she healed from the pain of losing her children and accepted the fact that she would never have one to call her own, a deep-seated hatred settled in her heart—and all of it was aimed toward Scott Mandrake. She would find a way to make him pay. Yes, indeed.

Gina took three years to carry out a plan that put the right people in place, and raked a fine-tooth comb over his business deals. She slowly, meticulously bought up stock in companies he targeted and eventually became a majority stockholder in Mandrake Equity Partners when a bad investment put him on the ropes and made him cash hungry. She gained the majority interest in all but one of his capital ventures.

She knew that someday his lack of morality would land him in trouble. She was patient. And finally, it did. All she had to do was point the Feds and SEC in the right direction. When he was arrested for securities fraud and embezzlement, the negative publicity caused friends and clients to shy away from him faster than anyone could say fifteen to twenty-five.

Gina walked into a sparse gray room in the courthouse that held only a desk and two chairs. She slipped into the seat across from him and focused on him as he attempted to conceal his shock and gather his thoughts.

The change in him was nothing short of amazing. The blond hair was limp; that normally pampered, tan skin was now as pale as Ivory soap; his once-tight build was a little soft around the middle. Evidently he hadn't hit the weights like everyone else around the place. But his eyes were the biggest change of all—dull and weary. Worry could do that to a man. Well, she was about to give him even more to chew on. Bad karma was such an absolute bitch.

"Sweetheart, I didn't realize that it was you," he said softly, finally finding his voice. "The lawyer just told me a few minutes ago that you were the one to retain him. I can't thank you enough."

Gina looked at him and raised an eyebrow, but said nothing. If she hadn't intervened, his crimes would have landed him in a federal penitentiary.

"All that time I asked him who helped me with the federal charges, and he wouldn't say a word."

She checked the small square glass in the door, waiting for a signal from the lawyer before she made her move.

"The moment this ... misunderstanding is all worked out," he continued, his eyes brightening with some of his old magnetism, "I'll give you back every cent, with interest."

Gina continued to look at him and only gave a cursory nod.

Scott reached for her hands, and she didn't bother resisting. "I'm sorry for the way I treated you. I was out of my mind to let you go." He shook his head as though that action alone could wipe away the stake he had plunged into her heart. "With losing the babies, I just—"

"You find out what a person's made of when they think you're vulnerable," Gina leaned in to whisper, as she clutched his hands in a vice grip. All the anger she felt came to the forefront. "Let me tell you something. I may have been down, but I wasn't the weakling you thought I was." She released his hands and slipped on her leather gloves, giving him a moment to wrap his mind around things. Prison must have dulled his wits because Scott was a lot slower at putting two and two together, so she added, "You made a critical mistake in underestimating me—and now..." She spread her hands. "Here you are."

She winked, and Scott's eyes widened in horror as the enormity of what she had pulled off, and the time in which it took to accomplish it, rammed home. "*You* put the Feds on to me? You made up those bogus charges?"

"I didn't have to make up anything," she answered smoothly. She looked up at the square window in the door in time to see the lawyer's quick nod. Her heart took a leap for joy. "I figured if I had misjudged you so badly in some things, then there was a good chance that you weren't honest in other areas of your life." Gina gave him the biggest smile she could manage. "It stands to reason that a man who would walk out on his wife at a critical time in her life was a grade-A slime bucket. All I had to do was bide my time, and all your dirty deeds came crawling to the surface. Your partners started singing the whole opera, encore included. You do notice that *they* didn't land in jail."

Scott ran a hand through his unkempt hair. "But you hired that lawyer to get me off on those federal charges."

"I never wanted you to do Club Fed kind of time," she replied, giving him a low, throaty chuckle. "No sweetheart, that would be much too easy. I want you doing State time. I want you to play with the big boys up there where some inmate named Duke can make you his house bitch."

Scott winced and drew back, closing his eyes before taking a long, slow breath.

"And for the record, I didn't actually pay for your bail. I used the money I made from taking your companies." She nodded at his angry expression.

Gina looked out of the window covered in steel bars, which allowed only a sliver of light to come in. "I run an outreach program that helps ex-cons learn a trade, get jobs, start their own businesses, learn other avenues of income." She brushed a manicured hand across his cheek and nearly cut herself on the stubble. "They have friends on the inside. They're going to treat you like you treated your family. And when they take special care of your tight little ass ..." She jabbed a finger in his chest and grinned. "Just think of it as me screwing you, the way you screwed me."

Gina slid a leather clutch under her arm. "Well, I have to go. You'll be given a public defender this time around. See you in what? About fifteen, twenty years? I'll bet you'll be *wide* open by then ... *husband.*"

Two detectives entered the room, and began reading him his Miranda rights and the new round of charges that would be brought against him. Scott's eyes flew open and locked on her; the anger radiating from him was palpable.

Gina gave him a parting wink and swept out the door to the sound of him screaming her name.

Chapter 25

Gina sat at the head of the empty dinner table and kept her gaze focused on the horizon. The last of the sunlight had disappeared, giving way to a blue so beautiful that could only be compared to some of the exotic places she had once traveled. As she waited for her guests, she picked up an article to take her mind off things, but it only caused her to worry about Madison even more. *Two hundred women and baby boys were gang raped over a four-day period not far from a United Nations peacekeepers' base near a mining district in eastern Congo. No one was killed in the attacks. Women and boys ranging from one month to eighteen months of age were systematically raped in front of family members or dragged into the woods and attacked there.*

She cringed, wondering if this type of violence against women and children would ever end. The article brought up memories of what happened to Mayre and her mother. *Would women ever be safe? Would Madison be all right?* Gina lowered her head, trying to stem the flood of tears that threatened to fall at the thought of her missing daughter. Her baby girl.

All these years, Gina had never received a call from the parents or their attorneys stating that custody had reverted back to her. That was the arrangement. Just recently something she couldn't put a finger on made her pick up the phone and call Solomon, only to find out that he had died under mysterious circumstances. Now she had every reason to be concerned with Madison's welfare. Gina phoned his lawyer, but the man was unable to explain why Gina hadn't been contacted upon Solomon's death. He requested she take up her concerns with Joan Engstrom instead. For that reason, Gina had her own lawyers investigate the matter. Unfortunately, even with all the money she threw into it, the process had been slower going than she would have liked.

The police didn't know Madison's whereabouts and didn't care since her parent hadn't filed a missing person's report. The private investigator she had hired hadn't turned up a single shred of information that Gina hadn't come upon on her own. After several failed attempts at reaching Joan Engstrom by phone and at her home in Niles, Gina took the first opportunity to find Joan's lavish photography studio, then stormed past the receptionist and demanded to know, "Where is she?"

"Where is who?" Joan responded without taking her eyes off the camera in her hands.

"Madison!"

"You mean that brat you left on our doorstep?" she snarled, giving Gina a sly smile. "I don't have the faintest idea. And I haven't seen her since Fat Ass up and died."

"Why haven't you filed a missing person's report?"

Joan gestured for her panic-stricken receptionist to return to her desk, then turned to finish packing the rest of her equipment before looking at Gina over her shoulder. "Why should I? She knows where she is. When she wants to be found, she will be."

Gina counted to ten, then moved in to corner the woman so she was forced to look at her. "Why didn't you call me when he died?"

"I didn't sign that contract. And I wasn't obligated to do a goddamn thing." Joan turned her back to Gina, snapping her cases until they locked. "She wanted to leave, so she left. End of story. And for the record, we made every attempt to contact you."

"I've kept that same 800 number for years," Gina shot back. "So don't give me that bullshit. You didn't even try. Neither did Solomon's attorney. You're probably sleeping with him, too."

Joan placed a strap over each shoulder and hoisted her bags before strolling toward the front of her studio. "If I hear from her, I'll have her to drop you a line."

"You do that," Gina said softly. "In the meantime, I think I'll do a little investigating of my own. You'd better make sure that every penny of Madison's money is right where her father left it. Because he certainly didn't leave any of it to you."

Joan's expression remained stoic.

"I have Solomon's original will. You know, the one that doesn't have all these strange new codicils that clear the way for you to have the money if she met an untimely death."

Only then did Joan's pale skin gain a little color. Her expression registered alarm before she was able to pull her features into an unreadable mask. But her tone was low and deadly as she said, "You need to stay out of my business."

"My daughter is my business," Gina snapped, bearing down on the smaller woman. "And if something has happened to her because of your negligence, trust me, this galaxy will not be big enough for the both of us."

"Get the hell out of my studio."

Gina left the place on Fulton and made another attempt to file a report at the Chicago Police Headquarters, but until she was legally declared the rightful guardian, she could not demand action. Gina had her lawyer working on the matter. Her case was bolstered by the documentation from Solomon and the original, unaltered will his lawyer was forced to produce, and it also gave her the cause for the police to look into Solomon's death.

At that moment, Gina's assistant, Debra, walked in and placed a set of five manila folders in front of her. "Ms. Wright, the doorman says your guests have arrived."

Now Gina only had a few more minutes to prepare her mind for what was to come. She questioned herself constantly about whether she had done the right thing in sending the invites to the women. But she could feel in the very depths of her soul that her youngest was in serious trouble. She had exhausted all her leads and needed fresh eyes, ears, and minds to put to the task. Each woman's profession could help Madison in some way.

Debra peered at her, placed a hand on her arm, and asked, "Are you all right?"

"I'll be fine. I'm just a little nervous, that's all," Gina answered, smiling slightly. The intelligent, resourceful woman with warm brown skin and tiny sister locs, always worried about Gina. Though Gina was more than touched by the sincerity, she couldn't unburden her soul to anyone.

"Are you sure you don't want me to stay?"

She gave Debra's hand a gentle squeeze. "That will be all for today. Thank you."

"Yes, ma'am. Good luck tonight."

Gina first peered at the summary on top of the full dossier that had been complied for each of her daughters

She had the top three floors remodeled and some of the units combined to make them into spacious condos that would house her guests permanently if they accepted her offer. In this way, she could build some type of relationship with her daughters, though they would never know who she was. She would keep her word on that.

Gina then traced a finger over the elegant invitation she had specially designed for each of her offspring. This one was to Madison, her youngest daughter. She held out hope that she would be able to place it in her baby's hand one day, giving her youngest a place in Mermaid Towers when she reached eighteen.

Madison needed her sisters. Bringing them together could either help or backfire, but with what Gina had found out about each of her daughters, she realized how much they needed each other.

Even more, Gina needed them—every single one.

Chapter 26

Friday - 6:45 p.m.

Gina walked into the cocktail room situated outside of the dining area of the parlor. A wide-screen television on the far wall displayed a re-run of a popular comedy. The faint sounds of Norah Jones singing *Come Away with Me* echoed in the room. Normally, that beautiful smoky voice helped to put Gina in a wonderful state of mind. Tonight, it just wasn't doing the trick. She switched off the music so she could listen for a moment. The glass window that separated the two rooms allowed her to take in the beauty of each of her daughters, who were partaking in a pre-dinner glass of wine and doing a wary dance of polite conversation among strangers.

Nikki was tall, thick, blonde with the color of a natural peach that accentuated sapphire eyes. She was dressed in a crisp pink button down shirt, sensible black slacks, and heels. A single strand of pearls graced her neck.

Nalina was a curvy woman of average height, with piercing dark eyes and a smoldering exotic beauty that reminded her of Prince's bad girl—Vanity. She was dressed in a seawater silk blouse, navy slacks, and killer stilettos.

Anjali, who wore a winter white dress that complemented skin that was a shade lighter than Nalina's, was a few inches shorter than her older sibling, and had dark hair that framed a heart-shaped face to perfection. Her eyes were soft brown and expressive, as though she had not learned to hide her emotions.

And then there was golden-skinned Vilay, whose jet black hair had been pulled back into a tight bun resting at the base of a graceful neck. Her lean, athletic body was a direct complement to an angular face with high cheekbones. Her dark eyes held an edge and element of mystery that bordered on danger.

Gina knew their backgrounds, marital statuses, and everything she could find out on paper or on the Internet, but getting to know each one personally while keeping her own secrets might pose a challenge.

"Good evening, ladies," she said, stepping across the threshold.

Conversation trickled to a halt as each one turned to face her. The picture they presented as a group was nothing short of astonishing. *These women came from my body?* She wanted to run to them and embrace them, but she took a deep breath and held her ground.

Looking into each one of their expectant faces made her tense up. She crossed the room and snatched up the glass from her place setting and took a long sip. When she put it back in its place, she said, "I had this whole speech prepared, but now it doesn't seem quite right."

"Why don't you start with this?" Vilay tossed the silver embossed invitation that held a cryptic message stating that she had an assignment for each one of them and made a brief mention of a real estate offer as a reward. It landed smoothly on the empty dinner plate at the head of the table.

A sudden ring of the phone signaled a call from the doorman, who had strict instructions not to interrupt her for any reason.

Gina crossed the room and opened a line on the phone on the console near the door. "What is it, George?"

"Ma'am, I apologize for the intrusion, but we have a situation."

She turned her back to the other women. "What kind of situation?"

"There are people down here demanding to see you. They're parked in the circular drive and refuse to move their cars. I was about to call the police, but I knew you would want to hear from me before I did that."

Gina stared at the abstract painting on the wall next to the glass doors, a small pang of worry filling her heart. "Who are they?"

"A Mr. and Ms. Kham, Sanjay Bhandari, Michelle, Srinivas Kasturi, and a woman named Alana Meister."

"Tell her that Christopher is on his way," she heard Alana say in the background.

"I heard her," Gina whispered before George could repeat the information. Her mouth went dry all over again; she had to get a handle on this new development. She turned to the girls. "Your parents are here and someone named Srinivas." She turned in time to see the women exchange wary looks before Nalina stood and shot an accusatory glare at Anjali. "Did you tell anyone else?"

"I promise you; I didn't," Anjali protested, getting to her feet. "I didn't even tell Anil. I told him that he had to trust me. I only said something to you because someone had to know where I was going. She could be a serial killer for all I know. That's when I found out that you were invited too."

"Then what the hell is Sri doing here?" Nalina countered, her eyes flashing pure fire. "And how did Mama and Papa find out? I certainly didn't tell them."

"Well, she certainly couldn't have told *my* parents," Nikki said, coming to Anjali's defense as she stood between them. "So, she might be in the clear."

Anjali nodded vigorously, inching toward Nikki under Nalina's blistering look.

Gina scanned their girls and said, "I really need this to be between you and me."

"I'd like to know why they're here." Vilay leaned her back on the patio door. "I say let them come."

Gina hesitated for a long while, then looked at the other women before asking, "Are you sure?"

They exchanged glances, then confirmed with nods and verbal consents.

"George, put them in the private elevator."

"Yes, ma'am."

Gina let out a long, slow breath and tried to calm her nerves. She had told each of the women this was a private undertaking. She certainly hadn't planned for this.

As Gina paced the length of the room, her mind was awhirl with thoughts. Finally, Vilay stood, snatched the invite from the plate, and blocked her path on a final pass in front of the patio doors.

"So what's this all about?" she asked, holding out the invitation. "Why do you need us?"

"Yes, that's what we'd like to know," Michelle Bhandari demanded as she walked into the room, followed by the Khams, Sri, Alana, and Sanjay, whose hot gaze lingered on Gina for more than a few moments. "How dare you break your word to us."

"They were never supposed to know," Alana whispered, the pain in her dark brown eyes tangible enough to touch.

"And we still don't know." Vilay looked at her parents, who were dressed in their traditional all black garments, looking as formidable as ever. "Why are you here?"

"I called them," Michelle said, with a haughty lift of her chin. "Sri went to Nalina's office to talk some sense into her. My husband threatened his life if he didn't bring his daughter back home safely." She threw a scathing look in Sanjay's direction, then an equally lethal one at Nalina.

Nalina glared first at her husband, then her father, but didn't say a thing to either one of them.

"Instead, he ended up following her to *this* place. She had been waiting outside of the building for a long time, so he called Sanjay to let him know that he would do everything he could to make things right between them."

"Fat chance of that happening," Nalina mumbled, plopping down on the nearest chaise, crossing one leg over the other, as Anjali shook her head. Sri grimaced and locked a worried gaze on Sanjay, whose dark brown eyes narrowed to slits.

"I overheard their conversation." Michelle frowned at her husband, who couldn't seem to take his eyes off Gina. "When I called Anil and he didn't know where Anjali was, I knew something was going down. Sanjay tore out of the house like a bat out of hell, and I knew that only one thing would make him move that fast and make him leave without telling me anything. You. So I was right behind him." Only then did she move forward to block her husband's view. "I wasn't going to let my husband near you without being nearby, you treacherous bitch."

Nalina threw a scathing glance at Sri, who inched back toward the door, almost as if he was ready to break and run—which is exactly what he did next. Nikki and Vilay shared a low chuckle.

"So how did they—" Gina gestured to the other parents. "know to come here."

"I called everyone else," Michelle said, perching on one of the dining chairs. "No way was I going to let you get away with this."

"Away with what?" Gina questioned in the calmest tone she could manage. "I had no intention of mentioning my connection to them."

"She's the woman," Nalina whispered, crossing the room to peer closely at Gina. "The woman you all never wanted me to talk about."

Michelle glowered at her older daughter. "And I still don't want you to. You shouldn't be here. I came to put a stop to this madness."

"What madness?" Nikki asked, looking first at her parents, then to the others, who were clearly unsettled. "What the hell are you all talking about?"

"They don't know," Ms. Kham whispered, a resigned smile on her face. They had all come here ready to string Gina up by her toenails, and their presence had been the very thing to reveal the secret that she aimed to keep. How would the women receive her if they knew the truth.

"And I wasn't going to tell them," Gina replied, leaning against the far wall so she could keep an eye on everyone. Well, except Sanjay. She couldn't look at him and keep her sanity. "I need their help to find Madison, my youngest child. Nicole is an investigative reporter, Vilay is a detective, Nalina has a social work background, and Anjali is aiming to be a counselor. Each one of them can help their sister in some way."

Sanjay moved to stand next to her. "I still do not understand why you called *them* of all people. There are so many other people who can help you."

Michelle placed a hand on her hip. "My thoughts exactly."

Vilay turned her body so she could scan each one of the parents. "First of all, I'd like to understand why all of you are so upset."

"I'm not upset," Ms. Kham said in a resigned whisper, while linking her hand with her husband's. "I think it's time the truth came out."

Vilay's gaze locked in on her mother. "What truth is that?"

Nalina looked first at the Khams and Vilay, then Nikki and her parents, then her own parents and Anjali.

"Nicole, we're leaving," Christopher Meister said as he burst into the room, extending a hand to his buxom daughter, who waved them off. "You're coming with us."

Nalina stood in front of Gina, then looked at Anjali, Nikki, and Vilay. "Isn't it obvious?"

The three of them stared at her for a long moment, then came to her side, trying to envision what she was seeing in Gina's face.

"The reason our parents are so upset is that … she's our mother. That's what they didn't want us to know."

"Whoa!" Nikki blinked several times to clear her vision.

Anjali's hand flew up to her heart as she staggered backward, shaking her head. "She … she never said anything like that."

Michelle shot an accusatory glare at Gina, who gave her a small, bitter smile as she met that glare head on. "Like I said, I wasn't going to tell them."

"Bull!"

"She couldn't be my mother," Nikki whispered as she dropped down into the nearest chair. "My birth certificate says Alana Meister is my mother."

Silence spread out for several spells.

"You were adopted by Alana," Christopher supplied. "I'm your natural father."

Anjali frowned at her parents, then shot a questioning glance at Gina. "So that means we were created in someone's test tube somewhere? In a lab or something?"

When no one said anything to answer the panic-stricken woman, Gina quickly answered, "No tubes, no labs, no artificial insemination.

The stunned silence that followed let Gina know that she had to pull the plug on this little operation before things went further down the drain. "I thank you all for showing up here uninvited. You all have done more in fifteen minutes than I would have accomplished in years, but it's time for you all to leave. I have business to attend to—the business they actually came for."

"You selfish bitch," Michelle spat. "You're not going to give us some crap about not telling them. I've already called my lawyer. We can sue you for this."

Gina didn't flinch at the caustic tone. "All I would have to do to rectify a breach of contract is return the initial payment you gave to me. I have that and then some." She stood and crossed the distance between them. "But here's where I would win—I told you that if you *ever* abandoned my daughters in any way, I would come for them. If you ever didn't want them, I specifically asked you to send them back to me, and I would welcome them with open arms ..."

"But we didn't abandon them," Michelle shrieked, as Alana vigorously nodded her agreement. Mr. and Ms. Kham just looked on, but their silence said so much more. Christopher could only stare at Gina, who said, "Why don't we ask them?"

Nikki smiled at her parents' discomfort. Their eyes practically pleaded for her not to speak on their shattered relationship. "This is the first time I've seen them in three years."

Nalina slipped into a seat across from the Khams and didn't bother looking at her parents as she took a long sip of wine. "You don't even want to know."

Vilay just shrugged and turned her back to everyone, finding a sudden interest in the view outside. The snow beginning to pummel the city was a lot less vicious than the blizzard blowing indoors. Maybe it was one of the reasons Vilay still had on her calf-length leather coat.

Anjali opened her mouth to speak, but shut it tight when Nalina looked her way.

"I wanted to be sure you all kept your promise to me." Gina scanned the solemn faces in the room. "You didn't. So if anyone should be upset, it's me."

"You have no right!" Alana shook her fist in Gina's face. "That abandonment clause was if it happened *before* they reached maturity."

"You misinterpreted it," Gina said smoothly, locking a gaze with each one of her daughters, who looked back in varying stages of shock, calm, indifference, and expectation. "They *never* stopped needing you. Just like I *never* stopped loving them." Gina shifted her gaze to the parents. "I would've kept my promise not to reveal my identity. I asked them here in their professional capacities. You opened the door to everything else."

Nikki shook her head, scowling as she looked at Alana. "Now it all makes sense. No wonder you could kick me to the curb so fast. You're not my real mother."

Alana came to take a seat next to Nikki and tried to hold her daughter's hand. "Of course I am, darling. She just carried you for us. I couldn't have children. She was our only hope."

Sanjay moved to stand in front of Gina, but froze when his wife snarled, "Don't even think about it." Michelle tried to turn her husband to face her, but he wouldn't take his eyes off Gina, who still wouldn't look at him. "It's over between you two."

"It was never over—just delayed by more years than I would like." He looked down at his wife. "Do you think I could not find her? She wanted her space desperately enough to walk away from everything, so I let her. She could have come and taken Anjali at any time. We did not have a contract for that child. So I let her go, and did not fight because you loved that little girl. I put my happiness aside for yours …"

"Wait a minute," Christopher yelled, pointing a shaky finger at Gina. "You gave them a second child … for free? And you wouldn't even consider our request? The people who first took care of you? The man who first loved …"

Christopher colored instantly, and backed up from Alana's shocked expression.

Vilay made her way over to her mother. "So what was your major malfunction?"

"Don't be disrespectful," Mr. Kham said, getting to his feet.

Ms. Kham jerked him back down beside her. She could barely look Vilay in her eyes as she said, "I miscarried seven children. Gina gave us the baby we wanted so badly." She reached out and touched a hand to her daughter's cheek. "A beautiful baby girl."

Vilay inched back, folding her arms across her bosom, "So she bumped uglies with dad—"

"Vilay, stop this crudeness." Mr. Kham's eyes narrowed to slits.

Ms. Kham gave her husband's hand a gentle pat to calm him. "Yes, he is truly your father."

"So the invitation said something about being awarded a condo here?"

Gina looked at Nikki and answered, "For your help, you will have full ownership of a condo. It's your property to do with as you will."

"In *this* building?" Vilay asked.

"Yes."

Michelle glowered at Sanjay, who didn't look away as she growled, "You bought this place for her."

Sanjay didn't bother to respond. He was still attempting to make eye contact with Gina, who still refused to look at him directly. If she looked into his eyes, she would lose focus. The moment he walked into the room, her heart nearly stopped beating. The love she had for him had not gone away. But she couldn't let it affect what she had to do right now. Madison.

Michelle switched gears and aimed her body in Gina's direction. "You may have left, but you've been a pain in my ass ever since."

"Hold up," Nalina whispered as reality set in. "You all had a relationship *outside* of her having the baby for you?"

"Oh boy," Ms. Kham quipped, causing her husband to swat her on her rear end. Her eyes widened in shock, and she glowered at him. He winked, and her shocked expression soon gave way to a stifled laugh. Their daughter watched the exchange and scowled.

Vilay tilted her head as she looked at Gina. "So let me get this straight. You had sex with him," she said, pointing to Christopher, shifting to Mr. Kham as she added, "Then my father." She gestured to Sanjay, "Twice with him and then some other dude?"

"Basically ... yes," Gina answered slowly, not liking the tone or how cheap Vilay made it all sound. She was bonded to these people and her daughters in a way no one could ever understand.

"Damn. And I thought I'd heard it all." Vilay motioned to Gina's tunic-clad form and locked gazes with her parents. "Must be nice to be in demand."

Gina flinched at her meaning. "It isn't like you're making it out to be."

"How else can it be said?" Vilay countered, anger lacing her tone. "You screwed them, had five children, then left us and just went on with your life. What part of *that* did I misunderstand?"

"These people wanted you," Gina snapped, looking at all of her daughters. "Each one of you. They *wanted* you. I loved you, but they wanted you. I wasn't going to have any children, but then I had Nicole, who brought joy to Christopher and Alana's life. When I went on to have my four other angels ... I knew I had done the right thing."

Her daughters were giving her their undivided attention. "Every time I placed one of you in their arms, there was this overwhelming love that came from them." Her voice wavered as she added, "Your parents went through hell to have you. And that's more than some people would have done."

She lowered her gaze to the Oriental rug. "The only child I ever worried about was Madison. And I have every reason to believe she's in danger."

No one said anything for a long while.

Though her vision was blurred by tears, Gina walked to a spot in the room where she could be in the center of all of her daughters. "All I needed was to know that each of you was really all right. Was that too much to ask?"

Chapter 27

Friday - 7:31 p.m.

The silence in the room was an entity all its own, as each person became lost in thought. This was too much information and too may players to process in a short time.

Ms. Kham looked at Michelle as if she wanted to strangle her for creating an unnecessary panic. This was more her fault than Gina's.

Sanjay moved toward Gina and wiped away her tears. "We should all get some rest and start the search for your daughter in the morning."

"What do you mean *we*?" Michelle fired back, gripping her husband's arm so he was forced to turn her way. "*We* are going home. I know where my daughters are, so *we* don't have to do a goddamn thing."

"This girl is their sister," he protested, pulling away from her steely grip.

"Someone they wouldn't have known anything about if she hadn't pulled this—" She waved her hand about. "This whatever it is. But noooooo, she had to play God."

Before Gina could react, Michelle's hand snaked out and landed across her face in a slap that caused everyone to gasp. Gina staggered backward and grabbed her face as the pain shot up to her scalp.

"I told you what would happen if you ever came between me and my husband," Michelle growled.

"And I told you what would happen if you ever thought you could whip my ass." Gina lunged at Michelle, landing a right hook to her jaw and a follow up to her stomach before the two women tumbled to the carpet.

She rolled back and held Michelle in a solid headlock as Vilay blinked, noting that neither her parents, Sanjay, nor the Meisters stepped forward to help. She nodded to the sisters, walked over to the dining table, grabbed a plate, and hit the first serving station. Nalina and Nikki looked at each other, stepped around the two women, and joined their younger sister.

Anjali stared at them and shook her head at their unmitigated gall. "How can you eat at a time like this?"

"It hasn't affected my appetite," Nalina snapped back.

"Mine either," Nikki replied, slathering the gravy over a small scoop of dressing. "I'm staying out of the way. Looks like that one was a long time coming."

Vilay grinned at Nalina and Nikki and said, "Five to one on Gina."

Nalina offered her fist for a power bump. "Not taking that bet. I'd pick her to win my damn self. That fight right there, looks like it's about more than just us."

"Word," Nikki said with a light chuckle. "Grown-ass adults acting like children. Pass the greens."

Anjali took a long, slow breath and trudged the few feet it took to join the others. "I can't believe this is happening."

"I'm sorry I accused you," Nalina said as her sister came near.

Anjali laid her head on her sister's shoulder as she piled one of the East Indian delicacies on her plate. "It's all right; it did look a little suspect."

"Don't look directly at them," Nalina whispered. "But are they still going at it?"

Nikki stole a quick glance in their direction and whipped back to the group. "Yep."

"Then let's ignore them like they would ignore us if we were throwing a tantrum."

The small group of women nodded and smiled at each other as they continued to eat.

Sanjay and Christopher had their hands full keeping the women separated.

Nikki took a sip of wine, scoping out the action from over the rim of her glass. "The animosity between those two speaks volumes."

Anjali toyed with the food on her plate, but stole glances at their parents when she could.

"So, our baby sister is missing," Vilay said. "What did she expect us to do?"

"That's why we're here to find out what she wants. She has to have some leads."

Sanjay was finally able to pull Gina and Michelle apart with Christopher's help. Both women struggled to get back and finish what they had started.

The women fell silent when Michelle shrieked, "You took my husband."

"I never took anything you didn't give," Gina countered, still struggling to get Sanjay to release his hold. "When I tried to leave, you brought me back. Sanjay didn't come for me—*you did!* I didn't want things to get too deep, but you were confident that he couldn't fall in love with me. So if you're going to hit somebody—you better start with turning your foot backwards and kicking your own ass."

Vilay let out a low, throaty chuckle.

Sanjay tightened his grip on Gina's arms. "Stop this. Don't antagonize her."

"I even took up … an outside interest," she said, gazing at Mr. and Ms. Kham, who she could swear were almost grinning. "And your *husband* nearly lost his damn mind. I went away, so don't blame me." Gina pulled away from Sanjay and glared at him, daring him to touch her again. Then she looked at Michelle. "We're talking years ago. Get over it."

"No, sweetheart, I'm talking right now."

Only then did Gina notice that Sanjay hadn't stepped anywhere near his wife, and that familiar spark of desire was in his eyes, which pushed aside the concern she saw there earlier.

Christopher felt Michelle's shapely bottom pressed against him and instantly released her and walked toward his own wife. "We need to get a good night's sleep and deal with things in the morning." He gestured for his wife to follow his lead. "Everyone will have a clearer head then."

Michelle glowered angrily at Gina as she asked Sanjay, "My husband, whose bed will you sleep in tonight?"

"Yours," Gina snapped, while trying to straighten her tunic and pants.

"I wasn't asking you." Michelle locked in on her husband. "I was asking *him*."

Sanjay stared at her a good long while but didn't say a word. Gina slipped past them and into the adjoining room.

"Don't leave," he said, following Gina. "There are some things we need to discuss."

Nalina hurried from the dining room table, moved past her father, and caught up with Gina before he did. She reached out to stroke Gina's skin as though she would disappear at a moment's notice. "I remember you," she whispered. "You used to sing to me at night. You said I was special."

Nalina stared into the face of a woman who was nearly her mirror image and moved the disheveled hair off her shoulders. "I thought I was losing my mind. My parents said it was all a dream. Then they warned me not to ask about you again. So I knew then."

Gina's eyes blurred with tears as she moved closer to the teary-eyed daughter who embraced her.

"I'll help you look for Madison," Nalina said softly.

"So will I," Nikki said, coming to stand next to Nalina.

Anjali nodded. "And me too."

Nikki reached out to embrace Gina, but Anjali hesitated several moments before she moved in to do the same. Vilay looked at them, then turned her back to them as Nikki said, "I might not understand why you did what you did, but I'm grateful that you brought me here. My parents gave me a good life, but they disowned me when they found out I was bisexual. So having a mother right now—one who accepts me and loves me unconditionally—would be super fantastic."

"We didn't disown you," Alana protested, placing a hand on Nikki's shoulder. "We just said you couldn't bring that woman to our home."

"And since *that woman* is a part of my life, how do you think I interpreted that? Huh? It meant I couldn't come home. That you rejected me." Nikki tried to hold back tears of her own as she shrugged off her mother's hand.

"I just thought it was a phase," Alana pleaded, looking to her husband for some type of help.

"I needed parents, not judgmental windbags. And that was a lot of nerve for people who rarely set foot in church."

Christopher tried to take Nikki's hand in his. "Come home and we'll talk about it,"

She snatched away from him. "You have put me off for three years, and it takes a night like this for you to say, we were wrong. We love you anyway." She looked first at Alana, then Christopher. "Yeah, right. We'll talk about it after I find my sister."

"She's not your sister," Alana countered, seemingly alarmed by the determined look in her daughter's eyes.

"We have the same mother," Nikki shot back. She flicked a look at Gina before again focusing in on her parents. "So that makes her my blood."

"*I'm* your mother."

"Only when I'm straight." Nikki joined Nalina, who was still next to Gina. "We'll be staying here tonight."

Nalina nodded, but Anjali grimaced.

Noticing that the Asian beauty hadn't made a move, Nikki ventured a timid, "Vilay?"

"So, what are you?" she snapped, those almond eyes narrowing to slits. "Our fearless leader? Someone who speaks for all of us?"

"Whether you come or not makes no difference to me," Nikki replied, but took comfort in the fact that Nalina and Anjali linked hands with hers. "We'll do just fine without you."

"Yeah, I bet. The blind leading the blind." Vilay held up a slim gold card and glanced Gina's way. "This is the key to my suite, yes?"

Gina nodded.

Sanjay scanned the group, and in typical take charge fashion, he said, "We should all be in this room by 8:30 in the morning and settle old issues, then move on to the more important problem at hand."

Vilay gave her parents a parting look, then threw up the peace sign on her way out the door. She only halted when Gina moved past Sanjay and approached the Khams. "You all didn't say much."

"Because you said everything, doll." Ms. Kham pulled the band from her waist-length locks and looked a few feet over at Vilay, who stood rooted to the spot, watching them closely. "She never quite bonded with me. Fought me tooth and nail on everything, but she loves her daddy something awful. So don't be too upset if she doesn't take to you. She never took to me either."

"I'm sorry for—"

"A little too late for sorry, Gina," Ms. Kham said, reaching out to stroke a hand over her face. "Do you realize what you've done?"

"I do now. But this wasn't supposed to happen."

"And there's no taking it back," Michelle growled.. "All these years and now you want to be trifling?"

"I just wanted my daughters' help. That's all. This had nothing to do with any of you."

"It's always about what *you* want," Michelle snarled as Mr. Kham came to stand close enough to curtail her movements if Alana couldn't keep her away. "Even the terms of the contract were always in your favor."

Gina looked into the eyes of each of the parents; most held angry glares, others had solemn expressions as though they, too, were trying to come to terms with the turn of events. "You got what you wanted," Gina said, taking a seat on the sofa before her legs gave out. "I gave up my daughters so they could have a better life."

"But did you really give them up?" Alana stayed by Michelle's side. "If that were the case, we wouldn't be here right now."

Ms. Kham gestured to get Gina's attention. "We'd like to stay and help if we can."

"Vilay is in suite 2201. She has plenty of room for guests."

"Thank you."

"I'd like to know how *they* ended up with two children, when we asked—no, practically begged—for a second child," Christopher said through clenched teeth as he bore down on Gina. "We were your guardians. We fed you, clothed you. We took care of you when you had nothing and no one."

"Yes, and you got paid plenty for it too. Ask Alana," Gina shot back.

Alana withered under his accusatory glare. "We took the risks. We needed to benefit too."

Christopher leveled a look at his wife. "What did you do?"

"I kept her as far away from you as possible," she said in a hard tone. "But you wanted her, wanted another child *only* by her. So it was up to you to persuade her to have it."

"And oh, baby, did he try," Gina said in a sarcastic tone. "Yes indeed. When you sent me to his office, I thought something was wrong with your daughter. No such thing," she winked at Alana. "You betrayed me with that last couple. They wanted a child strictly for it's parts. You knew I wouldn't do that. You just wanted me to see that having another for you would be so much better." She smiled, but it was one devoid of warmth. "But I have to tell you That parting gift he gave me was quite lovely. Thank you, sweetheart."

Christopher turned even more pale than Gina thought possible.

"You didn't tell her about that?" Gina snapped her fingers and said, "Aw shucks."

Christopher came to stand so he was directly in her face. "You would still be back in those damn projects if it weren't for us."

"Developments," Nalina corrected quickly.

"Same mistake I made," Michelle said to Alana, who was too shocked to open her mouth. "My husband kept fucking her long after her expiration date."

"How quaint," Gina said in a low tone. "You told me once to make what I could of things … and I did. He's really *in love* with me."

"*Was* in love with you," Michelle corrected.

Gina's red lips lifted into something that was neither smile nor frown. "If you say so."

Sanjay couldn't even look his wife in the eye. Instead his focus was on the possessive hand Ms. Kham had draped around Gina's shoulder.

"I will never forgive you for this," Michelle whispered.

"And I'm not asking you to."

Nalina put her body in front of Michelle and extended a hand to Gina. "Come, show me to my place."

Gina slid her hand inside and smiled at her daughter. "The condos have clothes, toiletries, and other things you might need. And the refrigerator is fully stocked."

Nikki gestured to the spread in the other room. "Is the food as good as this stuff?"

Gina shook her head. "None of it has been prepared."

"Then I'll be right back." Nikki made her way back into the dining area to get a plate to go.

Sanjay maneuvered around the Meisters until he had caught up with the group.

Michelle was right behind him. "Where do you think you're going?"

Gina pushed him back toward the cocktail room. "Stay with your wife."

"I don't need you to tell *my* husband to do anything," Michele snarled.

"Very well then. Goodnight." Gina followed the Khams, the Meisters, Nalina, Nikki, and Anjali out of the room while a short, heated exchange between Sanjay and Michelle echoed behind them.

Moments later, Sanjay reached them as they waited at the bank of elevators.

"What's the matter, lover man?" Ms. Kham taunted. "You still don't trust her with us?"

"In a word … no."

Mr. Kham shook his head and grinned as he shared a knowing glance with his wife.

"You all go on down," Gina said.

"Not without you, love," Ms. Kham replied softly, placing a hand to Gina's cheek. "I don't want you and Michelle to get into it again. She might not live to tell about it this time."

Two sets of elevator doors opened, but strangely enough no one stepped on.

"Sanjay, go back to her," Gina whispered, placing a hand on his chest before she reached up to touch the small shock of silver hair that looked strangely intriguing within the rest his dark strands. "I already have enough trouble on my hands."

"That makes two of us."

"I think this will be good for Vilay," Ms. Kham said to no one in particular, but it pulled Gina's focus from Sanjay. "She's always been searching for something—like we were never enough. Like what we gave her wasn't enough. Maybe this will settle the restlessness within her soul."

Gina looked at the petite, red-haired woman whose thin locks were just as beautiful now as they were when she first met the couple.

"She cried for you, you know," Ms. Kham said in a breathy whisper. "The day you left, she cried and wouldn't stop. Nothing anyone did could help. It was as if she knew, could *sense* she was losing something and couldn't voice her pain in any way except her tears." She placed a hand over Gina's, looking into her eyes as she said, "Give her some time to come to terms with things."

Gina nodded, keeping a wary eye on Michelle who appeared with Sanjay.

"You own this place?" Mr. Kham asked, still scanning the area as though unable to believe it himself.

"Yes. It's mostly slated as rental property. There are some businesses on the first level. The penthouse on the top level is mine. The only condos are on the upper levels, and they belong to each of the girls. They have adjoining guest suites. You should be quite comfortable tonight."

"Nikki's father said you grew up in the projects?" Nalina inquired.

"Yes."

"Which one?"

"The Robert Taylor Homes. One of the yellow brick buildings on 52nd and Federal. And I'm not ashamed of where I come from." Gina threw a scathing look at Michelle, who was trembling with anger or frustration—it was hard to tell which. "Unlike *some* people I know."

Nalina beamed. "That's where I live now."

Gina blinked and opened her mouth to say something but quickly shut it. Instead her stunned gaze flashed to Michelle, then to Sanjay, and back to Nalina. "You. Live. W*here*?!!!"

"5135 S. Federal. One of the 5th floor apartments."

Gina's gaze narrowed on Michelle and Sanjay. "She doesn't have money?"

"Oh, she has it all right," Michelle countered smoothly, a smug smile lifting her lips. "She wants to wallow in filth. Must be genetic."

"Don't talk about my mother that way," Nalina snapped, causing Michelle to flinch from the intensity of the words. "I chose to live there because it was necessary."

The elevator doors opened and closed without a single body trying to get on. All of a sudden, things were interesting again, and no one wanted to miss out.

Alana shook her head and chuckled as she took in their perplexed expressions. "Everybody's trying to get out of the projects, and your daughter's clamoring to get in them. How ironic is that?"

Michelle focused her anger on Alana. "To hell with you."

"How can I be of service to people if I don't understand them?" Nalina asked.

"You'll never understand *those* people," Alana said in a tone that matched the disgusted expression on Michelle's face.

"They are a community of people who look out for each other,"

Nalina snapped at the two women. "And now that the area means big money, they want my people out of there."

"They aren't *your* people," Michelle snapped.

Nalina faced her mother head on. "They accepted me unconditionally. They listen to me; they respect me. They didn't stand by as my father sold me into an arranged marriage as a means to reconnect with his long-lost family."

Gina gasped, felt a chill run through her. "Sanjay, you didn't!" Gina searched his eyes, hoping that what her daughter had said wasn't true. She knew from the PI's report that the girls were married early, but wasn't aware that it wasn't of their own choosing.

"An arranged marriage?! Virtual slavery?!"

Moments later, Gina's body slumped against Ms. Kham as her knees failed under the weight of that revelation.

Chapter 28

Friday - 7:49 p.m.

Sanjay lifted his chin so they were eye to eye. "Her husband is the son of a wealthy family with ties to my homeland. Arranged marriages happen all the time."

"And she just went along with it?" Gina asked.

"Papa didn't give us a choice," Nalina said in a heated whisper. "I had to do what Papa wanted, or he wouldn't love me anymore."

All the color drained from his face as he reached for his daughter. "How could you believe that?"

Nalina moved out of his range. "Because you know how to get your way."

Gina staggered backward until she ended up against a wall. "You did that to our daughters?"

"They're not your daughters." Michelle took two steps in Gina's direction.

Mr. Kham shifted quickly to blocked her path.

"Oh, we've already established who the mama is around this camp," Nalina taunted, coming to stand next to Gina. "So stop giving lip service." She gave Michelle a scathing look. "For all that strength you've shown tonight, you were submissive enough when the time came to bow down to what he wanted. Did I hear, 'Sanjay they're not old enough?' Did I hear, 'Sanjay did you ask what they wanted?' Not once!" She looked at Gina. "I bet *she* would have had the presence of mind to challenge him. She would have thought of my well-being, my happiness."

Michelle glared at Gina. "So now you've taken my daughter too? Having her take sides with you?"

"You can't change the simple truth that she gave birth to us," Nalina told Michelle. "But the moment you told me to put my big girl panties on, suck it up, and deal with it … you weren't my mother. You. Were. His. Wife!"

Michelle blanched at her daughter's caustic tone and looked away, but Nalina wasn't backing down. "I can understand it being a part of *his* culture, but it certainly wasn't a part of yours. You sacrificed me on the altar of an arranged marriage. Not once did you think about standing up for me as your daughter. So don't get all pissed off now." She turned to her father, who stood in the center of the hallway looking like a long-lost puppy. "Did you know that my husband called me a half-breed? Do you know what he said to me the moment after I signed that contract?" Nalina moved in to stand directly in front of Sanjay. "Sri said he was going to enjoy breaking in his little Black whore."

Gina flinched at hearing those words. They sounded so much like the ones Rakim had said to her so long ago.

Sanjay's hands balled into fists, a vein throbbed at his temple but Nalina continued. "Said that he wanted to fuck me on all fours so he didn't have to look at my face. Said that I should be grateful he married me because I wasn't … pure."

Nalina let out a small, bitter laugh at her father's angered expression. "Well, the joke's on him. I *never* let him have sex with me. I'm still as pure as the day I was born. They can have their family physician check me all over again. I'd go through that humiliation one more time just so they can see that I never let him touch me." She saw the tears well up in her father's eyes, and rounded him like a vulture on its prey. "You might want to put me back on the auction block, Papa," she taunted. "See how much I'm worth as a virgin."

Sanjay's expression crumbled. "Sweetheart, I am so sorry."

Nalina turned her back to him as Nikki and Anjali came to her side, each rubbing a corner of her back.

Gina held on to his shoulders. "Was being accepted by your family that important to you?"

"The Kasturis are good people," he protested. "They swore they would take care of them." Sanjay looked at Gina, then Nalina, then to his younger daughter. "Nalina is too much like you. Anjali is still married. And she seems all right."

"That's only because he and I have recently come to a good understanding. It didn't take an unfortunate accident for him to come to *his* senses."

Nikki's gaze narrowed on Anjali. "What kind of accident is she talking about?"

Anjali shrugged and lowered her gaze. "Something like the cast iron skillet that ended upside Sri's head."

Nikki stared at Nalina, grinning. "You didn't."

"Damn straight I did."

"Both of them. Just like you," Sanjay said with a weary shake of his head.

"So now you're faulting them for being strong like me?" Gina pushed him back. "I'm almost sure they weren't raised to be docile little women or to be second to anyone. You served them up to men who were nothing like you, who thought dominance was permissible, who considered your daughters inferior because they carry Black blood—my blood. And you thought that wouldn't be a problem? Are you serious?"

"I did what I thought was best for our family," Sanjay yelled, trying to lock gazes with her. He moved to take hold of her shoulders. "To have them know that part of their culture."

"They weren't raised as women in your country once were; today a good majority of East Indian women are making strides for independence. If you don't recognize that, then you're not paying attention."

"They need strong men to—"

"To what? To keep them in line? Like you tried with me?" Her hands balled into fists, as she tried not to touch him. She felt as though she could literally ring his neck. "They need men who will love them, not make them feel worthless. Michelle said you never made her feel that way. Why would you do that to them?"

Michelle leaned on the window ledge and looked out on the snow covered sun deck. "He wasn't the same when you left. That's how I knew I had made a mistake." She glanced over her shoulder at Gina. "I underestimated you. You were a snake, and I let you into my garden."

"Michelle, I apologized, and I meant it then," Gina said in a low tone, "but you're in my house now. And I'm not going to take too much more—."

"Or what? What will you do, Gina? Screw my husband again?"

"I won't have to. You're handing him over quite nicely—again. I'm sure Sanjay would prefer someone who isn't a bitter bitch right about now."

"Sanjay, get your whore before I give her something to think about."

Ms. Kham ran to Gina and held her in place.

"Stop it. Stop it. Stop it," Nalina shouted. She glared at each set of parents. "We have a sister who's in trouble. We don't have time to referee grown-ass people." She stormed out with Sanjay fast on her heels.

"Where are you going?" Michelle shrieked at him from the confines of Mr. Kham's arms.

"To right three of my wrongs."

Nalina whirled to face him, the tears welling up in her eyes. "Papa, I couldn't stay married to him any longer."

"I know, sweetheart," he said, pulling her into his arms.

This time she didn't resist, and the sobs were heart-wrenching. "Nothing I did pleased him. Nothing I could do would please him."

"Why didn't you tell me he said those cruel things? I would have ended it right then and there."

Nalina kept her head on his chest. "You were so happy among your people. I just wanted you to be happy, Papa. It always felt like you were missing something." She looked at Gina. "I didn't realize it was her."

"Did he put his hands—"

"No, he never hit me," she answered softly. "But his words, his actions right before the wedding made it painfully clear that he could never respect me because I'm Black."

Sanjay rubbed her shoulders, then pulled a tear-filled Nalina to his chest. "I'll take care of it. I promise."

"But you'll lose face with the Kasturi family, and we have to think about Anjali. She's still married into that family. You can't do anything that might jeopardize her."

Sanjay stared at her a long while before nodding. "I thought connecting you this way would"—he shook his head, grimacing as though trying to come up with some explanation that made sense even to himself—"give you some balance."

Nalina cupped his face in her hands. "Papa, don't you understand you and mama were all that we ever needed?"

Anjali nodded, too filled with emotion to speak. Sanjay held out a hand to her and brought her close.

Sanjay held her in his arms and rocked her. "I am so sorry, sweetheart. I do not know what I can do to make it up to you." He tilted her head so she had to look up at him. "My judgment was clouded. You are so much like Gina, and she was so easily led into one thing and then another. I tried to balance her, tried to tame her wild ways, and it drove her away." He looked at Gina, whose eyes were moist with tears of her own.

"You still love her?" Nalina asked in a voice just above a whisper, looking from Gina to Sanjay, like she couldn't believe it was possible after all this time. Anjali stiffed at those words.

"I will always love her, just like I love your mother."

"And aren't we just one big happy family?" Michelle sneered, rocking on the balls of her feet. "This time it'll be different. You have a choice to make, Sanjay. Me or her."

Sanjay's eyebrow shot up. "That is really no choice at all."

"There's always both," Nalina countered smoothly, casting a glance at Michelle. "It was that way before, right?"

"I will not share you with her again," Michelle said, ignoring Nalina's sarcasm.

"Then it looks like you have already chosen the path for us."

Sanjay turned and walked out with his daughters following him onto the elevator.

Gina locked gazes with Michelle. "Now tell me again about the difference between love and … in love."

Michelle stepped inside the elevator and flipped Gina the bird as the doors started to close.

Chapter 29

Several moments, the private elevator opened and Sanjay walked off, catching Gina by the arm as she made it to the small hallway leading to the entrance of the penthouse.

"What are you doing here," she demanded.

"You could have always come back to me."

Gina took several moments before moving a few feet away. "I wanted to be more than a woman who spread her thighs for you. I wanted you to see me, to really see me. Respect me for me. Love me for me."

"I always understood you." He stood behind her and placed his hands on her shoulders, stroking them softly. "Your drive to never know another day of poverty, to know what love truly was, to succeed even beyond your own expectations." Sanjay angled her and looked into her eyes, even though she tried to look away. "I was afraid that the one time you failed would be enough to make you do something to harm yourself. I might not have been able to bring you back from that kind of sadness. You were carrying so much already."

Gina allowed the tears to fall as she realized he truly did understand her. She had walked away from this man's love—not understanding that everything he had done was for her own good. "I wanted children of my own," she whispered, placing her hand over his as she leaned into his embrace.

"I would have given you as many as you wanted."

"But you said no more children."

"Your body had already been through so much," he whispered in her ear, pressing a hand to the lower part of her abdomen. "Your little womb needed a rest. More children would come later. I do not know why you could not understand that."

"I was losing myself in you," she said softly. "I couldn't think straight. I couldn't see myself without you. I had to let go or I would've been ... I would've been nothing more than your toy, someone you totally controlled. I couldn't live with that. I already had one man who wanted that very thing. I wouldn't bow down to him, and I wasn't giving in to you either."

Sanjay stared at her for the longest time before saying, "Maybe I was a little restrictive."

Gina cocked a single eyebrow.

"All right, too restrictive. I was jealous. I was afraid."

"Afraid?"

"I realized that Christopher was in love with you. He allowed his wife to separate you. And he was upset."

"Christopher?"

"Oh yes. That man had heat for you. Still does," Sanjay said with a shake of his head. "You signed those contracts without even telling me. I would have loved for you to have children only for me."

"But they would not have been *my* children. Just like Nalina and Anjali."

"At no time did we restrict your interactions with the girls."

"But they still weren't *mine*."

"You were part of the family, Gina," he whispered as he stroked her hand. "They would always be yours."

"Until Michelle decided something different," she said dryly. "She resented my relationship with the children."

"She resented your ability to have them." Sanjay moved a strand of hair from her face. "You gave us a gift and then blessed us with a second. And here is where I know you stopped letting your life become all about money and started opening your heart. You started caring about more than just yourself. Not once did you mention being paid for that second child. Not once did you make that part of your life a negotiation."

He tilted her chin and looked into her eyes. "I wanted to give you the world. I wanted you to never want for any good thing. Not money. Not love. Not pleasure. There was no contract for Anjali. You could have come and taken her at any time. But you did not do that because you loved us, because you loved … me."

Gina leaned into him and let him wrap his arms around her.

"You were so strong," he said, holding her close. "But I thought that someone would use you, would take away the purest part of you—your heart. I could not let that happen."

She pulled away to look up at him. "I've made some mistakes in my life. Some I've learned from; some I repeated because I didn't learn the lesson the first time—so it was like life said, 'Let's run that by her one more time.'" Gina shook her head, trying to push away the tragedies that she had endured. "There are only three things I regret: losing my twins, leaving you, and hurting everyone here today."

"Something good will come of it." He stroked a hand through her hair. "I assure you."

"I made another mistake bringing all my girls together. I've hurt them because I was selfish. I never once thought that the secret would come out. I planned to carry it to my grave."

Sanjay pulled her back to him and continued holding her.

"I'm not showing up here tomorrow. I'll find another way. Just tell them that I love them and that I'm sorry—so sorry—for what I've done."

Gina hurried to the door but didn't make it out of the entryway before Sanjay caught up with her and held her to him. That instant comfort brought more pleasure than all the times they had made love. She cried then, finally cried for her losses in a way she had never done before. Cried for all the time wasted. Cried for her twins. Cried because she had a daughter that needed her so much right now, but she was helpless. So very helpless.

"I love you, Gina. Always have. Always will." She buried her face in the smooth curve of his neck. "It is the kind of love that makes getting up in the morning something to look forward to. Come home, baby. Come home to me."

"I have to find Madison," she said after a few moments of his comforting touch. "She's out there hurting, thinking that nobody cares about her. I can't be with you or anyone else until I know she's all right."

"I understand," he said, stroking her back. "We will find her together."

"But she's not your daughter."

"She belongs to you, and that makes her important to me." Sanjay pressed a hand to her back and let out a long, slow breath. "Get some rest. Tomorrow you must address those people and your daughters."

"What will I say to them? Vilay and Anjali don't trust me."

"That is not true. They just don't know how to love you … yet."

Sanjay placed a tender kiss on her forehead, then watched her go into the penthouse. She gave him one last longing look before she closed the door.

Chapter 30

Mermaid Towers - Penthouse Suite

Gina slipped out of bed, glanced at the clock, and wondered who could possibly be coming to see her at two o'clock in the morning.

She pulled the door open and stared at Nalina. Those piercing brown eyes swept the area behind Gina before looking the older woman in the eye.

"Are you going to let me in?"

"I apologize," Gina said, inching back a little. "I'm just shocked to see you."

Nalina swept by her, walked into the foyer, then turned to face her mother. "Can I stay here with you tonight?"

"Sure. No problem." Her gaze narrowed on the young woman's disheveled form. "Is everything all right?"

"My parents are still fighting," she replied, covering a huge yawn. "I just need some sleep."

Gina didn't have to guess what Sanjay and Michelle were quarreling about. A reminder of an unlikely threesome had to be cause for the dissension. Only now did she feel a tiny bit ashamed of her part in making things worse. How would she have felt if a woman her husband loved, suddenly reappeared.

"You can have one of the guest bedrooms. Let me show you the way."

The foyer led into an elegant but cozy living room with two suede semi-circle sectionals facing each other, with a long, glass coffee table in between. The cream walls were adorned with paintings of abstract art done in warm colors and splashes of red throughout. But it was the pictures above the fireplace that made Nalina move in that direction rather than continue to follow Gina. She recognized herself on that wall. The images of her as a baby, then a toddler, then a toothless five-year-old were prominently displayed among photos of Anjali and what she could only assume were childhood photos of her other sisters. She scanned each one as Gina stood off to the side and lingered on the one of Madison.

"Who are they?" She gestured to another set of photos off to the side.

"My father and mother, Mama Bessie—the woman who raised me—and my little sister, Mayre."

"Do you keep in touch with them?"

Gina tried to quell the pain in her heart, "They're all gone. It's just me now."

Nalina nodded and looked off toward the dining room that had seating for six people. Five daughters, one mother. Five condos, one penthouse. Everything about Gina's place seemed to be about what she longed for. "I have so many questions."

"I know, sweetheart," Gina said softly, resisting the urge to touch Nalina. She was so absolutely beautiful, such a wonderful combination of her genes and Sanjay's. "We can talk tonight, tomorrow, any time you want."

"All right." Nalina quickly bypassed the trio of glass doors leading to an outside balcony that ran the length of the living room and dining room combined. "I'm afraid of heights."

Gina gave her a small smile. "So am I. I rarely go out there. And I have to talk myself into it each time."

They continued on past a private office, a chef's kitchen, two bathrooms, then the master bedroom, before entering a hallway with five open doors. "Take your pick."

The light from the open doors illuminated the hallway walls. Gina had each room decorated to mirror a country she had once visited. Nalina gravitated toward the red room with East Indian influences. "I'll take this one."

"Goodnight, Nalina. Sleep well."

"Goodnight … Mama."

Gina's smile was fleeting because tears filled her vision. She didn't know how to respond, so she said nothing.

Nalina extended her hand toward Gina, who took it and held on before pulling her daughter into an embrace that seemed to last an eternity.

Finally, Nalina whispered, "I remember you, Mama. Your voice. Your scent. I remember. I don't know how, but I do." She held her as though Gina would disappear in a blink. "Don't leave me again."

Gina stroked Nalina's back and the silken strands of hair that fell past her shoulders, as she rocked her daughter in her arms. "I'm not going anywhere. I promise."

The doorbell rang again, startling them.

Nalina pulled away and wiped away her tears.

Gina smiled, held up a finger, and tweaked Nalina's nose. "Hold that thought. I'll be right back."

"Okay."

She pulled the door open to find her blond, blue-eyed beauty on the other side this time.

"Can I camp out here for a minute?"

"Are you renting or buying?" Gina asked, letting her first born in and closing the door behind her. She nodded at the pillow and comforter in Nikki's arm and the cell phone she nearly dropped.

"Dad snores like a lumberjack. I think he's called every hog in the vicinity. Mom can take it, but I give up."

"Come on in. Nalina's here."

Nalina peered around the entrance to the living room like a naughty child. The two women stared at each other for a moment, then Nalina squealed, ran forward, and wrapped her arms around her buxom sister.

Nikki hesitated a few moments before she returned the embrace and looked over Nalina's shoulder at Gina before a smile appeared.

"Oh my God," Nalina gushed and pulled away. "You have to tell me absolutely everything. I've read every one of your articles. And to think, you're actually my sister."

Nikki laughed at the younger woman's excitement. "I'm still trying to wrap my brain around that one. Mom is livid," she said to Gina. "They refused to go home, even though I insisted. Now she's trying to play catch-up with me so she can have some leverage against you. People don't tend to change the way they feel about the lifestyle that quickly." She shook her head and tried to pull down the chemise that barely covered her generous hips. "Parents are a trip. Now it doesn't matter that I'm with a woman. Now all of a sudden, they want to meet Rocky."

"You have to tell me about her," Nalina said softly.

Nikki's smile was as wide as a ship's sails. "Cool."

"And I certainly want to know how you came up with that story on—"

The doorbell rang again. The two women turned to Gina, who let out a long sigh and grumbled, "What is this? Union Station or something?"

Anjali came across the threshold in seconds. She peered in, trying to see behind the woman standing in front of her.

"Is my sister up here?"

"Which one?"

Anjali grimaced, then scowled. "That's a very good question. I have four of them now, right? But I'm talking about the troublemaker."

"Forget you." Nalina rushed, yanked her sister forward, causing her to nearly trip over a flannel seafoam gown. "Get your tail in here." She hugged her, then asked, "Did Anil have a problem with you coming here tonight?"

"No, he urged me to come. Since we came to that understanding just recently, things will be a little different for us."

Nalina peered at her for a moment. "Do Mama and Papa know you're up here?"

"They were too busy fighting to notice that I left," she said, her eyes moist and sad. "Papa left your place to get away from mom; mom followed him to my place, and they've been at it ever since. I bet they'll be going back and forth between the condos all night."

The doorbell rang yet again. Gina rolled her eyes toward the ceiling. "Who wants to place a bet on who that is?"

"Vilay." The other three said in unison.

The more mysterious sister sauntered in to find the other three looking at her intently. "What?" was all she managed to say before the rest of the sisters broke into a fit of laughter.

Vilay looked at Gina. "I want to talk with you." She looked pointedly at the other women and added, "Alone."

Gina looked at her for a moment, took in the determined lift of chin, and said, "Girls, there are several guest rooms here, so spread out wherever you like. The kitchen's fully stocked and so is the bar."

"Who's up for a shot of tequila?"

Anjali's head whipped in Nikki's direction. "It's almost two o'clock in the morning."

"And what's your point, caller?" Nikki gave a low, throaty chuckle as she followed Nalina to the kitchen.

As Anjali filed out of the room behind them, Vilay gestured to the balcony. "I'd like to talk out there where we'll have some privacy."

Gina opened her mouth to protest, but Vilay was already unlatching the lock and stepping out onto the concrete landing. She wasn't wearing a coat. Maybe Vilay was used to the Chicago weather, but Gina couldn't handle it. She grabbed a purple throw from a nearby chaise and inched her way toward the glass doors. Finally, she closed her eyes, stilled her breath, and moved forward. She faltered at the threshold, and Vilay's hand snaked out to steady her.

"What's wrong?"

"Oh, nothing," Gina quipped in a sing-song tone, alarmed at how shaky her voice sounded. "Just a teeny little problem with heights."

"Then why the hell would you take the top floor?"

"I enjoy the view; it doesn't mean I have to come outside and be one with Mother Nature."

Vilay searched Gina's face, noting the flush of color and small dots of perspiration on her forehead. "We can go back inside if you like."

"No, I'm out here now." She put up her hands to keep Vilay from moving forward. "Just don't make any sudden moves."

"That's normally my line." Vilay took the snow covered tarp away and helped Gina into one of the padded chairs.

"Right. You're a cop."

Vilay removed another tarp and took a seat across from Gina, then chanced a quick look over her shoulder, scanning for signs of company. "A detective," she replied. Then, scanning the floor-length balcony, she added, "Nice place."

"Thank you." Gina tried to pull the wrap tighter; she was freezing.

"And the condo's nice too."

Gina gazed at Vilay a moment, then nodded.

"But you can't buy me that way."

"I wasn't trying to. I didn't do any more for you than I did for my other daughters."

"I'm not your daughter."

"Let Ms. Kham tell the story, you're not hers either." Gina focused on Vilay for several long moments and tried to keep her teeth from chattering. It was windless, but the bitter chill was a motha.

Finally Vilay tore her gaze away and looked out over the dimmed reflection of Chicago's skyline. "Aren't you going to try and convince me to accept you?"

"No."

Vilay's head whipped around. "No?"

"You've already made up your mind about me," Gina said in a tone filled with regret. "Nothing I could say right now will change that. I've learned when it's worth my time and when it's a waste of time. With you, it would definitely be the latter." Then realizing how cold that statement sounded, she softened her tone. "It will happen in its own time or not at all. Just like with your mother."

Vilay scowled at the mere mention of the woman who raised her. "That woman never cared about me. She wouldn't even look at me sometimes. Wouldn't lay a hand to discipline me. My father did that. Only my father loves me."

Gina knew that Ms. Kham loved Vilay. There could only be one reason for her not to touch her daughter. "Vilay, you don't know me from Eve's cat, might not trust me or my word, but that woman—your mother—miscarried several children trying to have just one child. She wanted you. And there's a reason she never laid a hand on you."

"What's that?" Vilay's almond-shaped eyes narrowed as she peered at the trembling woman, whose teeth had actually begun to chatter.

Gina realized Vilay was taking a serious liking to Gina's discomfort. But Gina was a lot stronger than Vilay realized. "I'm not at liberty to divulge her personal information, but I implore you to talk with her, tell her what you feel. Ask her why. I think she might tell you, especially now."

Vilay looked down at the hands she had folded in her lap. "I never felt comfortable talking to her."

Gina moved her hands from under the wrap and touched Vilay, which caused the young woman to look up. "Then try just this one time so you can get the answers you need."

Silence expanded around them. Gina looked over her shoulder into the warmth of her living room, then closed her eyes to focus and think warm thoughts. This conversation might take a while, but she'd be damned if she would show weakness in front of a woman who seemed to be a natural gunslinger. There was a small gun tucked in the back of her waistband, another at her ankle, hidden away where an inexperienced eye couldn't see.

"You sure didn't waste any time putting some distance between us," Vilay whispered after a long moment. "How is it that *they* actually remember you?"

Gina's lips lifted into a small, bitter smile. "And that's what you're really angry about, isn't it? That I didn't spend as much time with you as I did with the other girls?"

Vilay formed her mouth to protest, but instead she asked, "That Indian man—their father—was the sex that good that you kept going back to him?"

All thoughts of the chill in the air evaporated like a snowflake in July. "I take you for a straight shooter. You really don't want me to answer that question, do you?"

Vilay locked gazes with Gina, biting her bottom lip as she mulled that over. "I guess not."

"It wasn't about his dick, sweetheart," Gina whispered and leaned over to place a hand over Vilay's to keep them steady. The woman was just as cold as Gina was, but she refused to admit it. "There was a misunderstanding between your parents and Sanjay that made it impossible for me to stay. I was only planning to stay one more month anyway. If I didn't put some space between Sanjay and your mother, she was going to kill him."

"What kind of misunderstanding?"

Gina released Vilay's hands and took a long, slow breath. "Let's just say he … misinterpreted something. I knew if I didn't leave with him, your mother could have really put the screws to him."

"She's always been so … controlled." Vilay thought that over a moment, then shrugged. "I know something's off about my mother; she never seemed quite … I don't know how to put it."

"Did she mistreat you?"

"No, nothing like that, but it's like she never cared if I did anything wrong. She never laid a hand on me … You're smiling?"

"Trust me. You wouldn't want your mother to paddle your ass."

"What do you mean?"

"Nothing in particular," Gina replied with a shrug. "And it doesn't matter; that's all in the past."

Vilay looked over at Gina, and the vulnerability that was displayed on that golden face tore at Gina's heart. "Did you ever think about me?" Vilay whispered in a voice so soft it was almost as if she was afraid to say the words—and even more afraid of the answer.

"All the time. But only now do I wonder if that one extra month would have made the difference."

Vilay nodded but continued looking out at the few cars that zipped up Lake Shore Drive, as though something out there held the answers she sought.

"Did you want to talk about something else?"

Vilay shook her head.

"Why don't you go see what your sisters are up to?"

Vilay didn't move right away. Instead she leaned forward, bracing her hands on her thighs. "I have … sisters," she said slowly, as though acknowledging that fact out loud might mean someone would come and take it all back. She stood and walked to the glass door, but kept her back to Gina.

"Vilay?"

The younger woman froze with her hand on the latch.

"I know you're trying to make sense of it all, but if you ever feel the need to talk, I'm here."

Vilay gave the barest of nods, and instead of moving toward the sound of her sisters' laughter, she turned to look at Gina; her mouth opened, then closed.

Gina stood slowly and tried to steady her steps as she crossed the distance between them. She placed a trembling hand on the woman's back and waited. Vilay turned and laid her head on the smooth curve of Gina's shoulder.

She reached up and held her daughter close.

"I'll never understand why you did what you did," Vilay said softly. "But I'm glad to be alive. And for that I thank you."

Gina closed her eyes to keep in the tears that threatened. Laughter bellowed out to them, causing them to look at one another. "It sounds like they're getting into all types of trouble."

Vilay gave her the first real smile she'd ever seen. "Sisters do that, you know."

 *Chapter 31*

Gina stepped back into the living room and closed the door behind Vilay. Giggles and laughter echoed throughout the house. "I think they put a serious hit on my liquor cabinet."

Vilay grinned at the picture that presented.

"They're staying here tonight. Feel free to join them."

Vilay hesitated for a few moments, then moved closer to Gina. They followed the sounds to the room where Nalina, Anjali, and Nikki were spread out on the huge bed. Vilay took a seat on the chaise near the window, which had a direct line to the door.

"Girls, I'm going to bed," Gina said, giving them all a final glance. "See you in the morning."

"Thanks, Mama."

Gina halted at the door and said, "It's my pleasure." She swept out of the room.

Vilay glared at Nalina. "So it's like that already?"

Nalina met her look head on. "I hate to inform you, dear, but it's been like that all along. It's up to you whether you accept it or not. I have. I love my parents, but this woman … whether we like it or not, she's our mother. She did a beautiful thing in having us for our parents. I have to respect her for that."

"Nikki?" Vilay asked, posing the question to the woman looking at her from an upside down position on the huge bed.

The blonde rolled to the edge and put her legs over the side so she could sit up. "It'll take some getting used to, but yes, I've accepted her. She accepts me and my girlfriend. My condo definitely represents that—Hers and Hers throughout. My parents cut me off the moment they found out."

"Happens" Vilay asked.

"I love who I love. And I make no bones about it."

Vilay grimaced, then shifted her gaze to the youngest of the group. "Anjali?"

She shook her head. "I can't hurt my mother that way. Where's this woman been all of our lives? And now she comes back because she wants something from us?" Then she locked gazes with Nalina. "And it looks like she'll be the reason our parents get a divorce."

"For real?" Nalina scooted over until she was next to Anjali.

"That's what they're arguing about. Mama wants to leave because Papa wants to be with her again."

"I think there's more to it than that," Nikki offered. "It sounded like Michelle sanctioned their relationship at first, but now she's having issues."

"Well that's their business. I say pass me that bottle of Louie the 13th." Vilay accepted the crystal decanter from Nalina and poured three fingers worth into a crystal cognac glass. "Just the empty bottle of this alone is about five hundred bucks. The woman has great taste."

She topped off the shot glass and tossed the first round back. "I was never close to my mother, but I'm with Anjali. The jury's still out on Gina. There's something different about her, something I can't name. I want to stay away from her, but I can't. I don't even know why I'm still here."

"Yes you do. I feel it too. I'm curious about her," Nikki said. "Five girls—no children of her own. And I'm still not convinced we weren't conceived in some Petri dish or lab or something."

"That couldn't be the case," Anjali said emphatically. "Or my parents wouldn't be fighting."

"And my father's pissed that she was with your daddy a second time." Nikki's face crinkled at the thought. "The old-timers were a little freaky back then."

"We're talking about our parents here," Anjali whined like a five-year-old. "I am so trying not to get a mental picture of that." She held out her glass to Vilay. "I need another one."

"I would love to see those damn contracts," Nalina said, failing in an attempt to swipe her sister's glass. "I'm not sure how I feel about being a business deal."

"How much were we worth to them?" Vilay wondered aloud, looking at her sisters for an answer, knowing that they didn't have a clue either.

Anjali sipped her drink and looked at Nalina. "Evidently, it cost more than they could afford to pay."

The women fell silent as they realized that Anjali meant more than just money.

"So you're part Chinese or Japanese?" Nikki asked Vilay, taking a quick look at her phone and sending the call to voicemail.

"Neither," Vilay answered after taking a small sip of liquor. "My father's from Laos."

The other three just stared at her.

"It's near Thailand."

"I can't help but be amazed at how beautiful my sisters are," Nalina said with a wide smile as she slipped off the bed and pretended to slink down an impromptu runway. "We could take the fashion world by storm."

Anjali pulled at her sister's pajamas and yanked her back onto the bed. "Quit dreaming."

"Speak for yourself," Nikki replied, patting her blond curls. "I have what it takes, thank you very much."

"Any of you have children?" Vilay asked after topping off another shot.

"I have a girl and a boy," Anjali answered.

"For now," Nalina added.

Nikki looked at her. "For now? You want more children?"

"*He* wants more. Lots more. A whole damn tribe," Nalina taunted, ignoring the warning glint in her sister's eyes. "Just like my husband."

"But from the sound of things, sounds like you showed him a thing or two," Vilay said with a laugh.

"It started with trying to teach him to open the car door for me. I sat in the passenger seat for the longest time before he tapped on the window and told me to get out. I told him, 'I'm one of *those* types.' He got out of the car and went straight into the house. I slipped into the driver's seat of his beloved Porsche, took off, left it right outside of a chop shop, left the keys in the ignition, and didn't come back for a week."

The other women laughed, and Nalina could only shake her head. "His car was never seen again. Lord was he mad. I wasn't for training a grown-ass man. If I was going to be married to him, then he had to compromise too. I told him that any door that wasn't opened *for* me, meant that he wanted me to stay on the other side."

"My girl." Vilay gave Nalina a power bump, fist to fist.

"Oh, that wasn't the worst part of it," Anjali said, noticing that Nalina's eyes widened in horror, imploring her to remain silent, but Anjali ignored her. "One night while we were having dinner with our husbands' family, they got into a really big argument, and Nalina told everyone that she was still a virgin. You should've seen their faces."

"Anjali," Nalina warned.

"When she said, 'It might mean there's more wrong with his equipment than mine,' he was livid. Then he tried to explain that she wouldn't let him near her." Anjali giggled and squirmed as Nalina tried to cover her mouth. "His family was more angered by that statement. 'Let you?' they said. 'But you're the husband.'"

"He was supposed to court me," Nalina countered, giving up on keeping her sister quiet. She rolled onto her side and looked up at her sisters. "He didn't take the time to do it before the wedding like he was supposed to. So he was going to have to do it after."

"A virgin?" Nikki asked, looking from Anjali then to Nalina. "How long were you married?"

"Coming up on three years."

Nikki whistled and nodded with admiration, but took a quick look at her phone and silenced the vibration again.

"He had to *earn* me. I give my body to the man I choose. If I said he wasn't getting any, then that's just what I meant. He tried to … force me that night of that first argument," she said, causing the smile to disappear from Anjali's face when understanding dawned.

"And that's how he ended up in the hospital with a skillet upside his head and soaking his nuts for the rest of the week."

Despite every effort not to, Vilay joined the other girls in laughter.

Anjali stared at Nikki, tilted her head one way, then the other. "I'm just amazed that you have blonde hair and blue eyes. The only sign of Gina is that you have her lips and nose and a slight tan. Oh, and definitely a sister's rear end."

Nikki inched up on the bed to look in the mirror over the dresser. "I always wondered why I wasn't darker, since Alana was my mother. But seeing Gina didn't make it any different—now I have a whole new set of questions."

"Why did she do it?" Anjali wondered out loud.

Nalina looked at her. "Do what?"

"Have us, then give us to our parents."

"I would love to hear her explanation." Vilay removed her boots, took off her weapons, slipped down into the chaise, and settled in.

They continued to polish off the bottle of cognac as the women shared more about their lives, their successes, and relationships—or lack thereof—until Nikki interrupted. "Maybe we should do this when we're all here. We're still minus one."

Silence ensued for several moments.

"Madison's what? Fourteen? Fifteen?" Anjali looked at them. "Suppose she doesn't like us?"

"Come on now," Nikki said, gesturing to her thick form. "What's not to like."

"Woman, you have enough ego for all of us," Vilay said with a wry twist of her lips.

Nalina nodded as the doorbell rang again. The four women exchanged glances the moment Gina's footsteps hit the floor.

Vilay was off the chaise before the other three could move. They caught up with her, and she signaled for them to slow down and follow her lead. The four women tiptoed into the hallway and pressed their backs to the wall.

Vilay motioned for them to get down on the floor. "It's a man's voice," she whispered, as they each perched on the carpet.

Disappointment showed in their expressions. Had they really expected Madison to show up?

"Who is it?" Anjali inquired, causing the others to shush her so they could hear.

All four of them aligned their bodies along the wall and peered into the living room.

Chapter 32

"The girls are sleeping," Gina said to Sanjay as he brushed past her and entered the penthouse. "Why are you here?"

"I need answers."

Gina braced her hands on her hips. "Take a number and stand in line."

She trailed Sanjay to the living room and watched as he looked around, those intense eyes of his missing nothing. He wore one of the silk robes that Gina had purchased for Nalina and personally placed in her closet. She had done this for each one of her daughters, using the information gleaned from the private investigators.

Gina was certain that Sanjay was naked as the day he was born under that robe. The thought brought her an expected thrill, but also sobered her. It was an absolute shame that the man looked as though he had barely aged. Gina resisted the urge to touch him. Instead she looked down, noticing his bare feet; she let her eyes make their way up to the trimmed and buffed fingernails. He had always taken great care with his appearance.

"Go back to your wife, Sanjay," she whispered. "There's nothing for you here."

At first he seemed at a loss for words, or maybe he was just taken aback by her harsh tone. Finally he said, "We have settled things."

"In what way?"

"She understands my position. She also understands that it will not change."

Gina's heart slammed into her chest. They were back at the beginning. This was the man that she loved—still loved—no matter how she tried to deny it. But she couldn't do this again. Whether Michelle accepted their relationship or not, Gina would not travel that road a second time. Not with him. Not with anyone. She wanted her own man. She wanted to be a wife—not a mistress.

"I ran into the others when the doorman forced us to move our cars." He looked over to her. "Do you know what that red-haired dominatrix said to me?"

Gina took a seat on the sofa and shook her head, knowing by the scowl on his face that he meant Ms. Kham.

He came to sit next to her. "She said, 'If I had known you would be so careless with her, I would have kept her my damn self.' "

In the hallway, Vilay froze at that admission. She looked back at the perplexed expressions of her sisters and grimaced as she stood, whispering, "Maybe we shouldn't listen in on this."

Nalina pulled her back into place. Nikki gestured for them to remain silent.

"Michelle is leaving," Sanjay said, though there wasn't a tone of sadness in his voice—just resignation.

Sanjay stroked a hand over her face, then held her hand. "I never meant for it to feel like you were being controlled. You needed someone to guide you, Gina, to care for you. You were reckless with your body. When I saw those bruises, what they had done to you, it … it … it took me back to a time when my mother was …"

He released her and moved away, until his back touched the patio doors. "My mother was so beautiful," he whispered. "She had fallen in love with my uncle, though she told me they never acted on that love. My father found out and had her beaten within an inch of her life. It would have been more merciful to have killed her." His eyes grew moist, and for a moment Gina's heart skipped a beat. "He would let no one come to her aid. But I did, despite his threat to have me beaten too. I nursed her back to health. I know he found out, but I was still his favorite son, so he did not have anyone touch me."

Gina joined him and reached up to wipe away the single tear that escaped as he struggled to hold in his pain.

"My father had his brother killed. My mother died a few days after my father so gleefully told her the news. The fact that she died because of her love for his brother sent my father into a rage. I left India with just my passport and not much else."

Sanjay took her hand in his. "They found me and had the Indian embassy force me to return so I could fulfill the terms of a family agreement. By then, I had already fallen in love with Michelle."

His looked out over the dimly lit living room. "I escaped a second time and went to New York. I worked almost anyplace that would hire me until I had a better command of English and could afford to go to the university. I bought my first restaurant from a man who considered me his son. I never returned to India. I never wanted to. There was so much sorrow there for me. And there was so much love for me here."

Sanjay kissed the back of her hand and looked up at Gina. "I wanted you to know that you had everything right here with me—love, money … pleasure." He stroked a hand along her back. "I love you, Gina. That will *never* change. I love Michelle; that will never change either, no matter what she does with our marriage. I will never throw a love so deep back into a woman's face. It is like returning a gift without opening it. I will not do that to her or to you."

Gina's heart stilled as she took his true meaning. At least he was as honest as he always had been. "But didn't you throw that love back in her face by asking her to accept you with another woman?"

Sanjay was silent, closed his eyes against the truth of that statement. Obviously, he hadn't seen it that way.

"My baby girl is lost," she said, releasing his hand so she could put some distance between them. Gina went to the doors leading to another private balcony and pressed her hand to the cool glass. "She's out there somewhere, hurting, and she needs me. I can't think about this right now. I don't have the bandwidth to deal with your wife, or to be second in your life."

Sanjay rushed to her side. "We will find her, Gina. Have no fear. And you were never second in any way. Neither is she. I do not know why you both cannot understand that. It is not a race. It is exactly as we want it to be—love, compassion, caring … passion."

Gina looked away from him, feeling herself slipping into the melodic sound of his voice, the sincerity of his words, the heat of his gaze. "An arranged marriage, Sanjay. How could you do that to our children? They have a right to choose."

Sanjay threw up his hands. "I did not know what to do. Nalina, sweet Heavens." He ruffled his hair in frustration. "She was so much like you. She was into *everything*."

Gina looked at him and grinned.

"She was in trouble for smoking marijuana at a school. She would slip out to underground clubs when she was only fourteen. Then she was angry at some girl, so she wrapped her entire house in toilet paper."

"Charmin or Scott's?"

"Gina!" he said, scowling as he glared a warning.

"I'm just asking." Gina's shoulders heaved in an effort not to laugh.

Three sets of eyes focused on Nalina, who had the decency to look a little bit ashamed as she whispered, "She stole my book bag with all of my assignments in it. She had it coming."

Sanjay shook his head. "Then, there were boys calling all times of night. One of them was so angered by something she had done that he actually admitted to doing something he called a 68."

"What's a 68?"

"When I pressed her I found out that it is where he …" Sanjay grimaced as he tried to gather his words, "… did things to her, special things … and she owed him one."

Gina nearly doubled over, laughing so hard that she cried.

Vilay and Nikki covered their mouths to keep in the sounds. Anjali peered through the screen of her fingers and sighed.

"Gina, that is *not* funny," he chided. "I had to marry her off before she ended up pregnant or worse. I wanted her to have the family I couldn't give her."

Sanjay gripped her arms to hold her in place. "And then she carries these weapons—a gun and a switchblade. Her own husband is afraid of her."

Vilay stopped laughing long enough to hold her fist out for a power bump, and Nalina quickly obliged.

"I can see how you would think that marrying her off and trying to rein her in would work for you. But she's my child and yours." Gina pressed a hand to his face. "Adventurous—a free spirit. That's not something that would work for her. She has to make her own way, learn her own lessons. Anjali is different; she's a peacemaker, a mild soul, but oh so sweet, smart, and beautiful. She will always find a way to make even the worst situations better for everyone. That, too, is you and me."

Anjali looked over at her sister and turned away from the knowing smile on Nalina's face. The words had touched Anjali, and it felt odd that they would mean so much from a woman she barely knew. She tried to stand, but Nikki jerked her back down to the floor.

"Nikki is my analytical, happy-go-lucky, down-for-whatever girl. She's the type of woman you want with you when you're trying to figure life out."

Nikki beamed and gave her blond curls a pat, whispering, "Ahhhh, she knows me so well."

"That leaves Vilay," he said softly.

"She's my mystery, but one thing I know for sure—she's also my gunslinger. She thinks I didn't see it, but the girl had five different weapons on her last night. She's better than a man for anything that doesn't require a dick."

Three of the girls winced before slowly looking in Vilay's direction. Her shoulders were back; her head was tilted as she met their gaze head on and whispered, "Gunslinger? I like that."

Nalina pressed her finger to her mouth, urging everyone to be quiet.

Sanjay took Gina's hands in his.

"Two of my daughters accept me; one doesn't; one isn't sure. But the parents are all angry with me. Yet my doorman says that he had to give them all temporary spots in the garage since there weren't any spots open on 67th Street. That means they didn't go home last night. I don't have time to deal with them either."

Sanjay wrapped his arms around her and sighed. "I am going to stay here. We will address them in the morning. What is done is done. The adults will just have to get over it. But my daughters . . . our daughters . . ."

Gina lay in his arms and splayed a hand over his chest.

"I talked with them tonight. Begged them to forgive me for what I had done. I had no right, but I wanted them entrenched in a family that could protect them more than I ever protected you. And I did things the wrong way. I am truly sorry, Gina."

"I don't want to hurt Michelle any more than I already have. I'm not feeling her attitude right now, but she has a point, Sanjay." She moved out of his reach, walked toward the opposite sectional, and looked back at him. "She was with you from the start, and she feels different about you and me this time. And so do I. She's angry right now, but she hasn't really left you, and I doubt if she ever will—especially if she feels as strongly about you as I do."

"Do you still love me?"

That quiet tone and his vulnerable expression did her in. She went into his arms and allowed him to hold her. Finally, someone to share her pain, someone who understood her more than anyone else ever could. Someone whose very existence filled her with such conflicting emotions she didn't know whether she was living or dying.

"I'm tired, Sanjay. I'm so, so tired," she whispered, laying her head on his chest. "I just want to find Madison. I just want to know that all my girls are all right, that they are happy. That what I did was the right thing." Her chest heaved in an effort to hold back the sobs that threatened to weaken her ability to stand and to think. "I did do the right thing. The parents . . . they were supposed to be better than me. So much better. I failed my children. All of them."

"Shhhhh. It is all right," he cooed. "Let the tears flow. Let them cleanse your soul." He buried his head in the smooth curve of her neck and kissed her there before leading her to the sectional and holding onto her as if his very life depended on the connection.

Gina saw the flicker of four shadows on the opposite wall of the hallway; realized that her daughters were listening in. She opened to him, telling him about her mother and father, what had happened to them, to her and Mama Bessie. She told him about Rakim, and the events that led her to Alana and Christopher. She told him about Scott, about losing her twins. She told him how each one of her girls meant the world to her. The tears did not stop coming for a long time, but soon she had unburdened her soul to him—and to her daughters—then lay within his arms, finding a comfort that had eluded her all these years. She told him how she loved her daughters more than words could say and that she was so, so very proud of them.

"I prayed for you every night," Sanjay said softly, his hands warming her with every touch. "That you were safe and that whoever you were with respected you, loved you, cherished you as much as I did."

"You set the bar too high." She stroked her fingers across his face. "No one will ever be as good to me as you were."

"Are," he corrected and tossed a throw over their entwined bodies. "Rest now, my love. Just rest," he crooned. "We will handle whatever comes our way when tomorrow comes."

Chapter 33

The four women remained seated on the carpet, two on each side of the hallway, as Nalina wiped away tears of her own.

"Why are you crying?" Nikki whispered, scooting backward so she was up against the wall. She laid her head on Nalina's shoulder and wiped away her own tears.

"Did you hear what happened to her? She's so ... strong ... and beautiful." Nalina sniffled and wiped her face with the back of her hand. "I'm crying because I know if I were the one who was missing, she would come for me; she would rescue me. My mother did not do a thing to stop Papa. I had to rescue myself."

Anjali lowered her gaze to the hands she held clasped around her knees, which were pulled up under her chin. She, too, had tears in her eyes, but she was torn between love and loyalty. She loved her mother, despite what she had done. And she still loved Papa. Maybe things didn't work out for Nalina, but she knew that Anil could work out for her.

Vilay turned her head and quickly wiped her face with the edge of her shirt. When she looked back, a hardened expression was in place. "It still doesn't excuse the fact that she took money to have us. She wasn't being Ms. Altruistic. She doesn't get a pass on that."

Nikki took in Vilay's angry look. "That woman loved us enough to have us for people who were desperate, who would do anything to have a child. Do you know how truly blessed we are?" Her gaze shifted to Anjali, Nalina, then back to Vilay. "So many children unloved, unwanted—accidents, afterthoughts. And we were wanted ... and loved."

Nalina reached out her hand to Nikki, who took it and moved closer, holding her sister in her arms, though Anjali grimaced at their actions. "She would come for me, and that fills me with such peace. I can't describe it," Nalina said. "I'm connected to her—we all are. I respect it and embrace it. It's your loss if you don't."

Anjali scowled at them, then looked up at Vilay, who had peered around the corner to check on Gina and Sanjay.

Finally, Nalina pulled away and tried to stand. "Tomorrow our parents are going to be too busy pointing fingers and placing blame to do anything." She focused first on Nikki before looking at Vilay and Anjali. "I'm going to find Madison. Will you help me?"

"I'm with you," Nikki offered, placing her hand on top of Nalina's.

Anjali let out a long sigh before saying, "So am I." She put her hand on top of Nikki's.

They all looked at Vilay, who rolled her eyes heavenward. She really could do without the gang's-all-here movement since she preferred to work alone, but Nalina did have a valid point about their parents. She stood, and the others followed her lead. "Let's get some sleep and head out in the morning."

Nikki gave Nalina a smile, and she returned it full force. "Everybody's on board. We're going to find her."

Anjali shrugged and moved away from the three women. "I'm going back to the condo."

"Just stay here with us." Nikki reached out to stop her. "You don't want to disturb the love birds."

"Don't call them that," Anjali nearly shrieked, yanking away as she glared at Nikki.

Vilay looked around the corner to see if the outburst had disturbed Gina and Sanjay. "Keep it down, or we'll get busted."

They moved quickly to the red room. Nalina put an arm around her sister's shoulder and whispered, "Joy, this is going to happen whether you like it or not. Grow up."

Anjali plopped down on the edge of the bed. "I'm just wondering how my parents expect me to stay in my marriage if they can't stick it out in their own."

Nalina perched on the spot next to her sister. "I know it hurts, but this thing started long before we came into the picture." She ran a hand through the dark, silky strands of her sister's hair. "Being upset about it isn't going to change anything."

"This chaise is pretty damn comfortable," Vilay said, taking up her former space. "Nal, you don't mind if I stretch out right here do you?"

"Move over," Nikki said to Nalina, pushing her to the other side of the bed. "I think I found my own spot."

Anjali waited, scanning each of their faces before she climbed over Nalina and landed in the empty space between the two women. "No touching my ass, Nikki."

"Sweetie, you're family. Your ass is off limits. And I like girls with a little boy in them. Vilay should be the one who's worried."

"As if," Vilay shot back, as laughter echoed in the room.

Then all was silent for several moments before Nalina nudged Anjali and mumbled, "And no snoring."

"I don't snore," Anjali replied.

"And no passing gas either," Nikki mumbled.

"Good grief," Vilay huffed. "What are you, a bunch of dudes?"

Nalina pulled the comforter up to cover all three of the women on the bed. Before lying back down, she looked out of the window to the dim city lights then closed her eyes and said, "God, please watch over Madison wherever she is."

"Amen," Anjali whispered.

"Amen," Nikki echoed.

"Yeah, God. What they said," Vilay said, before snapping off the lamp and closing her eyes.

Chapter 34

Vilay rolled into the bedroom pushing a serving station filled with enough food for an entire football team. "Wake up, sleepyheads," she crooned to the three slumbering beauties splayed across the bed in varying stages of disarray. "I fixed breakfast."

"What time is it?" Nalina grumbled, putting the pillow over her head to block the sun.

"Too early to be talking, that's for sure." Nikki slowly rolled onto her back and stretched, causing the chemise to ride up further on her full hips. Nalina was sprawled out on her back, with Anjali curled into her side.

"It's two-and-a-half hours before that meeting is supposed to take place. We need to get out of here before our parents come looking for us." Vilay removed the tops from the serving dishes, allowing the scent of breakfast to sweep away the faint scent of liquor.

None of the women made a move, so she added, "I'd like to go down to the station and pull up a file on Madison."

Nalina sat up and wiped her eyes before yawning and making her way to the adjoining bathroom. "You make that move," she called out to them. "But I'm going to tap my own sources."

"What sources?" Vilay inquired, giving her a pointed look when their gazes connected in the mirror. Nikki ran in, used a hip to inch Nalina over, stuck her hands under the water, and lathered up with soap from Nalina's hands.

"I have my own connections," Nalina said proudly.

Vilay leaned against the door, folding her arms over her chest. "Are they legal?"

"I'm not telling."

"Figures."

Nalina splashed water on her face, rinsed her mouth, and turned to glare at Vilay. "Figures? What does that mean?"

Nikki scurried out of the bathroom and back to the tray.

"Exactly what have you been doing down there in the hood? Must be something that keeps you going back." Her lips spread into a sly smile. "And it's not just work either."

"Vilay, I know we're supposed to love everybody—especially family," Nalina said slowly, yanking the towel next to the sink and drying her face and hands. "But I'm beginning not to like you worth a damn."

Nikki was tearing into the food, as Anjali looked on. Nalina went over to the spread and filled her plate with eggs, toast, and fruit. She gestured to the bacon. "Is this pork?"

Vilay shook her head, lathered an English muffin with butter, and plopped down on the chaise. "There wasn't a single bit of oink in that fridge. I thought that was strange."

Nalina and Anjali exchanged a speaking glance. But Nalina froze for a moment and really took a good look at her sister, who hadn't changed positions since she came out of the bathroom.

The silence that filled the room felt like a weight being pressed on Nalina's chest. "Aren't you going to eat something, Joy?"

Anjali's lips trembled in an effort not to cry. She felt as though someone had reached in, pulled out her heart, and gave it a vicious squeeze. "Our parents are divorcing."

"So they have something in common with the rest of the free world," Vilay countered around a mouthful of food. "You'll get over it." She took another bite. "And anyway—"

An intense glare from Nikki and Nalina shut her down.

"I don't think you understand," Anjali said, sniffling as she scooted back down on the bed. "Nalina left Sri. Now I'm the only one stuck in a marriage that was not of my own choosing."

"But I thought you said you and your husband were working things out," Nikki countered smoothly.

"The fact that everyone expects me to do the right thing when no one else is doing what they're supposed to do isn't sitting too well with me." Anjali leaned back on her elbows and looked at the three of them. "My father put me in this marriage because of his problems with Nalina, and he's leaving his own. That's just not right."

"I think it's Mama that's hitting the trail, sweetheart," Nalina said, smacking Nikki's hand away, trying to keep her from stealing the last croissant off her plate. "You might want to rethink your position on that."

"I can't just walk away." Anjali looked down at her hands. "I have children with him."

"No one is saying you have to," Nalina countered. She put her plate to the side and went to put her arm around Anjali.

"And I ..."

Nalina stroked her back. "You what, Joy?"

"I actually love him."

Vilay held up her cup of coffee in a mock toast. "Well, that puts a real nice spin on the situation. Looks like you've got some thinking to do, doll."

Anjali flinched, then lifted her chin, but her eyes were filled with a sadness that was too deep to voice. She uncrossed her legs and stood slowly. "I'll be right back."

Nalina reached for Anjali's hand, stopping her for a moment before releasing her grasp. Anjali ran out of the bedroom.

No one spoke as Nalina went into the bathroom. While she took a shower, she thought things over and wondered what she could say to comfort her sister. When she came back out, she noticed that Nikki and Vilay were talking about the fact that perhaps Anjali might be more worried about something else. Nalina crossed the room, picked up a piece of toast, and put some eggs on top. Then she added a couple of slices of turkey bacon since Nikki had finished off her original plate—croissant included. "I think if she was going to feel some kind of way about anything, it should be that there was more to the relationship between our parents," Nikki said.

"Aw, please," Vilay scoffed. "As many skeletons came creaking out of the closet last night? My mother gets off on spanking some ass." She gestured to Nikki. "Her father still has the hots for Gina, and Alana isn't sweating it like Michelle is. I wonder what *their* little fetish is."

"Maybe we should leave Anjali out of all this at the moment," Nalina said, swiping Nikki's glass of orange juice before she could get to it. "She's dealing with her own issues right now."

"I agree." Nikki looked over at Vilay. "Can we find Madison on our own? Do you think she's been—"

"Gina thinks she's still alive," Vilay answered quickly, as a teary Anjali slipped back into the room. Her hair was wet, her face freshly washed, and the towel she had around her body barely hid the ample breasts and shapely figure.

"Where do we start, really?" Nikki dabbed a napkin at the corners of her mouth. "We only have a first name."

"Mama has to know something." Nalina walked over to her sister, lifted her chin, and pressed a kiss to the tip of her nose. "Lighten up, Joy. Everything's going to work out just fine." That little nickname brought a smile to Anjali's face, and she allowed her sister to put a corner of sandwich in her mouth. Nalina looked over her shoulder at Vilay. "There's an office right next to the blue room. Maybe Mama has something in there."

"Will you cut out all that mama shit," Vilay snapped, noting that Anjali nodded at that assertion. "You haven't known her long enough to call her that."

"Right now, I could use all the mothering I can get. And from the sounds of things, so could you. Might help you figure out which end is up," she said with a sly lift of her eyebrows.

Vilay glared at her so intensely that Nikki thought they might come to blows. She sighed heavily. "Why don't we just ask her? I'm sure she'll give us anything we need. She was planning on it anyway, right?"

"I agree," Nalina replied, watching as Anjali put a few items on a plate and began to eat her own meal. "We should move forward on our own. By the time the parents come to a decision, it might be too late. Alana and Michelle are ready to jump Gina every time she blinks."

Vilay put her empty plate to the side. "And Christopher and Sanjay won't be much help; they're too busy thinking with the wrong head."

"I resent that," Nalina protested.

Nikki shrugged and countered with, "I think she's spot on."

"I call it like I see it, doll," Vilay offered with a smug smile. "My parents are indifferent; they're probably going to be the most help in this but might have to stick around and keep the others from killing each other."

No one disagreed.

Nalina kept her focus on her sister. "As complex as it may seem, Sanjay loves both Michelle and Gina. I know he's going to help."

Nikki reached for the pitcher of juice, only to find there was barely a swallow left in the container. The grin on Nalina's face told her she relished getting to it first. "While we're out doing our thing, I think Sanjay will give Gina moral support."

"Or *oral* support," Vilay said with a chuckle, as Anjali's head whipped in her direction.

"Will you cut that out?" Nalina snapped, rubbing a hand over her sister's back. "That smart mouth of yours is going to get your ass kicked."

"You and what army?"

"You're not the only one who's packing, sweetheart," Nalina said, locking a steady gaze on Vilay. "Five weapons? Overkill. One will do it, hon. One will do."

"Put the claws away, girls," Nikki teased, going to stand in the center of the room to block their angry glares. "Let's find out what Gina has in her office, then make a plan."

Vilay checked her watch. "Then I'll go into the station and do a little research on my own."

"Oh no, sweetheart, we're going with you," Nikki said smoothly.

"I work better … alone."

"This is a *family* effort, babe." Nikki looked to Nalina. "If everyone goes off on her own tangent, it'll take longer to get results." She put her fist in the air. "All for one, and one for all."

"Actually, I'm going to pump mama for information and work another angle," Nalina said as she sat back on the bed.

"We should stick together," Nikki said.

"I've got connections," Nalina replied softly. "Better than the police."

"When we find Madison, what will we do?" Anjali put the plate back on the cart. "She obviously had a reason to run away from home."

"We'll deal with that later, li'l sis," Nalina said, rubbing the towel in her hair. "That's what you're around for—that psychology crap."

"But if the reason she's staying away is because something happened to her—something bad—then we must at least set her mind at ease that she'll be safe."

"She's right about that," Nikki said, looking at everyone. "I did an article on that once. Most children who run away from home are victims of some form of sexual or physical abuse."

"So are we agreed?" Anjali scanned the other women's faces. "We work this together."

"The three of you work it together," Nalina said softly. "I'll come back here when I'm finished. Make sure you keep your cell phones on."

"I don't have your number," Vilay said to Nalina.

"My sister has it."

Nikki whipped out her phone and said, "*This* sister doesn't. Let's all exchange info so that we're not depending on one person or another."

Nalina recited her number; the rest followed.

"Who's going to keep an eye out while I scope out Gina's office?" Vilay asked.

Nikki raised her hand.

"Figures Ms. Super Snoop would volunteer," Vilay grumbled.

"I'm going to clean up this mess." Anjali scooped up the crystal snifters strewn about the room and placed them on the table.

"No, *I'll* look out," Nalina said to Nikki. "You should hit the shower so you're ready to get dressed when we get back."

When Vilay slipped from the room, Nalina placed a hand on Nikki's shoulder. "You keep on her like a second skin. There's something sneaky about her."

Nikki gave her sister a head nod. "Word."

Chapter 35

Vilay was right on Nalina's heels as they walked back into the bedroom and closed the door behind them. She took a seat on the chaise as Nalina crossed the room to perch on the bed between Nikki and Anjali, who was toweling off her sister's blond curls.

A cell rang and Nikki looked at the screen and grimaced.

"Why don't you answer it this time?" Vilay snapped. "Whoever it is, is just going to keep calling back. That thing was vibrating all morning."

"I don't want to talk to her. It's over."

"Then be a woman about it and tell her so it'll be done," Vilay challenged.

Nikki answered with, "Rocky, this isn't a good time," then was silent as words spewed on the other end—angry words that caused Nikki's face to redden.

"I gave up my family for this relationship," Nikki said with a lift of her chin. "I'll be damned if I give up anything else."

The women shared a speaking glance of concern as Nikki continued with, "A child is not something a woman keeps putting off. If I hit sixty and want to learn to play the piano—I can do that. If I want to travel the world, I can do that too, but a child beyond a certain age does not happen. My eggs will be old enough to graduate from college on their own."

Nikki lowered her gaze, and lifted it only when Anjali placed a comforting hand over hers. "I love you Rocky, but I'm not giving up something I want for that love."

Silence again, this time Nalina put her arm about Nikki's shoulder.

"That didn't change because I fell in love with you. You're the only woman I've ever been with, but after you, I don't think I'll ever do this again."

Nikki bit her lip, then sighed her frustration, listening to what Rocky had to say, then replied, "Now don't get me wrong the sex is off the meter, and the friendship has been wonderful, but for a woman to tell me that I can't have a child, that does not compute."

Nikki closed her eyes, as Rocky implored her to reconsider.

"I'm done, Rocky. And I mean it. We're never going to see on the same level with this issue. Now there's nothing keeping you from going back to Atlanta. It's what you've wanted to do for a while. You just won't be doing it with me." She disconnected the call.

Finally, she looked up to the expectant faces of her sisters, all of which who circled about her and embraced her. "Thank you," she whispered. "That has been so hard. I thought being in a relationship with a woman would be a hell of a lot better than being with a man. I was wrong. It's actually harder because people don't understand it." She grimaced, lowered her gaze to her manicured hands. "No one could have prepared me for how my parents would react to the relationship. The cut me off immediately. I haven't heard from them or spoken to them in three years." She looked into the eyes of each on of her sisters, and said, "And now I have you. And I don't feel so ... "

"Alone?" Vilay supplied.

Nikki nodded. "Yes, that's the word."

"We have to find Madison so she'll feel that way too." Vilay peered at Nikki for a moment. "You all right to go ahead with this?."

"Yes, of course," she said with a smile. "Let's get to work."

"All right, I have her full name," Vilay said, flipping through the folders she had swiped, amid protests from Nalina.

"We shouldn't have taken them."

"She was going to give us the information on her anyway, so what's the difference?" Vilay scanned the first pages of documents. "Gina didn't care for this girl's mother at all."

Anjali slipped from the bed and crossed the room to sit next to Vilay, who immediately put a couple of inches between them. "Then why did she leave her there?"

"Looks like the father was the primary caregiver," Vilay replied without taking her eyes from the file. "The mother—her name's Joan Engstrom—didn't want children."

"What a cold bitch," Nikki said softly.

"I don't want children," Vilay fired back, whipping her head in the blonde's direction. "Does that make *me* a cold bitch?"

Nikki opened her mouth to speak, but Anjali replied, "No, it makes you responsible. Children can make you lose your freaking mind."

"Spoken from experience?" Vilay inquired in a soft tone.

"Ooooooh, yes."

Everyone laughed as Vilay passed the file to Anjali and slipped into the bathroom for a moment.

Nalina took a quick trip out of the room and came back. "Mama and Papa are still on the sofa."

"With their clothes on?" Vilay yelled from the bathroom.

"Hey," Anjali warned, looking up from the file.

"I'm just saying," Vilay replied with a sly grin that only Nalina could see. "Things might have gotten a little … *hot* last night."

"My father's not thinking about that right now," Nalina snapped, scowling at Vilay's reflection in the mirror. "He's concerned about her."

"Yeah, okay. You stick with that. You heard the same conversation I did. The man is still in love with her, and she's feeling him too." Vilay came to sit next to Anjali and gave her shoulder a gentle pat. "You're not in Kansas anymore, Dorothy. Papa and Mama number one are about to get it on."

Anjali shrugged off her hand.

"Will you leave her alone?" Nalina snapped. "Give me that." She snatched the folder and scanned the papers herself. "Gina hired a private detective, so we have a few leads here."

"Let's meet in the lobby in twenty minutes." Nikki polished off the last of Nalina's juice and scrambled off the bed, ignoring Nalina's glare as she grinned.

Without another word, the threesome tiptoed through the hallway until they were pressed against the wall. They peered into the living room.

"They're still asleep," Vilay whispered over her shoulder. "Must have been some night."

"Are they ..." Anjali turned her face, but not before a blush crept into her cheeks.

"No, they still have their clothes on," Vilay said dryly.

"I don't think she's in the mood for a little slap and tickle," Nikki quipped. "But I know someone who could use an outright slap."

"And I'd love to be the one to give it to her," Anjali mumbled.

Vilay gave them a wink.

The three women slithered past the sleeping couple, quietly closed the door behind them, scurried to the elevator and split up to their respective condos.

* * *

Fifteen minutes passed before Vilay and Anjali walked into the lobby. Nikki was already perched on the bench, having a chat with George. Vilay rearranged her black ankle-length coat over her weaponry, slipped on a pair of black leather gloves and a cashmere scarf as she said, "For an old girl, you sure do move fast."

Nikki came to her feet. "Who you calling old, heifer?"

"Well you are the *oldest*," she teased.

"Kiss my ass."

Vilay adjusted her coat, took a gander at Nikki's back end in motion, and grinned. "Doll, that's waaaaay too much ground to cover."

Even Anjali had to laugh at that one. Nikki flipped them the bird.

As they left the building, Anjali looked back at the doorman before moving down the small flight of stairs. "Strange twist of events."

"No doubt our parents are saying the exact same thing," Nikki said, pausing at the end of the circular drive to allow traffic to clear.

They crossed the street to a black SUV. As Nikki rounded the back, she took in the police medallion on the back of the truck and said, "I want one of those little things. I'll stop getting so many tickets."

Vilay gave a low, throaty chuckle. "Believe that if you want to."

Nikki slipped into the backseat as Anjali opted to ride shotgun. "Nice whip."

Anjali nodded, taking in the supple black leather interior. "Practically spotless."

"You're not the only one who can keep things neat and tidy. Strap up, please."

"That has a nice ring to it," Nikki said, laughing.

Vilay tsked her disapproval, saying, "Down girl, down."

They pulled out onto 67th Street and Vilay whipped a U-turn and headed toward South Shore Drive. Nikki looked back at Mermaid Towers one last time. "I came here expecting one thing, then find out a whole lot of stuff I didn't ever want to know."

No one spoke for a long while, as they traveled past the Metra Train tracks.

"I feel a little ..."

"Scared?" Nikki supplied for Anjali, who nodded.

"Me too." Nikki reached forward and curled her hand around Anjali's. "Suppose finding Madison means we don't like what we find."

"Let's not talk like that," Vilay said quickly, although inwardly she was thinking that very same thing.

Chapter 36

Riding up Yates Boulevard, Nikki sighed impatiently at Vilay's slow driving. "For someone who said we need to get moving, you sure are creeping." Nikki tapped Vilay on the shoulder. "Come on, Vee. Put the pedal to the metal."

"I'm doing the speed limit."

Anjali frowned at Vilay. "I didn't think the police actually did that."

"It's a school zone."

"It's Saturday. School's out."

Vilay picked up speed as they went up Yates to 103rd, past Jeffrey Manor and were soon parked in front of a square, red brick building with black-tinted windows and a spray of snow-covered grass out front. A set of circular steel sculptures in the center of the lawn added a hard edge to the place. White cars with powder blue stripes and red lettering were parked in all directions—a sure sign that the cops didn't have to obey the law, even if the good citizens of Chicago did. Nikki gestured to the cars and winked at Vilay, who grimaced and opened the driver's side door. "Stay in the car; I'll be right back."

"Bull," Nikki shot back and stepped out. "We're going with you." She gestured for Anjali to follow her and Vilay. The square lines and hard edges all spoke of the purpose of the place and were in direct contrast to the tastefully dressed women trailing Vilay.

The lobby was covered with vibrant artwork depicting Black and Hispanic people representing the community the station served. Patrolmen entered and exited through the back door that led to a larger parking lot. Some ushered their "guests" to the lock-up area off to the right, and others continued on to the three interview rooms toward the front of the lobby.

Ten officers in uniform blues sat at a series of square block desks—not one of the most coveted spots if you weren't nearing retirement. But it was a position Vilay had come close to being forced into on more than one occasion.

The commanding officers she had worked under in units before this one thought that she should be more willing to see the gray areas when it came to police misadventures. Vilay believed that if the people who were supposed to protect and serve couldn't be held to a higher standard than the criminals they brought to justice, then evidently she—or the brass—had forgotten what it meant to uphold the law and keep the oath that they had sworn when taking office.

Vilay's belief resulted in her being bounced from unit to unit as word got around and officers quickly learned that she was strictly a by-the-book kind of woman. That didn't sit too well with officers who didn't go by the book at all; some of them ripped out the damn pages or wrote their own story altogether.

Police brutality and sexual assaults were at an all-time high, and it had become the citizens' word against the officers'. The Internet and camera phones had done a bit to give citizens an extra boost, but they had not stemmed the tide of bad apples who thought that women who had been stopped for tickets or unarmed Black teens who found themselves on the wrong side of the law were easy prey.

Vilay soon came to understand that men and women who came face to face with brutal crimes and horrible acts against children were a little less concerned with what they considered "minor" incidents involving women who had spread their legs to avoid a ticket, citation, or jail. Adding insult to injury, some of those "incidents" had taken place in the back of a squad car while said officers were on duty. Vilay could now only shake her head at such gall, since having spoken out one time too many put her in a precarious position.

Andy, a pale-faced redhead with a scruffy beard, cast a wary glance over the two women who were scoping out the joint as they tried to keep pace with a quick-footed Vilay.

"Come on, ladies, we don't bite," he taunted, leaning back in the chair and giving a low whistle that caused the other four officers to look their way.

"Tell that to somebody who'll believe you," Vilay shot back.

"Hey, we're not *all* bad."

"I know. I know," Vilay said with a mild chuckle. "Just the ones that have a dick."

Anjali gasped. "You talk like that all of the time? Even at work?"

"Please. She's a saint most of the time." Andy shared a humored glance with his fellow uniformed officers. "That is, when she's not jerking off the commander or pissing up the food chain."

"Yeah, she's the kind of woman a man thinks about when he's dying," replied a sandy-haired, jowl-faced officer who gripped his heart as though having an attack. "Oh, Lord, I hope I don't meet another ball-breaker like her in hell."

"Let's hope your wife doesn't get there before you do," Vilay shot back, gesturing for the women to follow her. "She'll think screwing the devil is an upgrade. He might actually have the equipment to do her some justice."

The scowl on the officer's face and hoots that followed them down the hall made Nikki burst out laughing. "That was hitting below the belt."

"That's the point," Vilay said, opening a set of doors in front of them. "He doesn't *have* anything below the belt."

The pungent odor of onions hit them as they rounded the corner.

"What's up?" Miller asked around a mouthful of hoagie. He lifted it toward Vilay. "I thought this was your day off."

She waved her hand in front of her nose to ward off the smell. "I couldn't stay away."

"Yeah, a regular entertainment district, ain't it?"

Vilay's gaze swept across the room. "Any interrogation rooms open?"

"Sure. This place will light up like Navy Pier, being Saturday and all. But that won't happen 'til much later. So we have an empty nest. Who are these pretty little birds?"

She bit her bottom lip, trying to decide how to get the two women out of the way. "Could you show my friends to Room 2? I shouldn't be long."

"This way, ladies. The Emerald Palace awaits," he said, pointing to a small area behind them that had several sets of open doors. "Tea and scones will be along shortly."

"I don't doubt it," Nikki quipped at his mild sense of humor and fake English accent. "But do you at least have cable?"

"Ha! We wish."

Anjali stayed back and tugged on Vilay's coat sleeve. "We don't get to see where you work?"

"I don't want the rest of my fellow officers losing their minds."

"We can stand the heat."

"The guys might not be able to stand the heat you two put out." Under her coat, Nikki was wearing a killer body-hugging dress that was the color of her eyes. Anjali—a Bollywood beauty—was dressed more demurely in a cream blouse and black slacks, but that wouldn't keep the men from going wild for her sultry good looks.

"We want to know more about you," Anjali said in a voice so soft it was as if she was afraid that Vilay would pounce on her at any moment. Nikki appeared next to her, out of breath. "Hey, you all ducked out on me," she said, then added, "But she does make a valid point."

"What's there to know? I'm a detective, never married, and just found out that the person I thought was my mother really isn't. And that my real mother has slept with more than her fair share. Enough said."

Anjali pulled away, but not before Vilay could see the heat rise in her cheeks. She immediately regretted being so harsh. Anjali was the innocent soul of the group, and she didn't mean to hurt her, but Vilay had always been a private person. Now more people knew about her life than she preferred. But at least no one knew the one thing she didn't want anyone to find out. That secret would stay buried for the rest of her life.

"We want to see you in action," Nikki said, sensing Vilay's reluctance. "Is that too much to ask?"

Vilay flickered a look over Nikki and sighed. She moved forward into the elevator and gestured for her sisters to follow. Inside a slate blue room with exposed brick along the outside walls and desks lined back to back, men and a few women chatted animatedly, talked on the phone, or scribbled out reports.

All activity slowed, then came to a complete halt as they stared at the women walking in behind Vilay.

Cat calls and whistles came from the back of the room, where several men were gathered around one of the more handsome and boisterous of the group.

"My desk is over here," she said, swiping a chair from an adjacent desk to hold it out for one of them to take a seat. Nikki perched her rear end on the edge of the desk instead.

"Damn, she has *two* fine-ass women."

"See, I told you she went for the carpet, not the broom."

Raunchy laughter followed as Anjali frowned at the men and sat behind the neatly organized desk.

"See, that is what I *didn't* want," Vilay said dryly.

Anjali lowered her gaze, mumbling, "Sorry."

"I'll be right back." Vilay removed the notes from her pocket and held them up. "As Polaroid says, let's see what develops."

She sauntered past the leering eyes of her co-workers and into a back office, but didn't miss hearing, "We know who to send out to catch johns next time we do a sting."

"Naw, she's too classy for that," one of them taunted as he gazed at her stylish outfit. "She could pull in a couple grand a night."

"Maybe we can send her up north to the Gold Coast. That's where the real money is," Bill said, chuckling at his own humor.

Thomas reached down to touch the hem of the skirt that ended right above the knee. "Naw, they might mistake her for a cross-dresser."

Guffaws filled the air as Vilay leaned back in so they could see her and gave them the evil eye.

Her fellow officers had never seen her out of uniform, let alone in makeup and a dress. Gina had pegged her right on size, but wrong on preference. The condo's closet was filled with dresses and skirts. She had hoped to have a moment alone to slide by her Kenwood apartment and change into those much-loved trousers and a simple turtleneck sweater, but she didn't want to take her sisters to see where she lived. Now she realized how much of a mistake she'd made. She would probably never hear the end of today's fashion slip-up.

Co-workers always made assumptions about her sexual orientation because of her strong stature, tough demeanor, and because she never talked about her personal life. She wanted a good man as much as the next woman; she just didn't waste time trying to convince anyone to see her differently. It wasn't worth the effort. Now, who she thought she was happened to be a complete lie.

Bill had pulled out a seat at his desk for Nikki.

She smiled and slipped into it with a breathy, "Thank you, sweetheart."

"My pleasure."

"You wouldn't recognize that word if it jumped up and bit you in that flat ass of yours." Vilay swatted him on the rear and he did a little hop before getting back to his spot behind the desk.

Jeers and laughter trailed her over to the cubicle nearest the window.

"How's it hanging?" she said to her partner.

"My balls are damn near dragging the ground." Chuck gestured to the messages on her desk. "How about you?"

"At least mine are higher than that."

Chuck gave a hearty laugh and locked gazes with Nikki, who gave him a seductive smile and stared at him for several moments. Vilay waved her hand in front of him to break the connection. Finally he turned his focus to Vilay, and she looked down at the hoagie next to his monitor. "Too early for that many onions, dude."

"What'sa matter, baby," he slurred, trying to put his lips on her cheek. "You don't want to kiss me 'til I hit the Listerine?"

Vilay tried to shoo him away. "Only after a gallon, 'cause that's what it'll take."

Nikki cleared her throat.

Vilay sighed loudly, pointed first to the blonde. "This is Nikki," and then to the raven-haired woman who came to stand directly behind her, "and Anjali. Ladies, this is Chuck Washington. My partner."

"Washington?" Nikki said with a grin. "How did a white boy end up with the Blackest surname in America?"

"You know, I asked him that very same question." Vilay gave Chuck a sly glance before looking back at Nikki. "I still think he's lying about some things. Got a few drops of the good stuff flowing in his veins."

"Screw you."

"Is that even possible?"

His head whipped in Vilay's direction, but took in the smile she tried to hold back, and he grinned. Chuck leaned against the edge of the desk and kept his gaze on Nikki, who returned his look measure for measure.

Vilay was about to walk off, then thought better of leaving the two women alone and shoved a document into his chest. "See what you can do with this."

"When do you need it?" he asked, still watching Nikki, whose come-hither look was holding him captive.

"Now is good."

Finally, he tore his gaze away and took a gander at the notes. "What case?"

"Missing persons."

His right eyebrow went up. "We don't do missing persons."

Vilay stayed silent.

"No paperwork, huh?"

"Something like that."

"I've got your back."

She let out a long, slow breath and clasped a hand on his shoulder. "Thank you."

Chuck walked a few feet then turned to look at her. "Family? A sister or something?"

Nikki opened her mouth to speak but Vilay quickly supplied, "Or something. I'll be right back."

Vilay saw the look that passed between Nikki and Anjali. She went back toward an area near the cage and pressed her back to the wall. She closed her eyes and tried to focus. She could get fired for this. The department expressly forbade using resources for personal use. But this was sort of an emergency, right?

She would have to file a missing person's report and fill in as much as she knew. Then Gina could sign it, and it would be somewhat official, even if it wasn't enough to totally cover her ass.

A short while later, Vilay walked back toward her desk and froze. Her sisters had not only made themselves at home but were entertaining a group of officers. Chuck was giving the evil eye to all of the men who had Nikki's attention. Vilay shook her head, thinking, *Way to go girls. Stop crime fighting by showing a little ass.*

The men backed up, but only a little, as Vilay slipped behind the steel gray desk. "Ladies, cut it out. The men already don't know the meaning of work."

"Aw, that's cold," Bill grumbled, giving Anjali a thorough head to toe.

"So are last nights' murder leads." She thumbed toward the white board with several names written in red—all current cases. "Get to work."

Thomas, a burly man with thinning hair, gave one last lingering look at Nikki as he walked away. "All work and no—"

"Results," Vilay slipped in. "Use your other head for a change."

The two women grinned as Thomas gunned a finger at Vilay, who crossed one leg over the other and waited. Chuck finally left to go about the task he was given.

"How long?" Nikki asked, taking the seat next to the desk.

"Chuck's the best at searches like these. He used to work for the FBI before coming to this joint. His expertise and the fact that I didn't have all the years under my belt to make detective is the main reason they put me with him."

Nikki scanned the activity going on around them. Suspects were being walked in and thrust into chairs. A woman cried as she told an officer whatever tall tale that would get her point across and her boyfriend locked up. "A police officer, huh?"

"Detective."

"I wouldn't think—" Nikki began, then shrugged as she grinned.

"Think what?"

"You're just so … feminine," Nikki blurted, but her tone was just shy of sarcastic.

Vilay's gaze swept across the area, taking in the bustle of activity among the men with whom she served. Men who had families. Men who would give their lives for each other, but not for her; she'd landed the kind of reputation that didn't make friends on the force. Only Chuck had stuck it out. "Let them tell it, I was born with a medium-sized pair."

"And you just try to keep up the image."

"What do you mean?"

"Don't play dumb with me."

Vilay's head snapped to Nikki, who shrugged absently. "As soon as you walked in here, your body language changed. The testosterone factor kicked in."

"Screw you."

Nikki lowered her gaze to Vilay's thighs. "You probably could and might have the equipment to do it too."

"Last I heard, it was you that's been munching the carpet in your spare time," Vilay shot back. "So who are you to judge me?"

"Hey, ease up you two," Anjali scolded, glaring at them as others started looking in their direction. "We're on the same side here."

"I'm not judging you," Nikki countered. "I'm bisexual so I can call it like I see it. When you walk into this place, you deny who you are to blend in."

"And who am I? You don't even know me."

Vilay pushed back from the desk then stormed away. As she rounded the last row, she turned back and faced the two women. "On second thought, it's time to go. I'll do this on my own."

Anjali rushed forward to Vilay's side. "She didn't mean—"

"Oh yes she did," Vilay snapped, causing Anjali to move back. "And I don't have to answer to anyone, let alone a woman who uses her femininity when it suits her for the moment."

"At least I know who I am and what I am," Nikki said, crossing the few feet between them so they stood eye to eye.

"And that's supposed to mean what…exactly?"

"You haven't come to terms with the fact that being who you are is enough."

Nikki glared at Vilay for what seemed an eternity.

"Please don't do this," Anjali said softly, taking in the fact that everyone was focused on the three of them. "We have to stick together."

"We're going back to the house." Vilay tossed another angry glare at Nikki before whirling away. "I'll go it alone."

Anjali moved in front of Nikki so that they were eye to eye. "Just looking at you, no one would ever know how much of a bitch you are." She walked away, moving in the same direction as Vilay.

Nikki shuddered in mock horror. "Oooooh, the girl has bite."

Just then, Chuck came rushing up behind them. "Hey," he said, rushing across the distance to catch up with Vilay. "You pulled a live one."

The three women halted at the elevator.

Vilay accepted the sheets, scanned the pages quickly, and roared, "Well, I'll just be a good goddamn!"

Chapter 37

Saturday - 9:06 a.m.

The knock on the door spurred Nalina into action. She wrapped a silk band around her hair, gave her reflection one last look, then ran through her condo, wondering how the women had made it back so fast.

Instead of the women she was growing to love—and hate—and the one she had known all her life, Gina stood on the other side of the door; dressed full out in an L.C. Belton business suit that framed her curvy body to perfection. There were no two ways about it—the woman looked awesome.

"Nalina, where is everyone?" she asked, peering over her daughter's shoulder as though the others would mysteriously appear behind her.

Nalina scratched her head. "Well, see what happened …"

"Don't give me that bull. Where are they?"

"Are the parents still having a meeting this morning?" Nalina gestured for Gina to take a seat on the sectional.

"Yes, all of us—the girls included—are going to decide the best route to take for finding Madison. Everyone's upstairs except you and the rest of my daughters."

"I hate to be the one to tell you, but after last night 'the girls' don't want to be anywhere near that meeting."

Gina's eyes widened at that statement.

"By the time you all decide on anything, it'll be next year."

Gina opened her mouth to protest but wasn't given the chance.

"You all have too many issues to work out among yourselves," she said, extending her hand. "It's distracting from what's really important. Your daughter. My sister."

Gina looked at Nalina for the longest time, then sighed as she clasped her hand around her daughter's more delicate one. "So why aren't you with them."

"I'm waiting for one of my connections to get here, so he can help."

Gina nodded, taking that in.

"When you're done upstairs." Nalina lowered her gaze. "I want to talk with you. Ask your advice about something."

"I have time. They can wait." Gina reached out and lifted Nalina's chin with a single finger. "Go on."

"I have a problem. There's this man …"

Gina let out a low, throaty chuckle. "Don't most problems start with a man?"

Nalina released a nervous laugh.

Gina cupped Nalina's face in her hands and trailed a thumb across the high cheekbones before taking her hand again.

"I'm very attracted to him, Mama, but I shouldn't be. He stands for everything that I'm working so hard against." She looked down at their clasped hands. "He runs the building that I live in."

Gina's eyes narrowed to slits. "When you say *runs the building*, what exactly do you mean?"

"He has people there working for him. Illegal stuff and all that. I don't see how I can be attracted to a man like that."

Gina thought that over a moment. "What are some of his good qualities?"

Nalina told her mother about all the wonderful things that Dinero had done for her and for others. Told about a few of their little disagreements, and then ended with the heat that seemed to make her lose her mind whenever he was near. She also clued her in to her marriage with Sri, and how she knew there really was no comparison.

"So, if he wasn't part of the whole drug thing, he would be the type of man you would go for? A perfect … ten?"

"Oh, yes, Mama," Nalina gushed, "but the brother isn't just a ten, he's a god*damn*!"

Gina nodded and tried to keep from laughing at her daughter's enthusiasm. "Sweetheart, I'm going to tell you what God loves—the truth—and I'm going to keep it as real as I can. I'm not going to say you shouldn't be with that man because one thing's for sure, I've learned to let people learn their own lessons. But since you asked me … I'm a firm believer that a woman should never marry a man who has less to lose in a relationship than she does."

Nalina narrowed her gaze at Gina and tried to stem the tide of disappointment that filled her.

"But who you fuck is a different story."

Nalina could only stare at her mother as she took in her meaning.

"If you're going to sleep with him, let it just be about that. Don't let it happen on your turf or his. Have him take you to a five-star hotel downtown somewhere or maybe even outside of the city, which would be better. If he can't manage at least that, that should tell you something. Those places aren't four-hour nap spots or cash only. He has to put up something plastic—and with plastic, you'll get a little more about him than he knows you have."

Nalina peered at her, trying to understand. "I'm sorry, but I'm lost on this one."

Gina gave her hand a gentle pat. "When you work that first time out of your system, call back and get a copy of the hotel bill and use it to check him out—his real name, his real address. We can use that to see what else he's into."

Nalina slumped back on the sofa, staring ahead at nothing in particular.

"Now, on another note," Gina said, "realize that being with him could put your life in danger. Somebody coming after him might miss and hit you by mistake. Not to mention he *must* wear a condom when you sleep with him. No exceptions, baby. He has how many women in that building?"

Nalina shrugged.

"Well suffice it to say he has enough mileage on his dick to make it to California and back, with a full car of passengers along for the ride."

Nalina looked away; tears threatened to come, and she certainly didn't want to cry. But the truth was the truth, and Dinero wasn't a saint—never claimed to be one.

"Oh, sweetheart, I'm not trying to make you feel bad." Gina gently guided Nalina's head onto her shoulder. "But I don't want you to go in with blinders on either. You may like his … what are they calling it these days? Swagger?"

Nalina nodded slowly.

"But don't let that *swagger* put your ass in the hospital or the grave." Gina lifted Nalina's chin so that she could look directly into her eyes. "If you have to have him, make sure it's on *your* terms and on neutral turf. You feel me?"

Nalina laid her head back on her mother's shoulder and closed her eyes. "I just wish Dinero would get out of that life, you know? I want you to meet him; you'll see what I see." She reached up and wiped a tear that managed to fall despite every effort she made to hold them in. "He's so intelligent, and he's … he could get killed out there and …"

"Shhhh, sweetheart," Gina rocked her in her arms. "Nalina, it'll happen when he's ready. If you're going to have him, do it because it's what you want and don't make a single apology about it either."

"Do you have regrets about …?"

"A few, but only a few. And since I can't change the outcome, I'm living my life the best way I know how. That's all any of us can do."

Nalina leaned over, kissed her mother on the cheek, and pulled away.

"Dinero? That's Spanish for money," Gina said. "You might start by making it habit to call him by his given name, instead of his street name."

"D'Angelo? D'Angelo Michaels. Why would that matter?"

"You're acknowledging the person he can be; maybe reach him on some level." Gina leaned in to whisper, "Now, what are those other minions up to?"

Nalina just smiled and shook her head. She would not break her sisters' trust. "Don't worry about Madison, Mama. You and Papa take care of the parents; we've got everything else under control."

Gina's eyes became moist, but she looked out at the view of the Lake Michigan waters and took a deep breath. "Already getting into trouble. Maybe bringing you all together wasn't such a great idea."

Nalina grinned and winked. "We'll see. Won't we?"

* * *

As Nalina left the elevator and entered the lobby, her cell rang. She quickly opened the line and said, "Anil, are you calling me to chew me out for buying her another—"

"Does Anjali need me? Is she in trouble?"

Nalina stopped walking and turned her back to the doorman. "Why would you think that?" she snapped. "Just because she's with me? Damn, Anil. You know I never get her into trouble."

"Calm down, Nalina," he said in that accented English that reminded her of her Papa. "Sri came home and told the family that Michelle is not Anjali's biological mother."

"So?"

"That's a huge problem and grounds for annulment. Sanjay has to be married to the biological mother for the marriage to be considered valid and the children to inherit."

Nalina sighed and shook her head. "What else is up with you people?"

"Don't '*you people*' me," he shot back, and his angry tone made her tense up. "It's not going to make a difference to me. I want to talk with my wife. *We* will decide what *we* want to do."

Nalina stopped pacing the marble tile as realization sank in. "That slick bastard. Sri's only making waves because if the marriages are annulled, it's not going to look so bad for him. They'll let him off the hook for not consummating our marriage."

"I never thought of it that way."

"Anjali doesn't need to be hurt by your family any more than she already has been. I know how you feel about your family, but—"

"My wife *is* my family," he yelled. "Anjali is my heart."

Nalina breathed a sigh of relief. This was the first sign of any type of passion she had witnessed in her mild-mannered brother-in-law. "That's so good to hear because she loves you."

"Really?" he asked, the slight catch in his voice telling the emotion behind that one word. "That's the first I've heard of it."

"Then come hear it in person." She gave him the address. "I'll leave a key to my condo downstairs, and you can wait there until I return."

"Should I bring the children?"

Nalina envisioned her sister's face when she saw her family. "I think she'll like that. And bring the dogs too … and enough clothes and things for you to stay a while, keep you all out of the line of fire while you come up with your own plan."

"Will do. Talk with you soon."

"Hey, and there's some stuff for me in the freezer … bring that too."

"No can do. I ate your little goodies yesterday. And they were goooooood."

Nalina chuckled and disconnected the call. She walked out of both sets of glass doors and ran down the steps. Nalina crossed the street and made her way toward him. Dinero opened the door to his SUV, and she kissed his cheek and slipped into the passenger side.

When he was behind the wheel, he nodded toward the high-rise. "What's this place?"

"Mermaid Towers. My new home."

Seeing the scowl that came across his handsome face, she quickly added, "My mother—my biological mother—owns the building."

Nalina didn't miss the flicker of relief that flashed in those expressive brown eyes. "For a minute, I thought … I thought you were going back to him."

"Oh, honey, never that move. I don't make the same mistake twice." She looked over at him. "I know where I belong. I know who I'm supposed to be with."

Dinero leaned across the seat and pressed a kiss to her lips, then used his tongue to gently ask for complete entrance, which she gave freely. Her heart hammered in her chest. She arched toward him and he held onto her, growling, "Woman, if you don't cut that out, I'm going to—"

"Spank me?" she teased.

Dinero's eyebrow shot up before he roared with laughter. "You'd like that wouldn't you?"

Nalina shrugged, but she couldn't stop the smile that tugged at the corners of her lips.

"Now what was so important that you had to ring my phone so early in the morning?"

"Like that's really a problem for a man who never sleeps."

"Oh, I sleep," he countered, trailing a finger across her face. "I just don't snore as loudly as you do."

Nalina gasped and opened her mouth to protest, then said, "Do I really?"

"Naw, baby, you purr." He imitated the sound of a kitten. "But I like it. You can *rrrrrr* at me anytime."

She pulled his hand into hers and smoothed her fingertips over the massive digits, trying to formulate the words. Finally she gave it to him the best way she knew how. "Dinero, I need your help. And I'll give you anything you want. I just know that you'll be better at getting results than anyone else."

"So it's like that?"

She nodded but didn't make eye contact.

"Tell me what you need, baby."

She relayed the previous night's events, sharing the great news about her mother, her sisters, her troubling suspicions about her missing sister, and the eyebrow-raising exploits of her parents.

Dinero's expression, which he normally kept masked so that no one could gauge his feelings, went through a few transformations as she told her story. He finally looked at her. "Your parents did *what*?"

"You heard me right."

Dinero let out a long, slow breath. He couldn't contain his wide smile. "Damn, the old timers know what's up."

"Yeah? Just don't expect the daughter to be down with that program."

Dinero lifted her fingers to his lips and kissed them. "You wouldn't want to share me with another woman, baby?"

"I'm already sharing you ..."

Dinero tensed and locked a steely gaze on her. "Nalina, it's not like you think. I haven't—"

"And she's a deadly mistress, Dinero," she said softly, touching his cheek. "One who might take her pound of flesh before you're ready to give it. And then I'll lose you before we can get to that love thing."

Dinero let that thought swirl around them before he said, "I'll do you this solid. Ain't no major to put my ear to the vine and get the info you need. But I'm not going to charge you for it like that. When you come at me, it's all about you wanting me, not you wanting something from me. That's what's up."

He kissed her forehead and got out of the car to open her door. "Keep your cell on. I'll call you when I get something. Cool?"

"Cool."

She waited for traffic to slow down before running across the street to the building and the doorman held it open for her to enter.

"And what did I tell you about rolling around with all that jewelry?"

She threw up her hands in frustration. "But I just came from up—"

Dinero winked and drove off.

Chapter 38

Saturday - 9:14 a.m.

Vilay's SUV was parked across the street from the station behind a row of townhouses. Nikki and Anjali could barely keep up with her brisk stride. When they made it inside the truck, the two curious women searched Vilay's stony expression for some answers about what had transpired.

Vilay gripped the steering wheel and closed her eyes. Finally she let out a long, slow breath and rubbed a hand across her forehead before moving it down to give her temples some attention. "I'm in so much trouble it's not even funny."

Anjali touched a hand to her shoulder. "Why?"

"What's up?" Nikki leaned forward so her upper body was directly between the two women.

"Let's get back to Nalina first. I'm only saying this once."

Nikki gripped Vilay's shoulder and pulled it back toward the headrest. "Tell us what's wrong now."

Vilay glanced at the hand Nikki had on her shoulder before locking gazes with her. "Move it, or I'll move it for you."

Nikki let go of a curse but slumped in her seat, folding her arms across her chest.

No one dared speak as Vilay pulled out at top speed. Anjali extended her hand to Nikki, who took it and held it securely.

The tension was thick enough to spread from one end of Chicago to the other.

* * *

Twenty minutes later, they entered Gina's penthouse where Nalina was sprawled on the sectional taking a nap.

"Honey, we're home," Nikki crooned as she sauntered into the room and made her way to the bar. She pulled out a highball glass and a bottle of Bailey's and let it pour.

"Where have you been?"

All eyes flashed to Gina, who closed the door behind Vilay.

Nikki looked at Nalina. "You didn't tell her?"

Nalina sat up straight and rubbed her eyes as she shook her head.

"What happened at the meeting?" Vilay asked.

"Exactly what you all thought would happen," Gina answered dryly. "Chaos and craziness. Not exactly in that order. Only the Khams kept it together."

"Sounds like my parents," Vilay said, almost sounding proud of them.

"Pour me one of those, please," Anjali said to Nikki, ignoring Nalina's frown.

Nikki turned to oblige and saw Nalina put up her finger for one as well. Anjali gestured to make hers a tiny one.

"We went in to get a line on Madison." Vilay pushed Nalina's feet off the sofa and sat down. "Then I had to get out of there before one of my superior officers came looking for me."

"Why would they do that?"

"The FBI knows exactly where Madison is."

"What?" Gina crossed the distance between them in the time it took to blink.

"There's a sting operation in progress to catch the guy she's shacked up with."

"Shacked up?" Anjali said with a scowl. "But she's ... fifteen."

"She might be on paper," Vilay countered, taking a long sip of her drink. "But trust me, Trey Dawg's probably turned her out something wicked. She might've started out a little girl; by now, she's done things no grown woman wants to do."

All the color drained from Gina's face as she stumbled backward then slumped onto the cushions and stared blankly ahead.

Nalina punched Vilay in the arm. "You didn't have to say it that way."

"There's no other way to put it," she fired back. Then she noticed that everyone else had the same angry expression aimed at her as Nalina. "I could lose my job. Her name is flagged. They'll know that I pulled it up. Somehow this little girl's done something to get on the FBI's radar. And that ain't no small thing, doll."

Anjali sank into the seat next to Gina and put her arms around the weeping woman.

"The FBI knows where she is?" Gina whispered. "And they've done nothing to help her?"

Vilay nodded.

"Why?"

"Because they don't mind sacrificing one little girl if it means bringing down an entire drug operation." Vilay softened her tone as she went to kneel in front of Gina. "No wonder the police didn't do anything with your missing persons report. I don't know how she got mixed up with him, but she's in it real good. And the police can't do anything at this point if the Feds are involved."

Gina lifted her hopeful gaze to Vilay. "But you could do something, right?"

All eyes were on Vilay, who walked to the window and turned her back.

"Where is she?" Nikki asked.

"I don't know. My partner found just a little information. Enough to know that she was still alive a couple of days ago. As long as the FBI is in on it, we should stay out of it."

"I have someone working on it." Nalina clicked off her cell and sauntered over to the sofa. She perched on the spot next to Gina and joined her sister in consoling their mother, who reached out and clasped their hands. "All he needed was the dude's name. He'll get a location or at least narrow it down for us."

"You can't tell other people the information I'm giving to you," Vilay snapped. "Who is it? Some drug lord you're all hooked up with?"

Nalina was in her face before anyone else drew a single breath. "Let me tell you something, chickie. You might have rules to follow, but I'm about getting results."

"Do it again, hear?" Vilay said, jabbing a finger in her chest. "And I'll arrest you both for obstruction of justice."

Nalina looked down at Vilay's finger then back to her face. "You need to put that finger somewhere else before I do."

Vilay took another moment before moving away.

"And you need to go somewhere else with that obstruction crap," Nalina snapped. "I'll do what I have to do to find our sister."

Anjali looked up at both of them. "Please. This is not the time to be arguing. Can't you see what it's doing to her?" She looked pointedly at a heartbroken Gina.

"I never thought that something like this could happen to any of you," Gina whispered. "Your parents had money; they could give you everything, provide you with endless possibilities." Gina looked up at each one of her daughters. "None of you should have ended up like this. None of you. That's why I chose them for your parents. Rich people who went through so, so much just to have you." A sob ripped through her. "They were supposed to keep you safe. They were supposed to love you more than I thought I had it in me to give."

Nalina laid her head on Gina's shoulder and stroked her back.

"I'm sorry," Vilay said.

"My children were never supposed to know poverty. They were

never supposed to experience the type of pain that I went through." She looked at each of the women. "How did I get it all wrong?"

"You didn't get it wrong," Anjali said, tightening her hand on Gina's. "But life just isn't that controllable."

Gina wiped the tears away and looked at Vilay. "Now, why is it you think we shouldn't look for my daughter?"

Vilay cleared her throat as she gazed at each of the women, who were looking at her as though she held the keys to the kingdom. "Oh, nothing major. Madison Steinberg is also wanted for murder."

Gina blinked and shook her head as though to clear her vision. "Bring that by me one more time."

"There's a murder charge attached to her name."

"We definitely have to find her," Nalina said to Vilay. "Murder? A girl doesn't come from the sheltered suburbs and become a stone cold killer. There has to be a reason."

"I hate to be the one to tell you, but I've arrested them as young as ten. So age hasn't a damn thing to do with it. We pull her, and you won't get to see her but a hot minute before they haul her off to jail."

Gina leveled a stony gaze at Vilay. "We get her out, and she'll never see the inside of a jail cell. I'll ship her to Timbuktu if that's what it takes."

Vilay took a minute and flicked a gaze at Nalina. "Suppose she actually did it?"

"Suppose they actually deserved it?" Nalina snapped back. "Don't judge her until you find out the truth."

"What Nalina means," Anjali interjected with a warning glance at Nalina first, "suppose there was a good reason—self defense maybe. Then there won't be a problem, right?"

"If she actually committed a crime, I will have to take her in to sort it all out. I've sworn to uphold the law, and that goes for everyone."

"How quaint," Nikki quipped. "We actually land a cop in the family who's not on the take."

"We won't need a crooked cop," Nalina countered. With a pointed look at Vilay, she added, "And we won't need you."

Vilay let out a nervous little laugh. "Oh no, sweetheart, that's not the way it works. My ass is already in a sling since the moment I ran her name through the system. I'm going to see it all the way through."

"Who is she accused of murdering?" Gina asked, coming to her feet.

"Trey's right-hand man."

"Then she *definitely* had a good reason. I bet he's the one who got her into this mess in the first place." Gina put a hand on Vilay's arm. "Tell us what you know, and we'll do the rest. We can leave you out of this so you won't get into any more trouble."

"Gina, these are hardened criminals," Vilay said, taking the older woman's hand in hers. "What do you think you're going to do?"

"Go in and protect what's mine—something your fellow officers have failed to do."

"Who? You and them?" Vilay asked, gesturing to the other women in the room. "Pullease. You'll get killed."

Gina's gaze swung to Nalina. "How's your aim?"

"I can shoot the nuts off a squirrel at fifty yards."

Gina nodded. "Damn, that's pretty good."

"Not for the squirrel," Nikki shot back. "I'm not as good as Nalina, but I can hold my own, and I won't miss."

They all looked at Anjali, who held up her hands and said, "No. Absolutely not."

"And you can't go anyway."

"Why?" Anjali locked gazes with Nalina.

"Anil and the kids are on the way."

"Because …?"

"Sri told the family what went down. Now they're demanding that both marriages get annulled."

Anjali shook an angry finger toward her sister. "I knew I should've let you shoot him that night." Then she sobered as the enormity of the situation set in. "We can't get it annulled; we have two kids."

"In their mind, they were born of a poisonous tree. If they had known that Michelle was not our biological mother, the marriage would never have happened."

Nikki offered her drink to Anjali, who took it and tossed it back. "So you get your wish," she whispered.

"Honey, my marriage was going to end regardless. Sri took the coward's way out." The she released a profane to describe him and with Gina's shocked expression she added, "Sorry, Mama. But if they're both annulled, then he's vindicated in the fact that he never slept with me in all those years." Nalina moved forward, took the glass from Anjali's hand, passed it to Nikki, and said, "Don't give her anymore of this."

"Right now I need the whole damn bottle," Anjali protested, eliciting a gasp from Nikki.

Nalina winced, not only at her sister's caustic tone, but at the fact that she had never heard her curse. And she had done more of it in the past two days than she could remember. The shock she felt was mirrored in the faces of the other women. Nalina hooked her arm under Anjali's and moved her toward the door. "You need to stay here and have a talk with your husband because if he's the man I think he is, you guys will have to move out of the Kasturi place ASAP."

"It's not like we'll be out on the street or anything," she said, looking to Gina for confirmation who gave a slight nod, but it was Nalina who said, "Go on downstairs and prepare for your husband."

Anjali looked at Gina, opened her mouth to speak, but couldn't form a single word.

"Go on," Gina encouraged softly. "We'll do all right. Unless you can actually handle a weapon."

"A steak knife?" Anjali replied, looking at Gina with a hopeful expression.

Gina gave her a small bitter smile and shook her head. "You get an A for effort, sweetheart."

Vilay watched as Anjali walked from the room before turning to the remaining women. "And then there were four."

"Three and a half; you're not all in, Ms. Law and Order," Nalina snapped.

"You can't expect me to bend the rules just because I'm related to this girl."

Nikki moved in front of her. "Yes, we can."

"And that's where you'd be wrong."

Gina stood and walked to where they were holding ground. "Well, I have a few good women. Three decent shots," she said, swinging her focus to Vilay then to her other gunslingers. "I rather like those odds."

Vilay glared openly at Gina before folding and going to the door. "Okay. I'll go. It's going to be worse if I let you all go alone." She sighed. "I'll call Chuck and see if he has any friends with the FBI."

Chapter 39

Three hours later, Vilay made a left off Sheridan Road and slowed down. She was in the center of a tree-lined block in Evanston, Illinois. She placed her hand against the cool glass of the driver's side window and tried to get a handle on her next steps.

Agent Newhouse was expecting her—not a group of pissed-off women. The moment she slipped out of Gina's suite, the other two jumped in the next elevator. They piled out into the lobby with their coats, scarves, and gloves in hand. Nalina ran past Vilay and opened the door, saying, "After you, my dear."

Vilay had no choice but to bring them. Then when they called upstairs and filled Anjali in, she told them not to leave without her. Vilay turned to them after she parked in front of the address Chuck had given her. "Stay in the car."

"Like hell I will," Nikki said, scrambling out of the back seat.

Anjali lowered her window. "Hurry back."

Nikki and Nalina walked toward a modern two-story house with a white picket fence and freshly shoveled walkway.

Nalina looked over her shoulder at Vilay, who was still behind the wheel.

"You're not coming?" Vilay asked Anjali.

"You all might need someone to drive the get-away car. I drive faster than you do."

"You've been watching too many movies." Vilay left the keys in the ignition. A frosty wind whipped through her hair when she slid out of the driver's seat. The orange glow from the street lamps lit the way as the boots of her heels clicked along the concrete path. Meanwhile, Anjali had slipped into the driver's seat.

Chuck had done some checking of his own and called in a few favors. He was given the name of one man who could potentially pull Madison's ass from the fire. The FBI was territorial about their cases—sometimes their operations could cross into several different counties.

Sometimes fighting crime was one big pissing contest, and the only ones getting splashed were honest cops like Chuck and Vilay. No wonder the criminals were often steps ahead of the "good guys." They had better communications and delivery systems than law enforcement.

She moved past Nikki, whose hands were folded across her ample bosom, and Nalina, who was involved with picking an imaginary piece of lint from her coat. Vilay got a shock from the brass knocker as she lifted it from the base. She released it and wrapped on the steel door with her knuckles.

There was no movement in the house.

A few moments later, she knocked again.

No answer. She knocked a third time. Still no answer.

Nalina and Nikki grumbled and made their way back to the car as Vilay made one last try.

As she whirled on her heels to join her sisters, the driver side window of her SUV slowly lowered and a pair of hands signaled for Vilay to turn around. She froze and gathered her thoughts before taking a long, slow breath and turning back toward the house. The light next to the door illuminated the man's cool green eyes, which were the same color as the bathrobe draped over his out-of-shape frame.

A stampede of heels traveling up the concrete rang out behind Vilay.

Newhouse reached out to pull her inside and slammed the door before the others could make it.

"Out here a little late, Ms. Kham?" he asked in a tone that belied his irritation.

"My sisters and I need to talk with you."

"Sisters?" He peered out of the curtain to stare at the women on his doorstep. He took in Nikki's peaches and cream complexion, which paled next to the olive skin of the woman standing next to her. He released the curtain and ignored their attempts to get in as he turned to look at Vilay.

She smirked at his look of astonished disbelief, and said, "Mama was a rolling stone."

"What the hell are you doing here?" he asked, leaning against the wall of the foyer. "I told you I'd meet you at the station tomorrow." He glanced at the women. "And why on earth did you bring them?"

"I didn't have much of a choice; you won't either if they decide to take matters into their own hands. I'd like to keep them contained. Your information will do just that."

Newhouse thought about that for a moment, then opened the door for Nalina and Nikki to enter the mini-mansion whose décor reflected a masculine feel and taste.

"Should we thank him or smack him?" Nikki snapped, rubbing her hands together to get rid of the chill.

"Chuck said that you'd be a hard-ass," Newhouse said, giving each one of the women a pointed look. "But I can't discuss this case with you or them."

"Oh yes you will," Vilay warned. "We need to get Madison Steinberg out from under Trey's clutches."

"Can't do it," he replied with a regretful shake of his head. "She's going to be our key witness; that's the only way those murder charges will be dropped."

Vilay squinted at him for a long while, noting the sweat that peppered his forehead. "I know how your kind works. That murder charge is probably fake and you know it."

Newhouse flinched at the accusation. He ran a hand through his salt-and-pepper hair. Then he rubbed his chin as though weighing what he could and could not share. "We needed her go back in and plant the wire." He swallowed, hard. "She hasn't been able to get back out since then."

"You assholes!" Vilay's fist connected with the man's jaw, sending him backward. "She's only fifteen!" she yelled. "You put her life at risk. I don't care what you've got going on; you get her out right now."

"We can't do that without blowing the entire case."

Vilay moved forward to hit him again, but Nikki stepped between them, and asked, "Who do we need to talk to so that it *can* happen?"

Newhouse focused on the tallest of the group and relaxed his stance when he realized that another blow wasn't coming—at least not from her. "There's nothing you can do. They're not going to call off the sting because some teen whore is—"

This time Newhouse found himself scrambling to get up from the floor with the business end of three weapons pointed at him.

He lifted his hands in surrender. "We've been working on this case for two years, and you want us to roll over for some teen tail. No fucking way!"

Vilay lowered to the floor so that they were face to face. "That whore … is My. Fucking. Sister!!"

Only then did his eyes widen to the size of plates as he looked from one gun's barrel to the other.

Nalina cocked the hammer of her gun. "And when I take you down for this, I'm going to make sure I quote you correctly." She glared at him. "What do you say, Nikki?"

"The Feds using children to get the job done should be front page material. I'll get it to my editor by morning."

"She's press? Damn!" He attempted to get his footing but didn't quite make it, since the women—and their guns—were almost in breathing distance. "What the hell do you expect me to do?"

Vilay shoved a piece of paper into his hand. "Twelve hours" she said, leveling a withering look at him. "If you don't get her the hell out of there, we'll find a way to do it our damn selves."

The three women turned to leave.

"Wait. Wait!" he said, gripping Vilay's arm. "We need more time."

Vilay pulled away. "Time is something you *don't* have."

"I'm sor—"

"Say you're sorry, and your ass will be eating the carpet," Nalina growled, moving so that she was only a hairsbreadth from his face. "Because you're not sorry. You thought you wouldn't get caught. You thought no one cared about that little girl. We care."

Newhouse wiped the blood from his mouth with the back of his hand.

Vilay looked at the family pictures along the wall leading to the living room. "You have children, right?"

"Two girls," he replied, following her line of vision. "They're with their mother."

"And you left her—a defenseless little girl—in there with those animals so you could make a name for yourself and your unit." Vilay gestured to a strawberry blonde that had to be all of twelve. "Tell you what? Why don't we trade off my sister for your daughter? I'm sure it'll be all the same to Trey Dawg. Ass is ass, right. One is less important than the other." She came to stand next to Nalina. "And let me tell you something. If something happens to her because you all were thinking with your egos instead of common sense, I will take you down my damn self. Believe that."

Newhouse maneuvered around them and snatched a red folder from the desk. He held it to Vilay, "You didn't get this from me."

Vilay flipped it open, shifted the pages so that Nikki and Nalina didn't get a clear view. "You'd better make this right because I have two other women—her mother and another sister—who are ready to join these two and go OK Corral on your ass. Trust me, we're the most reasonable of the bunch."

"We didn't put her in there," he shot back. "She was already there. Quasi brought her in from the 'burbs. She agreed to help us with our case in exchange for dropping the murder charge."

"A charge that was probably bogus in the first place," Nikki offered.

"Just so you could secure her cooperation."

"And a deal made without her parents' consent," Nalina offered.

"Her mother never returned our calls," he protested. "And her prints were on the weapon."

"'And you never considered that he helped put them there?" Vilay said, moving in. "Did you think that maybe he had her hold the gun *after* he committed the crime."

Nalina and Nikki shared a look. They glared at Newhouse. They hadn't considered that fact.

"We do what we have to do to get criminals off the street."

"Even if you have to use a child to do it?"

"We figured she was just another runaway."

Nalina raised an eyebrow. "And that makes it all right? They don't need protecting?" When he didn't answer, she lowered her tone. "How … how is she?"

Only then did a flicker of compassion show in those green eyes. "Last report said she was fine. He hadn't harmed her. It devalues the property."

That admission was met with a chilly silence.

"So you'll keep my name out of it?" he inquired.

"Maybe," Vilay shot back, closing the folder.

"This thing is bigger than just me." He gestured to the folder in her hand. "This investigation includes at least fifteen gangs who move hundreds of kilos of cocaine, weapons, assault rifles, handguns, and sawed-off shot guns. We have seven states involved, twenty different branches of law enforcement. What do you expect me to do? Blow that all away?"

"All it takes to bring down a giant is to chop him off at the ankles." She lowered her gaze. "Yours will do just fine."

Vilay gestured for the women to hit the door. She turned to walk up the path from his house. "One of her sisters is a reporter with the *Sun-Times*. Remember that." Vilay glanced back over her shoulder just in time to see his panic-stricken expression. "You've got twelve hours to pull her out on your own or we handle this business our way."

Chapter 40

Sunday - 9:03 p.m.

The door slammed behind them. Vilay turned and jabbed a finger in Nalina's chest and then glared at Nikki. "If you *ever* pull a weapon in my presence again, I will arrest you my damn self."

"He deserved it," Nalina shot back.

"And he'll get his. But not by you." Vilay lowered her hand. "Put that thing away."

Anjali's grip tightened on the steering wheel, but she remained silent.

Nalina placed the gun in her waistband, as did Nikki, who grimaced when Vilay's steely gaze landed on the semi-automatic.

"Where did you get those?"

Nikki and Nalina looked at each other, and one said, "Gina." the other said, "D'Angelo."

Vilay shook her head, mumbling, "Lord, save us from women with guns."

"You have one," Nikki shot back, strolling behind the two of them.

"And I'm licensed to carry it. You're not."

Vilay's cell vibrated as she walked past them to get to the parked SUV.

"Detective Kham."

After litany of *Yes ma'ams*, and *No ma'ams,* Vilay's back rose and fell with a sigh as she said, "I'll be there within the hour."

She disconnected the call, leaned on the driver's side door, and said, "I have to get back to the station—pronto." She moved to a seat in the back. "I need to look over the information he gave us. Anjali, you drive. And put the pedal to the medal."

"What's to keep me from getting a ticket?"

Vilay flashed her badge.

"About time that sucker came into play," Nikki said with a grin. The tires screeched in protest as Anjali tore down the block.

"My captain got wind of what's going on," Vilay said as she underlined some points in the file. "She wants to speak with me." She looked over at Nalina, who was trying to scope out the file for herself. "I think you all should go back to Mermaid. It might take a while."

"We should stick together. We're stronger as a team." Anjali extended her hand to Vilay. "If your butt is getting reamed, then we'll be there with bandages."

Vilay slowly grasped Anjali's extended hand and gave her a small smile.

"Maybe there's something we can do," Nikki said, turning onto Lake Shore Drive.

"We gave him twelve hours." Vilay looked at each one of the women. "Things will have to go through the proper channels. No going off the reservation, ladies. Got it?"

"Got it," Nikki and Anjali replied in unison. Nalina turned her face to look out of the window. "Actually, you'll can drop me off at my office. I have to check on something."

Vilay stared at her for a long time before pulling out something from the pile. "This was taken three weeks ago. Here's our girl."

Anjali almost swerved into another lane trying to get a look.

"My God," Nalina whispered. "Even in a mug shot, she's absolutely beautiful."

"But look at her eyes." Nikki trailed a finger across the photo. "They're so sad. She's been through hell."

Vilay didn't open her mouth to say that hell would have been much kinder. She had deliberately put all of the material relating to the girl's interview at the back of the folder, away from Nalina's prying eyes. As hardened as Vilay was, it was still enough to make her heart hurt.

Anjali looked in the rearview mirror and locked gazes with the two in the back seat. "Should we show these to Gina?"

"Absolutely not," Nikki said, noticing that Vilay shook her head. "But we should tell her we're getting close."

"She'll want to know."

"She'll know everything soon enough." Vilay snapped the folder shut, much to Nalina's dismay. "No use worrying her any more than she already is."

* * *

The three women entered the familiar station once again. Vilay put them in one of the interrogation rooms and hurried toward her desk.

Chuck stuffed the last bite of Italian Fiesta pizza in his mouth and looked up as she slid into her seat. "Twice in a single weekend. We must have hit the jackpot."

"Save it."

He gestured to the file in her hand. "You need some more help on this?"

"Thanks for the offer. You've done enough. If anyone's going down, it'll just be me."

"How bad is it?"

"DEA, FBI, and family."

Chuck gave a low whistle. "Who's the biggest headache?"

"Family. Three women with enough firepower to put Dirty Harry to shame and balls that'll make yours shrink to the size of raisins."

"That's a vicious mental picture." Then one bushy eyebrow shot up as he asked, "Is Nikki one of 'em?"

Vilay grinned at his sheepish look. "Get off my sister, Chuck."

"Your … sister?"

She nodded, taking in his incredulous expression. "Anjali too."

Chuck rubbed his chin as he pondered that a moment. "And the girl?"

"Yep."

He let out a low whistle, then he leaned forward so they were eye to eye. "How the hell did that happen?"

"I woke up yesterday an only child," she said, passing him the contents of Newhouse's folder. I woke up this morning with more family than guns."

Chuck grinned. "So that means you can put in a good word for me with that gorgeous sister of yours?"

Vilay didn't have the heart to tell him that she had a better chance of sleeping with Nikki than he did. She didn't dare dampen his little fantasy parade.

"If you need me …" he began.

"Dude, I need your butt in the chair and your ear to the phone." She clasped a hand over his shoulder. "Keep pressing your buddy to make my deadline, and I won't have to do anything." She swiped a slice of pizza and held it up. "What's in this?"

"Ground beef and everything else."

She stuffed it while trying to work up the courage to take a hit from the C.O.

"He gave me all kinds of grief earlier," Chuck said, devouring the victory slice. "Why is he so cooperative all of a sudden?"

"He's not going to want my sisters all up in his grill. They don't care about procedures or going by the book. All they want is justice—the kind with its own judge, jury, and death sentence."

"Sounds a lot like you these days."

"You know, you might have a point," Vilay said over her shoulder as she made her way to the back offices. "Captain Wallace is expecting me."

"Yikes."

He didn't know the half of it.

Captain Toni Wallace had always treated Vilay fairly. Until Vilay, who had her initial start as an intern in the crime lab, had gained her footing within the unit, Wallace had put her onto working cold cases. That actually worked in her favor, since it was practically Vilay's specialty. She enjoyed solving murders using clues and leads that other officers had missed.

Vilay's biggest case involved solving the murder of a member of the mayor's extended family. A couple of years ago, Vilay's hard work freed a man from death row and put the right culprit behind bars. The fact that seasoned officers had missed vital clues that a rookie—a *crime lab* rookie at that—had caught made her an instant enemy within the rank and file. Her success had been noted in the news, and the mayor granted that single request for her to be put on the fast track to become a detective well before the standard age requirement. She'd been proving she actually deserved that concession ever since.

She walked into the cluttered office with glass windows on three sides. Either the entire department could see the captain drilling a hole in your ass, or she would draw the blinds and leave people guessing. This time, she left the blinds open. Not a good sign. Captain Wallace's long, dark hair was styled in a pageboy that complemented a heart-shaped face, gray eyes framed by thick lashes, and naturally pink lips. She was as tough as officers came. She was typically by the book, but she also knew how to blur the edges.

She gestured for Vilay to take a seat. "What the hell have you been up to?"

"I just tried to pull up information on a little girl who might be in trouble." It was no use trying to cover things up at this point. She needed someone up top on her side. "I didn't know at the time that the DEA and FBI were involved."

"I just got a call from the area commander, who chewed me a

new asshole. After that, the chief of police prepped me for a second one." She gestured to a notepad with Madison's name, date of birth, and Social Security number. "What the hell have you done?" Captain Wallace leaned back in the chair and studied Vilay for several moments. "Talk to me."

"Here's what I know," Vilay began, then laid out what they had found minus the information that Agent Newhouse had just given them. She ended with, "Her mother's a real estate mogul and philanthropist. One of her sisters is a reporter with the *Chicago Sun-Times*, and another has the ears of two aldermen on the low end who are really tight with the mayor."

Captain Wallace closed her eyes and sighed. "And the good news is ..."

"This is going to get mighty ugly if I don't get some results ... and soon."

"How ugly?"

Vilay lowered her gaze.

She swiveled in the chair, grimacing as she connected her own dots. "Damn. And I can't even pull you off the case and pretend that we were told to back off by someone else."

"I was never assigned to the case," Vilay responded. "Just did a bit of snooping that's all, and all of a sudden it's like everyone's on to this girl."

Gray eyes narrowed to slits as the captain peered at her. "Who is this child, really? Why are you so involved?"

Vilay looked over her shoulder to the interrogation room, and noted that Chuck was standing outside looking in on the two women she had parked there.

"She's my sister," Vilay whispered. "I just found out," she quickly added upon seeing the captain's perplexed expression. "I have four sisters, two mothers, and a father who's into something that I can't even wrap my head around. But this girl means a lot to people she doesn't even know yet."

Captain Wallace leaned back in her chair and tapped a pen on the desk as she looked at Vilay. "Who has her?"

"Some big time dealer named Trey Dawg."

Toni's eyebrows drew in. She swung her chair to the computer, pecked the keys for a bit, then looked at the screen. "We bagged him in a sting out here in Jeffrey Manor. Had a house full of girls that he worked up north on Rush Street and was a major distribution pipeline."

"That sounds like the guy. Then why isn't he in jail?"

"Probably copped a plea by giving up his suppliers." She clicked the mouse a couple of times. "We should have some info on him somewhere."

Vilay almost wanted to do a classic fist pump, but she contained herself.

"I hate to tell you that you've got your work cut out for you."

"It's a current case," Vilay said, noting the solemn expression that came over the woman's face. "Shouldn't be too hard to find something in the database."

"I don't think you realize what I meant," she replied, her tone foreboding. "We've updated to a new computer system. The fifth update in ten years."

Vilay's heart sank as she realized exactly what the woman meant.

"Nothing of the old case is on the computer except the arrest record. The rest is lost in a lump of pages that were schlepped downstairs. If you're going to do this, I want you to do it the old-fashioned way. No computers. No trail of what you're doing. And when the rubber hits the road, you do your best. Family or no family. I can only protect you if it looks like you were attempting to do the right thing. You hear me?"

"Loud and clear. But that's not enough time," Vilay said. "If it's all right, I've brought some … *unofficial* manpower with me. If anything's there, we'll find it."

Vilay stood to leave, but the captain halted her movements with a single hand. "Vilay, I like you as an officer, and I'm proud of the work you've done here. I've kept you above ground on a lot of things, and I'm giving you a little license on this. But I'm going to tell you flat out … you'll lose your badge if things go sour."

"She could lose her life," Vilay replied. "Sour would be mild by comparison. I don't care about making a name for myself. I care about bringing her out alive."

Captain Wallace handed over the notes from the desk. "We never had this conversation."

"What conversation?" Vilay grinned and walked out.

When she made it to where the women waited, Chuck had his head lowered. Vilay walked past him into the room and came to a halt.

Her sisters were holding hands as Anjali whispered a prayer not just for Madison, but for each one of them. Vilay was especially touched by the words of protection for her and other people in her line of work. She usually felt a deeper connection to guns than people. Vilay hadn't known these people for more than two days and they had damn near taken over her life. Yet somehow, it wasn't the intrusion she thought it would be. She had sisters! Four of them. And though they had their issues, she was bonding with them in a way that she had never done with anyone else.

Vilay waited for them to finish, and they looked up at her. She opened her mouth to sum up those five minutes in the captain's office but couldn't quite pull it together. What would she do if she lost her job? Police work was all she had dreamed of doing the moment she had made it through a horrible situation. A police officer and a Greyhound ticket agent had saved her life.

Nikki maneuvered around the table. "Come on, Vee, tell us."

"If we locate her, I have to bring her in."

"You didn't tell him that we—"

"No," Vilay replied. "Of course not. And *he's* a *she*." Vilay showed them the notes from her captain. "So not only do we have to find her, but we have to get the Feds to give us evidence she didn't kill that guy. Then we can clear her name."

Anjali came to stand next to Vilay. "How do we do that?"

"First, we find the files my unit has on him. We can't be sure that Newhouse gave us everything."

"Then what?" Nikki asked, perching her rear end on the edge of the table. "We show up to a drug dealer's house and say, 'Our sister missed a family meeting. She has to come home now. And, by the way, we think you framed her for killing Quasi. What you know 'bout that?'"

"Let's hope we can be a little more tactful than that," Anjali said, nudging Nikki's side.

"Personally, I say we shoot first and ask questions later," Nikki quipped.

Vilay heard a distant chuckle and knew Chuck was still outside listening in. She turned to Nikki and said, "Woman, what did I tell you."

Two pairs of eyes locked on Vilay.

"I mean it, Nikki." Vilay said, ignoring the fact that the blonde rolled her eyes heavenward. "Enough with that gangster act."

"I need a drink," Anjali whispered.

Nikki ran her hand through her curls. "I need more than that."

"You all need to keep a clear head. No Joy juice."

"Why did you have to put my name in that?" Anjali said.

Truthfully, Vilay had forgotten that Joy was her special name, so she added, "Because you're always the first one to suggest it and the last person to finish the bottle."

Nikki busted up laughing, as Anjali flipped Vilay the bird.

Vilay opened the door and shooed a laughing Chuck back toward his desk. It was like moving a five-ton truck. As she pushed in one direction, he steadily tried to come back. Their antics caused Nikki and Anjali to double over. Finally Vilay gave up. "Cut it out, Chuck. We've got work to do."

Chuck gave Nikki one last longing look, which elicited a small wave from Nikki before he trudged back to his desk.

Vilay hooked an arm under Nikki to get her moving toward the offices along the back end of the wall.

"Seems like material for a suspense novel," Anjali said to Nikki. "You should write about this."

"Only if it's a happy ending."

"Not all stories have a happy ending," Vilay said softly. "Even the fairytales."

Anjali placed a hand on Vilay's shoulder. "I'm so hoping that this one does."

Vilay leaned on the lobby desk counter and swiped the bread crumbs off Andy's blue shirt. "Have Hank turn on the beamers for the records room."

"How long do you think you'll be?"

Vilay looked at the clock just behind the desk. "About an hour."

Andy picked up the radio unit next to the phone console, but looked up at Vilay first. "Need some extra heat?"

"No, just some light."

"They'll be on by the time you get down there."

The women walked to the elevator as Andy's voice followed, "Eh, Hank. Wake up."

The silver doors closed and opened in the basement within moments. They stepped out into total darkness. Hank wasn't as fast on the switches as Andy believed he could be.

Vilay held the door open to the elevator so the light within would keep them company. Seconds later, the fluorescent lights came on row by row until the entire room was illuminated.

"This way, ladies." Vilay swiped her card, and the click of the lock made everyone relax.

A maze of beige and gray shelves filled the entire area. A single table with two chairs on opposite ends was close to the door.

"This place is huge," Anjali said, moving to stand behind the two women, who went farther into the room and left her standing there.

Vilay checked her notes, made her way down the third aisle, and scanned the numbers. "This is what we're looking for." She gestured to the notes, and they peered at the paper.

"Don't they have an actual filing system in this joint?" Nikki allowed her gaze to sweep over all the boxes that seemed to go on forever.

"They're moving these to long-term storage. Right now, everything's in a mix." She held out a document and pointed to a set of numbers. "This is what we're looking for."

Arriving at the last set of files, they turned right and headed for another row and spread out.

* * *

Several hours later, Nikki wiped her brow and rubbed her aching feet. "I should've worn jeans for this."

"I didn't say it would be soft work."

"Well, you didn't say it would be three hours of hard labor either."

"Quit bitching, blondie," Vilay turned and snapped at her. "You could have stayed behind—"

"Don't even say it," Nikki shot back, placing a hand on her hip. "I need a stretch."

Anjali gave Vilay a pleading look, noting that she agreed.

"All right, let's go for a cup of coffee."

They stopped long enough for two of them to put their heels back on, then turned and went up another row to make their way to the exit.

"Wait. Wait." Nikki stopped short in front of a white file box in the middle. "I think I found it."

Vilay looked up at the place Nikki pointed, then grabbed the ladder and wheeled it to the box. She stepped up, slid the box out of its place, took off the top, and rummaged through the contents. "I think this," she said, holding up several tattered manila folders, "is exactly what we're looking for."

"Let me see one."

Vilay passed it to Nikki. "But this is only part of it. We need the rest of his file too."

"Why?"

"Dealers tend to net out in an area and stay near their client base. When they move their operations, it's always to a place where they've laid a little groundwork. We have a general idea of the area, but something in here might give us the spot of a known associate or girlfriend."

Anjali took one page off the top. "You could get in trouble for this?"

"No more than I'm already in."

"You know, I thought you were this tough, uptight Asian chick. But really, you're a sister and all heart."

"Shhhh. Don't tell anyone," Vilay teased, giving Anjali a conspiratorial smile. "It'll destroy my image."

"You think we're close to finding her?"

"Closer than yesterday," Vilay said to Anjali. "At least we know she was all right a few days ago. That's a start."

"I think we should check in with Gina and Nalina," Nikki suggested, passing the folder back to Vilay. "Then start fresh early tomorrow morning."

Vilay scooped up the contents of the file, returned everything else to the box, then guided the women back toward the door.

Chapter 41

Mermaid Towers - Nalina's Suite

Nalina and Nikki were dressed in gear that was more suited to hitting the strip and picking up a few not-so-good men. Vilay's gaze shifted to them. "This is such a bad idea."

"It's been thirteen hours, and we haven't heard jack."

Anjali pouted as she looked over at them. "I want to go too."

"Absolutely not," Nalina countered. "You have children. And your husband would kill me if I got you involved in this."

"News flash. I'm already involved." She plopped down on the sofa and poked out her bottom lip, causing Nalina and Nikki to share a smile before they cleared their expressions. "And what makes you think it's any safer for you?"

"Nalina goes into the projects all the time," Nikki said, putting a pin in a long, blonde wig.

Vilay grinned. "Dressed like that?"

Nalina gave her the evil eye, which caused Vilay to bust up laughing.

"Don't you think you should tell Gina what's going on?" Anjali inquired softly.

"No," Vilay said, waggling a finger at Anjali. "And neither should you."

Nalina's phone rang. She looked at the display and quickly walked away from the rest of the women. "D'Angelo, what's going on?"

"Stay away from the Ida Bs."

"Why? We were just about to pay Trey a little visit. That man's been hiding in plain sight. What fool stays in the same area where he committed the crime?"

Dinero let go of a string of curses that forced her to pull the phone from her ear.

"Woman, didn't I tell you about traveling up in spots you aren't cleared to go?" he snapped. Then she heard him take a deep breath. When he continued speaking several moments later, his voice was calmer and his tone softer. "Lina, I'm only going to say this once ... keep your ass at the Towers. There's some things going down here that I don't want you caught up in."

"What do you mean?"

"All kinds of law enforcement have been creeping up the block all day. And they're not being cute about it either."

Nalina swallowed, trying to keep her panic at bay. "D'Angelo, is my sister in trouble?"

"Do you trust me?"

"Yes."

"Then, baby, let me handle this."

"But it's not just me, honey," she said, looking at the three women who had followed her into another room and were focused on her.

"Honey... I like that," he said in a low tone. "But you need to keep your sisters in check, baby."

"How? One of them works for the police. I can't tell her what to do."

"Damn straight," Vilay said, moving to stand directly behind her. "And who is that?"

"My friend." Nalina then filled her in on what D'Angelo said.

Vilay put a hand up to rub her eyes. "So, instead of going in for her, they moved up the timetable for the whole operation."

"They were probably scared we were going to screw it up," Nikki said as she perched on the edge of a chair near the two women.

"And they would be right," Vilay countered. "I should probably make a move anyway. Agent Newhouse's probably pissed off enough to make Madison pay for our little showdown last night."

Nikki gestured to her outfit. "We could still be useful."

"Trust me, the last thing those boys will be thinking about is ass. Put some real clothes on."

"Dee, are you safe?" Nalina asked him.

"Sweetheart, all my people have been out of RTH since you gave me the 4-1-1 last night. Cops are sweeping those areas too. But right now the Ida B's is where a lot of the heat is."

Vilay kept an intense glare on Nalina, studying her face and body language.

"I'm rolling near 39th Street right now, but wanted to scope out the place and see if I could get in real quick. DEA and FBI are trailing the mark, baby. It's about to be live at 5, news at 10. Do not—I repeat—*do not* set foot in this area."

"But she's my sister," she pleaded.

"If there's any way that I can go in, I'll do it. Don't you make matters worse by having me worry about you. Do you hear me, baby?"

Nalina looked at the other three women, who stared back with varying degrees of concern, anger, and determination.

"I said, do you hear me?"

"Yes."

"I love you," he whispered before disconnecting the call.

Vilay pushed Nalina back into the nearest wall. "You've been giving him my intel?"

"I certainly have."

"Why?"

"Because he can do things that you can't," she shot back, removing

Vilay's hand from her chest. "He's not bound by law to do the right thing."

Vilay smirked as she walked away. "And he can land his ass right in jail with the rest of the criminals."

Nalina bore down on her so that they were toe to toe. "You mess with my man, it's like messing with my money. Not too many people survive those moves."

Anjali looked at her sister. "You've been sleeping with this thug?"

"Not a thug, sweetheart," Vilay said with a wide smile. "A big-time drug dealer. Dinero. Real name's D'Angelo Michaels. I checked into him. Easy to locate in the system."

"But you're still married," Anjali whined, searching Nalina's face for some sign it wasn't true.

"I haven't slept with him." Then she grimaced, remembering that first night at RTH and added, "Not in the Biblical sense."

Vilay's eyes flashed with anger. "Riiiiiight. And I have a bridge in San Francisco I'd like to sell you. You sure can pick them, doll. The man has a rap sheet a city block long, yet you're giving him more play than you're giving us."

"Kiss my ass." Nalina pushed her away. "If he says for me not to go into that place, I'm not going."

"Like a good little whore."

The slap that rang out sent Vilay staggering backward to slump on the sofa. She jumped back up, but Nikki was in between them in an instant, ducking blows that almost landed on her instead of their intended target.

"Call me out of my name again, hear?" Nalina growled. "And we will roll up in this camp."

Anjali blinked and looked at Nalina as though seeing her for the first time.

"You know what? Forget both of you," Nikki said, sliding a cool glance to Anjali. "I say *we* go."

"I want to find out who the heck this guy is you've been keeping company with," Anjali said.

Nikki tapped Anjali's shoulder. "In or out, sister. Argue with her on who she's spreading it for later. You're forgetting the point here."

"I say we all go," Vilay said, giving Nalina a sly smile.

"He says we shouldn't go anywhere near the Ida B's."

"And who the hell is he to tell us anything?" Vilay snapped, coming to circle around Nalina.

"He's a man who isn't just speculating on where my sister is. He actually *knows*, which is a hell of a lot more than what you and the two musketeers have come up with."

Nikki let out a low whistle. "Well, she does have a point on that. That box didn't give us squat."

Vilay threw an icy glance at Nikki, who wrinkled her nose and grinned.

"Stop it! Just stop it," Anjali shouted and stomped her foot. "You all are forgetting what's at stake here."

Nikki's head whipped in Anjali's direction. "Just a minute ago, you were all on your sister's jock, so come off it, babe."

Vilay smirked at that admission.

"I'm so disappointed in you," Anjali whispered, moving toward Nalina. "And a drug dealer? Are you for real?"

"Joy, I don't need your approval for my life. Just like I don't need Papa's. Get over yourself."

Nikki nodded toward Vilay, who was focused on the other two women. "If the police are swarming that area, evidently your FBI dude came through."

"I wouldn't be so sure he'll do it in our favor."

"So do we go or do we wait?" Nikki asked, tipping some cranberry in with the seltzer.

Nalina perched on the sofa and crossed one leg over the other. "I'm staying away."

"Figures," Vilay quipped on her way to the door. Nikki was hot on her tail. Anjali stood frozen in the center of the room, looking from them to Nalina and back.

Nalina's cell rang, and the others turned to face her, then back into the living room.

A few moments later, she pulled the phone away from her ear. "Madison's on her way to University of Chicago Hospital."

"They got her," Anjali shrieked with joy.

"He says she's badly injured."

Vilay crossed the distance between them. "Do they have Trey Dawg in custody?"

"He got away."

"There's only one way in and one way out," Vilay countered. "How could he slip past the police?"

"He didn't," Nalina said, dropping down on the sofa before looking up at Vilay. "One of them let him walk right out of the building." She scanned the shocked faces of the women around her. "He's definitely coming after Madison."

Chapter 42

University of Chicago

The five women arrived at the hospital just in time to see D'Angelo being ushered toward a police cruiser by an officer in uniform blues. Nalina ran to the officers, demanding his release. She narrowly escaped being arrested herself, and that was only because Vilay intervened.

"He's not in cuffs, Nalina," Vilay said. "They just want to question him."

D'Angelo gave Nalina his classic smile and said, "Don't worry, baby. It'll be all right. Go see about your sister." Then he locked gazes with Vilay, who moved toward him. He leaned in and whispered some things in her ear. He looked at each one of Nalina's sisters, but lingered for a longer moment on Gina, then to Nalina before the officers shoved him in the car.

Vilay relayed the information she found out from him. Somehow, Trey Dawg got wind of Madison's involvement with the FBI. He had poured scalding hot water on her back as she tried to escape.

D'Angelo had burst into the apartment just as Trey was poised to give her a Sicilian smile—a knife slice from ear to ear. D'Angelo managed to stop the man before he did any major damage, but Trey escaped as D'Angelo called for help. Madison's injuries were more pressing than subduing a dealer and pimp. Knowing that the paramedics might not come up, he carried her out of the building and arrived at the curb a few moments before the ambulance pulled up.

As the squad car drove away, Nalina looked at the women. "I was only trying to do what was right when I got D'Angelo involved in this."

Nikki stroked a hand across her back. "She's alive, and that's half the battle."

"If he hadn't gone in when he did," Vilay added, "Trey would have killed her."

They made it to Madison's room and spread out around the sleeping girl. Soon they were discussing the events that led up to her being in the hospital.

"We shouldn't be talking about this here," Anjali whispered. "She can hear us."

"Sweetheart, she's doped up. Surely you cannot be that naïve."

"Vilay, go screw yourself," Nalina snapped. "If you hadn't been on that Dudley Do Right trip, we could've gotten her out ourselves, long before one of your people told him what she was up to. Long before he hurt her this bad."

"I didn't want to lose one of you," Vilay said, her voice wavering. "Not if I could help it."

Silence fell over the room at that heartfelt admission. It was the first time that Vilay had admitted that they meant anything to her.

"Let's just be here for her," Gina said softly, placing a gentle hand on Vilay's arm. "And we'll be the first faces she sees when she wakes up."

"All strangers," Nikki said dryly.

"But not for long." Gina touched her hand to Nalina's face. "I'm sorry about your friend. But we're not going to tear at each other. Right now, it's all about Madison getting better and making her feel safe." She looked at each one of the women. "Do you all understand me?"

The silence that followed in the ICU felt like a weight sitting on Nalina's chest. Nikki's lips trembled in an effort to keep back her tears. She felt as though someone had reached in, pulled her heart out, and gave it a vicious squeeze before putting it back in. A quick glance at the solemn faces of Anjali, Vilay, and Gina made her reluctant to say a single word.

* * *

The pain was so excruciating that they were forced to put Madison in a medically induced coma until she wouldn't need as much medicine. The angry pink flesh had been bandaged, and Madison was now laid out on her stomach.

Gina sat stoically, taking in the horrible sight of what had happened to her baby girl. She reached for Anjali's hand, stilling the fingers that were wringing frantically. A spasm of pain tore through her. A world of "what ifs" were rolling through her thoughts.

What if she had taken Solomon up on her offer to marry him and raise Madison. What if she had checked on Madison sooner? What if she had stayed with Sanjay instead of having that last child. What if. What if. What if.

The women took a round-the-clock watch over Madison for the next four days, waiting for the time when she would awaken. That series of green dots, single beeps from the monitor and the small, shallow breaths were the only signs of life.

Nalina ran into obstacle after obstacle trying to locate D'Angelo. It was like he had disappeared into some Alice in Wonderland type hole, and no one would tell her anything.

Vilay made a single call after Nalina broke down and asked for her help. She didn't come up with anything on her end either. Nalina stopped calling him, as there never was an answer, and his voicemail was full.

Then as they each sat around the room, lost in their own thoughts, a soft, "Who … who are you?" came from the bed.

The voice snatched everyone from varying states of worry and reflection, and all eyes were on the young girl on the bed struggling to turn over.

"We are …" Gina began. How could she explain their presence? Really? "I'm Gina Wright. I'm your mother. Your *real* mother."

Madison's soft brown eyes widened in shock. Anjali poured a cup of water and helped the young girl to take a few sips.

"My real mother?" she croaked. "What do you mean?"

"Your father and I … your father wanted you very much, and I had you … for him."

Madison blinked twice and swept a gaze over the other women around her bed.

"And who are they?"

"They're your sisters."

Madison looked first to Nalina, then Nikki, Vilay, and finally to Anjali, before bringing her gaze back to Gina. She raised a single eyebrow. "Sisters?"

All of the women nodded.

"I'm Nalina, and this is Anjali."

"I'm Nikki."

"Vilay."

Madison looked down at the hands that had grasped hers. She then focused on Gina. "And Joan?"

"Joan Engstrom? She was Solomon's wife. That's all." Gina reached out and stroked the perspiration from Madison's face. "When your father died, I was supposed to be contacted so that I could come for you, but no one called."

Madison swallowed hard and kept looking at the women who claimed to be her sisters. "Why do they look so … different?"

"They all have different fathers. Except those two," she said, gesturing to Nalina and Anjali. "But I am their mother, as I am yours."

Madison took a long moment to ponder that statement.

Gina moved from the chair, lowered the rail, and perched on the bed. She brushed the soft tendrils of hair away from her baby girl's face. "Your father promised that he would take care of you. I didn't expect that things would go this way. When I felt that you were in trouble, I searched for you. Then I brought your sisters together to help; it was because of them that we found you."

A tear escaped from those soft brown eyes as her gaze swept to each one of the women. She pulled her hands back from the two that held them. "Why would you all help me?"

"Because we love you," Anjali said softly, as three others moved closer to sit around her on the bed.

"You don't even know me," she shot back, giving them attitude—an instant flash of fire that gave Gina an inkling that Madison would be all right. She was a fighter.

"We didn't know each other until a week ago," Vilay said softly. "But we did know one thing ... we had to find you and make sure you were all right. We can learn more about you when you're ready to tell us."

Madison locked gazes with the woman who claimed to be her mother. She lowered her head so that the focus went to the white sheets.

"I tried to leave him," Madison whispered. "He said he would kill Joan if I did. But things got so bad ... so, so bad ... I just couldn't anymore ..."

"Shhhhh, don't try to talk about it right now," Anjali said, brushing the tears away. "There'll be time for that later."

Madison reached for Anjali's hand, then Gina's, and looked up at Nalina and Vilay, who moved in closer so they were in a semi-circle around the bed.

"I met Quasi at school," she said. "He worked in the cafeteria. I didn't know he was into drugs and stuff. He owed Trey some money, so he gave me to him to work off his debt. Then Trey killed Quasi so he couldn't take me back."

The nurse walked in, but Vilay flashed her badge and waved her away. The strawberry blonde slowly backed out the room and closed the door behind her.

"I tried to call my mother once when I was out on the street." Madison looked up at Gina. "She said whatever happened to me was good for me." A sob escaped as her grip tightened on Gina's hand. "Then I stopped wanting anyone to help me because I was too ashamed to go home. All the things I've done. I feel so …" She shook her head as though unable to come up with the words.

"He did things to me … terrible things, and there was nothing I could do to stop him. I just wanted to die. He said I wasn't pretty enough for him anymore." She looked up at them, then lowered her voice to a breathy whisper. "How could you want me as your sister? How could anyone look at me now?"

Vilay moved past Gina, sat on the bed, and put a hand to the young one's cheek. "Let me tell you something, Madison. There is *nothing* that you've done that will mean we won't love you. Nothing. Please believe that." Vilay's gaze swept to the four women as she said, "I wish I had these women there for me when I went through the things I did."

Madison tilted her head in Vilay's direction. She opened her mouth but closed it and shrugged as though she didn't have a right to voice the question that everyone in the room wanted to ask.

Vilay's bottom lip trembled as she closed her eyes. "I fell in love with a guy when I was sixteen, and he took me to Memphis. He changed the moment we got there. He kept me from my family. They do that so they can have control." Madison looked away, but Vilay lifted her chin so she could look directly into those tear-filled eyes. "I was scared, Madison. I was in a different city; I didn't know anyone, and didn't know what I could do. First, it was, 'If you love me, you'll take care of my boys.' Soon it was another guy, then another, and then another. One of them …" Vilay hesitated a long while before peeling off her coat; she then raised her blouse and showed the scars that crisscrossed her body.

The collective gasps that filled the room were enough to make Vilay wince, but it was Nalina's arms that went around her and held her securely; then Nikki joined in, holding her from the other side. Anjali and Gina were too shocked to move, and they couldn't even if they wanted to. Madison's grip on their hands was just that strong.

Vilay slowly relaxed and put her hands up to hold on to her two sisters. When she pulled away, the tears were almost blinding. "I, too, was afraid to leave because I thought he would kill me. I'm a police officer now, and everyday I see grown women who get stuck in situations like that."

"But how did you get away?" Madison asked, her hands gripping the sheets a little too tight.

Vilay focused on Madison and moved in to sit next to Gina. "He went out to get his next girl. He thought he had me doped up enough that I couldn't move. But I found the strength to get out of that bed," Vilay whispered, pausing only when Madison reached up to wipe a tear from her eye. "I didn't have any money. The woman at the window of the Greyhound station gave me a ticket to come home.

"It was eleven hours on that bus, riding on the edge of the seat because it hurt to lean back on the cushion. I kept looking around because I thought he was coming after me." Vilay shifted, and went back to sit on the bed, noting that Madison released Anjali's hand to hold onto hers instead. "I spent almost ten hours at Cook County Hospital before they even looked at me. It took a long time for me to heal. I was ashamed for my mother to see me like this. I didn't die from those drugs he gave me, and I refused to live my life in fear.

"I had to fight back on my own, get myself together, and get into a line of work where I could feel safe." Vilay looked around at the women in the room. "But you're not alone like I was. I'm here to help you." She scanned the encouraging faces of her new family and felt more empowered than she could put into words. "We're here to help you. And you're going to be just fine. I promise you."

"We're so happy that you're alive and safe," Nalina said softly to Madison, though she continued to rub Vilay's back. "You don't know how much we worried about you."

Gina looked up at the tubes that were going into Madison's arm. "Sometimes I would see young girls about your age and ask if they needed something, anything, anything at all. I would help them in whatever way I could, hoping that someone, somewhere was looking out for you." She stroked Madison's hand. "I couldn't bear to lose you again. And I don't want you feeling sorry for yourself. You still have so much life ahead of you. Think about what you want to do, and we'll do our best to make it happen."

"This might have been a rocky start," Nikki said quietly, "but you've got a kickass team behind you, baby girl. And we'll be there."

Madison tore her gaze away and looked out of the window to the sun pushing the clouds away for its turn in the sky.

"My mother." She quickly looked up at Gina and corrected herself, "I mean … Joan was so angry that Edgar paid so much attention to me. He was always like a second father to me. But when my daddy died, he really stepped up and Joan didn't like it."

Gina's expression went dark. Nalina gripped her hand to hold her steady.

"That's why I went with Quasi," Madison sobbed. "I thought he loved me. It's all my fault."

"No, sweetie." Vilay put her arm around her shoulder, taking care not to touch her wounds. "This isn't your fault. You didn't want this to happen. You didn't deserve for any of this to happen."

Just then, a nurse came into the room, followed by a slender man with hazel eyes that twinkled with mirth. He gave them an update on Madison's condition. He seemed hopeful for a slow but full recovery. His parting comment, "A loving family's support goes a long way toward healing."

"She has that," Gina said, scanning her daughter's faces. "And then some."

"I'm scared," Madison whispered the moment the doctor and his nurse walked out. "He's going to come after me. And if he finds out about you, he'll hurt you too. And he'll get away with it. Just like he does all the time."

Gina stood slowly, a steely expression on her face. "Madison, I promise you that won't happen. We're going to do everything in our power to keep you safe." She looked at each of the women, who nodded. "So don't you worry about a thing." Gina pressed a kiss to her daughter's temple. "I'm going to take care of a little business. Your sisters will stay here with you and take care of you. All right?"

Madison nodded but was reluctant to release her hand until Nalina took over.

Gina gave Nalina a pointed look, then left the room.

Nalina looked back at Madison for a moment, then a morbid thought clicked into place, and she froze. She had seen that look before—in her reflection the night that Sri had tried to rape her. He didn't know how close he came to death that night. She felt a tightening in her gut. Gina wasn't coming back.

Nalina kissed Madison on the cheek, then gestured for Nikki to take over her spot. She turned slowly and gazed into Anjali's eyes. She smiled as she mouthed the words, "Do your thing, Joy."

Anjali nodded, then put her focus back on Madison and continued offering comfort and a compassionate ear.

Vilay peered at Nalina for a moment, then stood and said, "I'll be back," and followed her out of the room.

* * *

Bustling noises behind her and the scent of two familiar perfumes alerted Gina that she now had company at the pick-up window of the hospital's pharmacy. She slipped the money and a card to the woman behind the window, turned her back to her daughters, placed the needles and the bottles in her purse, and strolled toward the elevator.

"Mama, where are you going?"

Gina locked gazes with Nalina as Vilay swung out and blocked the path to the open elevator.

"Don't do anything stupid," Vilay warned. "Let the police handle this."

"Like they did before? They knew, Vilay. They *used* her! You know how wrong that was on every level." Gina's chest heaved in an effort to get her emotions under control. "And now she can't feel safe. That's up to us. That's up to me."

Nalina put a hand on her mother's shoulder. "I can't talk you out of this, can I?"

Gina didn't say a word, but her look spoke volumes.

"She's going to need you, Gina," Vilay whispered, her expression laced with concern.

"She's going to need to feel safe."

Nalina reached up to wipe away the tears falling from her mother's face. "We're going to get through this."

"Yes, you will." Gina reached out and embraced Vilay, then held on to Nalina for a long moment.

She stepped into the elevator, and it closed behind her, but not before she mouthed the words, "I love you. I love you both."

Nalina looked at Vilay a long moment, then reached into her pocket. Alarm coursed through her and she whispered, "Vilay …"

She turned to take in the panic-stricken expression on Nalina's face.

"My cell phone is missing."

"So report it."

"That's not the issue, Vi. I had it when I walked out here," she responded, searching her pockets a second and third time. "There's only one reason why she would take it."

Vilay just looked at her.

"D'Angelo."

Vilay mumbled something Nalina couldn't quite catch as she ran to the stairwell and disappeared.

Chapter 43

Gina had the taxi pull into the empty gas station lot, gave the driver a generous tip, and walked over to where the commanding figure of a man in a dark leather coat awaited her. She hadn't wanted to involve her daughters any more than she already had, but seeing the fear in Madison's eyes and hearing what Vilay had been through had made the next course of action clear. D'Angelo, when all was said and done, was the man who could get things done. She had taken his number from Nalina's phone but used her 800 number to contact him. She knew that unfamiliar number was the only reason he had answered the phone.

"Thank you for coming."

"As if I had a choice," he said smoothly, giving her a quick onceover.

D'Angelo opened the door to his SUV, but Gina shook her head, saying, "This won't take long. Why haven't you called her?"

"I need to tie up some loose ends," he replied. "Can't do it with that woman on my mind."

Gina took a good long look at his handsome face—the milk chocolate skin. She peered closely at him, and recognized some of the features as belonging to someone she had known a long time ago.

"Where are you from?"

His dark brown gaze locked on her. "Right here in Chicago."

"I mean your people. Where were you raised?"

"Robert Taylor Homes."

Gina nodded, and for a moment her heart constricted. She would recognize those piercing dark eyes, that strong jaw line, and those lips anywhere.

"We didn't exactly come out here for a background check," he snapped, his eyes flashing with impatience. "What's on your mind?"

In one minute, Gina summed up what she needed, and D'Angelo shook his head. "Ma'am, I can't let you go up in there by yourself. I wouldn't let your daughter do it, and it definitely wouldn't be a good look if I let her mother do it."

"Then come with me," Gina said with a shrug of indifference. "Makes no difference to me."

His gaze swept over the area before coming back to her. "Wrong building, wrong people. That's just like declaring outright war."

Gina nodded a moment and took that in. "Then all you have to do is point me in the right direction. I'll take it from there."

D'Angelo leaned back on the driver's side door of his SUV and grinned. "You're definitely Nalina's mother."

"What makes you say that?"

"Mannerisms. But you look a lot alike. And you're stubborn too."

Gina smiled. He was certainly right about that, but she wondered if he knew how much he was like his own father. She realized that fate had a funny way of coming back with a calling card. What were the odds that a child of hers would fall for the son of a man she once loved? She would have bet a million to one that they would never have crossed paths.

"How's the little girl?" he asked, keeping his focus on a car that slowed down as it passed by the station. He hooked an arm under Gina's and moved her to the other side of the SUV to finish the conversation; away from open view of those passing by.

"She's alive, but she'll need some skin grafts eventually. But she won't feel safe until someone makes her safe. People have failed her in every other way. I can't fail her in this."

D'Angelo took a moment to ponder that and looked out over the Pershing Road traffic. "I'm not feeling right about this."

"I can understand that, but it's not going to change what I have to do. I'd prefer to do it with the right intel, and not have to fumble my way through this with people who are less … efficient."

D'Angelo's focus shifted to the group of men bunched near the entrance of the building.

"I'm just going to have a little talk with him," she said. "Make sure he understands that coming after Madison or her family—her real family—is a suicide mission."

"Trust me, he knows."

"I want to be certain of that. For myself," she countered evenly. She placed a hand over his. "You can understand that, right?" At his hesitation, she opened her coat and took a small silver box. "See, I don't have any weapons that would make him suspect."

"So what's with the needles?" he asked, glancing at the small packet hooked on the outside of her waistband.

"Medication. Diabetes runs in the family."

D'Angelo gave her a long, hard look and pursed his lips in disapproval of that obvious lie.

"He's in that one on the end. That's his home. The other place was all about business." D'Angelo gestured to the group of men gathered in front of the building. "They're not going to let you past the door."

"I have something he wants; he'll talk to me. As long as I can get through the front door."

D'Angelo looked at her a long moment, then shook his head at having to accept the inevitable. "Tell him that his partner, Vic, said you have a way to get him out of town. Vic was just picked up by the police, so Trey can't check that story. That might get you through the door, but between here and there, you'd better come up with something to float the rest of that lie."

Gina nodded and took a deep breath.

"And exactly how were you planning to get out of here when you're done?"

She just looked at him.

"Jesus," he mumbled, running a hand through his short-cropped hair. "Lina's going to kill me."

She put out a hand to calm him. "Sometimes we have to make the hard choices for the ones we love. I have to make sure Madison is safe. And I don't want anyone else with blood on their hands."

D'Angelo glared at her, and she could see the war he fought on whether to leave or join her.

"Let me talk to you about something," she said, moving closer to him. "Do you love my daughter?"

"Who wouldn't? She's the finest person I've ever known. She has heart. She has soul. She has ... passion."

"Then you come correct, young blood," Gina said, putting a finger to his chest. "It's nothing to just lay up with a woman; any male can do that. But it takes a real man to build a life with her."

"Build a life?" He shook his head. "We're from two different worlds."

"Then you have some hard choices of your own to make." Gina placed her hand back on his leather-covered arm. He looked down at it but didn't make an attempt to move. "You'll have to give up some things and so will she. What are you willing to give up to get what you want? When you turn fifty, are you going to be in this line of work?" She took a slow, steady look at him from head to toe, then focused on his eyes—his most arresting feature. "You have all this—the women, the cars, money—but do you have love?"

"I have ... Nalina."

"But do you really have her or is it just surface love?" Gina placed that hand on his icy cheek.

He flexed with that instant warmth but didn't resist.

"My daughter's torn because she feels some kind of way about you. Willing to take a little leap just to go with how she feels. Are you worth it? Are you worth her sacrificing her life to be with you? Because she can't ride the fence on this one."

A vein throbbed at his temple as he glared at her.

"What will it take to walk away and do something else with your life, really?" Gina searched his eyes for some sign she was reaching him. "Things are changing, and if you don't understand that, then you're not as smart as she gives you credit for. It's time to get out while you have your life."

"You don't understand," he said, his eyes boring into hers with an intensity that shook her to the very core. "There's more to my life than what you see. It's complicated … really." She felt that he wanted to say much more, but something was holding him back.

"I didn't say that it'll be easy. You've racked up some good karma and some bad. You can't get away from the bad, but you can lessen the blow you've got coming by balancing the scales. It's time for you to stop sucking the life's blood out of your people. It's time to open a vein and give some back."

D'Angelo sighed and tried to remove himself from her grasp, but she held on.

"Walk away from this. Walk away and do what you can to make sure the youngsters coming behind you get out of this alive."

She slipped a card into his palm, before he looked down at the hands she placed onto his face. D'Angelo tried to move away, but she held him steady, as though their connection was a direct transfusion of power.

"What makes you think that anybody would listen to me? Especially with everything I've done. I'd be a hypocrite telling some kid don't do drugs, don't sell drugs."

"You're the perfect person to say it," she countered. "You know firsthand what they're up against. They'd rather hear it from you than some suit-wearing bum who's only smiling for the cameras and lining his own pockets."

D'Angelo grimaced and shifted his stance as he looked at her. The uncertainty in his eyes made her know she had to press her point home. "It won't mean that everyone will listen, but there's going to be a chosen few who will make a different choice. And that's one less youngster on the street, one less in jail … one less body in the morgue. And that matters, D'Angelo."

She shook her head as she remembered one snippet of information. "D'Angelo. She says that your real name is D'Angelo. I'm going to call you that. It tends to happen when people are about to transition from one life to another." She took his hand in hers to get his focus away from the activity across the street. "You think your life matters to no one. It matters to her. I couldn't save your father from the life he chose."

D'Angelo's head whipped up to look at her, as he tried to break her grasp on his hand without hurting her.

"But I realized he wasn't able to participate in his own rescue. Fear kept him from leaving this place. Fear helped put him six feet under."

D'Angelo's lips moved, but not a single sound came out.

"What are you afraid of, D'Angelo Michaels? Are you going to let fear check your ass out of here before you can make your mark on the world?"

He looked over to the building, then back to her. "I can't let you do this, ma'am."

"And you can't go with me either," she said, giving him a slow grin. "What's the first rule of the street?"

D'Angelo released a resigned sigh. "When you're about to do some dirt, do it all by your dammy."

"I grew up in the same place you did, and I'll never forget that rule." She extended her hand to him; he took it and gave it a firm shake before she embraced him and slipped an envelope into his pocket. "I have to do this alone. I can't risk that you won't be around to take care of my daughter. She needs you. I'm counting on you."

"How did you know my father?"

"Rakim?" she whispered, feeling a twinge of sadness pierce her heart. "He was the one who didn't get away. I got out while I could, made a life for myself—one a lot of people might question, but it was my life, and I make no apologies for it."

She moved past him, then turned back to where he stood. "People often make one mistake when they're trying to make a change. Like in the movies, there's always, 'I'll do it after this one last score, one last hit, this one last time.' And it always ends up not working out the way they thought it would. You have more choices than your father ever did. Unlike him, you don't owe anybody a damn thing. So make a move, make it fast, and don't look back. You got that?"

After a few seconds, he said, "Got it."

She gave him a small, bitter smile. "One last thing. I've paid for the shit I've done. I'm still paying—gained some, lost some. It's coming back good right now, but I have one more thing to do before I can be at peace." She looked at the building, then back at him. "I want to know that my daughter is in good hands."

D'Angelo walked over to her, leaned down, planted a kiss on her cheek, then watched as she walked away.

Moments later, he whipped out his phone and made a quick call, then pulled his gun an trailed several yards behind Gina.

* * *

Friday - 4:02 p.m.

Vilay tore out of the hospital and ran to the cab sitting at the corner of 59th and Ellis. Nalina had finally received a call from D'Angelo, and now time seemed to be on fast forward. He didn't say exactly what Gina's plans were, but Vilay knew enough about Gina to know that she was on a justice mission. And she hadn't missed the fact that Gina had gone to the pharmacy before leaving the building. What had the woman done?

She banged on the window and said, "Hey, let's get moving."

The bushy-haired driver shrugged and continued with his meal. "I'm on break."

"Break's over."

He waved her off and rolled up the window.

She pressed the badge to the glass, then pulled back her coat to flash her gun. "If you don't get your ass moving, I will put a bullet in you and take the damn car."

Seconds later, they were tearing up Cottage Grove Avenue toward the Ida B. Wells projects.

* * *

The guards at the door of the low-rise project searched her, then alerted Trey to her presence. When he peered outside through a tiny crack in the door, she said, "I hear you've got a little heat on your ass and need to make moves. Vic sent me to help. I owe him a favor."

The men pulled back her coat, searching her body until they came upon something hard in her breast area.

"What's that?" the shorter of the two asked.

"Can I pull it out?"

"Slow. Real slow," he warned.

She reached in, whipped out her cell and showed it to him. "I've got one on the other side. One's for business. The other's for … pleasure." She smiled. "You need to check that too? 'Cause it seems more like y'all are just trying to feel me up. Last time I checked, guns weren't square shaped."

Trey Dawg said, "Naw, let her in."

He was tall—a menacing figure if she had ever seen one, and his eyes were beady and cold. He wore a lounging suit over his muscular frame, as though he were in an upscale north shore apartment rather than the heart of the ghetto. And he had nerve enough to think he was a little bit handsome—as evidenced in the care he had taken with his hair and beard.

One of the guards reached for the square object in the other side of her bra.

"I said, let her in."

She raised an eyebrow at the angered man, then swept into the place with two guards flanking her sides. She was met with the overpowering stench of weed and liquor. She took a short, shallow breath and braced herself for what she had to do. "Can you be ready to leave within the hour?"

"Why should I trust you?"

"At this point, who else can you trust?" She slipped off the suede gloves. "The police are hot on your ass. The FBI and DEA are closing in. And if I can find you, they're going to be right behind me. I thought Vic said you needed a way out of Chicago—and fast. We're doing entirely too much talking, so I guess he was wrong."

She reached into her pocket, pulled a business card from her gold case, and flicked it towards him. "Remember to tell your partner that he owes me one regardless of whether you take up the offer. Trust me, Vic isn't going down for any of this." She gave him a two-finger salute and turned to walk out. "I hope it all works out for you."

"Wait," he said, gesturing for the guards to block her exit. "Let's talk."

"In private," she said, giving him a pointed look. "Too many ears. Too many lips—all it takes is one wrong word in the wrong ears and the right amount of money in their hands. Then you'll have more wind and bullets on your ass than freedom."

Trey's gaze narrowed on her.

"It has to be just you and me." She wet her lips with the tip of a moist tongue. "Vic said he owed you one and that I'm supposed to see to all of your needs."

He scanned her from head to toe, and for a second, a flash of pleasure lit in his eyes. "Y'all give us a minute." He waited for the men to leave the room. Glancing at the card she had handed him, he said, "Yeah, I heard about you. Run that place for rehabbing ex-cons. Took some of my best soldiers. They said some bullshit about how they wanted to live right. Whatever the fuck that means. This right here"—he gestured to the powdery substance and the tiny crystal-like balls on the table—"is all the get right I need."

"You know, the best cover is an honest front, right?"

Trey Dawg chuckled. "See, I knew you wasn't legit."

Gina scanned the area, took a long look at the kitchen, then inched forward to peer out of the window, making sure there was no one else close enough to slip up on her. His guards were stretched out on the ground. She held up a hand, signaling that she needed more time. D'Angelo gave her nod. She finally focused in on Trey again, noticing that he kept as much distance between them as possible. She reached up and took out the pins that held her hair. When it fell down to her shoulders, his gaze followed every movement.

"I have a connection down in Natchez who's running a tight operation. G Man can work you in until you can start somewhere else. You'll have to be ready to leave with me," she said in a husky tone, lowering her lashes before looking directly at him. "You'll have to act like you're going to run a quick errand or something. None of your boys can come."

Trey nodded, but he was totally focused on her body. She smiled and slowly opened her coat, giving him a full-frontal view of the outfit that draped her body. The move, an invite of sorts, caused him to lick his lips in anticipation. Gina removed her coat and gently placed it on the back of the chair. She smiled at him, watching his gaze roam over her curves, and he moved in even closer.

"Vic said that I should do whatever you need," she whispered. "Said that you were the best at what you do." Gina lowered her lashes. She pretended to bat them seductively, but she was actually taking in the items along the kitchen counter. She ignored the fact that he reached out to stroke her breasts. "So what kind of operation were you running?"

"Drugs and ho's—the best kind of money." He moved in and palmed her ass, stroking the winter white cashmere slacks as though he had never felt anything quite so soft. "Easy come, easy go."

Gina nodded as though she admired the hustle and the fact that he was trying to arouse her. "Young girls, right?"

"They bring in the most money," he whispered in her ear, moaning when she reached down and massaged his erection. "Them white boys pay top dollar for young pussy."

She kept her gaze on him, unzipped his pants, and went inside his boxers, stroking until his breathing hitched. "And where do you get them?"

"Some from the 'burbs; some just get lucky and … land on my

doorstep," he said with a low chuckle.

"Lucky, huh?" She gave him a casual smile as he throbbed under her ministrations. "Would all of your girls feel that way?" She nodded to the slice of skin missing from his cheek.

"That ho cut me." His head rolled back, as his balls pulsed with a need to release. Gina looked down at his arms and saw the crude bandages that tried to cover the slices of skin missing from his upper arm.

For a moment she wanted to smile. Madison was definitely her daughter.

"But I got her good," he ground out, in between the hard strokes to his prized possession. "She ain't gonna be good for nobody. Stupid little bitch."

Gina felt him pulse with an oncoming orgasm. "Yes," she said in a sultry whisper. "I want to give you the right type of going away present."

"Is that right?"

She moaned a promise of things to come. He eyes closed allowing her complete control. She reached into her bra, extracted what she needed from that silver box. An unfriendly gaze arrowed in on him and his hazed expression. "Stupid little bitch, huh? That's not a nice thing to say about my daughter."

His eyes popped open. She squeezed his nuts hard enough for them to pop. He gasped for breath as the needle came down and jabbed him in the right eyeball. Gina quickly pressed the plunger, emptying the contents into his shaking body. She snatched a dirty towel from the floor, rammed it in his mouth, and pressed him downward. Gina had to struggle to keep him from thrashing about and alerting his guards.

Trey jerked upward and went sprawling across the room until he bounced off the wall and landed on the kitchen table. His eyes rolled back in his head as the first set of drugs took effect. Gina followed with the second and third doses, which rendered him unable to move. She put a pot on to boil, then retrieved a solid pair of butcher knives and a rolling pin from the kitchen.

Gina grinned down at him spread out on that rickety wooden table like Christ himself and said, "Madison sends her regards."

Chapter 44

Vilay pulled up in front of the building just in time to see an officer slap a pair of handcuffs over Gina's wrists. She flashed her badge and ran toward them. "Hey, I've got this. I'm the one who called it in."

"But she's our collar."

"Stand down; this is part of an ongoing investigation." She gestured to Newhouse's scowling form. "Our unit's in on it, and so are they."

Newhouse gave them a quick nod and glared openly at her. The officers glanced at her badge—probably committing the number to memory to report back to their superior officers. The shit would hit the fan from there, and it would probably all land on her. They filled her in on the scene, and just as quickly she laid into Newhouse for mishandling the case.

"Take her, and get out of here," Newhouse said through clenched teeth. "You can snap my head off some other time."

"If you had waited," Vilay said to Gina as she ushered her to the nearest squad car, "it could've been done in a way where it was justifiable homicide. Someone else could have taken care of the problem."

"It's not the same," Gina replied without an ounce of remorse in her tone. "I wouldn't feel it, wouldn't feel any satisfaction."

"It wasn't about you," Vilay shot back, gripping the arms of her coat, shaking her just a little. "We all felt it, but don't you realize that by doing it this way, you take yourself out of the picture? When Nikki needs you. Anjali needs you. Madison needs you. Nalina needs you. When … when I need you?"

Gina locked gazes with her and saw the truth and pain in her eyes. And only then did she feel a moment of regret—but only a moment.

"We all wanted a piece of that man," Vilay growled. "You didn't have to let emotion into this. I could have handled it. There's enough evidence for the FBI and DEA to make sure that he got what was coming to him."

Gina thought about that a long while. "You're right. I was thinking with my heart instead of my head."

Trey Dawg's guards were being ushered into squad cars. The paramedics wheeled a stretcher toward the ambulance. The crowd gathered around the building let out a collective gasp when the spectators saw the state Trey was in. Some looked over to where Gina and Vilay stood, and Vilay could almost swear there was a mixture of fear and admiration in their eyes for the classy woman standing next to her.

"I have to take you to the station and book you. I can't get around that."

Gina touched her hand. "I wouldn't want you to."

"I can understand why you would want to peel every inch of skin from his body," Vilay said softly. "But did you have to put the rolling pin all the way up his ass and leave it that way? You know somebody else has to pull that thing out."

Gina looked over at Vilay, who was trying real hard not to smile.

"Don't say anything without a lawyer."

Gina nodded and asked, "How is Madison?"

"Asking for you."

Gina lowered her gaze to the snow-covered ground, and the tears began to flow. "She's safe now. She has all of you. And you all have each other."

"I'm not saying that I don't agree with what you did," Vilay whispered, wiping Gina's tears before they froze. "I just think you could have waited so we, as a group, could have come up with a better plan so none of us would end up in jail."

Seeing the tender gesture that Vilay had made to the suspect, one of the first officers on the scene came over and inquired, "What's your relationship to the suspect?"

Vilay hesitated only a minute before replying, "She's my mother."

* * *

Nikki disconnected the call and blew out a breath. "You won't have to worry about Trey Dawg anymore."

Madison's head whipped up to look at her. She pushed aside the remaining bites of the burger and fries that Nikki had snuck out to get her, amid Anjali's protests.

"He'll never hurt anyone again. The cops just arrested Gina."

Anjali looked at Madison. Then she said to Nikki, "She shouldn't hear this."

"We can't treat her as some little kid," Nalina replied. "She's been through too much. She needs to know some things."

Nikki then shared what Vilay had told her.

The silence that fell over the room was unsettling.

"Madison, you understand what she said?" Nalina finally asked.

"She killed him?"

"No, but she came damn close," Nikki replied, almost sounding proud of that glad fact. "That man won't be able to move any time soon, if ever." When she described what the injuries he sustained would actually mean, Madison's shoulders visibly relaxed as she asked, "My mother did that?"

Nikki and Anjali nodded. Nalina answered with a soft, "Yes."

Then for the first time her sisters had ever witnessed, Madison actually smiled.

* * *

Later that night, Anjali, Nalina, and Nikki were sprawled out on the chairs in Madison's room.

They were awakened by a harsh voice that demanded, "I need to speak with my daughter."

All gazes shifted to the door and landed on the ivory-skinned woman dressed in all white and the ebony hued man standing right next to her. Madison shifted on the bed and looked to her sisters as though pleading for help.

"Alone."

"That's not happening," Nalina said, going to stand next to Nikki at the end of the bed. "Whatever you have to say to her, you'll have to say to all of us."

"I'm so sorry," she said, trying to move around them to get to Madison. "I didn't know."

"You knew," Madison spat. "You just wanted me away from him," she said nodding toward Edgar, who glared at the ice queen.

Nikki bore down on the woman, forcing her to back up. "Did you know that she didn't leave that monster because he threatened to kill you?" Nikki jabbed a finger in the woman's chest. "You? The mother who didn't even have the decency to tell her real mother where she was."

Joan put a hand to her chest and backed away from Nikki but landed on Nalina.

"If it takes five days, five weeks, five months, or five years," Anjali said, rising slowly from her spot on Madison's bed. "I'm going to see that you pay for what you've done."

Nikki came to stand next to Anjali. "So keep looking over your shoulder. You never know when one of us will be right behind you."

"She was the one who left with him," Joan shrieked, a shaking fist aimed at Anjali's face. "She's a whore just like her mother."

Anjali slapped the woman so hard she reeled back and slumped against the wall. "Call my mother a whore again, and you'll be picking your teeth up from the ground."

Nikki and Nalina exchanged a surprised look. All gazes shifted to Anjali, whose skin was flushed with anger.

"All this because you were jealous of a little girl," Anjali said. "You cared more about money and pleasing that man than the safety of another human being. Doesn't take many words to say who the real whore is around here."

Joan backed away, glowering at all of them. "I'll be back with my lawyer."

"No you won't. Her real mother has this under control," Nalina said, holding onto Madison's hand. "She doesn't need your half-ass attempt at mothering. We're her real family. And we love her."

"Legally, she's still my daughter," Joan threatened, lifting her chin. "I'll take her to court."

"And it will be the ugliest battle since the McCoys and the Hatfields," Nikki fired back, holding onto Anjali's arm so she wouldn't lay a hand on the woman again. "I'm sure the media will love it—you being famous and all. He left everything to his princess. If Madison died, all of his money would come to you. You wanted her dead because you were jealous and greedy," she spat, as Joan's eyes went wide with shock. "Wanted Trey Dawg to finish her off. I'm sure you don't want the world to see what the real Joan Engstrom is like. Might lose some of those famous clients. People don't like to be associated with cold-hearted bitches. Especially ones that leave their children in the arms of a predator because it suits them."

Her lover moved forward and tried to lead Joan away. But Nikki stopped them at the door saying, "Call security. No, better yet, call Vilay." She pulled back her blazer and showed him the weapon she held. "You're not going anywhere until she gets here to deal with you."

"You can't hold us here."

"The hell we can't," Nalina said.

"She lies. She lies all the time," Joan said, her fist mere inches from Nalina's face. "And you have no rights. I'm her mother."

"Before you go all Mama Bear on us," Nalina said, wiggling her fingers in mock fear, "remember that when your cub called you for help, you turned her away. And remember this one thing—she *stayed* in that hell hole because he threatened to kill *you*. She loved you even though you didn't deserve it." Nalina pointed toward the door. "Now stand down before I put my foot somewhere it truly belongs."

"I'm the only one with a legal right to be here," Joan said with a haughty lift of her chin, though it was evident in her lover's anxious expression that he didn't agree with her sentiments.

"She has four sisters who are going to take very good care of her," Nikki said. "She doesn't need you."

Joan lifted her chin and glared at each one of them. "You all don't have any say here. I'll make sure the hospital is aware of that."

"They already have the paperwork they need," Nalina said, dismissing her with a wave. "Your lies won't work here. You've got nothing coming lady."

"Where's Gina?"

"She had a little conversation with the man who hurt Madison," Nikki said, giving her a sly grin. "He probably won't live to see tomorrow. Now that's a *real* Mama Bear for you. I want you to stick around until Gina gets back. I'm sure she'd loooooove to have a long talk with you too."

Joan lost every ounce of color she had, but it didn't keep her from trying to make a hurried move toward the door.

"And Joan," Madison said, which caused the trembling woman to turn back to face her. "After my real mother shows you what she's made of, I want your things out of my house tonight. You won't see a dime of *my* money."

Joan stiffened with anger.

"I'm sure daddy wanted it that way."

Chapter 45

Eight Months Later
October, 2003

The teal waters of the Atlantic Ocean were calm under the Bahamian sun. Gina and her daughters were spread out on loungers soaking up the warm rays. The coral stone of the Atlantis Royal Towers provided a surreal backdrop and luxurious accommodations for their family vacation. The women had been there for a week with one more to go.

"You took her to a shooting range," Anjali said, glaring at Vilay.

Vilay chuckled at her sister's indignation and adjusted the silk wrap around her body. "She has to learn more than just how to cook and clean, Anjali."

"But a shooting range? She's too young." Anjali looked over at Gina, who was stretched out on a lounge chair wearing a two-piece bikini that accentuated a body that had received appreciative stares from men and women alike. "Mother, talk some sense into this woman."

Gina lifted the sunglasses from over her eyes. "Don't ask me," she countered smoothly. "I learned to shoot when I was six."

"Good grief." Anjali gave a weary shake of her head. "What is this world coming to?"

"Every woman should know how to handle a gun, even if she never has to use it," Vilay replied.

Gina accepted the lotion Madison gave her and spread it over her legs. "My grandmother always said, 'Put a Smith & Wesson in a person's face, and it can start a conversation or end one.'"

"She ain't never lied." Nikki caught the quick glance exchanged between Vilay, Gina, and Anjali, and gave them a brief nod.

"Hey, let's get something to eat." Vilay gestured to the snack shack just at the end of a winding concrete path. "There should be something we can sink our teeth into."

Madison scrambled off her lounger and traipsed behind Nikki and Vilay.

"How is she doing, really?" Gina asked Anjali, who moved over and settled into the lounger beside hers.

"It's slow going, but she's learning to trust again. She knows that we're really there for her. She still sleeps better if Nalina is in the bedroom with her, but more and more, she's coming into her own."

Nalina's gaze followed her three sisters until they were out of range. "Nikki's teaching her to journal so she can get it all out of her head. When she's through, maybe she'll turn it into a novel or something. She wants to help other girls so they won't make the same mistakes she did." Nalina looked off at a couple strolling hand in hand toward the lazy river, then quickly looked away. "She's doing all right in school; she struggles with math, though."

Gina gave them a smile. "So did I."

"And this new math is a killer. It doesn't look anything like the stuff they taught us," Anjali said, smoothing on more sunscreen.

Nalina's expression became solemn. She constantly worried about her baby sister, but more than that, she missed D'Angelo something fierce. She tried not to let her pain affect other people, but each day that went by with no word from him, the more sullen she became. "Her first tests came back negative for everything. She'll still have to be tested every six months for the next few years."

"And we'll help her deal with whatever comes," Gina countered smoothly.

Nalina sighed softly as she leaned back on the lounger and retrieved a novel from the glass table next to her.

Gina looked at both of them, taking in Anjali's sad expression and Nalina's frustrated attempt to find her page in the romance novel she'd been struggling to read all week. "In the meantime, she can still lead a normal life."

Nalina looked up to see a couple snatching a kiss as they walked along the stone path. She shoved the novel underneath her chair and turned away from Gina and Anjali for a moment. She wished waving a magic wand would make it all go away—the pain she felt, the agony that Madison had gone through. But life had a strange way of putting a rocky road where there should be a smooth path, or putting a curve where a straight line would have made things so much easier.

"You're thinking about D'Angelo," Gina said quietly, rubbing a hand over Nalina's bare arm.

Nalina nodded and struggled not to tear up. "Mama, I can't get him out of my mind. He just disappeared on me." She turned onto her side, focusing on her mother. "I thought he loved me. Not knowing what's happened to him makes it even worse. I guess it's best that I stick with my own kind and leave the thug loving to the books." The bitter tone lingered in the air, and it was enough to make Gina tighten a hand on her daughter's arm.

"Sweetheart, let me tell you what I've learned about love and life," Gina said, sitting up so she could look Nalina directly in the eyes. "The heart doesn't look at a person's bank account; it looks at the soul and spirit. There isn't a 'my kind' to stick with. I've been with the best of men—millionaires, men at the top of their game. What I found is that they all have their flaws—jealousy, possessiveness, and freakish natures—just like everyone else."

She wiped away the tears sliding down Nalina's cheeks. "The only difference is perception. They look good on paper, but add stress or money, and you'll see what folks are made of. They're strong. They're weak; they're sinners; they're saints. But they're all human."

Gina placed the floppy straw hat on her head, bent it forward to block the bright sun, and settled in as though ready to take a nap. "Some people think I'm an angel—ask those ex-cons who are living good lives now. They say I'm a goddess, when all I am is a woman living my life the best way I know how. Sinner and saint. I take life like it comes, and I don't have time for regrets. Regrets don't change a thing."

She locked gazes with Nalina. "You remember that. Cherish the time you had with him. I've been telling you from day one that you have to believe in the love he had for you. You just have to have faith that he will come to you when it's time."

The trio was on its way back with a tray of food and beverages in hand. Madison chatted happily along the way, her skin much darker than it had been a week before. She wore a full body bathing suit, and her curves were turning heads left and right. The sisters never let her go anywhere without one of them. Overprotective? Yes. But she loved every minute of it and knew how to back them off when she needed her space.

"Look at Nikki. Happy and pregnant and so damn intelligent," Gina said to Nalina.

Nalina laughed at that statement. "You're just saying that because she's your daughter," she said, frowning as Vilay handed her items to Madison and pulled out her cell.

Gina chuckled as she mused, "She might not be so happy to find out that I invited her parents to come."

"Why would you do that?"

"She needs to heal, and Chuck insisted. Her baby is going to need all the love it can get. People make the mistake of recreating the same issues over and over, and healing with her mother and father will only make things better."

"What if she isn't feeling you on that?"

"Then I'll fall back on every mother's motto."

Nalina swung a gaze at Gina, one eyebrow raised.

"Because I said so, that's why."

Nalina let go of a small laugh. "Did you invite Madison's mother too?"

"And catch another case?" Gina huffed. "That cold, deceitful, heartless--."

"Mama, don't get yourself worked up," Nalina warned.

Gina sighed, continuing with. "She didn't have a loving bone in her body. Not even for her husband."

The others had almost made it back. Gina watched their movements along the path.

"Vilay. Her strength, her integrity. I can't say enough about how beautiful she really is. When she started giving, she started growing. And that's how she was able to mend her relationship with her mother. She laughs so much now; she seems like a totally different person."

Nalina scowled as she looked at Vilay's retreating form. "Where is she going with that cell phone? This is supposed to be a family vacation. No outside anything."

"Let her be." Gina stilled Nalina's anger with a simple touch. "I know you girls are still angry at Vilay for arresting me."

"She didn't have to do that."

Gina gave her an indifferent shrug as she sat up and placed a hand on Nalina's shoulder. "I didn't give her much choice. I knew what I was doing. I didn't care either way. And Vilay did help me."

"Yes, right into a jail cell," Nalina said sourly.

"But only until I made bail."

Nalina folded her arms across her full breasts. "If she hadn't turned you in, there wouldn't have been a trial."

"Sweetheart, I wasn't innocent by any stretch of the imagination. And how do you think that evidence disappeared so that the case was thrown out?"

Nalina's expression went blank.

Gina smiled, stretched out on the lounger, and placed the sunglasses back on her face.

"Vilay did that?"

"So give her a break." Gina looked down at her bare left hand.

"Why do you keep looking there," Nalina asked."

"Because I know you're worried about your sister and the fact that the Kasturi family is still pushing Anil to get an annulment."

"He's not going through with it. Sri's just angry because I signed those papers and Kalyan immediately asked me to marry him."

"Well, why wouldn't he? Just because Sri didn't see your value, doesn't mean that another man won't. What did you say?"

"I told him that I was flattered but I couldn't because I was already in love with someone else. He seemed to take it in stride. Sri was livid."

The two women shared a laugh. "You know, the Kasturi family was only half right," Gina said. "Anjali is not the child of Sanjay's mistress; she *is* his wife's child."

"I don't understand."

Gina unhooked the chain from around her neck and slid off the ring. She slipped it on and wiggled her fingers, displaying a platinum band.

"You and Papa got married," Nalina said in a breathy whisper. But it was loud enough for Anjali, who had been pretending to be asleep on the lounger across from them, to sit up and take notice.

They shared a look—Anjali's expression was pure confusion, and Nalina's was one that showed acceptance. Gina inclined her head at both of them. Nalina smiled, but it didn't quite reach her eyes. She was happy that her parents had found true love after all this time, but it only accentuated the fact that she was all alone now. "Congratulations, Mama."

"Yes," Anjali whispered, wearing a distant, dazed expression. "Congratulations."

The others made it back, and Madison scanned the tense faces of her two sisters, then frowned at the tart taste of her lemon slush. "I should've tried raspberry. I'm going to hit the water slides. Who's game?"

"Let me finish these and I'm with you," Vilay said around a mouthful of nachos slathered in melted cheese.

"I can't do the slides," Nikki said, "but I can watch you both make complete fools of yourselves."

Madison gave her a sly grin. "It's no different than watching your wide behind waddle down the hallway."

Everyone chuckled behind that, causing Nikki to blush and waggle her finger at Madison. "You know, you're not too old for me to put you over my knee and spank that ass."

Madison shuddered in mock horror as she sat on the edge of the lounger and swiped a sip of Nikki's raspberry slush, giggling when she narrowly missed a playful punch. Then she curled up next to her oldest sister, who held onto her and kissed her forehead.

"But I don't understand. When did all this marriage thing come about," Anjali said, bringing the conversation back to their original point.

"Michelle tried to leave—divorced him and everything—but she came back a few months later. By then we were married. She had to accept it. He loves both of us, but he made it a point to let her know that he was in love with me and only wants one woman. Me. It shows a lot of growth on his part, because before he would have tried to have both of us."

Nalina shook her head and looked off at the ocean's waves. She had noticed that whenever events put the three of them in the same space, Gina and Michelle weren't the bitter enemies they once were, but Gina seemed more at peace with things than Michelle. Now she understood why. Michelle only realized she had made a mistake after it was too late.

Gina suddenly placed a hand on her heart and took in a deep breath. "Nalina, I need you to go back to the suite and get my meds."

"Meds? What meds?" Nalina's gaze narrowed on her mother, who finally looked away under the intense scrutiny. "You want me to go all the way back there? For what? Really. You've never mentioned you were on any type of medication."

"Would it help if I said please?"

"Why don't you ask Madison? Her legs are younger."

"I'm about to hit the waterslides, big sis. You know, those big, looooong things over there," she said gesturing to the replica of an Aztec pyramid "Those things you're *afraid* to get on."

"I'm not afraid," Nalina said in a huff. "I just don't see the purpose in it."

The women passed a look between them, along with a few smiles.

Nalina folded her arms across her full breasts. "Why not Anjali?"

"No can do, my sister," Anjali quipped. "Anil's keeping the kids in the next suite so I can have some 'me' time. If they see me, it'll be all over."

"I'll go for you, *if* you promise to go on the slides with me," Madison taunted, nudging Nalina in the side.

"Shoot. I'll be back." Nalina scooted off the lounger and slipped on a sarong.

Anjali took off after Madison, with Nikki right behind them. Vilay lingered a moment, then tried to catch up with the other three women. She looked back over her shoulder at Gina, who gave her a slight nod.

"Y'all be careful now," Gina called after them, noticing that Nalina threw a scathing glance at the foursome trekking up the concrete path leading toward the slides and lazy river.

Nalina trudged up the stairs, past the shark ray tank and all the lush greenery, then onward through the building until she made her way to the top floor of the West Wing of the Royal Towers.

She slid the key in the slot, stormed into the luxurious Sapphire suite, and froze when she recognized the lone figure standing in the living room.

"D'Angelo?" was all she managed to say before her legs became too weak to stand on.

Chapter 46

Anjali, Vilay, and Nikki followed Madison as they all ran into the suite. Gina entered right behind them, quickly slumping down on one of the four sofas in the room. "She was right," she said between shallow breaths. "That *is* a long-ass walk."

When they saw D'Angelo scooping Nalina from the carpet, Nikki said, "Oh my. This went well."

"Give her a moment," D'Angelo said smoothly, brushing the hair from Nalina's face. "She'll be all right."

"Madison, get a cool towel." Gina walked over and lowered until she was level with Nalina's body.

Vilay looked down at Nalina, taking in her flushed face. "I didn't think she was the fainting kind." She gave her sister's face a gentle pat, then a harder one. "Come on, girlfriend. No time to punk out now."

Nalina's eyes fluttered open. Still a little dazed, her gaze locked on the handsome man holding her in his arms. His white shirt, slacks, and sandals gave him an air of breezy calm that was a far cry from the confusion she felt. She tried to form words but could barely get a solid breath.

"It's all right, baby," he crooned, grinning down at her. "It's all right."

"She won't have to go to the hospital? She'll be okay for her wedding to D'Angelo, right?" Madison asked, looking up at Gina.

Nalina jerked up as everyone's gaze shifted to D'Angelo. Their silence was cause for alarm. She looked to Nikki, Anjali, then Vilay and Gina, who were all scowling at Madison, who said, "Ooops."

Nalina closed her eyes to keep the room from spinning. She held out her arms, trying to balance herself as realization hit.

Nalina peered at them, then punched Vilay in her arm. "You knew. You *knew!*" She took in the expressions on the women's faces. None of them were as surprised at D'Angelo's presence as she had been.

"We couldn't tell you," Vilay shot back as Madison slipped out of the room with Anjali following close behind. "You had already made things worse with all your attempts to find him." She rubbed her throbbing arm. "Damn, you can hit."

Nalina put a hand on her hip and glared at Vilay who added, "If you knew he was alive, you would have been on the hunt all the more."

"Damn straight!" Her eyes locked on D'Angelo. The anger subsided, and the tears began to flow. "How could you do this to me? How could you let me go on believing that something had happened to you? I thought you were … I thought you were …"

"Shhhh," he crooned softly, curling her into his arms as he lowered back down on the sofa. "Because it was necessary, baby. I had to tie up a whole lot of things so I could come to you with no strings, no baggage, nothing that would be a problem for me in my new life."

Anjali tried to catch up to Madison, who walked back in and held up a beautiful wedding gown. Her soft brown eyes relayed her feelings of happiness. "See, I picked out your dress."

"Could you wait until I ask her first?" D'Angelo said, trying not to show his frustration.

"Oh yeah, I forgot about that part." Madison plopped down on the nearest seat and lowered the dress to her lap. "So ask her already, and let's get this party started."

D'Angelo slipped out from under Nalina and dropped to one knee. "Nalina Bhandari, will you marry me?"

"Can I get back to you on that?" she fired back, a shadow of annoyance crossing her flushed face. "I need some answers first. How the hell did you get out of jail?"

"I was never in jail, baby. I was working undercover, baby. Have been for three years."

Her eyes widened to the size of plates; her breathing came in short bursts. "Are you kidding me?"

"Made it easy for me to run that area, since my people are from there." He reached into his jacket and pulled out an FBI badge that showed he at least hadn't lied about that or his name.

"Why didn't you tell me?" she whispered, her voice breaking just a little. "We were close enough."

D'Angelo raised a single eyebrow. "*Were?*"

"Why did you let me believe all that stuff about you being in the drug business? You could've told me the truth. I wouldn't have said anything to anyone."

"It was personal," he said, trailing a finger across her cheek, wiping away the last of her tears. "I wanted to know that you loved me no matter what. That you loved me for me."

She smacked his finger away. "I'm not feeling that love so much right now." Sobs tore through her instantly. He tried to embrace her, but she shoved him away. "Do you know that I could hear the sound of my own heart breaking? It felt like there wasn't enough air to sustain me. That every single nerve in my body had managed to stop working—and when they did work, it was nothing but more pain."

"And if I can help it," he said, bringing her back into his arms, "you'll never feel that way again. I had to finish out that case, testify against key players and I didn't want any of them to connect me to you or anyone in your family. I had to keep you safe." He ran a hand through her hair. "Now answer the question, woman."

She looked at all the expectant faces before focusing on him. She shook her head. "It can't be this easy for you. Not after what you put me through."

Vilay stepped forward. "Girl, if you don't marry that fine-looking piece of law enforcement, I will." Vilay pointed first to Nalina, then to D'Angelo. "Quit fronting and do the damn thing."

"Yes, what she said," Anjali chimed in.

Nikki patted her curls and said, "And hurry up, 'cause my wedding's tomorrow."

"Oh, please," Nalina shot back. "You could've done it any time. Certainly before that bun in the oven became a full loaf."

Nikki looked at Nalina for the longest time before saying, "I couldn't be happy if you weren't happy. I didn't want you looking like a lost puppy in my wedding photos." Nikki settled into the nearest chair. "Chuck's always wanted to do right by me, but I waited until D'Angelo could get here and do right by you."

"And you *will* do right by her, young man," Sanjay said as he stepped into the room. Michelle walked in behind him.

"Papa. Mama!" Anjali shrieked at the same time as Nalina. But only Anjali ran into his arms for a hug, and then extracted one from an expressionless Michelle, who gave Gina a thorough once-over before scanning the tense faces in the room.

"I most definitely will do right by your daughter," D'Angelo said, shaking Sanjay's extended hand.

"Oh no, my brother." Nalina's gaze swept across everyone. "This is so not happening today."

"What do you mean?" Madison looked from Nalina to D'Angelo and back. "There has to be a wedding. You love him. And he really loves you."

"It takes more than love, sweetie."

"But at least you love him, right? He came back for you. That's way more than Quasi ever did for me. He used me and left me in that horrible place ..." Madison's bottom lip trembled as she struggled not to cry.

"You love him, right?"

"Sweetie, it takes trust and honesty. And he hasn't been honest with me." She flicked an angry gaze at D'Angelo, whose calm manner was pissing her off even more. "I don't know who he is."

"Yes you do. You know in here." Madison placed her hand over Nalina's heart and pulled away. "You're just using that as an excuse."

D'Angelo slipped into the seat behind them and gave Madison a slight nod.

"That's why I'm with you every night. I'm there because you're crying. I'm there when you're praying for him. I'm there when you're praying for strength. God answered your prayers, and now he's here, and you're playing hard to get." Madison shook her head. "And I thought *you* were the grown up."

Nikki let out a low whistle behind that, eliciting an angry glare from Nalina.

"And this is grown folks' business," Nalina snapped at Madison, straining with an effort not to cry at her baby's sisters heartfelt words. "Stay out of it."

"I thought this was *family* business. I am family, right?" The baby of the family looked at everyone else and took in the round of nods. "And with what I've been through, I'm grown folks too." She shook her head at Nalina, the disdain she felt plainly evident in her expression. "Making him wait, when you know you want him. You are so full of it."

Madison tossed the dress over the chair and stormed past her but made it only to the door before Nalina said, "Madison."

The teary-eyed youngster froze, then looked over her shoulder to see Nalina retrieving the wedding dress. "Will you help me get dressed?"

The smile that graced the girl's lips was enough to put a tear in everyone's eye. She scanned the range of expressions from her sisters, then she looked to her mother as she whispered, "I can believe in happily ever after again?"

Gina was too choked up to do anything but place a hand over her heart and incline her head.

Vilay put her arm around Madison's shoulder and said, "Indeed, baby girl. Indeed."

Nalina made her way to D'Angelo and pressed a kiss to his lips, which brought a smile and another apology for hurting her the way he had.

Gina watched her five daughters disappear into the master suites. Laughter and excited chatter echoed in the room, and she smiled at Sanjay, who returned it full force. Michelle gave her a fleeting smile of her own. Sanjay walked over to where Gina sat and took her in his arms as she cried tears of joy.

Evidently, things hadn't tied up quite as tidily as Gina would have liked, but her daughters were safe, together, and each enjoyed some form of happiness. In a way, her life had come full circle. One of her precious daughters was about to marry the son of her first love, Rakim. And she was now married to the only man she had ever truly loved—Sanjay.

Somewhere Mama Bessie was smiling down on her and those five beautiful daughters, saying, "Beauty, strength, and brains, baby. That's how it's done."

Naleighna Kai

is the national bestselling author of the provocative novels: *Was it Good For You?*, *Open Door Marriage* and *Every Woman Needs a Wife*. She started writing in December of 1999, independently publishing her first two novels before acquiring a book deal with an imprint of Simon & Schuster and most recently a book deal with an independent publisher founded by two national bestselling authors She is a contributing author to a New York Times Bestseller, an award-winning author, and The E. Lynn Harris Author of Distinction.

Naleighna works for a major international law firm and is the CEO of Macro Marketing & Promotions Group, the Director of Marketing & Promotions for Brown Girls Publishing, as well as the marketing consultant to several national bestselling and aspiring writers. She is also the brainchild behind the annual Cavalcade of Authors events which takes place in her hometown of Chicago. Naleighna pens romance, contemporary fiction, erotica, and speculative fiction and is currently working on her next novels: *Slaves of Heaven* and *She Touched My Soul*.

Find her on the web at www.naleighnakai.com, www.thecavalcadeofauthors.com and on Facebook and twitter under Naleighna Kai.

also by Naleighna Kai

"Open Door Marriage *is a page-turner from start to finish, uniquely written to explore the emotions of three people who have bonds that seem unbreakable. That is, until they are tested in a relationship that causes their families, religious leaders, and the public to be up in arms. Naleighna Kai has written a provocative novel about a relationship that is as complicated as it can get."* – Valarie Prince, best-selling author of the novel, *The Virus: When Love Becomes Deadly*

A chance encounter lands NBA star Dallas Avery back in the arms of the woman of his dreams. A woman he hasn't seen in years. A woman he soon discovers just so happens to be his fiancée's aunt! But Dallas' fiancee, Tori, isn't ready to give up all that she's worked for, so she makes him a shocking offer – go through with the wedding and she'll still allow him to be with the one woman he now can't seem to do without. Dallas will get a family, something her much older aunt, Alicia can't give him. Tori will get the lifestyle she clamors. And Alicia will get the love she's longed for all her life. Everyone will get a little of what they want. . . and maybe a whole lot of what they don't.

The details of the trio's love life play out in the tabloids and on talk shows, making Dallas the center of an NBA scandal. And eventually, the doors slam shut on this open marriage and Dallas is forced to make a choice to end the chaos. But moving on is easier than it looks and by the time all is said and done, secrets will be revealed, passions will be extinguished, and everyone's lives will be forever changed.

www.naleighnakai.com

Years before, Delvin and Tailan complicated their lives by bringing another woman into the relationship to bear his children. When threatened with losing the family he always wanted, Delvin was given an ultimatum: either leave Tailan, his high school sweetheart, and marry the surrogate; or lose the child he's always wanted. He made that life-altering choice, breaking Tailan's heart, in spite of the fact that he loved her like he loved no other woman.

Now seven years later, fate has given Delvin four days to right old wrongs, and he'll use everything in his power to win Tailan back. Unfortunately, Tailan is harboring a secret that she's kept not only from him, but from the world. His determination to have her will turn the tables and make him have to either share Tailan with another man or walk away from the strongest love he's ever known.